SCHOOL FOR PAGAN LOVERS

RUTGERS PRESS
fiction

OTHER BOOKS BY EDMUND KEELEY

Fiction
The Libation
The Gold-Hatted Lover
The Impostor
Voyage to a Dark Island
A Wilderness Called Peace

Nonfiction
Modern Greek Writers (ed. with Peter Bien)
Cavafy's Alexandria
Modern Greek Poetry: Voice and Myth
R. P. Blackmur: Essays, Memoirs, Texts
(ed. with Edward Cone and Joseph Frank)
The Salonika Bay Murder: Cold War Politics and the Polk Affair

Poetry in Translation
Six Poets of Modern Greece (with Philip Sherrard)
George Seferis: Collected Poems (with Philip Sherrard)
C. P. Cavafy: Passions and Ancient Days (with George Savidis)
C. P. Cavafy: Selected Poems (with Philip Sherrard)
Odysseus Elytis: The Axion Esti (with George Savidis)
C. P. Cavafy: Collected Poems (with Philip Sherrard and George Savidis)
Angelos Sikelianos: Selected Poems (with Philip Sherrard)
Ritsos in Parentheses
The Dark Crystal/Voices of Modern Greece (with Philip Sherrard)
Odysseus Elytis: Selected Poems (with Philip Sherrard)
Yannis Ritsos: Exile and Return, Selected Poems 1968–74
Yannis Ritsos: Repetitions, Testimonies, Parentheses

Fiction in Translation
Vassilis Vassilikos: The Plant, The Well, The Angel (with Mary Keeley)

SCHOOL FOR PAGAN LOVERS

EDMUND KEELEY

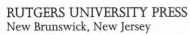

RUTGERS UNIVERSITY PRESS
New Brunswick, New Jersey

Design by Liz Schweber

Library of Congress Cataloging-in-Publication Data

Keeley, Edmund.
  School for pagan lovers / Edmund Keeley.
      p.   cm. — (Rutgers Press fiction)
  ISBN 0-8135-1935-7
  I. Title.   II. Series
PS3561.E34S3   1993
813'.54—dc20   92–28943
                                                              CIP

British Cataloging-in-Publication information available

In Memoriam
Doreen Arditi Gilbertson

1

I HAVE A SURE MEMORY OF *WHAT MAGDA SEVILLAS* LOOKED LIKE when she arrived by taxi at my home on the outskirts of Salonika for our first tutorial session that March afternoon in 1938. It was an unusually warm day for March so far north in Greece, and she was wearing a green cotton dress that had short sleeves and a band of white at the edge of the sleeve and below her throat, not lace but a cotton strip that matched the narrow white belt around her waist. As she came up the walk, the dress was soft and tight enough to let you see the outline of her thighs. Her hair was light for a Greek girl, what the local people would call blond but an American would say was light brown or, more accurately, copper, with occasional gold threading, and her skin appeared to be unusually white, almost a foreigner's skin like mine, without any olive tinting. She stood there for a minute looking at our house, studying it, and when she raised her chin as she gazed up at the stork's nest on our chimney, she showed the full stretch of her neck, slender and delicately shaped and longer than any I'd seen in someone her age. Her features were delicately shaped too, the eyes large and wide apart, the nose sharp and a touch long, the mouth small but with full dark lips. Though she was almost three years older than I was, on first sight she looked to me young enough not to belong to the more distant adult world that my parents lived in, but at the same time, she looked old enough, beautiful enough, to be a little frightening.

I had been in Greece for the best part of a year when my lessons with Magda began. My father had moved his family there early in the summer of 1937 to head the farm machinery division of an American-sponsored vocational school for Greek village boys. He wasn't so much an educator as a fixer. Though he'd been principal for a while at a high school where my mother once taught English, he would have been content to spend his life running the farm in upstate New York that my mother inherited if only there had been enough income from that to buy all the machines he needed to keep himself busy. There wasn't nearly enough income, so when an offer came along that put a whole collection of old machines and a good selection of the latest ones under my father's command, he packed up my mother, my brother, and me and put us on a ship bound for the port of Piraeus, with our final destination the Macedonian city of Salonika.

I was sixteen at the time and had a lot of old friends in my local high school and a few new arrivals that I had hoped to cultivate, a girl just down from Buffalo in particular, so I was quite content to stay where I was. None of us in the family had ever heard of Piraeus or Salonika, and my mother seemed even less happy than I was about this middle-aged move to a Balkan country that my father had arranged, especially in view of all the war talk that you heard in 1937. But however much she got to express her opinion, and that was a lot, I was never asked for mine, nor was my younger brother asked for his. That isn't the way things worked in our family or maybe in any other family that had to move out of the depressed parts of upstate New York during those prewar years.

My brother, Sam, and I had problems adjusting to our new country at first, especially at school. When my father decided to move his family to a city whose name I didn't even know how to spell, he hadn't bothered to ask anybody what you could do in that city to educate two boys as hostile to their new situation as Sam and I started out being, though Sam proved to be more adaptable than I was. Since he was twelve and a half years old to my sixteen when we made the move to Greece, I lay that to his broader ignorance of what might be in store for him from minute to minute rather than any special strength of character. But I could hardly be called the best judge of my brother at the time, fond of his spunky nastiness as I learned to be. My mother, who was more concerned than my father about our education, sought what advice she could as soon as we were on the scene, first of all from the American Consul in Salonika. His opinion, and the consensus among the few Americans in the foreign community, was that the best school in town for foreign children of our age was the German School, which was where his oldest son Jackson had gone for several years before managing to get himself transferred to Anatolia College, where at least some of the classes were taught in English.

The German School was in fact a terrible school, especially for those foreign students who had never heard of the Third Reich, which is where the teachers were trained in educational discipline and international diplomacy before being sent abroad as missionaries of Hitler's new world order. But the problems that came with their view of life and its recent history were not the immediate ones for Sam and me. Our first problem was having to learn yet another language besides the one we spoke at home and the other one we spoke outside the house with our local friends. That meant mastering a new script that was almost as foreign as the one on the street signs and shops in the city while also learning to spit out a guttural strangeness in sounds that had to seem natural if you hoped first to catch up with the class you were put in on probation and then maybe move up a grade. This was a possibility more on my mind than Sam's because my date of birth fell between grades and I could have easily been a half year ahead of myself rather than starting out a half year behind. But whatever my ambition to move up in that school or even to stay comfortably where I was, I did not do well enough with the German language. In fact, I did so poorly that I found myself threatened with losing even more time than I'd lost starting out.

I was about a month into the second half of the school year when I was called into the principal's office to get the word that, as the new term had progressed, my work at school had become quite deficient in the view of several of my teachers.

"Perhaps deficient is too strong a thing to say," the principal said in his slowest German when he saw the expression on my face. "Let us say that your work is perhaps well below what is thought to be your ability. Do you understand what I am saying?"

"Truly I understand," I said in my most somber schoolboy German.

"So let us then say that the problem is not ability or attitude but a failing to achieve the proper balance that would result in sufficient knowledge of our language. Do you follow what I am saying?"

"I am following," I said. "Entirely. I mean, deeply."

Compared to most of those he commanded, the principal was thought to be a kindly soul, a man who had a nervous laugh but no harshness in his voice, his head shaped like a shiny gourd with a low fringe of curls so that he seemed almost a clownish figure, and except for his allowing the worst of the teachers to have their way, a man generally popular with both the students and their parents. The news he was bringing me came as no surprise, since it had been obvious for some time that my distaste for the German language and some of the people who used it officially in that school was creating both a writing and a speaking block that made it difficult for me to express myself in class on those few occasions when I found the heart to speak at all or was called on to do so. And my performance on written tests had become disastrous, more often than not a chance to work out a private syntax and handwriting that completely baffled the teacher who had to decipher what I wrote and even baffled me after the agony of producing it was over.

The principal went on to explain that he would have to take the matter up with my parents, because he wanted, before it became too late, to spare both me and them the embarrassment of my having to repeat my first year at the school without much chance of making up the time I'd lose that way. From my point of view, serving time in the same class had become only a degree more alarming than moving up to serve time in the next grade at the school, but I knew my parents would be grimly upset by a failure like that, especially since I'd just turned seventeen. So I answered the principal as soberly and correctly as I could, promising to do my absolute best from then on to take my schoolwork more seriously.

"I am not certain that will be quite good enough," the principal said. "We will have to consider the matter with your parents. Perhaps we will have to think of some special private lessons through the remainder of the school year."

The tutor chosen for my private lessons, Magda Sevillas, was a senior in the German School two years ahead of me and a year older than the others in her class for reasons that remained obscure but were surely not academic since she was not only graduating at the head of her class but was among the few women students preparing to go to the University of Salonika to major in foreign languages in anticipation of entering the teaching profession. Her future plans were a matter that she discussed not with me but with my parents when they interviewed her, at the principal's suggestion, as a potential private tutor who might give me the kind of cram course in German at a reasonable cost that would not only get me through the school year but possibly give me an advantage in the next. That allowed a little more than two months for her to perform this miracle. Still, after the interview with her, my parents were apparently convinced that if anybody could save the day for me, it would be this intense, bright, and well-mannered girl, who was actually a woman in their eyes, fully in command of herself. And whatever she might accomplish, it would be without great expense to my parents since she would be doing it mostly as training for her future while picking up some pocket money, though that isn't where they put the emphasis when they faced me with the news of their decision.

My mother did most of the talking, and in the beginning she did her best to appear sympathetic about my problem. She allowed me full credit for the difficulty of doing advanced high-school level work in a language foreign to my own while living in a country which spoke yet another language foreign to my own. And she was quite aware, she said, that Sam's relative success in mastering German was partly a consequence of his being three years younger than I was, still at an age when foreign languages entered the mind more easily and naturally. But, she said—and here my father began to nod in agreement—there was really no other choice but for me to accept the tutoring that she and my father had arranged if I didn't want to lose all I had put into my first year of school in Greece and find myself falling way behind my age-group. End of conversation.

I was upstairs in our house looking out of the front bedroom window well ahead of time that afternoon in March when Magda was due to arrive for our first tutorial session. Sam, who was fascinated by cars, was there too, tracking her taxi a good kilometer before it reached the school gate. The arrival of a taxi in those pre-war days was enough to make the deaf-mute coming along the road outside our house from the opposite direction pull up his donkey cart and jump down to hold the donkey as close to the side of the road and clear of danger as he could, though the taxi was now stopped well ahead of him and gave no sign of going anywhere. Close at hand, it struck Sam as an undistinguished automobile, in fact boringly out-of-date, and he didn't even wait for Magda to step out of it before he took off for the soccer field to get in some practice until sunset, when all the underage inhabitants of the school we lived at were called in by their parents to avoid the mosquitoes that came out with the dying sun to spread what Sam called the dreaded disease of malaria. Sam was an expert on diseases and physical deformities, having secretly read most of the medical book for family use that my mother had brought with her from upstate New York. Rabies was his favorite. Even if you were only scratched by a rabid cat or dog or goat but didn't admit it, Sam said, the result would be a progressive madness that had you suffering first from extreme depression and talkativeness, then choking paroxysms at the sound of running water, and finally a maniacal excitement that caused you to zigzag down the road with a foaming mouth as you tried to bite anything in your path, even your friends and relatives, until the police could get to you and put you in a cage or shoot you dead on the spot the way they did any mad animal.

After watching Magda come up our walk and stop with her copper-tinted head so elegantly poised to look up at our resident stork, I had a feeling that things between us might not go as easily as I wanted them to, though at the time I had no idea why I felt that way. And our first tutorial session turned out to be less than a great success. One problem was that after my mother called me down from the upstairs bedroom to meet Miss Sevillas, as I was supposed to call her, my mother insisted on hanging around, not in sight, just outside the doorway into the living room where she could hear most of what went on, though she may not have stayed there as long as I imagined her doing. Another problem was the setting. Our session took place in my father's study, which had books lining the walls wherever there weren't windows, a desk, and a coffee table, the place very neat because my father was never in there, but with only a couch and an easy chair to sit on. This meant that I either had to sit beside Miss Sevillas on the couch or catty-cornered to her, with one end of the coffee table between us. After I shook her hand, which was as cold as mine, and after my mother left us alone, Miss Sevillas suggested in Greek that I sit on the couch and she in the easy chair so that I could look at her and watch her shape the exact sound of the phrases we would be working with in our oral drills. She said this would not only help me with certain especially difficult words but also with the general rhythm of German, all part of a new approach to language teaching that interested her and that would be a regular part of our tutorial sessions.

Words and rhythm were less of a problem during that first session than watching Miss Sevillas shape the language. She had a book with her that she said was rather experimental in that it put the emphasis on the spoken tongue through the repetition of phrases from everyday life, with little attention, at least in the beginning, to questions of grammar. She soon found out that I was beyond the beginner's stage, but she also found out, when she finally flipped through the book and went on to the more complicated phrases farther along, that I sometimes had trouble following what she was saying when she would tell me to look at her and repeat the German phrase after her, following the sound and rhythm of it as closely as I could.

"So," she said at one point with a little sigh. "Let us try once again. Please repeat after me: In order to bring about the immediate stopping of the train when serious danger is imminent, the rip cord to be found dangling from the ceiling is to be pulled."

"In order to stop the train immediately when there is danger, the I-don't-know-what dangling from the ceiling is to be pulled."

"You are not looking at me again. Please repeat once more. Slowly. In order to bring about the immediate stopping of the train when serious danger is imminent, the rip cord to be found dangling from the ceiling is to be pulled."

"I don't understand what's dangling from the ceiling," I said in Greek.

"No. In German please. Remember, we don't speak Greek any longer."

"I can't tell you in German because I don't know the word."

"The word is rip cord. The thing you pull when you think you're in danger on a train. But maybe this sentence is too long. We will move on to the next for the moment. Now, in German please, repeat after me: Improper use will be punished."

"Something will be punished."

Miss Sevillas sighed. "Not something. Improper use. All you have to do is listen carefully and watch what my mouth is saying."

"I can't do it," I said.

"That's because you're not looking at me," Miss Sevillas said in Greek. "Watching me helps to fix it in your mind. Why won't you please watch me?"

I couldn't tell her that looking at her in that dress with her long white legs turned sideways against that chair and her head bent forward toward me so that I could see every brown speckle in her green eyes, this while her lips made shapes I'd never dreamed could make lips so sensual, was affecting my breathing and making my stomach tighten up all the time. I had to settle for a lie, which was actually a truth that had nothing to do with my problem.

"I hate German," I said. "I can't stand the language."

That made Miss Sevillas smile. "Po, po," she exclaimed in Greek. "That's a very violent attitude. Do you really feel that way about the language of Goethe and Schiller?"

"The language of who?"

"In any case," Miss Sevillas said, still smiling. "I don't want to strain your hatred the very first day we meet, so I will leave you with an exercise to work on for Friday that won't require your having to look at me."

"It isn't your fault," I said. "Really. I just have trouble sometimes getting the language out. But I promise to work on it."

"Well maybe next time I'll bring along some poetry to read to you so you see that German can sometimes be as beautiful as any language when it's used well and when you don't resist letting it touch your heart."

I was in despair after she left. I felt I had made a fool of myself and insulted her, this girl, this woman who seemed more sensual despite her formal manner than any creature my adolescent imagination might have invented and who spoke in the face of my idiocy with a gentleness and a conviction that simply mocked my lying effort to be clever. When my mother asked me—so casually that I could have strangled her—how I had gotten along with Miss Sevillas, I had to fight against the impulse to say that there was no need for me to answer her question since she had overheard everything that had gone on during our session. I held back and settled for saying that I thought Miss Sevillas was really a fine teacher for someone her age and that we had hit it off very well. I didn't add that my opinion was maybe a bit partial, since what I brought out of that first session was not so much what Miss Sevillas had taught me about the German language as an unfading image of Miss Sevillas herself that haunted me through the night and into the next day and into the night that followed.

Our second session two days later—we were scheduled to meet three times a week until she could report real progress—didn't do much more than the first to ease my language difficulty, but it worked wonderfully to liven the bittersweet uncomfortableness that

I felt in the presence of Miss Sevillas. This time she tried a different approach with me, delaying the drill part of the session until she'd made an effort to challenge my dislike of the language by reading me German poetry. That was not a thing I objected to. I had read my share of English poetry during my last school year in upstate New York and had actually come to like some of the Keats and Tennyson and Browning that our teacher recited for us in her cheerful high voice, her hand sometimes waving the rhythm along or softly beating it out on her desk. The difficulty was that Miss Sevillas suggested I sit on the couch beside her for this portion of our lesson so that I could follow the written word as she read from her book. She caught me hesitating.

"Please, Henry," she said in German. "What is the problem now? Please sit down so that we can get started."

"I hate the name Henry," I said in Greek.

"So much hate. So many problems. That is your name, isn't it?"

"It's my official name, but I don't like it much," I said. "Especially the way it's pronounced in German. Or even in Greek."

That was at least a half-truth. I'd always had trouble with my name, not so much my last name, Gogarty, but the name Henry, which wasn't ever used by my family except for official purposes outside the privacy of our home, where I was called Hal from the day I was born. I found out in later years that my mother had picked both the official version and the one she normally used from her love for Shakespeare during the years she taught high-school English, just as the name Sam had come out of her love for Samuel Johnson. But once I reached Greece, neither Henry nor Hal worked well for me, and Gogarty not at all. There is no true "h" in Greek, just a guttural sound that approximates it as in the German "ach." And since a man's surname in Greek normally ends not in an "i" or "y" sound but in an "is," I lost most of the Irish in me as far as my Greek friends in Macedonia were concerned and became Chal Gogartis to the local population.

Miss Sevillas was studying me. "I'm sorry my pronunciation upsets you in the two languages I know best. Maybe you can teach me to say your name correctly in English."

"I didn't mean anything personal," I said. "Anyway, if you don't mind, I'd rather be called by my nickname, which is Hal."

"Hal. Good. We will call you Hal from now on since that is what you prefer."

She was still pronouncing the "H" too harshly, but hearing her say the name sent a shiver through me.

"Now will you please sit down?"

She patted the seat beside her on the couch, as she might for a child. I sat down beside her and waited. She flipped through her book and laid it open, holding it between us, slightly more over her thigh than mine, which I was straining to make sure didn't edge over to touch hers. She smelled deliciously of lemon.

"This is a poem by Goethe," she said in German. "Very famous in Germany. I think it is easy enough for you to understand, but I do not want you to think about the meaning at first. Just listen to the sound. We can think about the meaning later."

And she read a short poem about how quiet and breathless it was over all the mountains and something about birds singing in the trees, but since in my sharpened discomfort I barely heard it the first time around, I asked her to do it again and this time learned that the birds weren't singing but were asleep, which made more sense.

"That's beautiful all right," I said in Greek.

She put the book down. "Why are you trying to make things so difficult for me?" she said in a way that made her sound really hurt. "Why can't you say that in German?"

"I don't know," I said. "For some reason it sounds false in German."

"Try. Please."

"The poem is truly beautiful," I said in my most solemn German.

"And you understood it?"

"Truly," I said.

"Tell me what you understood."

"I understood that there is quiet in the mountains and that the birds are asleep in the forest."

"Excellent. And what about you?"

"Me? I don't understand."

"You in the poem."

She took the book up again and read the last lines to me.

"Do you see that there is a you at the end of the poem?"

"Truly," I said. "There is a you."

"And what is the you doing?"

"Waiting?" I asked.

"Not exactly. The poet is telling you to wait, soon you too will be quiet like the mountains and the birds. That is the point."

"Truly," I said. "I see it entirely now."

Miss Sevillas smiled. "Let us try another. Perhaps one a little more difficult."

She read a longer poem full of words I had never seen before, what struck me as a terrible poem. Those words in it that were familiar—river, ocean, forest, mountain—weren't held together by any verbs that made sense to me, and then suddenly a father came into the poem out of nowhere, which threw me off completely. But the way she read it, the heart she put into it, was enough to make you want to cry.

"That was wonderful," I said when her voice trailed off. "Truly."

"It is a great poem. You recognize the form?   Fourteen lines, Petrarchan?"

"I think we had that form in school in America," I said.

She must have seen that I had no idea what she was talking about, but she didn't press me.

"It's the last lines that are so moving," she said in Greek, really to herself. "The wave returning to flash on the rock, a life made new again."

I could see that those lines had some special meaning for her and that it saddened her. She closed the book abruptly and stood up.

"Now to serious work," she said, and went around the coffee table to sit in the easy chair.

I felt that I had been dismissed, turned aside, just at the moment when she might have let me see something about herself that would have made her more approachable, whether girl, woman, anything but this unattainable schoolmistress type who knew so much more than I did and who made me feel so awkward and foolish.

Some weeks before Magda entered my life to begin my adult education in the language of erotic mystery, the political climate in and around the German School pressed me into learning the language of underground dissent and the virtues and vices of exclusion that came with it. My first knowledge of politics—anyway, of political propaganda—had come from two of the milder teachers in the school. The stout blond woman who taught geography and history in something close to a baritone voice was generous enough to the new foreign students to skip the required oral report on the difference between the three maps of Germany we were meant to memorize—Before World War I, After World War I, and Greater Germany of the Future—and allow us to draw them as best we could on the blackboard. And either out of kindness or the sense of defeat that is supposed to come with age, the music teacher, a gentle white-haired tenor who appeared to be almost totally deaf, chose not to notice that some of us failed to join in singing the German national anthem or the required medley of traditional Tyrolian songs we couldn't half understand.

But a harsher, more complicated political education began one late fall afternoon while I was sitting on the curb opposite the school gate waiting to head home with Sam, who was lingering in the yard hoping to try out for the position of lower division goalie. A parade went by as I sat there, several hundred high-school students of both sexes but with the sexes separated into platoons, marching down the center of the street so that the streetcar line had to be shut down for half an hour. They were all dressed in blue and white like the Greek flag in front of them, the boys wearing short puttees and crossed white belts on their chests, all of them singing Greek marching songs that I hadn't heard before. The only other time I'd seen a parade of people that young in uniform was when a group of German students from the upper classes at our school had come out in khaki to march around the yard for some visiting official from Germany. But these Greek marchers were more nonchalant about it, not always in step, and you could see that they weren't taking themselves that seriously because they talked to each other between the singing, and some of the boys at the end of the parade waved to me as they went by.

When I asked the sour, pinched man who ran the cafe on that side of the street what the holiday was, he shrugged and said: "What holiday? That's just for General Metaxas."

I nodded with full understanding, though I had no idea who General Metaxas was. I had to wait until I got home to ask my father. All he told me was that General Metaxas ran Greece, but he said it in a way that made the General appear not the dictator he turned out to be but a man that I had no need to give a second thought to. And I didn't, anyway not until Herr Trauger, our calisthenics instructor, announced later that week during the gym period that the school day was going to be extended by an hour for those in the upper division—this meant me but not Sam—so that there could be a new special drill session at noon that would bring together those Germans who were qualified to be part of the Hitler Jugend program and those Greek nationals in the upper division who now belonged to the allied Greek youth movement called Neolea.

Herr Trauger was once a fencing champion, and though he didn't look athletic, he was lithe, and he could do exercises with complete precision. Whenever he'd finish demonstrating an exercise, he'd pick up his riding crop and walk back and forth in front of us with his back slightly arched, as though he was on horseback. If you got up close to him, which wasn't a thing you'd normally choose to do, you could see that he had a white scar that ran from behind his ear to the corner of his mouth. He was said to be proud of that scar and this was why he was always bareheaded in winter and walked with his head slightly tilted so that the scar would catch the light. When we were in the yard for calisthenics, Herr Trauger allowed no room for casual talk, relaxed posture, or lack of coordination. Calisthenics was a military exercise that he patiently explained was meant to build the mind while it built the body, not only essential preparation for those non-foreigners who would be admitted to the Hitler Jugend, but basic training for the human spirit. Those who were weaker than others and less physically endowed could learn to keep up with the rest by a mixture of concentration and dedication, and any failure in this regard revealed by conversation with one's neighbor or stopping to rest before an exercise was completed or expressing frustration in one's native language meant a trip to The Wall.

The Wall was a stretch of stuccoed masonry about ten feet high that separated one side of the closed-in yard from the buildings next to it. When you were sent to The Wall, you had to step out of line and march smartly to the front of the gym class, then cross over to stand at attention facing the stretch of stuccoed masonry on that side of the yard. You then had to put your arms out in front of you to touch the wall with your fingertips, elbows absolutely straight as though in a double-armed salute to the Führer, and lean on your fingertips against the wall, with your back stretched out to form as straight a line as you were able. You waited in that position for Herr Trauger to come over in his good time and help you assume a better angle and a straighter line, guided by his riding crop, until you finally found that you had to give up and go to your knees.

I was sent to The Wall only once during my first term at the school, and that was for swearing out loud in Greek, the subversive language, which I had mastered during the summer and fall on a village level almost to the point of being a native curser. But true subversion came with Herr Trauger's announcement that the German and Greek students in the upper division would now be exercising together during the extended noon hour while the rest of us in the upper division were supposed to go home during that period and be back sharply on time for the afternoon classes.

Going home at noon was out of the question in my case. A trip of that kind early in the morning and late in the afternoon was cruelty enough. Going home meant a seven-kilometer walk from the end of the streetcar line at a place called the Depot across open fields where the sheepdogs that came at you on the run with bared fangs would stop short of shredding your arm or leg and settle for violent barking only if you stood perfectly still and gave them no sign or smell of fear until the shepherd finally came up over the ridge ahead to call off his drooling killer. Then there were the Gypsies who sometimes put up their tents along the main path and would send out a gang of their dirt-smeared offspring to make sure you didn't get through their temporary piece of countryside without handing over whatever you might have in coins or disposable clothing, even if that came down to your ripe handkerchief or your filthy cap. And even when I'd found the path clear, I'd had to contend with Sam's obsession to explore the cone-shaped burial mound on the last stretch home, a dark and evil monument to someone's ancient folly with an endless selection of tunnels that led nowhere a normal adult would want to go but that had served a generation or two of nomads for an easy outdoor toilet.

What Herr Trauger's announcement did at first was make me angry over being excluded from the chance of meeting some older Greek students of both sexes I might not get to know otherwise, which would at least have given me more of a chance to talk in the new street language that I was coming to know almost as well as my own. Why were the German students the only ones allowed to join in with those relatively casual boys and girls in the new Greek youth movement? All of us had to do the same calisthenics, all of us could learn to march if we had to. And what were those of us who couldn't go home during that free period supposed to do? But when the small group of the excluded foreign students with the same lunch problem were brought together with others of their kind by the school principal the following day, we suddenly had the makings of a resistance cell even if we didn't know it by that name. There was Faruk, the son of a Turkish diplomat; Lars, a Dane whose father worked for one of the local tobacco companies; Marcel, a Lebanese who had a Greek mother and whose father was a silver merchant; and Stephan, whose parents belonged to the Salonika Jewish community but who qualified for admission to the German School because he had a Spanish passport.

We came together for the first time in the cafe across the street from the school after the principal had explained to the full contingent of so-called foreign students that we should not consider the rules of limited participation in the new joint program of training any reflection on us personally and certainly not on our parents. In fact, he said, our parents, being of various other nationalities, were likely to be embarrassed if they were to find us taking part, even as observers, in a youth movement that was a cooperative effort meant strictly for German nationals and their Greek associates. That was why a classroom would be set aside for those of us who wished to stay at the school and study rather than go home during that part of the lunch hour that would henceforth be devoted to the special training program.

If there was any resentment over this news, it remained unstated, because no one of us at this meeting raised a question about what the principal had said to us, and in the case of five students in that room, no question about it was given any chance to be raised at home either. That became clear the following day during the extended lunch hour when the five of us found ourselves waiting out the special noontime drill in the cafe across the street. We spoke only in Greek, as was right for our subversive mood. By the end of that first free lunch period we knew that each of us for his own reasons was not about to make use of the classroom set aside for noontime study but was ready to join the others in sharing the gift of time and liberty we had been granted by the principal: almost two hours without discipline, constraint, violent exercise, regulated recreation, moral lecturing, and all the other forced training in attitude that went with our assigned work. For these two hours, life in the city would be ours to make of it what we wanted.

The first order of business was finding a place where we wouldn't be under surveillance by anybody, including the cafe owner, who was with us in spirit so long as we supplemented our lunch with what he had to offer from behind his counter but was not much interested in having us just hang around to discuss the state of the world and our role in its future. It took us close to the Christmas recess to find our private winter quarters. We knew that nothing appropriate was likely to turn up between the waterfront and the spread of relatively new residences along the streets leading up to the lower border of the old city, so we concentrated on the steeper area between that border and the prison grounds at the top of the city walls. The old city up there had the look of a Greek island village, with narrow winding streets that seemed to be designed against strong winds and unfriendly visitors, though most of the houses were in the Turkish style, with closed-in wooden balconies overhanging the street. Then, as you went farther up, things opened out a bit and the style became more rural, the houses sometimes independent of each other, with walled-in courtyards and occasionally with a shed for animals attached to the house. There was no traffic in the streets up there and sometimes no street, just a stone path for mules and donkeys that often led to a fenced-in dead end.

All we were looking for was four walls and a covering of some kind, whether a deserted house or hut or shed, with enough room for everybody to sit comfortably, enough light to read by when that was what we chose to do, and enough cleared space in the center to allow us to build a small fire. What we ended up with wasn't entirely satisfactory: an abandoned one-story cottage on the outer edge of the old city, actually just four walls that had no roof or windows and an earthen floor that was littered with garbage. It seemed possible only if the winter stayed mild, though there was an annex to it that could provide additional protection, a stable shed where goats had once lived, the roof made of stripped branches that came down too low to let you stand upright and the floor covered with a mixture of straw and dung. The yard outside was only partly walled in, and it seemed to be merging with a plot of ground next door that looked as though it might have once been a vegetable garden but that had now been taken over by a rich mix of garbage and trash dropped there over the years by whoever passed by.

We managed to clean out the floor of the cottage in time for the Christmas recess, but we didn't get to use our new quarters until mid-January. With most of our energy given to climbing up there in the first place, then to building a small fire that was both safe and hot enough, and then to putting it out carefully before we headed downhill again so that we didn't become a serious threat to the neighborhood, what time we had left was taken up by talk. We covered a number of subjects during our first weeks up there, but the two I remember as the ones we came back to more than once were war and women.

The war talk began when one of us broke an unspoken rule against mentioning anything that went on in the school building or the yard across the street from the cafe that was our daily starting point. It was Stephan who broke the rule by telling us one noon that he was thinking of asking his parents to let him drop out of the German School because Herr Trauger had sent him to the principal's office two weeks in a row for no reason at all except maybe the way he looked at Trauger, a thing he said he couldn't help because he hated the man like nobody else in the world. And of course the principal had just shrugged off the whole thing without bringing up the fact that Stephan was Jewish or questioning what Trauger was up to. All he'd said with his nervous laugh was that Herr Trauger could sometimes be a little touchy because he had personal problems.

"The only problem Trauger has is being a Nazi," Lars said.

"He may be a Nazi but that isn't all he is," Faruk said. "He's sick in the head. I mean being a Nazi, whatever that means, is no excuse."

"It means for one thing that you love Hitler and hate Jews," Lars said. "My father will tell you everything else it means if you're really interested."

"Why do they hate Jews so much?" Faruk said.

"Because, masturbator, they're Semitic rather than Aryan," Marcel said. "Like we Lebanese. And maybe like you Turks."

"I don't think we're Semitic," Faruk said. "We're Moslem."

"That's how much you know," Marcel said. "A lot of Semites are Moslem. Some Lebanese even. Those who aren't Christian like me."

"Well, the Nazis are supposed to be Christians too," Stephan said. "Like most Germans who aren't Jews. Only the Nazis are different."

"Nazis are Nazis," Lars said. "They think they can conquer the world."

"Well, they won't if the French have anything to say about it," Marcel said. "Have you heard of the Maginot Line?"

"Of course I have," Lars said. "I'm not saying they're going to conquer the world. I'm just saying they think they can."

"Who cares what they think?" Marcel said. "History is on the side of the French."

The conversation died because the rest of us didn't know enough about history to challenge Marcel, who was some months older than we were, even those of us who had been held back by our initial language deficiency, because his deficiency was long-standing and based on the principle that German was a barbaric language compared to French or even Arabic, an advanced attitude that served to make him our undesignated leader from the start. That evening I decided to work on my ignorance, so I made my way down to my father's machine shop to see what I might be able to pick up from him. My father was working on the insides of some kind of motor that I'd never seen opened up before, all coils and wires and screws spread out on his worktable in a great mess that he seemed to understand but that was still giving him trouble, as I could tell from the spread of perspiration on his shirt under the armpits and the set of his lips. I knew it wasn't the best time to interrupt him with questions about current history, but I did so anyway, because the thing had been eating at me all afternoon. I asked him point-blank if in his opinion the Nazis were capable of conquering the world.

"Is that what they're feeding you at that school?" he said, glancing over at me without changing the pitch of his head.

"No. It's just a thing some of my friends are talking about."

"Well, don't you worry about the Nazis," my father said, taking up a coil for close examination. "The Nazis aren't going to get anywhere in the end. The British will take care of that."

The subject came up again a few weeks later when the German School called a half-day holiday and a special program in the assembly hall to celebrate the union of Germany and Austria, with non-Germans excused from the celebration. That was early in March, when it was still cold out but not enough so to keep our group from heading off during that free afternoon to climb up Mount Hortiati at the back of the city. We took a bus as far as the village named after the mountain and then climbed into the forest above it. The trees thinned out eventually so that you could get a full view of the city below and the bay beyond it, and then beyond that, the open sea. The air was sharply clear that day, the beach along the bay's inner rim showing a clean line, the few white houses above it and the bluff at its outer end brought close in by the light's purity, as was solitary Olympus in the far distance, one of its twin peaks covered by snow and the other by a bright cloud that hardly moved the whole time we were up there. We stayed until the sun went down and the leftover light began to die on us, so that it looked like we might run into trouble if we didn't head back to the village and the main road. There was something sweet in the air as we started downhill, maybe from the pines behind us or the purple thyme along the way, and when the sweetness began to fade, we slowed down and sat for a while above the village to take in a last long feel of that open space. Nobody said anything while we were sitting there until Lars stood up suddenly at the far end of the jagged line we'd settled into. He picked up a rock and hurled it sidearm in the direction of the road the way you might skip a stone across the surface of the sea.

"They're going to have to put us back in a geography class if it keeps on going like this," he said.

"Geography?" Faruk said. "That's lower level. We're through with geography."

"The point is, masturbator, they're changing the map of Europe. You should hear my father on the subject. My father says now that they have Austria, they're going to keep right on going into the Sudetenland and out the other side until they reach Russia. Unless they decide to go the other way into Denmark and Holland."

"And who's going to let them do that?" Marcel said. "You think France is just going to sit there and let Germany do whatever it wants?"

"They're doing what they want," Stephan said. "My father gets reports."

He made it sound as though he knew things he wasn't free to discuss. He'd told us once with a certain pride that his father had diplomatic connections of some dark kind, but his tone was different this time.

"What sort of reports?" Marcel said.

"About outlawing the Jews inside Germany," Stephan said. "Closing businesses. I don't know what else. And who's doing anything about it?"

"Well, that's inside their own country," Marcel said. "You can't do much about what happens inside a country. Not with somebody like Hitler in charge."

"Why can't you?" Stephan said.

"I don't know," Marcel said. "Never mind Hitler. Take Mussolini. Take Metaxas."

I don't think any of us fully understood what he meant, but he seemed to be on to something.

"My father says it's just a matter of time before the British settle the whole thing," I finally said.

Everybody turned to look at me.

"The British?" Marcel said. "What can the British do?"

"Well what can the French do? The same sort of thing."

"Masturbator, please, don't make me laugh," Marcel said. "The French have the Maginot Line. What do the British have?"

I had no idea what the British had or didn't have, so I just shrugged as though the whole thing was a matter of opinion.

"Anyway, we can count on a lot more strutting around the yard by you know who," Lars said. "So we'd better be on guard for the worst."

Stephan stood up now too. "Three months more is all," he said. "Then the whole bunch of them can strut through their own shit as much as they want."

He headed on downhill. The rest of us followed a little ways behind. We knew that what he had in mind wasn't just the end of that school year and that he was telling us he wouldn't be back at the German School when classes started up again in the fall. It didn't leave a good feeling, and though we couldn't talk about it, everybody must have realized that it meant our group wasn't going to hold together indefinitely. Stephan still showed up at the cafe after that, but not regularly, and when he did, there was a new pride in him, an independence in his manner that distanced him from the rest of us, though nobody was ready to blame him for that or do anything about it. And then Marcel began to show up less and less too. That may have been because he felt he was getting too old to hang out with us, even if Lars and I had also turned seventeen by then. It's more likely that Marcel realized he'd lost some standing with our group over the issue of women, in particular the episode with our classmate Sara.

The issue had begun with some casual talk during one of those winter days when we'd found that it was too windy to build a safe fire in our roofless cottage and had moved to the goat shed next door. It was dark in that shed and crowded, so each of us had cleared a place for himself on the ground, pushed away the dung and lined a hollow with straw to sit in. There was nothing to do in there. You got bored very quickly if you didn't talk about something interesting, and maybe not being in a circle and not having to look at each other all the time made it easier to talk about the more delicate or controversial or enticing subjects. What we ended up talking about that day was the possibility of bringing one of the girls from our class up there. Faruk was against it because he said both his mother and father told him women couldn't be trusted. Marcel claimed that the right kind of girl could be, and that he in fact knew one or two. Stephan argued that in that school we weren't allowed to get to know girls well enough to find out who was the right kind and who wasn't. And Lars wanted to know what would happen if we did find the right kind.

"I mean what would we do if one of them did come up here with us," Lars said. "Take turns?"

"What's wrong with that?" Marcel said. "If she's willing."

"Not me," Faruk said. "I wouldn't trust her however willing she is. She'd tell everybody in that school and just get us in trouble."

"That, my beloved masturbator, shows how much you know about women," Marcel said. "You think they're so different from us? You think they don't want it as much as we do? Most of them, anyway. And once they've done it, you think they're going to tell anybody that they have?"

"And what would the others do while one of us was at it," Lars said. "Just stand around and watch?"

"Did I say that?" Marcel said. "Why are you trying to make me out to be decadent? We could take turns in here, and the rest could wait next door. Sometime when it isn't so cold."

Nobody said anything. You might have concluded that they were actually thinking it over, some of them anyway, and that included me. I began to have a strange feeling, too new to place exactly, a mixture of excitement and fear. And since nothing more was said on the subject one way or the other, the assumption seemed to be that we'd all more or less agreed to go along if Marcel came up with the right kind of girl. It must have been two weeks into February when Marcel announced, as we gathered together in the cafe, that Sara had accepted our invitation to meet with the group and was ready to pay a visit to our cottage the first decent day that came along. And that happened the following week, after the Vardar wind had finally died down and the sun had been out long enough to warm the air, unusually so for late February.

Sara wasn't exactly a stranger to our group. She was a short girl, with black hair that almost reached her waist, and a full figure that she didn't mind showing off by the tight sweaters and skirts she wore. There was a rumor that earlier in the year she'd had a boyfriend in one of the upper classes at Anatolia College, because she'd been spotted in a sweets shop along the route up there sitting with a boy at least two years older than any one of her classmates. The possibility of her having had an older boyfriend put her in a special category of worldliness that was enough to rouse the envy of some of the girls in our class and the keen interest of some of the boys, so that she was one of those about whom there had been gossip. Nobody seemed very surprised when Marcel brought up her name, and nobody asked him what he'd said to her about the visit to our hideout or what she'd said to him about it. We took for granted that he knew what he was doing.

The four of us had been sitting in our cafe waiting for over half an hour when Marcel showed up with Sara, and during that time we'd talked about anything but what was actually on our minds. When the two of them came in, we sort of nodded hello to each other, Sara smiling but not really, and there was very little talk during the climb up to the outer edge of the city except between Marcel and Sara, who were walking side by side ahead of us, turning every now and then to say something to each other that we couldn't hear. The whole trip up there didn't feel natural, probably because it was the first time we were bringing a stranger along with us, but also because we didn't know exactly what lay ahead. And the general mood didn't change much once we got up there, though Marcel and Sara seemed to be on friendly terms by that time. He showed her the cottage and the grounds, then stood back to let her poke her head into the goat shed, about which she didn't say anything we could hear but made a face that said a lot. Marcel settled down beside her against the back wall of the cottage while the rest of us occupied ourselves with building a fire.

"What do you spend your time doing up here in the cold?" Sara said to Marcel loud enough for all of us to hear.

"We talk a lot," Marcel said.

"About what?" Sara said.

"You know," Marcel said. "What men talk about."

He suddenly reached inside his coat and brought out two cigarettes. He offered one to Sara, but she shook her head. Marcel lit his. He'd never smoked before in front of us, but he seemed to know how to do it.

"What do you talk about when you get together with your girl-friends?" Marcel said. "I bet it's the same kind of thing."

"I don't really have any girlfriends," Sara said. "One or two maybe. But not at school."

"Anyway, you must talk about the boys you go out with and what you do with them," Marcel said.

"Not me," Sara said. "I don't talk to anybody about that sort of thing."

Marcel took a long drag on his cigarette. "Well, that's the best way," he said. "You should keep things like that to yourself."

Faruk had the fire going well now, and the three of us who had been gathering wood for it formed a kind of half circle and concentrated on feeding it more than it needed to be fed. Marcel studied his cigarette, then flipped it into the fire.

"What would you say to our taking a little walk?" he said to Sara. "Or going next door."

"It's nice here," Sara said. "Now that the fire's going."

"Well it's nice next door too," Marcel said. "Not as exposed."

"You mean that goat shed?"

"It may not seem so great just from poking your head in there, but it's really very comfortable."

"It smells of goat manure," Sara said.

"What's wrong with a little goat manure? It's perfectly healthy. When you were growing up in your village you must have eaten goat meat and drunk goat milk from the same kind of goats we have here."

"Well that doesn't mean I have to like their smell," Sara said.

Marcel stood up. "Then let's just take a walk. The point is, we don't have all the time in the world."

"I thought the point was for me to meet your friends," Sara said.

"Well go ahead and meet them," Marcel said. "Talk to them. I'll be waiting next door."

He sauntered off, trying to make it look nonchalant, and disappeared around the corner. Sara just sat there looking at the ground. It was very embarrassing. Lars finally went over and sat down beside her.

"Are you and Marcel sort of going together?" Lars said. "Because if you are, maybe the rest of us should leave the two of you alone awhile."

"We've been out together in the afternoon a few times, if that's what you mean," Sara said.

"I just wondered if there was something serious between the two of you," Lars said.

"Well, I like him," Sara said. "At least I think I do. But sometimes he acts strange. I don't think I understand him."

"The point is, what did he tell you that he had in mind about coming up here?"

"He said he wanted me to meet his friends. His special friends, he said. I thought that was a thing he wanted and that it would be a nice thing for me to do."

She got up suddenly and came over to kneel in front of the fire to warm her hands. Then she opened her overcoat. She was wearing a red sweater that reached up to her neck and folded over there, and the sweater was held in tight around her waist by a wide black belt so that her breasts stood out above it. I thought she looked beautiful kneeling there with her black hair falling down over her shoulders.

"Well, maybe we'd just better let the two of you be alone a bit," Lars said. "The rest of us can start on down the hill."

He signaled us with his head to get up. Sara was still looking into the fire.

"Well, I'm not going next door," she said. "You can be sure of that."

"What you do is up to you and Marcel," Lars said. "We'll see the two of you in class."

"I mean it," Sara said.

The four of us headed on down the hill, and we finished out our lunch period in the cafe. It was hard for me to figure out how I felt about that outing, I guess disappointed and embarrassed at the same time. But I didn't know exactly why I was, and though I really felt sorry for Sara and the way Marcel had talked to her up there, I also felt something else about her that made my stomach tighten and that took a while to go away. When we went to class that afternoon, Marcel and Sara were both there. He never told us what had gone on after we left. In fact, he never mentioned Sara again. I ran into her in the school corridor later in the week while she was getting a book out of her locker, and as I stood there trying to figure out what I should say to her, she brought the book down and held it close against her chest with both arms wrapped around it as though it was something to cuddle.

"Your friend Marcel doesn't know as much as he thinks he knows," she said to me, trying to smile. "At least about somebody's feelings. And making use of them."

"I know what you mean," I said. " I—"

"I don't think you do," Sara said. "But it isn't really your fault. Or your other friends. It's my fault for trusting him when I should have been smarter."

"I can't say that I really trust him either," I said.

"That's up to you and him," Sara said. "All I know is I won't let that sort of thing happen to me ever again."

I wanted to tell her that I wouldn't let it happen to me ever again either, but I couldn't then, and though I saw her in the corridor once in a while after that and though she was friendly enough toward me in a rather distant way, I could never bring myself to tell her what I wanted to or even talk about much of anything after we'd said hello.

It wasn't long after Stephan and Marcel began to withdraw from the group regularly that I became so preoccupied with my German tutorial sessions that I began to withdraw as well. After the first very awkward drill exercises, my sessions with Magda began to go much better through March and into April, when it sometimes became warm enough and the days long enough to allow the two of us to sit out in the garden below my house. I had waited some weeks before I found the courage to ask her if I could call her Magda, and she seemed to grant me that privilege as a reward for the progress I was making. "Why not?" she'd said with a shrug and a half-smile. "Since it seems we've found that we can work together without being enemies. But please, not in front of your parents."

I chose to read a degree of conspiracy into that last remark, and it thrilled me at the time, but there was nothing in Magda's manner to justify my making very much of it. She was still formal and proper during our tutorial sessions, as though she needed that for confidence, and I was careful not to take advantage of this one early concession she'd made, rarely saying her name out loud, except to myself when I was alone and couldn't help myself, or didn't want to.

After our first attempt to get into Goethe's poetry, Magda lent me the book she had read from that day and suggested that I look through it as the spirit might move me, not as required homework, which would come from the phrase book and certain writing exercises she would begin to assign. The poetry, she said, was simply for whatever pleasure I might get out of it since that was what poetry ought to be for. But this didn't keep me from having a problem about the book for some time. It sat there unread on the dresser in my room beside the Bible my mother had given me for my seventeenth birthday, the kind of Bible that had room at the back for you to record the main events in your life from birth to confirmation to marriage to the births of your children. That Bible had also sat on my dresser unopened because there was nothing in my life that I felt I could record except maybe the date and place of my birth that my mother had already inscribed in there for me, and the date I'd started my lessons with Magda, which didn't seem a thing that should be recorded in a Bible, given the nature of my persistent frame of mind.

What got me to take up the book of poems seriously after the one time I'd leafed through it with barely controlled boredom was a plot I conceived when I happened to pick it up again one day and came across a poem by Goethe that I learned, after a conference with my mother, was a thing called a "sonnet." It clearly matched the one which had so moved Magda that afternoon when she'd left me sitting by myself on the couch feeling awkward and foolish. This sonnet was not as confusing as that one, but it took a lot of work with the dictionary and some help from my mother before I had all the words clear in my head, and though I can't say that I grasped the meaning of everything in it, I got enough of a hold on it after a great deal of practice to be able to recite it from memory with only a mistake here and there. The most important part of it, anyway, was the beginning, where some kissing was mentioned, which is what had put me on to it in the first place, and that part I could get through without a hitch.

The poem was called "The Farewell," at least that was how my mother translated the German title. The gist of it was that the "I" in the poem had a craving for a thousand kisses but had to settle for one as he said farewell to somebody, and this made for a bitter parting that was deeply painful to him, but after thinking that he had lost the heat of his desires, he had a vision that told him he hadn't really lost a thing and every joy that had gone was his again. I thought this poem at least hinted at what was on my mind, and even if Magda didn't get the message in it, or chose to pretend she didn't, I figured my having learned most of it by heart would be an impressive step forward. So I saved it for one of those late April afternoons when we could sit out in the garden until it turned mosquito time, and then I sprang the poem on her.

We had come to the end of our tutorial session, and we were just sitting there on the wicker chairs that my mother had set out in the garden earlier in the month, waiting out the few minutes before Magda caught a ride into town with the school's evening bus. She suddenly put the drill book on the ground on top of some papers and moved out to the center of the patch of lawn that the gardener had created back there and sat on the grass with her arms around her knees to look out toward Salonika Bay well beyond the lower end of the school grounds. I didn't go over and sit beside her as I wanted to. I just stayed put where I was and said behind her back that I had something for her. "What's that?" she said, turning to glance at me. "This," I said, and I recited the poem, stumbling only once as I got toward the end and maybe not getting all the words exactly right but close enough so that there was no reason to choke up.

Magda sat there staring at me. Then she shook her head.

"That's unbelievable," she said in Greek. "Did they teach you that in school?"

"In school?" I said. "I learned it by myself."

"You did?"

"From that book you gave me."

Magda stood up and brushed off the back of her skirt. Then she came over and stood in front of me. I thought she might kneel there for a second and embrace me, kiss me on both cheeks or something, but no such luck. She just stood there looking at me as though I was this strange overgrown kid she hadn't seen twenty times before.

"You mean you memorized that poem on your own? Just for the fun of it?"

"Well not exactly just for the fun of it," I said. "I thought, you know, that you might be impressed with my progress."

"I am truly impressed," she said, back in German again, which threw cold water on the whole thing. "You have certainly made a great deal of progress. I know that your parents will be very pleased."

"Who cares about my parents?" I said in Greek, half under my breath.

Then she did kneel down, smiling, and actually touched my knee with her hand.

"You shouldn't say things like that about your parents," she said in Greek. "They're only trying to help you."

"Sure," I said. "They're all right. They just don't know what's really going on inside me most of the time."

Magda stood up and went to sit down on the grass again, turned a little more toward me now so that I could at least see her face.

"You don't know how lucky you are," she said. "There are parents and parents."

"You have problems with yours?"

"My parents are hateful," Magda said, and as she did so she glanced away from me, as though what she had said didn't call for further conversation. But of course I couldn't leave it there.

"How is that?" I said.

Magda just shook her head and didn't say anything. She was still looking away. I decided to go over and sit beside her, but before I could get there she was up and gathering her books and papers.

"Would you like to walk with me to the bus?" she said.

It was the first time she'd suggested I do that, and it was what I had to settle for, which left me with a kind of brooding disappointment since that took only five minutes and we didn't talk about anything really interesting on the way. But there had been times when I'd felt worse after being with her, and she'd said enough while we'd been sitting out in the garden to stir my imagination about what it was in her life that would allow a girl as careful as she seemed to be about manners to say a thing like that about her parents and to look the way she had when she said it. I decided I would try to follow up on that, and the only way I could think of doing so without making her suspicious was to see if I could dig up any information about her from Jackson Ripaldo, who lived in one of the few villas on the road above the general area where Magda lived and who, I assumed, must have known her during his time at the German School.

Jackson was not what I would call an intimate friend of mine at that particular time, but even though he was older than I was, I felt comfortable with him because we used to shoot baskets together sometimes at Anatolia College on weekends. From his talk you got the sense that he was not only wiser than you were about the ways of the world, at least when it came to women, but knew that there were certain secrets that men had to keep between themselves. I never had any trouble getting my father to drive me up to the College and leave me there for a visit, because Jackson's connection to the American consulate made him highly desirable in the view of my parents, who supposedly saw his parents as the cream of the small American community in that city. Of course they didn't know that Jackson's language on the basketball court, at least in Greek, was right out of the village dung heap, and conversation with him in any language could turn dirty the minute you gave him an opening to move in with his knowledge of sexual practices, whether in the country we were living in or remoter places.

I decided to bring up the question of Magda on the basketball court while we were playing one-on-one rather than in his house, because it would seem more casual that way and there was no chance of being overheard out there. Jackson was shorter than I was but faster, and he got in more practice than most of us outsiders because he lived close enough to that court to get there on his own any time he felt like it, but I managed to keep up with him until I got into the subject that had brought me up there. My hunch turned out to be right. Jackson knew a lot about Magda, more than I wanted to hear.

"Yeah, she was one of the smartest in her class two years ago and they gave her one of those prizes they give out at Christmastime. Why do you want to know? You got the hots for her or something? She's a little old for you, buddy, isn't she? I mean she must be nineteen or twenty by now."

"She's tutoring me in German," I said. "I see her two or three times a week these days, so I'm just curious about her."

"Well, if you've got the hots for her, forget it. She's all hooked up with some guy. Or anyway, she was. It created a big scandal."

"Magda?" I said. "Are you kidding?"

Jackson faked me out completely and went in for an easy lay-up.

"Why should I kid you? She got involved with one of the teachers up here at Anatolia."

"She got involved with a teacher?"

"Hey, let's play, O.K.?"

"What kind of teacher?"

"How do I know? I think he taught Greek up here. Or English. Anyway, they got rid of him."

"Because of her?"

"I don't know if it was because of her. Maybe he was just a shitty teacher. All I know is that her father raised hell about it."

I went over and sat on the bench at the side of the court, pretending to be pooped.

"You're not giving up already?" Jackson said.

"I've got stomach cramps."

Jackson went on shooting baskets by himself. "You've got the hots for Magda, that's what you've got."

"You're crazy," I said. "She's almost three years older than me."

"A clear case of testicle fever," Jackson said. "For which there is only one cure."

"What's that?"

"A visit to the Vardar district. The only cure. Ask any Greek in your neighborhood."

"I don't have to ask any Greek," I said. "I know all about the Vardar district."

"But you don't know what's vital about the cure the whores down there give someone with testicle fever."

"What's so vital?"

"They teach you how to fuck and forget," Jackson said, swishing one in.

"Where did Magda's father raise hell?" I said.

"He raised hell up here with some of the big shots at the College for one thing. And they say he was told to go home and mind his own family business."

"So what was the big scandal?"

"Your friend Magda dropped out of school for two weeks. Just disappeared. I guess she went off somewhere with this guy, then got bored and came back on her own."

I stood up and stretched myself with some exercises as coolly as I could.

"How do you know she went off with the guy?" I said.

"I don't know. It just figures. All I know is that after that you didn't see her around much. I think her father locked her up for a while. And she dropped out of school for a year, which is why she's older than the others in her class."

"Locked her up?"

"At home. Wouldn't let her out except when he got around to letting her go back to that school. Only I'd pulled out of our local German asylum for the criminally insane by that time, so I really can't speak for what happened to her after that little episode."

I went over and started shooting baskets again, but I can't say that my heart was in it. Jackson creamed me. Then he got bored and gave up. The trouble wasn't only what he'd told me. He'd also seen something in me that I hadn't planned on showing anybody, and I swore that this one-sided love affair, this overheated erotic obsession with my German tutor, was finished once and for all.

My resolution to cool things off with Magda lasted through the next tutorial session and the one following it. For her part, Magda was friendlier than she had been, I suppose still touched by that poem I'd memorized to impress her. But from my point of view, it was all business when we were together, all a matter of my repeating this and that in German in imitation of her rhythm, whether it was how you get to the train station on the right around the corner or the pharmacy on the left a short distance down the street. And I managed to keep my concentration relatively steady when it came to the grammar exercises, even when I was called on to identify the subject and object of a sentence that had one or the other so far out of any natural order that you had to wonder how native-born Germans managed to learn to speak to each other early in life without tripping all over themselves. Anyway, there was no time out for any bullshit about personal matters—that is, until my resolve broke down again over the subject of the school we were both forced to attend.

This happened during the third session, a week or so after I'd learned about her secret life from my friend Jackson. I have to admit that the information he'd given me provoked confused feelings, not just anger and jealousy, which were natural enough, but a new kind of erotic revery that was much more disturbing. When my mind would clear of the resentment I felt against her for turning out to be not much different from Sara or other girls I knew at that school, I found myself picturing her doing all kinds of things with her dark-haired, mustached, olive-skinned lover, which is what I assumed he would be, being Greek. And in the end this would drive me wild with hatred and longing, to the point where my mind would suddenly clear sharply and go on to something else, the way you wake yourself from a nightmare.

We were sitting out in the garden again the day the conversation turned to the German School. It was Magda's fault for bringing it up. I was just getting into the lesson as usual, trying to work out a sentence that had a subject on one page and the verb that went with it far down the page following. At the time we were sitting catty-cornered again with a wicker table between us, and Magda suddenly took the exercise book out of my hand and closed it not quite gently enough to keep it from making a sound that startled me.

"Now tell me what's wrong, will you please?" she said very sweetly and in Greek.

"Who says anything's wrong? I just find that the stupidest sentence any human being would want to think up."

"I'm not talking about the sentence. I mean what's wrong with you. In general."

"There's nothing wrong with me in general."

"Did something happen at school to upset you?" Magda said, her voice still a bit too sweet. "You're just not the same person."

"Actually, I'm doing all right in school these days. Though I can't say I like everything that's going on there. But that's nothing new."

"What's going on there that you don't like?"

"The way they've begun treating some of my friends. Stephan, for example. Just because he's Jewish. He's decided to drop out of school before the year's even over."

"You don't have to tell me about that sort of thing," Magda said. "I'm Jewish too. Half of me, anyway."

"You're Jewish?"

"What's so surprising about that? There are a lot of us in Salonika."

"I know that," I said. "I just thought you were Spanish or something. Your name sounds Spanish to me."

"Portuguese, actually. My father was the Portuguese Consul for a while even though his parents were Jewish and he was born in this country. But my mother's Greek."

"No kidding? Your father was a Consul?"

"Honorary," Magda said. "Which is why they don't dare pick on me at school. It's just my father who picks on me."

She stood up at that and went over to look at a spread of sweet peas that were coming into bloom on the outer edge of the lawn. She'd offered me an opening, and of course given the mood I was in at the time, I wasn't either cool or clever enough to let the thing just close up again. I went over and stood near her, a little behind her.

"I heard your father locked you up," I said.

She whirled on me. "Who told you that?"

"I just heard it," I said. "And I heard you ran away with somebody for two weeks."

She was turned around now and just stood there looking at me, and the way she was looking made me feel like easing sideways and bending low to hide among those sweet peas until I was clear out the other side of the garden and on my way south heading for the cow barn as quickly as I could.

"What you heard isn't true," she said. "I went off by myself. But whatever I did isn't anybody's business."

"I'm sorry," I said. "I know it isn't really anybody's business. And I didn't believe it anyway."

She turned back and bent to smell a cluster of those new flowers, which gave off a scent strong enough to break through the sweet stench of cow manure that would come wafting over that garden whenever the wind came up out of the south.

"People can be very cruel," she said. "They talk too easily. Especially in this town. So just don't believe everything you hear."

I wanted to go over there and kneel beside her and kiss her hand, tell her that I was ashamed of what I'd said, tell her to hit me for it if she wanted, as hard as she could, but if the tears came it wouldn't be for getting what I deserved, it would be from the joy of having heard her say that she'd gone off not with a mustached, olive-skinned lover but by herself. Instead I stood where I was and told another lie.

"I didn't believe what I heard," I said. "Not any of it. I only mentioned it because I, well, I respect you, I really mean it, and I thought you ought to know what some people were saying behind your back. That's all."

She reached over then and ran her hand through my hair to ruffle it. I was so surprised by the gesture that instead of grabbing her hand and kissing it, I sort of pulled my head back, and by the time I realized what I'd done, what kind of insanely wrong message that might have sent her, it was too late, the hand was gone.

"Well, don't worry about it," Magda said. "Someday I'll tell you the whole story. When you're a bit older and our lessons are done."

She said that with a little smile that I took to mean she only half meant it about my having to get a bit older. And I also chose to see what she'd said as implying that she had some kind of continuing friendship in mind beyond the classroom, which allowed me to ignore any other implications that might have changed my mood, which was bordering on hysterical elation. She didn't ask me to walk her to the bus, but I did anyway, and then I kept on going down to the cow barn to watch the afternoon milking. Seeing those cows that had been shipped over from America always raised my spirits any-way, I suppose because they were the same Guernseys and Holsteins I'd learned to milk in upstate New York during the summer months I spent helping out on the family farm that my grandfather had created out of thick forestland. He'd started out with ten acres and had ended up with nearly a thousand, which brought in enough income to get his children through college, though he himself al-ways talked poverty and never seemed to have any extra cash lying around that wasn't in small coins, at least not when his grandchil-dren were in the room.

But what occupied my thoughts among the cows that particular afternoon was not the old familiar longing to be back on my grandfather's farm where nobody worried much about telling me what I could do or not do and where I was free to travel the land as I chose. What occupied me was the less familiar longing to be alone with Magda so that I could hear what she'd called the whole story and then try to tell her some of my own. I felt I had to arrange that desperately soon, before she went off God knows where for her summer vacation only to disappear after that into what seemed a place so remote and closed off from my life as to be a nunnery or a prison, that is, the local university. And I had to work out some way of getting to be with her outside our makeshift classroom, because she had made it clear as the lessons got more difficult—and I'd played right into her hands recently—that there wouldn't be time any longer for much personal talk during our tutorial sessions, which would end in a few weeks when exam time arrived for both of us.

It finally came to me that a cow barn at milking time wasn't really the best setting for thinking through my problem. A church would have been better, because my situation seemed so complicated at that point that I felt what I really needed was a peaceful place to ask for some kind of divine intervention to bring me understanding. But in those days there was no church at the school where my father worked, just an assembly hall filled with rows of straw-seated chairs. The students would gather there on Sundays to sing evangelical hymns like "Come to Jesus" and "Count Your Many Blessings" and "Bringing in the Sheaves" in a rich, full-voiced Greek approximation of English from the worn hymn books that had been left there by the Christian missionaries who had founded the school long ago and who apparently didn't know or care that the students who sang so radiantly in that mostly incomprehensible language belonged to a Christian church that had almost two thousand years of belief and ritual going for it by the time those hymn books in English arrived on the scene. As I walked out of the cow barn I decided I had no choice in a country as ancient as this new one I found myself in but to play it safe when it came to calling on higher powers for help, so I settled for making a deeply sincere wish and crossing myself three times the way I'd seen local women in black do at weddings and funerals.

THE BREAK I NEEDED TO HAVE MAGDA TO MYSELF FOR AN AF-ternoon came early in May when our school suddenly announced a special holiday to permit a joint drill on the school grounds for the Hitler Jugend and the new Greek youth organization. This was to prepare for an afternoon ceremony that was to include band music and speeches on a huge platform erected at one end of the school yard. We were told the speeches would have something to do with the way Germans were being mistreated in the Sudetenland and their right to independence. At the same time, the Greeks would be celebrating some treaty they'd signed with Turkey. Those who wouldn't be taking part in the drill because they weren't German or Greek would be excused from school for the full day.

This gave me only two days' notice to work with. My first move was to try and get my father involved, because I knew that my plan for taking an afternoon off with Magda was bound to fail if I didn't have somebody from the older generation to help make the idea at least believable, and my father was not as shrewd about human relations as my mother was, though he also had a tender side to him that you could usually count on and that sometimes came out in odd ways. I remember Sam telling me when he came home with a broken elbow one day not long after we'd arrived in Greece that my father had gotten in a shoving match with the army doctor who was supposed to be the finest bone specialist in Macedonia but who caused Sam unbearable pain when he bent my brother's elbow back and forth to see if it was really broken. Besides the advantage of my father's good nature, I felt I might have a reasonably easy time getting my way with him these days because I sensed that he felt a little guilty about having taken Sam and me out of school in the States in order to get himself a job abroad that didn't allow him much time to give his family. On the Monday that the ceremony was announced for Wednesday, I tracked my father down in the farm machinery barn, which is where he normally hung out even after the school day was over.

He was working on a new monstrosity that had just arrived there from the States, a giant contraption called a combine, the first of its kind in Greece, as he announced to us one evening at dinner, an engineering marvel that could do all at once what three other giant farm machines couldn't do as well alone. He was working with a wrench high up on top of it, so that I had to make my pitch louder than I would have liked, explaining to him that Wednesday would be a day off at school to celebrate the cause of the Germans in the Sudetenland, and since I had a tutorial session that same afternoon with Miss Sevillas that I could hardly afford to just drop, I wondered if he might be willing to drive her and me out to the beach so that we could work together out there on my German without costing her a chance to get a little suntan during the course of her day off from school. I could be pretty certain that if my father did agree to drive us out there, he wouldn't stay around long, because one thing he was definitely not keen on at the time was lying around on sand, surely out of the question when there was a novel monstrosity to play with back home.

"What beach do you have in mind?" he said, as though he'd barely grasped what I'd just explained.

"Any beach," I said. "Out along the bay. Where everybody else goes."

"And what has that got to do with this ceremony about the Sudetenland?"

"Nothing," I said, my voice getting louder. "That just gives us foreign students a day off."

"Well, I'll have to check with your mother," he said. "I'm a little busy now. And there's plenty of time to discuss it before Wednesday."

"The thing is, I'll have to make arrangements for this special tutorial session tomorrow at school. Because that's the only time I'll get to see Magda, I mean Miss Sevillas, before we get that holiday, since she's not due out here until Wednesday, which is the day she probably won't be coming out because she has the day off."

My father stared down at me without seeing me at all.

"O.K., I'll do my best," he said so that I could barely hear him. "I just can't think about it right this minute."

I knew I had him on my side after that. He would most likely forget about the beach idea completely until I brought it up again, and if I delayed doing that until the last minute, he wouldn't have a chance to discuss it with my mother. And when I finally did bring it up, he'd feel so guilty about having forgotten his promise to do his best that he'd drive Magda and me out there to the beach without a word and leave us there alone for at least the better part of the afternoon so that he could get back to put in more time on his combine. It was Magda who wouldn't take to the idea easily, that I was certain of.

I figured the first problem would be getting to her the next day simply to discuss it. I had rarely run into her at the German School, because her senior class was usually let out at a somewhat different time from those lower down in the system, and she would sometimes take advantage of the special after-hours study periods for those preparing to go to the University. Besides, after my conversation with Jackson Ripaldo, I hadn't felt much like hanging around to find out who her friends might be, male or female, but especially male. And once she and I had reached a certain understanding about her past, I didn't want her to get the idea that I was still spying on her. But on that Tuesday, I had no choice. It was wait for her until she got out of class in the afternoon or miss her completely. To be certain that she didn't slip by me because of bad timing, I skipped my last class that day, a thing that surely would have caused problems for me if everybody in authority at that school hadn't been so tied up with putting on a good show for the cause of Greater Germany the following afternoon.

I was watching for Magda from the cafe across the street when she came through the school gate arm in arm with another girl and with some others following behind. There was no way I could cross the street and just walk up to her in the middle of that crowd to tell her what was on my mind. I watched the group of them move on down to the streetcar stop on their side of the street a ways beyond the gate, and at that point the group broke up, with some of them crossing over to the stop going in the other direction. Magda stayed on the far side with those of her friends waiting to head out of town toward the Depot and the crosstown street called the 25th of March, which eventually came out to where she lived on the way to Harilaou. Since I couldn't very well cross over at that point and try to squeeze on board the streetcar behind her, I had no choice but to try and do what I'd seen Greek kids and even men get away with time and again, that is, climb aboard the bar that hung out of the back of the thing like a narrow stiff tongue. I waited until the streetcar passed by the cafe I was in, and while it was standing at the stop opposite loading up, I cut across the street and climbed aboard that tongue just as we took off and the conductor turned to busy himself with those who had come on board in the normal way. The trouble was that a character just a little shorter and scrawnier than I was had already stationed himself on the tongue when I arrived there.

"Christ and the Virgin," he said when I jumped up behind him and grabbed the back window screen to hang on. "Are you trying to kill me?"

"Don't give me any trouble," I said, "or we're going down together."

"How can I give you trouble? I can't even breathe."

"Just keep still and we'll be all right."

"I'm keeping still. What do you expect me to do when you've got yourself glued to my ass?"

I could smell him now. He hadn't washed in weeks, and the black, stringy look of his hair told me that he must be a Gypsy or something like it, let loose to travel through the city as he chose for whatever cash he might beg for or just collect. If the streetcar hadn't been picking up speed at that moment, I'd have jumped off then and there and taken my chances on the next one that came along, but before we started slowing down again, that raunchy character slithered out from under me and made a practiced run for the curb. I looked back to see him give me the Greek five-finger sign meant to bring me a bad fate by relieving me instantly of each of my five senses.

I stayed with the streetcar all the way to the 25th of March Street stop, keeping low so the conductor wouldn't spot me, and managed out of pure luck to time my jump at the end so that I got off the tongue well ahead of the stop without killing myself. I was waiting on the corner when Magda crossed to transfer to the streetcar heading out to Harilaou. Despite the Gypsy kid and his attack on my fate, the gods had seen to it that Magda was by herself at that point.

I don't remember that she said anything when she first saw me, though that could be because I was too nervous for my mind to record things as it normally would, but I do remember the way she stood there staring at me, stopped in her tracks. And I could tell from her look that she knew I wasn't there by accident. That was a thing I liked.

"I thought I might run into you here," I said. "On your way toward Harilaou."

"That was clever of you," she said in Greek, always a good sign. "Why did you want to run into me?"

"About tomorrow's tutorial session," I said. "I thought we might take the opportunity to hold that session on the beach since we don't have any school."

We'd started walking side by side up the 25th of March Street but that made her stop again.

"On the beach?"

She looked at me, sort of smiling, sort of tolerant, I wouldn't say exactly tenderly. "You're out of your mind," she said.

"What's so crazy about that?" I said. "We can go through what we have to cover out there just as well as we can in the garden and still have plenty of time for a swim or just lying around."

"My father would never allow that," Magda said. "Unless I brought him along. And it would bore him to death. Not to speak of what his being there would do to me."

"Well how about my bringing my father along? Wouldn't that amount to the same thing?"

She was really smiling now, and since we'd started walking again, I felt her close beside me, our arms not quite touching but close enough to make me deliriously uncomfortable.

"I didn't realize that you'd become so fond of German that you'd give up a holiday with your friends just so you wouldn't miss a lesson with me."

"Well, it's important at this point," I said soberly. "It's getting near exam time and I have to know what I'm doing."

"I think you know what you're doing," Magda said. "Anyway, it's out of the question. How could I possibly explain it to my father?"

"You can say it's a family outing. Since my father will take us out there."

"And what about your mother?"

"Well, I'm not sure about my mother. Isn't one parent enough?"

Magda shook her head. "It's mad," she said. "I mean I appreciate the thought, honestly. But it's out of the question."

An insane idea occurred to me. "Well what if I get my father to talk to your father. Sort of invite you formally."

"To the beach?"

"Well, if your father's so difficult, why do we have to spell it all out? Why can't you just come over to our house for my lesson the way you would anyway and we'll take it from there."

"I'm surprised at you," Magda said. "You mean I'm supposed to deceive my father?"

She had stopped again to look at me, and there was no escaping the playfulness in her voice this time. We'd almost reached the sign for the next stop on the 25th of March Street, and I knew I was about to lose her. I decided what the hell.

"You don't have to deceive him," I said. "Just don't tell him."

Magda was silent. We came up even with the sign and stood there.

"Well, coming to your house for a lesson is one thing, and going to the beach is another. I suppose if you're willing to give up your friends for the holiday, I owe you the lesson at least. Anyway, here's my streetcar."

I eased my elbow against her arm a little awkwardly as a parting touch that I hoped would say all that needed to be said, but at the last minute I remembered to call out to her that the time of the lesson had to be changed to two o'clock instead of four. I couldn't be sure she heard, because she didn't turn around, but when she climbed up into the streetcar, she gave me a little wave before going inside to take her seat.

The next day Magda was at our house at two sharp, but the truth was that I myself had not had an easy time arriving at that hour with sufficient peace of mind to greet her as calmly as I would have liked. The most serious obstacle proved to be my mother, who lived in another world when it came to my recreational needs. She began the morning of my holiday from school by suggesting at breakfast that I take some time out to wash the family car. I didn't have any objection to that, it would only take up an hour of my life, and I figured that along with the small addition to my allowance of drachmas it would bring in for possible use later in the day, it might put her in a more receptive mood when I got around to informing her about my afternoon plans. But as soon as I had the car washed and before I'd worked out clearly what I was going to tell her, she let me know what plans she herself had for my afternoon.

I was up in her room at the time collecting the drachmas she owed me for the car wash, and she was sitting in her bathrobe in front of the mirror running a comb through her blond hair, which was still wet from the shampooing she'd just given it. Her face, which I had always thought fairly beautiful in a round, full-cheeked, cream-rich sort of way, looked red and puffy to me now. It showed the weight she'd put on since coming to Greece, and the strain of coping with the new life my father had brought on her. After she'd doled out the money and I was still standing there looking at it and then at her, trying to determine if her mood was right for the subject I had in mind, she said that even though it was a bit sudden for my school to have announced this holiday we were having, she was pleased that it would give me some free time that afternoon to work with her on my English grammar correspondence course. This correspondence course was a thing that she had assigned both Sam and me earlier that spring, when my trouble at school—trouble which after all had nothing whatsoever to do with the way I handled English—gave my mother the idea that my brother and I might be losing touch with our native language now that we were spending so much time speaking either Greek or German with our friends.

"I don't think I'll be able to work with you on my English this afternoon," I said. "I have my German tutorial session with Miss Sevillas."

"This afternoon?" my mother said. "Doesn't she have a holiday too?"

"Well, we thought it wouldn't be a good thing to just drop my German lesson with her so close to final exams."

"Then we could do your English grammar exercises after you're through with Miss Sevillas."

"I don't think that would work either," I said. "Miss Sevillas's father has invited us to an outing on the beach. After the German lesson, that is. Or along with it."

My mother turned to look at me. I pretended to be adding her drachmas to my other drachmas and then counting what was there. It was a pathetic sum.

"This is the first I've heard of an outing," my mother said.

"Well, it was sort of a last minute thing. In view of how sudden the holiday was announced."

"Suddenly," my mother said.

"How's that?"

"Suddenly announced," my mother said.

"However," I said. "The point is, you're not expected to have to go along. It's just for the younger generation. Because Miss Sevillas thought we could work on the German a bit more while we were out there so as not to lose this opportunity."

"Is Sam invited too?"

"Sure he's invited," I said. "I just think he'd rather stay here and play soccer."

Which was entirely the truth. Sam would be no problem. He was not only a fanatic about soccer, but like my father, he hated sand. He'd told me once, somberly, that sand was full of germs and that getting crud from a beach into your toes and ears and other cavities could make you impotent some day.

"Well, then, we'd better work on the English course right now," my mother said. "As soon as I'm dressed."

"That's fine by me," I said. "We've got until lunch time."

It wasn't fine by me at all because I had a few other things to take care of before lunch, such as pulling my swimming gear together and finding my father to remind him of what he'd half promised, but the only choice I really had at that point was to work on the English grammar exercises, and the cooperative attitude that this forced on me seemed to help me ease out of a potentially dangerous situation.

"I don't understand why this outing is just coming up now," my mother said, as though to herself.

"It isn't just coming up now," I said. "I mentioned it to Dad two days ago, when he promised to drive us out there. I thought he would have told you."

That worked to end the complication with my mother, because there was no chance she wouldn't believe I hadn't told my father about it or that he hadn't forgotten to pass the word on to her. And if I felt a touch of guilt in having betrayed my father by making use of a weakness in him all too familiar to the rest of us, that was counteracted by the lift in spirits I suddenly felt in having solved the problem of getting around my mother. All that remained now was the moral and logistical problem of getting Miss Sevillas into the family car.

I found my father down at the piggery, where it turned out there had been a crisis earlier in the day when the boar had injured himself trying to climb over a low wall to get at one of the sows. My father had gone down there with the vet to check things out, and luckily the boar's injuries were not that serious or my father might have spent the whole of the afternoon helping to tend that pig, as he was known to do whenever one of the farm animals was in serious trouble or having a difficult birth—a thing I'd watched him cope with more than once on my grandfather's farm. He was standing there wiping mud off his hands with a rag, his shirt wet with sweat and his forehead deeply lined.

"I don't mean to bother you," I said. "I know you've got problems down here. But I thought I'd better warn you that Miss Sevillas may be coming over here early today so that we have plenty of time for a cram session once we get out to the beach."

"She's coming today?" my father said.

"Like I said on Monday. It's a holiday for us, so we thought we'd have a really long lesson out at the beach."

"Right," my father said, still cleaning up. "Am I supposed to be taking you out there or something?"

"That's it," I said. "Around two o'clock, if she gets here when she's supposed to. Which is half an hour from now."

"Well all I have to do is change my shirt. I'll meet you up at the house."

"The point is, I'd be grateful if you could make a point of telling her right off how much you and Mom appreciate her giving me this extra time today even though it's a holiday and especially how much the two of you appreciate her invitation."

"What invitation is that?"

"For me to join her family at the beach. So that we have the extra time I mentioned."

"Sure," my father said. "I do appreciate it. I'm just sorry that it isn't a holiday for me but just a normal working day. Which means I can't stay out there with you very long."

"I understand," I said. "But if I were you I wouldn't mention that right off, so she doesn't get the wrong idea about your having to leave. She can be a little sensitive."

When Magda arrived at two instead of four, I took it as a very good sign. Not that I'd had an opportunity to expand on why the early hour was better if we were planning the trip I had in mind, but beach or no beach, her arriving like that gave me two more hours than usual before the evening bus was scheduled to go into town, and that was a thing she knew as well as I did. But what really made my breath come short for a second was seeing her climb out of her taxi with a bag on her arm that looked suspiciously, grandly, larger than any pocketbook and made out of colored canvas. I found myself staring at that in a way that made me take too long getting around to shaking the hand she held out to me.

"Don't look so surprised at this," Magda said. "I thought you told me your family was planning a trip to the beach."

"Right," I said. "I just wasn't sure you were going to make it. I mean go along with the idea."

"I worried about it," Magda said. "Then I thought why not? I've worked hard for two months and so have you. I just didn't tell my father."

"That's great," I said. "Really great. The only thing is that my mother decided not to come along because she has too much work around the house. And my brother has a soccer game."

Magda was studying me. I don't know exactly what was going through her head because at that moment my father came skipping down the steps of our house wearing a clean cotton shirt but the same old pants and heavy work boots that had done a lot of time in the piggery. He reached out his hand to Magda, and I stepped back.

"I want you to know how much Helen and I appreciate your family's invitation and the time you're spending with Hal," he said. "As I know Hal here does too. I mean we're really grateful in general for the help you've given him. Really appreciative. Especially giving up part of your holiday like this. And I'm just sorry it turns out to be a work day for me so that I can't take the time for a swim myself. But let's not worry about that. Let's just follow me around to the garage here and climb on in the car and get going."

I didn't have the courage to look at Magda. I let my father motion her out in front of him and I just followed behind, hoping that whatever was making him ramble on that way would finally choke him up and be replaced by his normal shyness once we got ourselves inside the car. And that's what happened. Hardly a word passed between the three of us going out to the beach. Magda, who was sitting in front, turned at one point to give me a look that told me what my little plot was likely to cost me by way of renewed suspicion on her part. Aside from that, she seemed to me as radiant that day as the first time I'd seen her coming up the walk to my house, though now dressed more informally in a white blouse that was open at the neck and in a bright blue skirt. Her bare arms were no longer as white as they had been, which meant that she'd already been out in the sun often that spring, and her hair seemed to me to have turned lighter, with more gold glint in it and also longer, so that it reached her shoulders. She would flick her head every now and then to make the hair twirl sideways and back again, flick it unconsciously it seemed, as though she was trying to shake something off her mind. That made me want to reach out and touch her hair to quiet whatever might be bothering her and at the same time to get the silken feel of it. But of course there was no way I could do that with my father there, even if he was concentrating on the road now in order not to lose any time getting out to the beach so that he could turn around as soon as possible and get himself back home.

We didn't have to go very far beyond the road leading up to my father's school in order to find open country that was cultivated on the left of the road, with brushland leading down to the sea on the right, but the places where a more or less decent road would bring you out to the public stretches of beach were farther out, and that was territory unfamiliar to me. When my father turned to ask me exactly where it was we wanted to be dropped off, I threw out the only place name I could remember having heard in connection with bathing facilities out there.

"Ayia Triada," I said. "Isn't that the place your family usually goes, Miss Sevillas?"

It was all or nothing at that point. She either chose to go along with me and my charade, accepted the idea of being out there alone with me without being chaperoned by her father or my father or anybody else, or she chose to betray me, which would not only end that day but any future days I might hope to have with her, at least of the kind I had in mind. I didn't see any way in between.

"No. It is Perea where we are going to meet the others," Magda said to my father with her terrible accent in English. "A little after Ayia Triada. But the road to Ayia Triada is better. You could take us on that road and we could then walk by the beach from where you leave us."

It was pure genius. She'd not only figured out what I was up to but appeared to suspect that my father wouldn't be likely to want to spend much time walking on sand, especially the way he was dressed.

"That sounds good to me," he said. "Only if it wouldn't hurt your feelings, I might just turn around at the first place and head on back, because I've got some workmen coming in this afternoon to help me make the final adjustments on our new combine."

He went on to explain what a great piece of farm machinery a combine was, how important for Greek agriculture, and how much he hoped Miss Sevillas might want to come out during the harvest to see it in full operation.

"I would like this very much," Miss Sevillas said. The sweet hypocrite.

When my father let us off at the Ayia Triada taverna, he promised to be back before mosquito time to pick me up and anybody else who wanted a ride, then swung around to head back down the road at a clip that made you think some army unit out there was taking potshots at his rear tires. I tried to carry Magda's beach bag for her as we headed out across the beach. She wouldn't let me touch it.

"You lied to me," she said in Greek.

"I wouldn't exactly call it a lie," I said. "All I did was say—"

"It was exactly a lie," Magda said. "You told me that your family was going to the beach and that I was invited to go along. And then you pretended to your father that it was my family who had invited you to go along with me."

"Well, if I'd done anything else, I never would have gotten you to come out here."

"And you think that's an excuse for lying to me?"

"I'm sorry," I said. "I don't know why you're so upset. You seemed to go along with the idea. I mean, pretending that your family was really out here."

That was when she stopped me in my tracks and stared at me.

"I have to tell you something," she said. "That is very different and I want you to understand it. I lied in order to protect your lie, out of what I thought was loyalty to you. What you did was to try to deceive me."

"I'm sorry," I said.

She was still staring at me. "If we're going to be friends, you must never lie to me again like that. Do you understand?"

"I'm sorry," I said.

"No, it isn't enough to be sorry. You must swear that you will never lie to me. Because if you don't swear, I will never trust you. And that will be the end of it."

"I swear," I said.

I think she could see that I meant it, because she finally turned away and angled off toward a stretch of beach with nobody on it. I followed a little behind, feeling like a child who had just been whipped. I knew Magda must be right about the difference she'd pointed out, but I couldn't sort it out clearly enough to say anything to myself that would make me feel better about what I'd done. At the same time, there was a part of me that realized what she now expected of me, so uncompromising, amounted to an admission that she had already put me in some special category that wasn't fully covered by the simple word friend, at least not as I'd always thought of it. She didn't say anything more until she'd found a spot that she liked close to the water and had plunked down her beach bag and taken off her shoes.

"Is this all right for you?" she said sweetly.

"Fine," I said

She sat down and tucked her skirt under her, then opened the bag and brought out the German phrase book.

"You must be joking," I said.

"Not at all," she said. "Why would you think I'm joking?"

"You can't mean that after all this, we're going to have a German lesson."

"Why not?" Magda said. "I thought that was the whole point in coming out here early."

"I'll die," I said. "I can't speak German now. Please."

Magda was smiling at me. "Well, I don't want you to die. That would be very embarrassing while we're way out here alone. What is it then that you had in mind?"

"I thought we might just talk," I said. "You told me at one point that we might just talk."

"About what?"

"You said you would tell me the whole story someday."

"And you think today is that someday?"

"I don't see why not," I said. "There's nobody out here to bother us. I mean, overhear us."

"And I'm just supposed to trust you now, is that it?"

"Well, I swore, didn't I?" I said. "What more can I do?"

Magda put away the phrase book. Then she took out a bathing suit and a beach towel.

"Well, first I'm going to have a swim. And then I'm going to think about it."

I was sitting there on the sand beside her and there was nobody within two or three hundred feet of us but also nothing any closer that might serve for a place to change, so I didn't know what to do with myself.

"Do you want me to take a walk?" I said.

"Not unless you want to," Magda said.

She had loosened her blouse and now had her beach towel wrapped around her full length and was managing with great skill not only to get everything off under that towel without my seeing a thing but to collect it all together without getting sand on it and to stash it away in the beach bag. She bent over with the towel still tight around her and picked up her one-piece bathing suit.

"Now would you be good enough to look the other way just for a minute?" she said. "Because putting this thing on isn't quite so easy."

I looked the other way. Then I stood up and took my mother's beach bag a short ways down the beach and sat there with my back turned until I heard a splash in the water. Magda was swimming out to sea in a slow crawl that she must have spent all of her almost twenty years practicing, because she moved through the water so gracefully that she hardly raised a ripple in it. I took out my towel and laid it across my lap to try and be decent about changing into my swimming trunks, but the towel wouldn't stay in place, so I finally just threw it aside and did what I had to do in the open. Nobody was watching me anyway, and by the time I got into the water, Magda was so far out there ahead of me that I decided to take my time trying to catch up with her and just let the water relax me a bit.

That wasn't easy, because the water was still cold at that time of year, with a bite to it that I wasn't used to after knowing only lake water at summer camp in upstate New York, but it did serve to wake you up and clear your mind. I gave up trying to swim out as far as she'd gone. In fact, I didn't stay in that water more than ten minutes, so that I had my things gathered up and was parked back at Magda's beach bag by the time she came out of the sea, wading in at the end with her shoulders turning this way and that, and then, as she moved onto the sand, running her hands through her hair and then holding it in tight to get the water out.

I couldn't take my eyes off her as she came up the beach toward me, because it was a new way of seeing her. She was wearing a black bathing suit that showed her shape clearly against the brighter sea and sky, and what I remember about that image of her was how much smaller she seemed, at least at that distance, not any part of her, because her proportions had the same balance as when she was fully dressed, her legs longer than those of most Greek girls and her hips tighter, her breasts delicately shaped. And that image of her had the effect of making her seem suddenly younger too. The other thing I remember is that when she came up to me, holding her hair in tight against her head again, I could clearly see the dark brown hair under her arms, and the surprise of that was that I felt myself wanting to touch her there.

Magda sat down beside me and reached into her beach bag for a bottle of sun oil, sweet-smelling and orange-red, and worked some of it slowly into her neck and arms and then the front of her legs. She still hadn't spoken to me as I watched her.

"You'd better put some on too," she finally said. "It's dangerous the first few times you're out in the sun. Even during this season."

"I don't usually burn all that easily," I said. "But I wouldn't mind trying some of that."

"All you Anglo-Saxons burn more easily than we do," she said. "I've seen it. And you don't know what our sun can do to you."

That irritated me. I didn't like the distance she was trying to put between us with this talk about Anglo-Saxons. It cut sharply across my mood, and she must have seen it.

"Here," she said, handing me the bottle. "But first I need your help."

She spread her beach towel on the sand and then stretched out on it full length, belly down, arms against her sides.

"Rub some in wherever I'm exposed," she said. "But do it gently please."

How could I not do it gently? How could I find a way to lay my fingers on the back of her neck and her bare shoulders so that she would even feel it? And how could I run my hand along the rounded curves and dips of one leg all the way from her heel to where her bathing suit cut across to stop me and then keep going down the other leg all the way to the heel again? I don't know how I could do it, but I did. And I have to admit that the more I got into it, the easier it became, the more firm my hand and the more sure my pleasure in it.

"That was nice," she said, rolling over to sit with her legs drawn up. "Now I'll help you if you want."

"That's all right," I said.

Magda was smiling at me. "Not even just your back?"

"All right," I said.

I dipped into the bottle and ran my hand quickly over my face and shoulders and then over my chest and belly and the fronts of my legs. I spread my own towel out on the sand. It was ridiculously short, but I flopped down on it anyway, with my arms crossed under my chin to keep my face out of the sand. When Magda started working on my shoulders, I could feel myself tensing up under her fingers so that I was certain she knew what that was doing to me, but she went right on, gently but not all that gently, and I slowly found myself relaxing a bit until her hands moved along the sides of my chest, under my arms, a thing that made me shiver.

"Now," she said, twisting the cap shut on the oil bottle. "I'm sure it's foolish of me and I'm sure I'll regret it, but I've decided to trust you and tell you what you want to know. And the reason I'm willing to do that when it's not really in my nature to be so foolish is because I don't feel it's right for you to go on thinking of me only through the scandalous rumors you've heard. But if you ever betray me by telling anybody else what I've told you, anybody at all, that will be the end. I will never talk to you again."

"I won't betray you," I said.

"I know you think you won't," Magda said. "Everybody thinks they won't when they say it. Then they find they can't wait to tell somebody."

"I won't tell anybody," I said. "You made me swear."

"That was about lying. This is about betrayal."

"I still swear," I said.

"All right then, I'll take the chance. This is the story you seem to want to hear. I mean the true story."

She didn't look at me much while she was talking, so I could see that some of it must have been still painful to her, but she kept her voice steady and her tone more or less casual. What she told me was that the previous year she had decided to learn English along with the German and French she already knew, so that when she got to the university, she would have a better choice of what foreign literature to study, especially since she was—and here she glanced at me—getting a little tired of so much concentration on German. So her father had arranged for her to get special lessons in English from a teacher at Anatolia College who had been brought in to supplement the classes in English there because he had a degree from England even if Greek was his native language. And these special lessons were sometimes at her home and sometimes at the College, depending on her schedule and his. Everything had gone fine, she said, he was a good teacher, a nice man, quite good-looking, and she was learning a lot of English until she realized that she was falling in love with him and he with her, and that made it difficult for her to think of him as a teacher any longer or even to work with him.

"You fell in love with this man," I said. "Just like that?"

"No, it wasn't just like that," Magda said. "It took months. But once it happened, there was no turning back. So I had to stop the lessons."

"And this man was in love with you?"

"So he said. And I believed him. Especially when he told me that he wanted to marry me as soon as I was finished with my schooling and he had a firm position."

The problem, she said, was that she couldn't tell her father why she had stopped the lessons, so she had to pretend to go on with them, and that meant that she still met regularly with her English teacher, which is what he wanted anyway and what she was too weak to resist, and so they became lovers.

"How? Where?" I said. "What do you mean, you became lovers?"

"No, you're going to have to let me tell it as I want to without interrupting me or asking me to tell you things I don't think you should hear."

"I thought you were going to tell me the truth. I thought it was going to be the whole story."

"You'll have to understand that there are certain things nobody should tell anybody else, personal things, because if I were to do that it would be a kind of betrayal by me. Even when it involves someone you come to hate."

"You mean your father?"

"No, I mean this man. But you're pushing me ahead of myself."

So the long and short of it was that she and her teacher would meet as lovers wherever they could find a place to do so, which sometimes had to be out in the open, and that resulted in somebody seeing them together at one point and telling her father about it. And what her father did then was look into this teacher's history and discover that he had a wife and a young son in Athens, which the father was pleased to reveal to his daughter the first chance he got.

"That was the terrible part," Magda said. "The cruel part. My father didn't give me any warning. He didn't tell me what he knew and didn't know or show any interest in my feelings. He just called me into our living room and sat me down there and said 'I thought you would like to know that your friend has a wife and child in Athens.'"

"My God."

"So that was when I decided I had to run away. From all of them. Including my mother, who just sat there when my father said what he said and stared at me as though I was a complete disgrace to the family. Which I suppose I was. But that didn't make it any easier for me to stay in that house."

"Where did you run away to?"

"I've never told anybody that," Magda said. "I just went away where I couldn't be found and two weeks later I came back."

"And you're not going to tell me either, is that it?"

Magda smiled at me. She had been sitting there with her arms around her knees, gazing out at the sea and rocking softly as she spoke, and now she reached over with one hand and touched my cheek. Then she took her hand away again and went back to gazing out to sea.

"I suppose there's no harm in telling you that it was Thassos," she said. "In a village high up on the island."

I wanted to lean over and kiss her then, I wanted that very badly, because I knew that she had tried to show me in her reserved way that I was more than just a pupil of hers now, and I was grateful for that. But what if she had also begun to see me as more than just an ordinary friend? That idea frightened me, and since gratitude wasn't all that I was feeling at that moment, in fact, the least of it, I found that I couldn't move. Then I put my hand out suddenly and touched her hair, just a light, momentary touch, hardly a caress, but I could tell from her not turning to look at me, not even shifting her gaze a fraction, that she knew what I meant by that touch.

"I'm going in for another dip," she said, and she stood up to head down toward the sea.

When my father arrived to take us back, we were sitting at a table in the taverna sipping a heavily carbonated and hypersweet version of lemonade called gazoza, which is as far as Magda would go when I suggested we might try the taverna's resinated wine. When my father sat down at the table with us, he churned around in his seat so much that he ended up digging his chair into the sand at a awkward angle. Magda could see that he was restless and suggested that it might be time for us to head back, especially since what she called "the others" had already gone ahead some time since, and that served to conclude our afternoon's outing without further small talk.

But it had really petered out earlier, after Magda and I had changed back into our regular clothes and had moved to the taverna, where we sat opposite each other with very little that was important to say to each other, certainly nothing about what was still on my mind. It was as though the concession she'd made to my personal interest in her by telling me the story of her love affair was as far as she planned to go in that direction, in fact, was maybe a step too far, as though she'd shown me more of herself than I had any right to know. I don't think she was embarrassed by the scandal of what she'd told me, however awkward that must have been for someone with her background. She had too much pride for that—too much pride not to accept the consequences of the choices she'd made. It was just that once she'd done her bit to satisfy me, she didn't seem at all ready to be pressured into making any new choices that she didn't feel comfortable with, even if she may have been a touch flattered by my increasingly intense preoccupation with every part of her that she'd let me see.

When she showed up at the end of the week for our next tutorial session, it was all business again, as though there had been no excursion to the beach, no suntan oil, no intimate talk, no touching, casual or otherwise. Halfway through the session I couldn't stand it any longer. We were into some fairly complicated phrases in the more advanced drill section and I found myself beginning to choke up on certain words.

"I know some of this is difficult," Magda finally said in Greek. "But this is an important word and you should get it right. The word at the end of the phrase is pronounced 'Weltanschauung.' 'Weltanschauung.' Which means philosophy. More or less. And that's why it's important. Now let's try the whole phrase again."

The phrase she said in German was something about finding out what the last conclusion of wisdom is if you wanted to know Goethe's philosophy. I slurred over the "schauung" part again.

"We will pass over that for the moment," Magda said in German. "Let us try the next one. Repeat after me: 'Only he earns himself his freedom, as his life itself, who must conquer it every day.'"

"I'm sorry," I said in Greek. "I can't say that. Anyway, I don't believe it. How can you conquer your freedom every day? Let alone your life. I mean, it's hard enough just trying to get along with your life from one day to the next."

"We're not here to argue philosophy," Magda said. "And those happen to be the dying words of Faust, who knew a bit more about life than you and me."

"I don't care whose dying words they are. They don't make sense as far as I'm concerned."

Magda put the book down. "All right," she said. "What's the problem today? You're just not yourself."

"I may not be myself but you're not yourself either."

"Really? What makes you think I'm not myself."

"You're so cold," I said. "When I thought we were supposed to be friends."

"Poor Hal," Magda said, trying to smile. "Of course we're friends. But right at this moment I'm your teacher."

Just hearing her say my name was almost enough to make me forgive her, but not quite.

"So that's it?" I said. "You're either my friend or my teacher, right?"

Magda sighed. "It's very difficult for me. I can't confuse the one with the other the way you seem to want me to. Not during a lesson."

"Well let's forget the lesson then and just talk."

"We can't forget the lesson. You only have ten days left before the exams begin."

Magda sat there looking at me. Then she reached over and touched my hand.

"Please be good," she said. "What will your parents think? I mean, I have a responsibility to them as well as to you."

"My parents won't know the difference."

"They will if you fail your exams."

"I'm not going to fail my exams," I said. "So don't worry about that."

"You must never say you're not going to fail something. That's hubris."

"That's what?"

"Hubris. Too much pride or self-assurance or something like that. The gods get jealous of it. At least in this country."

"Well let's say your gods over here give me a break and everything goes well with the exams. What happens after that?"

Magda stood up and walked to the edge of the lawn. "Then I have my own exams and after that the university entrance exams and after that I don't know what."

"So that's it," I said. "This lesson and two more and then that's the end of it?"

"We'll just have to see," Magda said. "Why can't we concentrate on what we have to do right now? That's the important thing."

"For you maybe, but not for me."

Magda turned around. She had a strange look on her face, a kind of sadness that I couldn't figure out.

"I knew we were taking a wrong turn," she said. "Now it's too late."

"What's too late?" I said.

"You can't see me as a teacher any longer. And that makes it impossible for you to work with me and me with you."

"I can work with you fine," I said. "But I can't work with you if you're just going to disappear after two more lessons."

"The point is, you want me to be more than your teacher. Which is very flattering, but it makes what we do here impossible."

She was too fast for me. I decided I had to cool things down again if I wanted to keep from losing her completely, which meant not coming quite clean with her.

"I just don't think it's right for supposed friends to end things abruptly like that, with two more lessons and then everything is over. Can't we get together at least once or twice after that?"

"Well, will you try to concentrate on the lessons that are left if I promise to see you once afterward? That is, if you pass all your exams, so that we can think of it as a graduation celebration for your having been such a good student?"

"God, you sure don't make things easy. But all right, it's a deal."

She came back to the table. "Now let's try the phrase with 'Weltanschauung' in it once more. Do you think maybe you can say it correctly now that we've made this deal, as you call it?"

I worked like hell over the weekend and into the next week, looking into the lessons ahead to get a jump on them, practicing the German phrases as best I could on my own, but when it came to the tutorial session on Wednesday, it was not a great success. We were both stiff, trying too hard to be the good teacher and the good pupil, not at all natural with each other. And behind my stiffness there was hidden panic, because I wasn't at all sure any longer that I would do well enough in the final exams that were waiting for me. And even if I got through that, I couldn't see what future the two of us had with only a single meeting afterward and that one to be arranged not because she and I were now the kind of friends who had shared intimacies but because I had supposedly performed in school the way my young green-eyed teacher wanted me to. I lived with a keen sense of doom.

"Is it really so serious?" Magda finally said in Greek toward the end of the session. "Whatever it is that's bothering you? I mean, you look as though someone has died. And this thank-you letter I want you to compose for me is supposed to be at least amusing."

"I don't think it's amusing. I think it's ridiculous."

"You don't like the idea of telling Miss Schenkendorf and her family how much you appreciated the picnic in the Black Forest that she invited you to on Ascension Day? We could make it some other day if you'd rather."

"No, I don't much like the idea whatever the day."

"Well what kind of letter would you like to write Miss Schenkendorf?"

"I'd like to write Miss Schenkendorf a letter telling her that she has beautiful green eyes and hair with gold in it."

"That's very romantic. Fine. Let's compose that kind of letter if it will amuse you."

"And I'd like to tell Miss Schenkendorf that she can be cruel sometimes, even if she did invite me to a picnic with her family."

"Cruel. How so?"

"Because she can pretend that nothing happened during the picnic except drinking a terrible kind of lemonade."

"So what else happened during your picnic with Miss Schenkendorf? In German please."

"Forget it," I said. "What's the point? It's a stupid exercise. I'd rather repeat phrases about philosophy."

"I know what you'd really rather do," Magda said gently. "You'd rather go swimming and lie on the beach. But we can't always do what we want to do, can we?"

"We can at least be honest. And not go on pretending that you're nothing but my teacher when there's more to it than that. At least for me."

I couldn't look at her after that. I knew I'd gone too far again, but I couldn't do otherwise. And I guess Magda realized that I'd become a hopeless case at that point. She didn't say anything but just gathered up the books in a neat pile on the wicker table and sat back in her chair to stare at them.

"I suppose what this means is that you've graduated," she said. "And that means no more lessons. Because I can't take money from your parents if I'm no longer teaching you."

"Well, we don't have to go that far," I said. "Can't we just relax a bit and not be so cold with each other all the time?"

"No, if we're going to be honest, the lessons have to end, because I simply can't be your teacher any longer. Whether we talk Greek or German or English or the language you like to talk most, which is looking at me as though your best friend has died."

"I can't help it," I said.

"If you can't help it, you can't help it. And I can't help not being your teacher any longer. Which means that I'll have to tell your parents that I won't be coming here again because you've graduated out of my tutoring class."

I don't know how I'd managed to get myself trapped with no way out, but that's where I felt I was, and that made me behave like a maniac. I picked up the German phrase book and started going through it, reading phrases out of the final conversation drills more or less at random, reading deliberately at first with slightly exaggerated pronunciation to make it seem to sound right, then speeding up as much as I could short of stumbling all over the place. Magda finally reached across the table to squeeze my arm hard.

"Please," she said, still in Greek. "What in God's name are you trying to do now?"

"Reviewing our phrases. Some of the harder ones. Trying to get them absolutely right."

She was half smiling. "So now you've become your own teacher, is that it?"

"I was hoping you might still want to correct me when I get things wrong."

Magda shook her head, still half smiling. Then she came over and bent down to take my head in her hands and kiss me lightly on the cheek. Just a peck—almost formal, though not doing it on both cheeks in the Greek style made it seem more intimate. I went right back to repeating phrases, speeding them up, though, making more and more mistakes, in fact, deliberately making mistakes so that Magda, back in her chair now, finally couldn't resist correcting me. And that's what we did till our time ran out.

Magda was the kind of person who sticks to what she says she's going to do once her mind is made up, and I think that gave me the courage to do the same, only I wasn't quite as open about it at that point in our life together. When I walked her to the bus, she told me that she wouldn't be coming out later in the week or anytime after that, and she said there was no point in arguing about it, because that was the way it had to be. But she also said that she was willing to have a final review session with me if we met at her home rather than mine and did not consider it a real lesson for which she would be paid, an arrangement that she was perfectly happy to let me explain to my parents as best I could if I would feel more comfortable taking care of this necessary detail myself. About that, there was no argument. I took it as a conciliatory gesture that was meant to soften the unassailable firmness of what she had decided. More important, it strengthened my own resolution to use the final review session she had offered to kill any lingering problem she might have with our student-teacher relationship. Clearly as far as she was concerned, that relationship was now over, and as far as I was concerned, that was fine by me.

What I told my parents, meaning my mother, was that I would be gone the whole of Friday afternoon because Miss Sevillas had scheduled a final marathon German lesson at her place to review all that I had learned so far, and it was likely to go on until I missed the last bus home out from town. This meant that I would need some taxi money, as well as whatever payment Miss Sevillas was still due for her tutorial sessions. My mother didn't look exactly happy about this arrangement, but she also didn't grill me. I think she considered me a desperate academic case at that point, and anything that might save my family the embarrassment of my failing the year at school must have seemed to her to justify this sudden odd change in the normal routine. Besides, she liked Miss Sevillas and trusted her. I didn't tell my mother that Magda wasn't willing to accept any payment for the final lesson in her home, because I had in mind spending some of what Magda was still owed on a present for her, and whatever was left over after that would be used for the private graduation outing I planned to invite her to after we'd had our review session, which I intended to keep short and sweet.

Magda and I had agreed to meet at two on Friday to allow us plenty of time for the review, but I was out in front of her house a good half hour ahead of schedule, having already spent another half hour buying her a silver filigree bracelet with embossed rose petals at a small shop on the 25th of March Street. The shop was run by a shady fast-talker who had some sort of connection to a Syrian souk where they made the finest filigree in Damascus and who wasn't above squeezing what he thought he could get out of a young foreigner relatively new to his country until he saw this one heading for the door. At that point he said he would have to settle, at considerable personal loss, for whatever drachmas I could bring up out of my pocket, which was half of what I had with me, though only my other pocket and I knew that to be the truth.

Magda's house was fancier than the others in her neighborhood, and the style of it made it look more Italian than Greek. It was a one-story cream-colored house, with a tall peaked roof made out of red tiles and intricate blue trimming cut out of wood running along the edge of it from corner to corner. It was in a good neighborhood compared to some others, but not the best in the city, and it was only the look of Magda's house next to those beside hers that made me think her family must be relatively rich—that and her having chosen to go to the German School instead of where she could have gone for nothing under the Greek school system.

I wasn't about to go up and knock on her door that early, so I wandered around the neighborhood to see what it might offer for a place to sit with her once I got her out of the house, and the best thing I could come up with was a sweets shop full of Turkish pastries and cakes covered with chocolate and cream that had a few marble-topped tables both inside and out on the street. I knew it would have to be inside or nothing for her, and nothing was as likely as not. But the main thing I had in mind was finding a way of luring her into taking a walk with me maybe up toward the village of Kapudgida on the way to Anatolia College, where there was some open country and a chance to give her my present in relative privacy. One thing I had going for me was the quality of the day, warm as you could want, and the air so clear that distances were deceiving, with the mountain beyond that section of the city now standing out so sharply against the uncluttered sky behind it that it seemed no more than an hour's walk up the long hill that would lead you there.

The woman who came to the door when I knocked at 1:55 was a small lady with dark hair rolled into a bun and brown eyes speckled with green. She didn't really look like Magda, even a much older Magda, but I figured there was enough likeness there to make her Magda's mother, and while she was leading me into the living room to sit me down on a bone-hard settee, that's who she said she was. Her Greek had a funny "r" sound in it that I'd heard before, which somebody had told me meant people who talked that way were either upper class or French in background or had a speech impediment. Mrs. Sevillas told me that her daughter would be down in a minute or two, at which point she would leave the two of us alone, but she wondered if I wouldn't like a sweet in the meanwhile.

One thing I'd learned from the occasional visits my family made to the homes of staff at the school where my father worked was that you never refused a sweet in a Greek home. It didn't matter how terrible it might look coming at you, whether a chunk of Turkish Delight with enough powdered sugar on it to make you choke or a solid green fig floating in heavy syrup or a sticky white substance on a spoon that had the consistency of molten chewing gum. You ate it as delicately as you could while the woman who brought it stood over you waiting with a tray, and when you were done you put the little glass dish it came on or the water glass it was submerged in back on the tray without dropping the messy spoon you'd balanced on the little dish, because if it landed on the rug or some part of your clothing, the damage could be terminal. And once the sweet was safely gone, you drank the water that had come with it and commented on how delicious it was without asking for a second glass of water to wash away the remaining saccharine excess of it or its bitter aftertaste.

"You are American," Mrs. Sevillas said as she stood over me watching, and it wasn't put as a question.

"Yes," I said—without looking up, because I was trying to cap-ture in one spoonful all the preserved cherries glued to my little glass dish so that I could get it all down in one swallow.

"But you are not Jewish," she said.

"No," I said. "Protestant. Anyway, my mother is."

"Protestant," Mrs. Sevillas said, again not as a question.

"But out here, I'm not sure what we are," I said. "I mean, there's no particular church for us as far as I can tell."

I must have sounded apologetic or something, because Mrs. Sevillas told me I didn't have to apologize.

"I'm not Jewish either," she said. "My husband is, but I have never converted. I don't see the point. You're born what you are born and I was born Greek Orthodox."

"Well, I suppose that sort of thing is a personal matter," I said seriously, somberly, not knowing exactly why I'd said it that way or what I meant by it.

"I suppose," Mrs. Sevillas said vaguely, studying me. "Can I get you another sweet?"

"No, no thanks," I said. "Really. I'm pregnant."

"You're what?"

"I mean, full out to here. My Greek gets away from me sometimes. Really delicious cherries. Thank you so much."

I got the little glass dish and the spoon back on the tray without trouble, though my hand wasn't what you'd call steady. Magda was standing in the doorway now watching me. She tried to take the tray from her mother as Mrs. Sevillas passed her in the doorway but she was brushed aside. Magda was carrying our German drill books under one arm. She came over and sat beside me on the settee.

"I'm afraid I embarrassed your mother," I said. "I was trying to show off my Greek and I used an expression I'd heard over at our school which didn't come out quite right."

"It doesn't matter," Magda said. "I can tell that she likes you. Though you wouldn't ever know it from the way she looks."

"Well, I think I should apologize."

"Nonsense," Magda said. "What difference does it make? She knows you're a foreigner. Now let's get to work. We have so much to cover today that I wonder if we shouldn't—"

"I wonder if we shouldn't skip the whole thing," I said, looking her straight in the eye. "I mean, what's the point? I either know what I have to know by now or it's too late to do anything about it."

"That's hardly the right attitude to take just before your exams. In fact, it's idiotic."

"Then I'm idiotic," I said. "Besides, you're the one who said you couldn't be my teacher any longer. And I can't say I feel much like being your student. Not on a day like this."

"So you want to go to the beach, is that it?"

"Well, I wasn't thinking of the beach exactly. I was thinking of our maybe taking a walk up the hill toward Kapudjida. And if you insist, I don't mind taking the drill books along and working a bit in the open air if we can find a place to sit for a while."

"Kapudjida?" Magda said.

"Isn't that the village up there?"

"Do you know that they stoned the Apostle Paul in that village? And they still stone strangers who pass through there."

"Well they won't stone me or I'll stone them right back. And I know how to throw. I used to play on a team where I had to throw a ball as hard as a stone back and forth all afternoon."

Magda was smiling now. "What sort of team is that?"

"It's an American game," I said. "I can't really explain it."

"So you would protect me by catching the stones and throwing them back, is that it?"

"You're making fun of me," I said. "I didn't say I'd catch the stones."

"Anyway, you're impossible," Magda said. "You're always trying to find ways to avoid studying. And to get me places I shouldn't go."

"I've only tried once," I said. "So far."

Magda sighed. "All right, we'll go for a walk. Anyway, it makes me nervous to have my mother walking back and forth out there. As though you are some sort of prospective husband she'd allowed me to be alone with for a minute."

"She thinks I might become your husband?"

"Not you. I mean in general. Like all mothers, she thinks the time has come for me to think about getting married. And I know my father thinks so too."

"Getting married?" I said. "With whom?"

Magda patted my hand. "Not with anybody in particular. Just in general."

"I thought you were going to the university?"

Magda stood up. "I am. If they allow me. And they'd better."

The tone she said that in bothered me, but she didn't give me a chance to follow up on it because she went out to tell her mother something that I couldn't hear. What she told her not only worked to get us out of the house but saved me from having to face the lady again after what I'd blurted out in my village Greek.

"I told my mother that we had to stop by the pharmacy to get something for your stomach trouble, and since she's getting herself ready to go into town to meet her canasta group, we don't have to worry about when we get back. As long as it's before my father comes home from work."

I wasn't sure whether it was the truth of things or just my rising hope, but I saw enough conspiracy in what she had done to make my mood as resplendent as the day. And once we were in the street, Magda turned toward the road that headed uphill as though we had already agreed to go in that direction. We went right by the sweets shop I'd thought might end up being the best I could do for privacy, and I didn't even bother to bring that idea up. When the houses thinned out in Harilaou and we were clear of the few at the beginning of the uphill road, Magda let me take the books she was carrying, and she linked her arm in mine, though she would drop it back to her side when the occasional car or truck went by, which wasn't often.

I don't know how long it took us to get up to the edge of Kapudjida village, because time that afternoon seemed to be on a different scale, speeded up mostly, yet with moments when it was suddenly suspended while we stopped at the edge of the road to look back at the city and the bay beyond it, or just to catch our breath, mine coming short in ways it didn't normally. And when Magda would turn beside me to look back downhill, that would give me a chance to take in her face as I couldn't possibly have done if she knew I was studying her that way. Her skin had turned light brown from our day at the beach, and maybe from other days I didn't know about. Our walking uphill brought a shine to her high forehead and moisture above her lip that just drew your attention to the lovely curving fullness below it, the lips a little open, and when she wet them with her tongue, I would have to look away and try to think of something else before she caught the hunger in my look.

We didn't go straight into the village because Magda seemed to know a path that skirted it, and her knowing that bothered me, though I didn't say so. When we got a little above the village, she now holding me by the hand and sort of leading me along as the path we were on narrowed, we came to a hillside that dipped down gradually to a ravine that had a stream running through it. There were still some poppies on the hillside, and other spring flowers I didn't know, and the grass was tall.

"We can go down to the stream if you want and sit there to do our review," Magda said.

"You've been down there before?" I said, trying to be casual about it.

"Once," Magda said.

"Then I'd just as soon not," I said.

Magda let go of my hand.

"That's silly," she said. "And it isn't fair to me. If you're going to ask me questions like that with some motive of your own and you want me to answer you with the truth, you mustn't hold it against me when I answer honestly."

"I don't hold it against you," I said. "The idea just makes me a little uncomfortable."

"Well, it shouldn't," Magda said. "You don't own my past. Nobody does."

I guess she saw that what she'd said cut into me, because she took my hand again.

"Come on," she said. "This isn't the kind of day for brooding."

When we got down above the stream, we found that there was hardly any water in it, so it wasn't worth climbing down the steep side of the ravine to get there. We sat above it, back from the edge where the grass began. I put the books I was carrying on the ground beside me, on the opposite side from Magda. Before she could say anything, while she was sitting there leaning back on her arms with her legs stretched out in front of her toward the edge of the ravine, I swung around suddenly and lay back with my head in her lap. I think I really startled her, because I could feel her thighs tense under my head, but she didn't move, not until one of her hands was on my forehead, brushing the hair back.

"You know this isn't right," she said, but her hand didn't stop. "Not at all right."

"I know," I said.

My eyes were closed now. I could feel the rise and fall of her breathing against the side of my head, and when I turned it slightly into her, I could smell the clean cotton of her blouse. Then, as I turned my head back, I suddenly felt her lips against my closed eyes, first one and then the other. I still didn't open them. I reached up and felt for her face, and when I found her lips to run my fingers along the outline of them, she caught my hand and put her lips against my palm. I opened my eyes then to look up at her, but hers were closed now. When she let go of my hand, I raised myself to lean on one arm so that I could move my hand to her neck to run my fingers down the length of it. She waited until I got to the open V at her throat before she held my hand there, just for a second, and then she took her hand away to unbutton the top button of her blouse. When I tried to undo the next button, she stopped me by holding my hand tight against her, then raised my hand a bit so that it was resting against the place she had bared, and she let my fingers move inside the collar of her blouse along the curve of the bone there and down to the rim of her brassiere. I was trying to work my fingers under the tight rim when she took my hand away and brought it up again to hold against her lips, and that was as far as she let my hand travel that day.

Our hillside above the stream did not prove to be the secret garden of love that my daydreaming made it in the days that followed, because the second time I went there, some two weeks later, I waited until the sun was nearly down before deciding finally that Magda wouldn't be meeting me there after all. Our arrangement had been to get there separately and to meet up in the same fairly secluded spot above the ravine. We were to spend more of the afternoon there than we had the first time, at least that was my plan. Then, when the sun was getting low, we were to go down to the pastry shop near her place, where we'd stopped on our way back from the ravine for a quick lemonade that had given me a chance to slip my tissue-wrapped present into her lap, which had startled her almost as much as finding a filigree bracelet inside the wrapping. This time she was to treat me in turn to my graduation present, and this new beginning in our relationship was to include the heavy licorice drink called ouzo, providing I had done well enough in my exams by that time to be assured of moving on up to the next class at the German School. I did well enough—nothing to brag about, but well enough to earn a prize for having shown the most improvement among my classmates during the course of the year, which is a thing that depends on how badly you started out to begin with and therefore is the kind of prize you'd just as soon not receive in public with your parents and the whole school community watching.

I hadn't seen Magda at all during the two weeks that had gone by. At our last outing on the hillside, after the kissing and touching were over and we'd both cooled down enough to talk, my head back in her lap, we'd agreed to this one more meeting in private after she was through at the German School and had a break before she had to face the university entrance exams in late June. And it was during this meeting that we were going to discuss soberly where we were headed and what we planned to do about it, since Magda refused to discuss the subject—so she'd said—while I was obviously in a mood to want more of her than she was ready to give and she herself was too torn about where we'd arrived already to think clearly.

A number of thoughts came into my head during the three hours I waited on that hillside the second time, occasionally getting up to stretch my legs and to wander along the edge of the ravine, even climbing down to the dry stream at one point and making my way along that for a while to see if a little exercise might relieve my state

of mind. Of course my first thought was that Magda had stood me
up, because that would have been the simplest way of solving the
problem she still had with my ripe obsession and the apparent embarrassment she felt about where it was leading the two of us. But
even in those cooler moments when my anger took over from my
hunger, it didn't quite make sense to me that she would choose not
to show up and at least tell me in her reserved and sensible way how
awful my desire made her feel and what she had decided was finally
necessary in dealing with it, despite her also having revealed, when
her guard was down, that she could take pleasure in what that desire
made me do. Standing me up without a word was simply out of
character for someone who always spoke her mind and acted on
what she spoke.

But if her problem with me wasn't the likely cause of her not
being there to meet me, what was? Had somebody seen us out there
together that day as they had once seen her with her former lover, or
seen her in another place with somebody else, so that, innocent or
not, it had led to another vicious confrontation with her father that
resulted in her being locked up again? Or was she suffering from
some illness that had her so blotched or so confined that she couldn't
get in touch with me? Or had there been a terrible mutilating accident earlier that afternoon on the road leading up to where we were
to meet?

Whatever way I turned to look at the thing, I found something
threatening that made me turn in a different direction, and that only
made me end up feeling worse. It almost got to the point where I
didn't want to find out what had happened, which may have been
just a way of saving myself pain, since I couldn't figure out what I
might do to get to the truth. Except maybe by going up to Magda's
front door and knocking on it to face her mother or her father, an
intrusion by a foreigner, whether suspect or not, that might just
make Magda's situation worse and was not likely to help my morale.
That might be a thing I had to do eventually, but the thought of
doing it at that moment sobered me enough to get me back to the
village of Kapudjida and heading off for home in the opposite direction. That is, until I remembered Magda's aunt who lived at the

beginning of the uphill road, as Magda had pointed out to me when we went by there on our walk up to the village that first time.

All I knew about the aunt was that she was the sister of Magda's mother and that Magda would visit her whenever she had to get away from her parents and wanted to talk to somebody who would listen to her without always judging her, so that over the years she had come to think of the aunt as her real mother. The aunt had never married but wasn't exactly the spinster type, according to Magda, though only one generation away from a Macedonian village near the Yugoslav border and Greek to her bones. Magda said that she felt she could tell her aunt anything, and sometimes did. She said that this was the one person who'd helped her get her self-respect back after that business with the teacher from Athens. Still, that didn't mean this lady I'd never met might be ready to open up to an American adolescent she'd never met, especially one who was almost three years younger than her niece and who came around looking for the kind of personal news that only a potential lover or bride-groom ought to have the right to ask for. Unless I played the stu-dent-teacher role a bit longer than I really had the heart to do at that point. But just thinking about how I might still bring it off got me heading downhill again and eventually had me cutting over toward Harilaou, and by the time I reached the foot of the hill, I'd con-vinced myself that I had no choice but to knock on the lady's door.

The aunt's house was a simple one-story square-faced box of a house in white, typical of that neighborhood, with two windows for eyes behind twin balconies and a red-tiled four-sided roof with a lid over it, perched up there like an undersized hat. The shutters were closed on the windows, but I figured that might be because they were facing the afternoon sun, which wasn't down yet. She had a fenced-in garden in front of the house, with rosebushes and plum trees and a stumpy palm tree on either side of the tiled pathway leading up to worn stone steps, gray like bad teeth. When I reached through the grating to raise the latch on the gate, I got the feeling that I was trespassing on private property that I had no business violating, but I went on in anyway.

The person who answered the door didn't look at all like a sister

of Magda's mother, at least not to me. For one thing, she had gray
hair, and though it was tied up into a bun behind her head like her
sister's, there were combs in it that showed, and there were a lot of
loose strands here and there which told me that this woman didn't
have the same degree of vanity in her. Also, I couldn't see any green
in her eyes, which were dark brown, and her face was lined in a way
that made her look ten years older than Magda's mother.

"Yes?" she said, showing only her face in the doorway. It seemed
from her gaze that she took me for a creature from a very distant and
hostile land, maybe because of my blond hair—even if it was actually a brownish blond to my mind, not that much lighter than Magda's
gold-threaded copper—maybe because I was wearing a T-shirt that
said "Camp Cory, Lake Keuka, N.Y.," though I figured the most she
could make out of that was meaningless letters in a language foreign
to her own.

"I'm Magda's pupil," I said.

"Magda's pupil?"

"Just once in a while," I said. "I live at the American School on
the way to Sedes."

"Sedes? You mean the village?"

"Yes. Near the military airport."

"Well Magda isn't here," the lady said quietly.

"I know," I said. "I was supposed to have a German lesson with
her and she didn't come for that, so I got worried."

The lady opened the door further. She was wearing a kind of
house dress that she held closed with one hand below her neck
though it was buttoned all the way up, and there was a silver cross
on a chain at her throat.

"You're the American?" she said.

"Yes," I said. "Anyway, the one she teaches German."

"She's told me about you," the lady said. Her eyes dropped. Then
she stepped back out of the way. "Please."

I can't remember when I've felt quite as awkward as I did the first
ten minutes I was sitting there waiting for her to bring in my little
glass dish of sticky sweet stuff, unless it was the five minutes after

the dish arrived with a honeyed green walnut on it that I didn't recognize and took in whole. I managed excruciatingly not to gag, and the lady didn't say a word until I had the spoon and the dish back on the tray she was holding in front of me.

"Magda has gone away," she said.

"Gone away?" I said, trying to sound cool. "Where?"

"I wish I knew," the lady said. "If I knew I would go to her."

"You mean she went away without telling you where she was going?"

The lady shrugged. "She didn't tell anybody. And I can't say that I blame her. Except that I'm worried about her."

"But she has her entrance examinations for the university. She was already studying for those examinations when we had our last lesson."

"There aren't going to be any examinations for the university," the lady said, turning with the tray she was holding to take it out to the kitchen. "Her father won't let her go to the university."

"Won't let her go?" I said to the doorway.

When the woman came back she sat on the edge of the straight-backed settee I was sitting on, but she left a lot of space between us.

"I don't know what I should tell you and not tell you," the woman said. "Magda seemed to be fond of you from what she told me about you, so I suppose I can tell you that there is no point in hoping that she will give you any more lessons because nobody knows when she will come back."

"You mean she's run away again?" I said.

The woman was studying me. "So you know about the other time," she said.

"A little bit," I said. "Not the whole story."

"Well I don't know the whole story myself," the woman said. "And all I know this time is that her father wanted her to marry a gold merchant she'd never even seen."

"Marry a gold merchant?"

"Of course it's ridiculous. Her father isn't a bad man, just a fool, and I would have run away myself. But I can't tell you where she's gone and I don't think anybody else can either."

The woman stood up and went over to a window to open the shutters.

"A gold merchant? What kind of gold merchant?"

The woman shrugged. "How do I know? Anyway, it isn't any of my business or any of yours. It's just very sad. Because they don't understand that Magda is special."

"You mean she really won't be going to the university?"

"How can she go to the university when her father insists that she marry a man she's never seen? And if it isn't this man, it will be some other. That is, if she ever returns to this city of the damned. At least damned for people her age."

"I can't believe this," I said.

"Of course you can't. You're an American. You have different customs. But what I'm telling you is true."

I had to get out of there. I could see that the woman was trying to be gentle and understanding with me, but she was still a complete stranger, and her living room was even more foreign than Magda's. This one was full of shaggy rugs and pieces of woven fabric and knitted pillows that must have come from her family's village, and on one wall there was a spread of photographs of men and women and children posing stiffly in formal dress belonging to some other century. It now made Magda seem that much more distant from me. And I was afraid if I stayed any longer I would give away what I was really feeling, confused as it was, my mood crossing from the edge of despair to the edge of elation and then back again, because along with the sensations that came with learning that Magda had run away, I had a feeling that I knew where she had gone and that I was the only one who knew.

The woman was going on about how Magda's father no doubt had her best interests in mind, as did her mother, but neither of them realized that Magda was different from others her age, and anyway the world was changing, changing rapidly, etc. All that while I was searching for some excuse that would get me out of there. I spotted a clock in the center of the buffet at one end of the room and I used that to discover suddenly how late it was and the very serious problem I would have with my own parents if I didn't find a taxi as soon as I could to take me home. The woman said she understood, and she got up from the settee so quickly that it was clear she didn't feel any too comfortable herself talking about Magda and her parents with this young foreigner. Still, when we got to the door and she gave me her hand, I felt like squeezing it instead of just shaking it, as though she and I we were now on the same side. But the lingering strangeness in her place and the look of her as she lowered her eyes to avoid mine made that a thing I couldn't do.

I got home from this visit with Magda's aunt to find that there was no one in the house, a sign that luck was with me. I figured my mother must still be at her Friday tea and sewing session with the staff, which meant that Sam would stay late on the soccer field, and I wasn't expected home in any case until it got dark because of the imaginary basketball game between the Foreign Community and Anatolia College that Jackson was supposed to have organized for my after-noon away. I didn't have any plan at that point other than packing a change of clothes and my toilet articles in a knapsack and gathering up what cash I could find before setting out to look for Magda. There was no need to waste any time arguing with myself about what I was doing. Whether or not my hunch about where Magda was hiding out proved to be true, I was certain now that I had to act on it and head for the island of Thassos. That's what she herself would have done, and if I hadn't learned as much as I should have by that time under her guidance, one thing I was beginning to learn from her was that there were certain choices you simply had to make and stick to without thinking about what they might cost you or anybody else. Wasn't that why she'd decided to run away again, and to do so without waiting to give me the word?

I still hadn't used up all the drachmas I had left over after buying the filigree bracelet for Magda, but I doubted that what I had on hand would get me very far, so I went up to my mother's room and found the purse she kept in her dresser drawer and emptied the purse of all the cash in it without stopping to count what was there. I thought I might leave a note saying that I was just borrowing the money and would work to pay it back when I had a chance but there wasn't a pencil handy, and I was under pressure to pack my things and get out of there before anybody came home.

When I got downstairs again I went into my father's study and found the shelf with his *Encyclopaedia Britannica* and picked out the volume with the atlas in it that I'd studied when he first told us we were going to the country called Greece. I ripped out the map on that page as carefully as I could and put it away in my pocket. Then I took a pencil out of his desk drawer, but there was no clean piece of paper in there, so I wrote out a note on the back of the Foreign Community of Salonika phone list: "Gone off on serious personal business. Will be in touch. Don't worry. Love. Hal. P.S. I borrowed a map and some cash." I put the note in the middle of the dining table with an empty milk bottle to keep it in place and went out the back door.

WHEN I WAS SAFELY THROUGH THE GATE OF THE SCHOOL
where my father worked, I decided to head
for town across the fields, staying within sight
of the school road and then the main road
into town in case I came across sheepdogs or
Gypsies, but far enough away to hide if I spotted
a car coming after me down either road. I
reached the Depot without any problem and
got on a streetcar going into the center of
town and out again in the general direction
of the railroad station beyond the harbor. On
the way in I changed my mind and got off to
cut over toward Vardar Square, where you
were supposed to be able to catch a bus for
the towns in the direction of Athens near one
side of the square or Istanbul near the other,
depending on whether you were headed out
of town to the west or the east. A look at my
Encyclopaedia Britannica map showed me that I
was headed east, because my plan now was to
catch a bus to the town of Kavalla, and from

there, a ferry to the island of Thassos. If there was one place Magda might have gone knowing I would figure out where she was, it had to be the same village high up on Thassos that she'd told me she'd gone to the last time she'd run away—and, so she said, told me alone. Of course that could have been a reason for her not choosing Thassos or the same village this time, but I decided if she'd gone somewhere else I didn't know about, that was worth finding out as well, even if it might point to something I didn't want to learn.

I had to ask more people than I cared to show myself to before I found the station where the bus for Kavalla was housed, and by the time I got there, the man selling tickets at a desk inside the station was closing up for the night. He said the next departure for Kavalla was at 6:30 A.M., and he gestured toward an empty bus parked outside. I bought a ticket for Kavalla, and stood around until the man had put away his work for the day and was ready to lock up, and when he spotted me still lingering in the street outside, I figured I'd better not hang around there any longer in case somebody back home eventually came up with the idea that my note might mean I was on my way out of town. I thought the safest thing would be for me to come back there at some point during the night and hide out in the back of the parked bus until it got around to taking off.

That gave me a few hours to kill. There wasn't much choice when it came to finding a place to hide out in that part of the city short of sitting in a cafe somewhere until it closed. I could have headed uphill toward the other end of town and maybe camped out for a while in our old lunch-hour courtyard, but that territory and the motley crew I used to hang out with there now seemed part of a different life I didn't feel easy returning to. One place close to Vardar Square where I figured I wasn't likely to run into anybody I knew was the red-light district called Bara. I didn't know exactly where it was, but it didn't take me long to find out, because everybody else in the area knew, and nobody seemed to care that I asked, as though it was a natural thing for someone my age to be looking for on a Friday evening. It also turned out that the street names they gave me for boundaries were the kind you didn't forget, Aphrodite and Bacchus streets. The first area was more expensive, I was told, because the women worked in houses and were young—fifty drachmas a go, plus five drachmas for the prophylactic—while in the second area you could get what you were looking for at half the price because the women there worked on their own and were all over forty.

It was a sleazy district compared to any other in that city. The streets down there didn't follow a straight line the way they did in the heart of the city but curved this way and that in their own pattern, some of the houses two-storied Turkish types, brick stuccoed white but peeling off in places, with a potbellied railing around the balcony on the upper floor or the whole of the floor projecting out over the street. The shutters were mostly closed and in need of paint and even slats sometimes, and the street was in need of a serious washing because you could smell the urine along one side of it long before you found out why it was there. That news came with the more popular houses, where you would find customers hovering outside, though they would hover only a minute or two on the way in—men of all ages but generally my age and up, though not very far up—sometimes in groups of two or three but usually alone, every one of them pretending to be very cool and smoking a last cigarette, which they would take a heavy final drag on and flip out into the street in a long red arc before moving up to knock on the door of the house. And those who came out would light up a cigarette as soon as they hit the street and cross casually to the other side to take a leak without looking in either direction first.

Not all the two-story houses were in business, at least not that night, and the only way you could tell for sure which of the one-story houses on the cheaper street had some action was from the few that had a front stoop where you would find a woman or two sitting out to get some air with their dresses drawn up and their knees spread. They seemed to me older than most of the men I'd run into, sometimes thinner than they should have been and sometimes heavy, but I didn't really get close enough to any of those who showed themselves outside to see exactly what they looked like, though there was a thing in me that made me want to, and that was part of the mystery of the place. The farther you got into that area, the more conscious you became of other smells besides urine, one of mildew or stale dampness, and another that reminded me of vinegar and that I later learned came from a red liquid which the women washed themselves with to protect themselves from the men who protected themselves simply by urinating.

My idea had been to wander through that district first to satisfy my curiosity and then to find myself a private section of wall I could lean up against to take a long nap. One thing I was dead set against was getting myself in a situation where I might pick up some kind of disease, or even where I might have to worry about whether I had— not with the possibility of finding Magda in her island hideout the following day. Given my distant attitude, I hadn't counted on running into anybody along those grubby streets down there who would take me for a serious customer, but I had no sooner parked myself up against the wall of one of the less dilapidated houses on the second street I'd turned into than the shutters opened above me and a lady as old as my mother leaned out over me wearing a kind of chemise that was very light, with thin straps on the shoulders. If it was a thing meant to protect a woman from the chill of the night, it failed completely in the case of this woman at least as far as one breast and a good part of the other were concerned.

"Can I do anything for you, light of my life?" the woman asked with a friendly smile.

"No," I said. "I'm fine. Just trying to catch myself some sleep."

"Well, my little piece of Turkish Delight, I can help you with that if you'd like. I can wake you up and then put you to sleep and then wake you up again as much as you please. And if you want to spend the whole night in my arms and sleep like an angel blessed by the Holy Virgin, I can arrange that too for a special price."

"No, I'm really fine," I said, sliding up by the side of the window and scraping my back on the broken stucco in the process. "I'm really on my way to get myself something to eat."

"Well, I can help you with that too," the lady said. "I can offer you the sweetest milk-custard pastry you're likely to taste in your lifetime, and I wish you a long one. And if the pastry isn't good enough for you, I can give you sugared almonds to suck on as you celebrate the best wedding night you're going to know before some plump village girl swallows your blond soul forever like a golden caramel."

"That's kind of you," I said. "And I thank you for your offer. The problem is, I'm engaged."

"All the more reason to have a last meal with me. Not that you wouldn't be welcome here anytime after you're married, but I can see that you're the type who believes that eternal love lasts forever, and it may take a long while before you get over that."

I slung the knapsack over my shoulder and smiled at her. I didn't know what to say, but I figured I had to say something neutral that wasn't insulting, and since it was still relatively close to Easter, I said "Christ is risen" and turned away.

"He is truly risen," the woman said. "But what has that got to do with you and me, my tender piece of shish kebab?"

I put a finger to my forehead as a kind of parting salute and took off down the street. The next one over brought me out to some open space and a building at the far end of it with a lot of broken windows and missing doors that must have been an abandoned repair shop or truck garage, because there were rusted car parts here and there. I found a corner to hole up in, and though all that talk of food reminded me that I'd moved right on through the dinner hour without a bite to eat, I decided I had to hold off and fast myself for a while, anyway until I was safely out of town. I don't know how long I slept. It was totally dark in there when I woke up, and mostly dark outside as well. My watch said it was three, but it was a watch with a mind of its own and not reliable. I skirted the Bara district on the way back to Vardar Square, which was pretty deserted, and headed over to the bus depot for Kavalla. The bus waiting there was locked. So was the office. I was still half asleep and really hungry by then, but I decided to walk down to the harbor area until daylight told me I'd better get back.

It was a melancholy time of night. You got the sense of being the only thing alive in those streets except for the stray cats and dogs and occasional scurrying rat, at least until you came out to the bay where there were a few caique captains getting their boats ready to go out and gather in their nets or set out for early morning travel. I sat down on the edge of the dock and watched them for a while, then took a walk along the full length of the quay, down to the White Tower and back.

That cleared my head. I'd woken up worrying a bit about the trouble I must have created back home by going off without telling anybody what I was really up to, Sam included, but the closer I got to getting out of that city, the more certain I became that I was doing the right thing, and this gave me a sense of freedom. I'd also become certain by then that I was going to find Magda on that island, though I can't say that my reason for being so sure was completely rational. I convinced myself that Magda would not have gone off without finding a way to let me know what she was up to unless she meant for me to figure it out on my own. I took it to be a kind of test she'd set for me—not just of how clever I might be, but of my faith in her and my will to act on that faith. She would have known how important that hillside rendezvous had become in my mind and how difficult it would be for me to believe that she had simply stood me up. If I did believe it, well, that would put an end to a thing not worth the struggle for either of us. But if I worked out a way of finding out what had really happened and took the chance of doing something about it, that would show her the value of my belief in her. Walking along the quay, I let this strong conviction that I would find her take over my imagination and begin to heat it up so that I couldn't think of anything else but an image of her on that island and my being there with her alone. By the time I got back to the bus, I was no longer hungry or tired.

I was the first to get in the bus after the driver, and I went for the rear seat, where there would be the best chance of keeping low and maybe stretching out eventually. While the bus was loading up, I drew a middle-aged woman dressed in black and a young girl of six or seven. The girl was so fascinated by the blondness of my hair that she would stare at me whenever she thought I was looking away, and whenever I'd catch her studying me and smile back at her, she'd blush and bury her head in the woman's bosom until the woman figured out what that was all about, and after a quick lecture on the need to be polite to foreigners however strange they might look, gave the girl a swat at her head that would have sent a less practiced dodger reeling into the aisle.

The seat beside me stayed empty until we were well out of town and cruising northeast into the early sunlight, with the brightest yellow wheat fields I'd ever seen on both sides of the road edging up the slopes of the high hills ahead of us until they turned green to the horizon with a forest of pine, and oak, and wild pear trees. The forest was broken only here and there by a cluster of whitewashed mud-brick and stone houses among plane trees or cypresses, which usually meant that a village was hidden away there in a valley between the low-lying hills or in a cleft between those higher up. Once in a while there would be a fallow field that a shepherd would use to get his flock moving toward the mountains to the west where there was summer grazing, and sometimes the bus would have to stop to let a flock that had taken over the road get across, the shepherd whistling high and long between his teeth to keep the sheep going, though his dog would do most of the work for him by turning in the strays along the rim of the flock to drive it ahead in the right direction. There were also loaded mules and donkeys to slow us down all along the road, because it seemed they were used to having the road to themselves and would take their good time getting out of the way or form a line along the edge that would force the bus to keep closer to the sheer side than looked healthy to anybody new to the ways of that countryside. And sometimes approaching a village around the bend ahead you'd come across a family or two transplanting tobacco plants they'd brought out from their homes to the fields to grow and ripen for the later summer harvest. The men and the women and even some half-grown children would all be bent over and working side by side down the rows in parallel formation and paying no heed to each other or the passing bus except for a quick glance once in a while that told you how lucky they thought those on the bus were to be out of the sun sitting down and on their way somewhere else.

The empty seat beside me was taken by a man older than my father who got on the bus as we'd begun a fairly steep climb between the last hills before we reached the Serres plain. The man was carrying a crate that had two chickens in it, which he put on the floor to block the aisle, and then set a basket on the seat between him and me, a deep one that was covered by woven cloth which kept you from seeing what was inside it but that allowed you to know that one thing in there was some kind of ripe cheese. After he'd made his claim to more than his share of our seat, I must have made an adjustment to try to give myself more room, because the man apologized about the basket. He explained that it was part of his contribution to the wedding of his niece in Serres, where his brother's family would have to feed people for three days, and this was just a beginning but at least it was the beginning of the end.

"This is his last daughter," he said. "The last of three. Now his sons are free to get themselves married and that makes my brother a free man again as well."

I wasn't quite sure what he was talking about, but I nodded wisely.

"I didn't have any daughters," the man said. "I was lucky that way. Not that I don't love my nieces, but it's been an expensive business, not just the dowries, but the agents you have to use to arrange it. Especially this last niece who came out of her mother as the kind who can turn your heart to stone if you look at her too closely and who has remained a virgin so long that the husband-to-be is in danger of finding worms in her womb."

It wasn't a conversation I much cared to get involved in, and not just because what the man had to say on the subject made me uncomfortable but because I felt it would be best not to let him or anybody else know too much about me while I was on the run, so I nodded again and then closed my eyes as though the climb we were in, one hairpin turn after another, was getting to me the way it clearly was getting to most people in that bus. Silence had taken over as we curled up those high hills from one village to the next, and it wasn't broken until the driver had to stop to let out several people who needed to vomit at the side of the road, which led to a lot more getting out to vomit next to them. I was dying of hunger again until that happened. When we started another climb, the man beside me decided that the best medicine against car sickness was eating, so he broke into his basket and came up with a heavy round loaf of black village bread that he sliced in half, then cut two large wedges out of, one of which he handed me.

"It will do you good," he said. "God's best medicine."

I thanked him and took it, and I had no trouble getting it down. The bread was pure wheat with all the bran left in, thicker than any cake, and it had a sweetness that no ordinary sugar gave you and that left room for you to taste the salt and the yeast that had been added, along with a taste of the soil where the wheat had grown. The man now took out an earthenware pot with goat cheese in it, a kind I'd never seen before, soft enough to dip his bread in and about as ripe in the open air as you could stand to know.

"Take some," he said, passing me the bowl. "It's kopanisti. I made it myself."

"Thanks," I said, handing it back. "I don't think I can manage that right now."

"Go on," he said, the bowl under my nose. "You won't have any trouble managing this. It's as pure as any cheese that's made because I watched over it myself."

I had no choice but to dip my bread in it.

"You're a foreigner," the man said. "I can see that. Only a foreigner would hesitate to eat cheese like that."

I didn't have any trouble getting that down either, as pure goat as the bread was pure wheat, and I managed to keep it down even after he explained that he'd made it the only safe way by using his own goat milk and sealing it for a year in the reversed skin of one of his own slaughtered goats so that it could ferment there inside the hairy womb he'd made and no danger of getting somebody else's germs trapped inside.

"You're not from here," the man said, handing me another wedge of bread. "I can tell. But you speak the language like a Greek. So your parents must be Greek."

"I learned to speak from my fiancée," I said. "Her parents are Greek."

"Your fiancée? You're too young to have a fiancée."

"It's different in my country," I said. "We get married very young."

"What country is that?"

"Alaska," I said.

He was studying me, so I closed my eyes again, still chewing on the bread.

"This is exceptional bread," I said. "You don't find anything like this where I come from."

"Is that right?" the man said. "What God won't let you learn if you keep your ears clean. And where are you on your way to so far from Alaska?"

"Kavalla," I said, glancing over at him. "My father's in the tobacco business. I'm going out there to pick up some samples for him."

The man put the cheese back in his basket. He shook his head.

"I should have been in the tobacco business. I had a chance and lost it. I'd own this bus and a few more if I'd known then what I know now."

I guess the conversation had depressed him, because he shook his head again, then took some light woven cloth out of his basket and spread it over the chicken crate—he told me that was to make the chickens think it was night so they would stop talking to each other— and stretched his legs over the crate to take a snooze. I was depressed now too, and it wasn't just the slow climb with its endless dizzying turns and the bus sputtering and sometimes rocking around the bends so that you couldn't be sure at any point that it wouldn't just fail to make it this time and thereby deliver you head-on to the eternal valley quicker than you wanted to go. All that made-up talk about my fiancée ended up making me feel that I was fooling myself more than that poor villager. I wasn't ready to give up my conviction that I was meant to find Magda at the end of the road ahead, but if it turned out that she was really there, what help could I be to her after that? How was I supposed to save her from what her father had in mind when just about everybody else in that country would take it to be his right to do what he was doing? Propose marriage to her myself? I couldn't even begin to shape an image of her face responding to that idea, let alone her father's. Or should I try to convince her that she had to run away with me to some other country when most countries to the north were heating up with war fever and those to the east and the west suspicious by nature of things coming out of Greece?

Whatever thought I came up with seemed to bring me to a dead end that blocked my hope. But I wasn't about to turn back. I couldn't— it was as simple as that. And since I couldn't, I decided I would have to live with my uncertainty about what lay that far down the road and settle for what the gods might have in store for me day by day. Surely that was where Magda found herself right now, and if it was good enough for her, it was good enough for me.

This decision brought much relief. I found that I could sleep now, cramped in that backseat as I was—and sleep deeply to make up for the strain of the long hours that had gone by since it had become clear to me that Magda was not going to meet me at our rendezvous on the hillside. I woke up finally as the road flattened out and we speeded up to cross the Serres plain, where the river going through it must have flooded regularly because there seemed to be more swampland than cultivation. My friend with the chicken crate told me the mosquitoes along that route were a menace with their malaria, so I shouldn't plan on camping out except in the mountains, and when I told him I didn't plan any camping until I'd done my business in Kavalla and was ready for a short vacation, he said the best place for that was the island of Thassos, the greenest paradise in the Aegean. He said one thing I had to be sure not to miss if I ever got to that island was the ancient statue of Silenus, which showed an erection the size of his arm and would bring me what I needed for a healthy love life in the future if I scratched myself some powdered stone from that erection and drank it down with unwatered raki. I told him I'd certainly keep that in mind if I ever happened to make it to that green paradise.

We said good-bye when the bus reached Serres, and I used the man's departure to establish a new angle that was good for more sleep until we came to a coffee and toilet stop after the climb up to Alistratos, where there was a full view of the Drama plain, almost all the way south to Kavalla, with high mountains on the far side, some still with snow on their peaks. The road stuck to the foothills of those mountains all the way to Philippi, an easy ride through open fields, with nothing but the ruins there at the end and a cone-shaped hill with a castle on it to remind you that you weren't the first foreigner to feel more at home in that landscape than maybe you had a right to feel.

Something told me it might be a mistake for me to go all the way into the bus stop in Kavalla, so when we suddenly came out above the sea on the upper edge of the town, I asked the driver to let me off. I made my way through by the back streets a good distance above the harbor where there was a fleet of bright caiques lined up for business, and I joined the main road heading out of town to the east toward the stretch of coast that my *Encyclopaedia Britannica* map told me would eventually lead to a village that provided the shortest crossing to the island of Thassos. But getting there took me almost as long as the bus trip out of Salonika. I picked up a ride with a truck on the main road east, but once I got off that and headed south again toward the sea on a narrow dirt road, the best I could do was a two-hour ride on an oxcart from one village to the next, and a spell on a farmer's spare donkey that had a wooden saddle which left me raw in the groin after a mile or two and didn't seem much fun for the donkey either. After that I just walked.

It was hot in the open sun, but not too hot, and the sky was the clear blue that the coastal people say you find only in late spring before the summer heat and dust move in to haze up the air. I felt good out there on my own in open country, free in a way I'd never felt back in the city or even at the school where my father worked. There were no houses to speak of outside the occasional village and only a few people working the fields, most of which were small squares of wheat or barley left to ripen on their own or uncultivated plots still showing poppies and broom along their edges and yellow and white daisies everywhere else.

The whole way down to the shore I could see the island of Thassos ahead of me, taller than I'd expected, all forested. I suppose it could have been my overripe imagination, but my first distant view of it, before I could make out the intersecting curves of the mountains there, took the shape of a woman lying on her back with her hair spread out behind her and a small island close by for a discarded pillow. The closer I got to the fishing village I was headed for, the more it seemed that Thassos was just an abrupt high extension of the flat mainland, until I came up close to the village and had a clear view of the spread of sea I had to cross, deep blue offshore against the lighter sky. I decided I would go for that water before showing myself in the village, so I turned away from the road to follow the curving edge of a field planted with broad beans, and this brought me out to a stretch of beach that was completely deserted. I hit that beach on the run and was out of my clothes and into that water swimming fast without once stopping to catch my breath, and when I finally flipped over to rest and look back, it seemed the whole shoreline and the country behind it was new country I could claim for my own as much as the next man. I floated out there awhile until the cold sharpness the sea had at first was entirely gone, and then I swam in slowly until I could stand on the sand bottom with clear water to my waist and wash myself clean of everything I'd brought with me from the city and the road I'd left behind.

It took me some searching and no little bargaining, but by late afternoon I'd found a caique captain who was willing to take me across to the island for less than half the drachmas I had on me. He turned out to be a refugee from Asia Minor, a bitter-looking man who apparently had a chip on his shoulder against all governments, domestic and foreign, but also a pair of hands that were grounds for envy, the fingers thick as two of mine and the whole hand toughened by the ropes he handled so that they looked as hard as wood. He didn't seem to have much time for small talk with a stranger, which was fine by me because it saved me from having to answer questions and make up a story about where I was going or why. I spent most of the three-hour trip in the bow of his boat with my head on a coil of ropes, watching the island come nearer and sometimes checking out the sails that were rigged unlike anything I'd learned about at camp in upstate New York but that the fisherman handled with enough skill to keep us moving straight ahead at a steady clip despite the shifting angles of the wind.

As we cruised close in, I got out my map, which showed only two villages on the island, neither of them the port but one of which was called Panagia, named after the Virgin Mary. I don't know whether it was pure hope on my part, but I seemed to remember Magda's saying that she'd gone into a church dedicated to the Virgin Mary at some point during her stay on Thassos in order to light a candle and clear her head of very evil thoughts about her parents. Given only two villages on my map to work with, I figured Panagia had to be my first choice after I'd checked out the port, a thing that didn't look as though it would take me much time, because all it had to offer were a lot of fishing boats in the harbor there and some shops for provisions but few houses and no hotel that Magda was likely to spend time in. I still covered the whole of it just in case, then had a quick look through the ruins at the crossroads beyond the port village where the dirt road headed uphill toward Panagia, because they'd told me along the waterfront that the crossroads was where I'd find the standing slab of marble with the carved relief of Silenus on it. It was there all right, with its huge erection almost invisible because the best part of it had been scraped away over the years, but I didn't go down the steps that led you to a closer look since I figured I'd better keep clear of that kind of magic until I knew exactly what I might use it for.

It was a hard climb up to the village, very steep in places, especially near the end when I took what I hoped was a shortcut up a cobblestone path that was made for mules. Though the sun was low, my shirt was soaked through by the time I got to the houses on the outskirts, so I washed out the shirt in a stream that ran for a ways beside the cobblestone path, then hung it over a branch to wait for it to dry out a bit. I was taking my time now, because I didn't know exactly what I was going to do when I got into that village. From where I was sitting it looked as remote as any I'd been to, surrounded by fir and oak and chestnut trees that spread out to more of the same as far as the ridge of the mountain behind me and down to where the shore would be if you could see it. The houses that stood out between the trees were all whitewashed, with the same slate roofs and stone chimneys, and no sound coming from there, no movement, no sign of any life at all. It was as still as a monastery or nunnery. If Magda was there, what would she be doing now? What was there to occupy her time? I couldn't see how she could stand being so alone in a place like that. Or was that the whole point? And if it was, how did I fit into this new solitary life of hers? I picked up my damp shirt and readied myself to head on in toward those houses to try and find out.

I reached the central square by aiming for the largest plane tree I could see. There were two small cafes there and a place that was first of all a grocery store but had a few tables outside where you could get some prepared food. It was too early for anybody to be sitting there, so I decided to try to pick up some information from one or the other of the cafes, and if that didn't work, wait for the dinner hour and see if anybody who wasn't a local resident turned up for dinner. There were two old men playing backgammon in the first cafe, talking to the dice to make them roll out what was needed and slapping down the counters on the board as violently as they could manage, which made me think they wouldn't welcome being interrupted. At the second cafe, I went up to the lone customer sitting there, a man in bad need of a shave. I asked him point-blank if he'd come across any strangers in town.

"That depends on what you mean by strangers. If you mean local strangers, that's one thing. If you mean people from another country, that's another thing."

"I mean local strangers. Greeks."

"Well, that depends on whether you're talking about Greek men or Greek women."

"I'm talking about a Greek woman from Salonika. My sister, as a matter of fact."

The man was studying me, as though trying to decide if I looked at all like any other stranger he'd come across in town.

"And about how old would your sister be?"

"She's nineteen years old," I said. "Into her twentieth year, that is. And close to being in her twenty-first year."

"Well, there's a difference between nineteen and twenty and twenty-one," the man said.

"Of course. But it depends on how you count."

The man shook his head. "No. It depends on when you were born."

I suddenly got the feeling that this man was the local philosopher, with nothing better to do with his time than debate whoever came along with a will to argue, and that wasn't my mood.

"You're right," I said. "Thanks for the lesson."

I was all the way to the door when he said something to my back that made me turn.

"If you're still interested in what I may know or not know, I think you'll find your sister near the spring around the corner. A woman maybe twenty years old, with hair not quite as light as yours but not much darker either."

"The spring? I must have missed it coming in."

"Of course you missed it if you're a stranger. They have it fixed so that it comes out of a tree. With a brass faucet."

I stood there waiting.

"But the water is the best you'll find on this mountain. And I'm ready to swear to that if you don't believe me."

"I believe you," I said. "And you say my sister's near the spring?"

He made me turn back and approach him again.

"In the house that looks like it was made for a midget," the man said. "But not one of those who actually lives here. And we have several."

"Thanks," I said. "I'll find it."

"Only you won't find her in that house but in the room the crazy woman who lives there built on to it. For putting up strangers and foreigners and who knows who else. Priests and cripples and people with diseases and just about anybody you could name who makes it up here. And I don't mean to insult your sister, because she's too young to know any better. But the crazy woman who owns that place has not got a good name in this village, I can tell you that."

I just smiled at him and got out of there, because I knew I was home now. I didn't have any trouble finding that spring, and not much trouble finding the right house, though there were a lot of small houses in that village, one floor each and squat compared to those with a second floor that was shaped to project out over the street. This one had an addition that was in a different style from the rest of the house: flat-roofed and the brick still exposed, as though whoever had built it had run out of money at some point. The added room had a single window facing front, with the shutters closed. I didn't see that I had any choice but go up and knock on the front door of the house. The woman who answered had some kind of foreign accent and was wearing a burgundy dress with large flowers all over it. She looked at me without the slightest surprise, as though that village high up in the middle of the remotest island in the northern Aegean was as likely a place for a blond American in a damp T-shirt to land as the middle of Lake Keuka, N.Y.

"I'm looking for my sister," I said. "Magda Sevillas."

"She's sleeping," the woman said.

I just stood there.

"I'd rather not wake her," the woman said.

"Fine," I said. "I'll just go over to the square for a coffee and come back in an hour or so."

"No need for that," the woman said. "I'll make you a coffee."

And that's what she did, a Turkish coffee in a little cup, that you had to sip carefully and only so far down if you wanted to avoid getting a mouthful of grains and that had a sweet bitterness which was still new enough in my experience to be unpleasant. While I put on an act of savoring each sip of the stuff, the woman told me a little about herself without my having to ask. She introduced herself as Natasha Somethingorother, from Russia originally, a White Russian, she said, and a trained nurse who had never been allowed to practice her profession in her new country because they didn't recognize her qualifications here. Still, she'd found a place on that island where she could practice in a way that was even more satisfying than working in a hospital because people came to her of their own free will, by word of mouth, and there was nobody around to tell her what to do or not to do when she knew better, and she was free to use her own cures.

"Is Magda really sick?" I said as I got rid of the coffee cup.

"Not the way she was the last time she came to me," the woman said. "But she still needs sleep and quiet."

"Do you know exactly what's wrong with her?"

"It's personal," the woman said. "And when it's personal, I don't ask for more information than I'm given and I don't give out anything I'm told. Not even to relatives."

That ended the conversation. The woman took the coffee cup away, and while she was doing that, I looked up to find Magda gazing at me from the doorway to her room. She was wearing a beige bathrobe that barely reached her knees, and she looked a little paler than when I'd last seen her, but the gold was still in her hair, and her eyes were the same translucent green. I don't know how long she'd been watching me, but I could tell that she'd had some time to get used to the idea of my being there.

"So you found me," she finally said. "I knew if anybody was likely to, it would be you."

"I'm ready to go right back if you don't want me to stay," I said. "I'm not here to make things difficult for you."

That made her smile. "I didn't say I wanted you to go anywhere."

"I mean, the last thing I want is to interfere with your privacy."

"Is that the last thing you want?" Magda said, still smiling. "After all the trouble you must have gone to getting here?"

"I mean, I just want to help in any way I can."

"Well, let's start by being honest with each other. When I decided to come here, I thought you might figure out where I'd gone from what I told you. But I wasn't at all sure you'd try to find me. And now that you have, I'm glad you came."

"Maybe it was stupid of me, but I had to," I said. "You look pale."

"It wasn't stupid," Magda said. "And I may look pale but I'm really all right. I just haven't seen much of the sun recently. And I don't think I've ever been as alone as I've been the past few days. Especially since I didn't see any way for it to end."

"Well you don't have to worry about that any longer if you don't want to," I said.

Magda stood there gazing at me from the doorway. "I'll get dressed," she said. "And we'll take a walk."

The woman in the burgundy dress must have been waiting for us to finish talking, because she came back in the minute Magda turned away.

"I expect you'll be spending the night here," she said.

"I don't know," I said. "I haven't had a chance to discuss the question with my sister."

"I think it would do her good. I can put another bed in her room or you can sleep out here."

"We'll see," I said. "I don't want to cause any trouble."

"No trouble either way," the woman said. "And either way I won't charge you as much as you'd have to pay in a hotel if there were a hotel. So you just let me know."

Magda came out wearing the same blouse and skirt that she'd worn the afternoon of our visit to the hillside above Kapudjida, and my seeing her like that made me hold my breath a moment and look away. When we got outside, she went straight for the spring built into the plane tree and knelt to drink some water, then cupped her hands under the faucet and asked if I wanted to drink. I knelt and drank out of her hands. The water was sweet and cold. When I was finished, she took her hands away and patted water on her face and neck, and I decided to do the same. While I was kneeling there she touched my shirt.

"It's damp," she said. "I'll wash it for you."

"I washed it on the way up here. In the stream that runs by the cobblestone road."

"That water isn't always clean," she said. "Tomorrow I'll wash it for you with soap."

We didn't talk as we walked on up toward the square, but before we got there she linked her arm in mine.

"I told the woman you were my sister," I said.

"I know. I heard you."

"I didn't know what else to say."

"It was clever of you," Magda said. "It makes things easier."

"I hope so."

"Though she isn't fooled for a minute."

"I also told that to a man in the cafe over there."

"Good. That means it will be known all over the village by tomorrow morning."

"I'm sorry."

"Don't be sorry. I wouldn't be able to walk with you like this otherwise. Not in this village."

"Well, it isn't exactly a lie," I said. "I think of you as a sister sometimes."

"No you don't," Magda said. "But it doesn't matter. We can pretend if it makes you feel more comfortable."

I didn't know where we were going, so I let Magda guide me over to the grocery store with the outdoor tables. It was still early, so we had the place to ourselves. Magda said that she hadn't been eating much the past few days but was suddenly hungry, so we went inside and ordered stuffed tomatoes and peppers and fried goat cheese to go with the olives and bread and local wine that the owner had brought us when we first sat down.

"I want you to know that I came here not because of anything having to do with you," Magda said. "I didn't meet you when I was supposed to because I wasn't in Salonika. I was already here. And there was no way I could let you know that I had to leave as suddenly as I had to."

"I know," I said. "I talked to your aunt."

Magda smiled. "You really are clever. I thought you might think of going to my aunt eventually."

"What else could I do? There wasn't anybody else I could talk to. And I was certain something serious must have happened."

"Then you know why I'm here."

"I think so."

"And you know why I can't go back. Ever."

"Well, you can't stay here forever either, can you?"

"That's the trouble," Magda said, looking away. She seemed close to tears. I reached over and touched her hand.

"Don't worry about it," I said. "I'm ready to take care of you for as long as you'll let me."

The tears came now. Magda smiled at me through them. Then she took my hand.

"Are you ready?" she said. "If you are, you're as good a pupil as a teacher could want. But I'm afraid I haven't been good to you because all I've done is help you to grow up too quickly."

"You're not my teacher any longer, so don't worry about it."

"That's also the trouble," Magda said. "Since I'm not your teacher any longer and not your sister, what am I?"

"Don't worry about it."

"I just don't want to take advantage of your feeling for me and the weakness it brings out in me."

"Why does it have to be a weakness? Why can't it be just what it is?"

Magda let go of my hand. "I don't know," she said, looking away again. "I'm still very confused. All I know is that I hate my father and my mother for what they are trying to do to my life, and yet I don't know what I can do about it. There's no place for me to turn."

"Yes there is," I said.

Magda turned back. Her face softened, and the tears came again. She leaned over suddenly and kissed me lightly on the mouth. Then she sat back in her seat and reached for the bread.

"Let's begin by getting our strength back at least," she said.

She broke off a hunk of the dark bread and passed the loaf over to me, then went for the black wrinkled olives and ate them one after the other as though they were cherries, then caught her breath by eating some bread. I poured the wine. When the tomatoes and peppers and fried cheese came, she filled my plate and then hers. We both ate what was there until there was nothing left but olive pits and bread crumbs, and I can't remember when food, any food anywhere, tasted as good as that did. I got up to go inside and pay the bill, but Magda grabbed my arm to stop me.

"I'm not going to let you spend your money after you've come all the way here on your own to find me," Magda said.

"I want to spend it," I said. "I have no other use for it."

Magda wouldn't let go of my arm. "We'll discuss this tomorrow.

Tonight is mine. Besides, it's the custom in this country to pay for a visitor."

"Not when he's your brother," I said. "You're my responsibility until you get married, and I'm not going to let you get married."

"Is that right?" Magda said.

"Not to a gold merchant or anybody else."

She let go of my arm. "You mustn't joke about that," she said. "The idiocy of it still hurts me."

"I didn't really mean it as a joke."

"In any case," Magda said. "I'll let you pay tonight if it makes you feel better, but beginning tomorrow, we share expenses."

I went inside to pay the bill, beaming to myself over the idea of a shared beginning tomorrow even though I had almost nothing in my pocket left to share. When I came out, Magda was standing at the edge of the earthen plot set off by potted geraniums to form our outdoor restaurant. She was gazing out over the still empty square. She didn't turn to look at me when I came up beside her and put my arm a little stiffly around her waist.

"You must be exhausted after your trip here," she said. "I'll go back now and arrange for the woman to move in a bed for you."

"You don't have to do that," I said. "I can arrange it."

"I think it would be better if I did the arranging," Magda said. "Especially if you think you'd be more comfortable having it moved into my room rather than her living room."

"I'd be more comfortable," I said.

She turned then to look at me, her face still pale and deadly serious, but there was something new in her look, a kind of shyness, that made the blood run out of me from head to toe and then slowly return until my face felt the full flush of it.

"I'll go on ahead and arrange it then," she said. "You come along when you feel like it."

I watched her move across the square. She used to have a way of walking that was full of purpose, at least when she was coming up the front walk of my house for our tutorial sessions, but her way of moving now seemed less sure, gentler, more girlish, and she kept her gaze on the ground in front of her so that it made her seem more pensive than determined. At one point she gave her head a little flick to make her hair twirl as though ending some thought, and that was a thing I recognized, but she still didn't raise her head to look up as she walked, and she didn't turn once to see if I was watching her.

I decided to explore the village awhile before going back. I headed uphill from the square because the road was broader that way, passing between some of the few houses that had an upper story overhanging the road, and this brought me out to a clearing with huge plane trees and a spring that was fed from three directions. Behind the clearing there was a church with a bell tower beside it. The bell tower had a clock in it that said nine o'clock, which was an hour ahead of my watch but must have been close to right because the sun was already down behind the mountain ridge that ringed the village and the light was thin.

It was a large church, all whitewashed, with a slate roof and a cupola at one end. There was a strip of Greek lettering over the gate, and I made that out to say "The Sleep of the Virgin." I wanted to go inside and have a look, but the gate turned out to be locked, so I kept on climbing up the hill behind the church until my shirt was damp again and the light almost gone, and then I circled around the village and took a different path back to the plane tree with the spring water coming out of it. I stopped there to have a long drink and wash under my shirt a bit before crossing over to the Russian woman's place.

She'd left the front door unlocked for me, and there was a kerosene lamp lit with a low flame on the mantel above the fireplace. Magda's door was closed, but it wasn't locked. It was dark in her room, and as far as I could see there was nothing in there except two narrow beds on either side of a tall piece of furniture that I figured served for a closet, and a chair at the foot of each bed, though once I got used to the light, I saw another low chest near Magda's chair that had a basin on it and a large water pitcher beside the basin. Magda was in bed with just her head outside the sheet and bedcover. I couldn't tell whether she was asleep, but her eyes were closed, and they stayed that way while I got undressed and climbed under my sheet and cover, wearing only my underpants. I lay there looking up at the ceiling, trying not to breathe too loudly, and I lay there a long time. I have no idea how late it was before I finally fell asleep, nor any idea how long I slept before I felt Magda's hand touch my cheek. She was kneeling beside my bed. I took her hand and kissed her open palm.

"I can't sleep," she said.

"I couldn't either at first," I said.

"You were breathing loudly," she said. "I'm not used to hearing that."

I let go of her hand. "I tried not to."

"I didn't really mind," Magda said. "I liked the sound of it after a while."

Her hand was stroking my cheek now and then my neck.

"I think I could get used to the idea of having a little brother in my room," Magda said.

I decided to throw back my sheet and bedcover. Then I edged over a little and lay sideways. Magda was still kneeling there looking at me. I could see now that she was wearing some sort of nightdress that was open at the neck. She stood up suddenly and pulled it over her head, and before I had a chance to see all I wanted to see, she came in beside me and pulled the sheet up to cover herself.

"Just lie still," she said when I tried to put my arm around her.

I didn't move, and she didn't either. Then I felt her lips on my cheek, and then her hand came up to hold my chin so that she could brush her lips against mine, but when I tried to kiss her, she moved her lips away, and then I felt them on my neck and along my shoulder. I didn't know whether she was being shy or teasing me or what, but when I started to say something, she put two fingers against my lips.

"We have to learn about each other," she said. "So don't be in too much of a hurry, little one."

I lay back and waited. She pushed the sheet lower so that her lips could move down to the top of my arm and gradually across my chest, brushing against one nipple and then the other. Her hand touched my belly button under the sheet and then my underpants and that made her hesitate. When I reached down to take them off, she moved away to the edge of the bed on her side.

"No, not yet," she said. "It's your turn to let me catch up."

So I did what she had done, as slowly as I could manage, down her neck and across her arm to her breast, barely touching her nipple with my lips and then turning my cheek against it to feel its hardness press against me, then across to the other breast, brushing it lightly one way and then the other, but when I tried to move my hand below her belly button, she caught it and made me look up at her. She had her eyes closed now and was shaking her head. I decided the time had come to take off my underpants, and after I'd done that, I lay back and let her have her turn again. She ran her hand over me gently as far as it could reach without pausing very long anywhere but shaping the way it moved so that it covered everything in its path, as though her hand had become her eyes, and then she brought her hand up and took my free hand and put it on her belly to signal the start of my turn. I couldn't make mine travel as lightly as she could make hers, and when my fingers moved through the fine hair between her thighs and came to where she was wet, I hovered too long where she was most sensitive there, because I felt her shiver and tighten, and then she took my hand away and guided it along the inside of her thigh. She brought my hand back to let it hover again but held it so that my touch was right for her. When I tried to go on to the other thigh to finish my turn, she eased my hand back where it had been and made me keep it there so that she could move against it, slowly at first, then freely, her breathing quicker and quicker until it stopped suddenly and became a long sigh. I was lying against her now and I felt her hand come down and hold my penis lightly, too lightly, so I did what she had done, moving against her hand, my breath now as short as hers had been, and when I felt I couldn't hold back much longer, I put my hand over hers and guided it so that it brought my turn to an end.

I was embarrassed by the wet mess I'd made half on her and half on me, but when I reached down to try and find my underpants at the bottom of the bed to use them to wipe it away, Magda brought my arm back and used my hand to spread the wetness thin on her belly and then used her hand to do the same for me.

"It isn't dirty," she said almost in a whisper. "And if it really bothers you, we can worry about it in the morning."

We lay still for a while, and when I finally put my arm around her and drew her to me to kiss her the way I thought I should, she didn't resist but used her free hand to turn my face so that she could kiss me back in her own way, a more open kiss, her tongue playing with mine, and then she brought her arm around my waist and left it there. We both fell asleep after that, though she did first, and when daylight came, I woke before Magda did and lay there gazing up at the ceiling with Magda's head on my shoulder, wondering how a night could ever be sweeter than that had been. After a while I tried to slip my arm out from under her without waking her, but it didn't work. She opened her eyes and looked at me, so I leaned over and kissed them closed again. We lay quietly until she said, "I'd like to get up and wash." I eased my arm out and reached down to find my underpants.

While I was doing that, Magda slipped out of bed. She picked up her nightgown and went over to sit on the edge of the bed opposite with the nightgown on her lap and her arms crossed in front of her. She looked younger that way than I'd ever seen her, but as I sat there on my bed in my underpants opposite her, I suddenly felt awkward, and I didn't know why. I lay back on the bed and gazed up at the ceiling.

"I can't wash if you're going to lie there," Magda said softly.

"I wouldn't look," I said. "But if it will make you feel better, I'll get dressed and go outside."

"Just for a minute," she said. "Then you can have your turn. I'll show you how you have to do it so you don't waste water."

I put on my shirt and pants and went out in my bare feet to wait in the living room. Sitting there depressed me. I suppose Magda was right to want her privacy, but after we'd been so close all night, it seemed to put distance between us, and I couldn't get used to the idea. I got up from the settee and tried to occupy myself by studying the pictures on the wall, but they were mostly revolting scenes of mountains and valleys with snow all over them and prancing deer. I could hear the Russian woman doing something in her kitchen, but luckily she didn't come into the living room while I was standing there. When I sat down again, Magda opened the door to our room and signaled me to come back in. She was wearing panties and a brassiere. She took my hand and closed the door behind us, then led me over to the commode, or whatever it was. I could see now that there was a large earthenware jug on the floor beside it, with a doily for a cover.

"There's plenty of water in this village," Magda said. "But it isn't easy for Natasha and me to fill up all the jugs for the rooms and the toilet outside and carry them here, so we try to save as much water as we can."

She raised the doily and reached inside the jug to bring out a dipper.

"You fill the basin with this, and then you use my soap and cloth to wash yourself, and when you're done you empty the basin outside the back window there. And then you fill the basin again with clean water to get rid of the soap, but that should be all the water you have to use."

I stood there gazing at the dipper in her hand.

"What is it now?" she said.

"You're treating me like a child," I said. "I know how to wash."

"Well, I thought you might not know how to wash in a village like this one," Magda said.

"If it's so different from washing anywhere else, maybe you'd better show me how to do it then."

Magda smiled now. "You're a devil," she said. "Very clever and very awful."

"I'm just trying to learn," I said.

"No you're not," Magda said. "I know what you're trying to do."

"Well, how about helping me wash my back at least. Where I can't reach."

"Oh, all right," Magda said. "Take off your shirt."

I took off my shirt. Magda filled the dipper from the jug and emptied it into the basin, then put the basin on the floor.

"Kneel down," she said.

I knelt down in front of her.

"Please be good," she said, "or you'll have to do it by yourself."

She pushed the basin around behind me, then picked up the washcloth and soap from the commode and knelt behind me to wet the cloth and soap it. The cloth was cold on my back at first and made me flinch, but as Magda worked it across my shoulders and down the sides, all business at first but gentler as she came to the small of my back, I relaxed into her motion with my head back and took in the full pleasure of it. When she was done, she wrung out the washcloth to get rid of the soap and started over again.

"No, it's my turn," I said and swung around to try and take the washcloth and soap from her.

"You can't take the soap from me," she said. "If you do that in this country it means we're going to have a terrible fight."

"Well, leave it in the basin then."

"But I've washed myself already."

"Not your back. Not everywhere."

"Oh, all right."

I picked up the basin to empty it, but Magda stopped me.

"You can use the same water," she said. "Only you have used it, so I don't mind."

She knelt in front of the basin and took off her brassiere. I knelt behind her and worked on her back the way she had on mine, only I took longer, and when I reached the small of her back I went up under her arm and washed there too and then let my hand reach around the front of her.

"Please don't do that," she said.

"I can't help it."

"I'm very sensitive there."

"So am I."

Her head was bent back now, and her eyes were closed, and she didn't stop my hand when I moved to the other side of her back and came around the front of her again. I don't know what had gotten into me, but I couldn't stop myself. I let the washcloth drop away and just stayed there with my hand. And then I brought the other hand around too.

"You really are awful," she said quietly.

"Maybe we should go back to bed," I said.

"We can't do that," Magda said. "The woman will be waiting with our breakfast."

"Can't we let her wait?" I said, leaning forward so that I could wrap my arms around her and kiss her neck. She didn't say anything when I straightened up but let her head come back against mine. Then she broke the grip I had on her and stood up to go over and sit on the edge of my bed.

"What we're doing is dangerous," she said. "If we're going to do it, I have to be able to trust you."

"You can trust me," I said.

"You say that but I don't think you have any idea what I'm talking about."

"Well, tell me then. You can tell me anything."

"I mean that I don't want to become pregnant. My life is compli-cated enough already."

"What do you want me to do then?"

"It's what I don't want you to do. Unless you have protection."

"I don't have any protection. How could I? Would you expect me to bring that sort of thing with me when I couldn't even be sure you wanted me to find you in the first place?"

"I'm not saying you should have it with you. I'm just trying to explain why I have to trust you. Do you understand what I'm say-ing?"

"I think so," I said. "But it doesn't really thrill me to talk about it this way."

Magda was gazing at me, smiling now. "Come here," she said. "If you don't want to talk about it, I guess I'll have to show you what I mean."

I went over and stood in front of her. She shook her head as though saying something to herself, then undid my belt and unbuttoned my pants. When I went to pull down my underpants, she stopped me and did it herself, letting her cheek rub against my belly. Then she held me close against her and raised her head to kiss my throat and then my nipples. I held her head there so she wouldn't move away until I was ready.

"Now lie down," she said. "On your back, so I can watch you."

I did that, and she took off her panties and knelt over my hips with her hands on my chest. She moved very slowly against me.

"You can come in when you want," she said, looking down at me, "but you can't stay there to the end. Do you understand?"

"Yes."

"Do you want to come in now?"

"Yes. Please."

"I have to watch you," Magda said. "In case you can't help yourself."

"You can watch me. I don't mind."

"And if I close my eyes, promise to hold back until I can watch you again."

"I promise," I said.

Her eyes were already closed, and I could tell from her breathing that they were going to stay that way, so I held on as her rhythm quickened, and when it finally slacked off and she opened her eyes again, I closed mine and held her hips so that I could move freely inside her until I had to ease off and then stop completely to keep my promise. I felt Magda's hand on my penis as she sat back on my thighs. I kept my eyes closed, and when she was done with me, she wiped me clean with the top edge of the sheet, then bent forward and kissed me gently on both cheeks, almost as she would in saying hello or good-bye.

"I know it isn't the best way for you," she said. "But it's just our first time like that. Maybe we can make it better."

"I don't mind," I said.

"But I do," Magda said.

I pulled her down beside me and held her there. She turned my face so that I had to look at her squarely.

"I don't want you to think that I'm difficult or that I don't know what it means for you to have come all this way to find me and how good you've been for me. I just can't believe that I'm good for you."

"Well, maybe you should start believing it. Because I believe it."

"You're still so young," she said, shaking her head. "How can you really know what you should believe when I don't know myself?"

"I'm not so young," I said. "Not anymore."

"I realize that," Magda said. "It's the thing that worries me most."

She stood up and gathered her panties and bra and went over to the other bed. She sat there looking at me, then at the floor.

"You can stay while I wash again and get dressed if you want," she said. "I don't mind any longer."

But she didn't move from the bed.

"I'll go see about breakfast," I said.

I got dressed and took my shoes and socks with me. I figured I'd go out to the spring and wash the socks since they were the only pair I had with me and check out the toilet on the way. The Russian woman was still keeping her distance, so I let myself out the front door and went around back to find the toilet. It was the Turkish kind, with two low steps for your feet and a hole in the middle and squares of newspaper on a nail where a roll should have been. I wasn't about to go in there and squat in my bare feet, so I headed over to the spring, and after I'd washed out my socks, I didn't see how I had any choice but to wring them out and put them on wet. I'd changed into my best shoes back home, but after all the walking I'd done on my trip to that village they looked like the kind you find sticking out of trash cans, so I decided to wash them inside and out too, even if they were mostly leather. I squished on back to the toilet and looked it over again, then decided I'd hold off until after breakfast and head for a private place in the forest.

I went inside and found Magda sitting in the kitchen with the Russian woman. Whatever the two of them had been talking about, my showing up killed the conversation. The woman brushed the hair back from her forehead and went over to the sink.

"Would you like some fresh milk?" she said, turning to me. "It's still warm from the goat."

"I think I'll just have one of these apples here," I said.

"The milk will be good for you. Magda is having some. It builds up your strength."

From the way she said it, I got the impression that she wasn't speaking as just whatever kind of nurse she was but as somebody Magda had taken into her confidence. One part of me didn't mind that at all, but another did.

"They have cows in America," Magda said without looking at me. "I don't think they have goats."

"They have goats," I said. "They just don't have them where I come from."

"You come from America?" the woman said.

"Didn't Magda tell you?" I said.

The woman looked at Magda.

"Yes, I told her," Magda said.

I stared at her across the table. Magda leaned forward and spoke to me suddenly in German.

"If we're going to stay here like we are, I couldn't go on pretending. Not to a woman who saved me from killing myself once."

"You don't have to explain," I said in Greek. "Just as long as you let me in on what's going on."

"I'm sorry," Magda said softly. "I would have as soon as we were alone."

"I have two kinds of preserves to go with your bread if you don't like goat milk," the Russian woman said.

"Oh, all right, I'll try the goat milk," I said.

Magda and I sat there on opposite sides of the table without saying anything. Then she reached over and took the apple out of my hand and cut it into four sections. When she'd cleaned each one, she fed me the first, then took one herself, then fed me another.

"I think you should go down to the sea today," the Russian woman said. "It will do Magda good to get some sun."

"That's fine by me," I said.

"It's quite a distance, but you can come back as late as you want, because I'll leave something for you to eat on the table here."

I suddenly felt very good. It wasn't just the idea of having Magda all to myself for a day. It seemed that she'd managed to ease me into this little family of three that she'd created, and I saw no reason why this day couldn't be followed by another and another after that. I took a second apple and cut it into sections the way Magda had and offered her the first piece. She caught my hand and bit into my thumb just enough to make it hurt a little, then swallowed the section of apple I'd given her. When the Russian woman put the cup of goat milk in front of me, I saluted her with it as though it were a glass of wine, and I sipped away at it steadily without showing that I really thought it a sorry substitute for the sweeter mixture of Holstein and Guernsey that over the years had made me grow a head taller than almost anybody else in my class at the German School. When Magda dipped her bread into her milk, I did that too. And when the fried eggs floating in olive oil arrived, I got those down as well and used what bread I had left to clean my plate because the Russian woman said that olive oil and eggs were even better than goat milk for building up one's strength.

It was already noon when we got down to the sea, because the path that led us there had its own sense of direction, often climbing uphill on its way down, and anyway, we were in a mood to take our time. The path went through woods mostly, with an occasional break that brought us out to a rock bluff above the sea, closer every time and therefore tantalizing, but not so much so that we didn't stop whenever we felt like it and sit down to look out to the east across a great spread of blue that showed a distant border to the north and nothing except open space straight ahead. Sometimes while we were sitting there Magda would point out trees I didn't recognize and name them in Greek, or show me the difference between pine trees that seemed much alike. And from her last visit she knew most of the wildflowers we ran across, because the Russian woman had taken her on walks to study them and gather those she thought useful for cures, along with certain healing herbs and greens. I learned too many names to remember, all in a language that wasn't my own. One time I began gathering up the wildflowers along our way to take back with us so that I could identify them later and see if they had a name in English that I recognized, but when I told Magda what I was doing, she said they wouldn't last long enough.

"How long is not long enough?" I asked her.

"That depends on when you decide to go home," Magda said.

"Well, that depends on when you decide."

"I'm never going home. I told you that."

"Well, then I'm not either," I said.

She leaned over and kissed me, little kisses on my cheek and mouth and chin and the other cheek.

"You're sweet," she said. "But sometimes you don't make any sense."

"I'm serious," I said.

"I know you are," Magda said. "But let's not be serious. Not today. It will just spoil everything."

She stood up and brushed off her skirt. I took the wildflowers I'd gathered and sprinkled them over her hair, then dropped a few down the front of her blouse.

"What are you doing?" she said, retrieving them.

"Trying not to be serious."

She stuck one of the flowers she retrieved behind my ear. Then she tugged at my belt and dropped another into my pants. I tried to grab her to tug at her skirt, but she pulled away and was gone, racing down the path ahead of me, and by the time I caught up with her, the flowers were gone from her hair. She held my hands to keep me quiet while she caught her breath, then went on ahead again at her own pace. She stopped once and waited so that I would listen to a bird that she called a nightingale but that sounded to me like an escaped canary, and another time she let me go on ahead and then disappeared behind me into the forest to do what she called her "tshisha." The next time we came out to a clearing, we were above a cove that had its own quarter-moon of beach separating it from a broad stretch of sand that curled along the coast for what must have been a mile. There were some olive trees at the far end of that open beach but no house or hut that I could see. Magda took hold of my hand again.

"We'll go down below here where nobody ever comes except by sea," she said. "But be careful to step where I step."

She was wearing sandals, but she handled them like ballet slippers, toeing her way from rock to rock above the brush and skipping back and forth across the gully we were following in a pattern that seemed to be a dance already set in her head. She turned only once to see if I was following her, and when she jumped from the last foothold onto the sand, she spread her arms wide toward the sea, as though there was somebody out there to give her applause, then stripped where she was without turning around and went for the water.

I decided I wouldn't follow her in right away. I sat down on the back edge of the sand and watched her swim out a ways, then stripped and piled my clothes beside hers. I picked up her sandals and my shoes and went down to the edge of the water to wash them clean of the dust they'd gathered coming down the mountainside. After I'd set them out side by side to dry in the sun, I lay down in the shallows with my head on my crossed arms just out of the water to gaze up at the sky and then to close my eyes with the wonder of where I was and who I was with. There was no sound now except the slight wash and roll of the sea as it came in to lick the sand around me and then brush back across the small pebbles it exposed, pause, then come on in again, and way behind me, where the trees began shaping the forest above the shore, a dense sound of cicadas beating against the heat. I don't know how long I lay still, but those soft rhythms must have worked on me until I heard nothing and felt nothing, no coolness along the length of me, no pressure of light against my eyelids or the heat on my forehead that came with it, nothing but the fading contentment of being there.

It was a sudden coolness on my face that brought the light back. I found Magda kneeling beside me, cupping water against my forehead and wetting my hair.

"You'll get sunstroke lying here like that," she said. "You're too blond for this sun."

"Then shade me," I said.

"How?"

"Like this."

I brought her face down to shield mine, and while I was at it, I kissed her the way she'd last kissed me.

"That won't help the rest of you," she said, leaning over me with her elbows straight. "You still burn even if there's water between you and the sun."

"Then you'd better shield the rest of me," I said.

"You mean like this?"

She flung a leg over mine so that she was kneeling above me.

"I don't think that's enough protection," I said. "The sun comes in at the sides."

"You want too much," she said, as I raised my head to kiss her where she couldn't protect herself. "We'll drown like this."

"I don't think so. Not if we're careful."

She slid down on top of me full length. "We can't do this here," she said. "We're exposed to the sea."

"Do you want me to burn to death?"

"No. You mustn't burn to death and I mustn't either now that you've woken up the wrong gods in this heat."

She ran her tongue along the lids of my eyes.

"I didn't mean to wake any gods. It's just that there's no other cool place for us to be."

"It's too cool," Magda said, raising herself on her arms, then closing her eyes when I began to take advantage again of all the territory she'd exposed. "Can you move back on shore a bit so that our legs don't float?"

"Not unless you move with me."

"You'll have to stop what you're doing and hold me then."

"How's that."

"You're holding me too tightly. We'll drown."

"That's because I'm afraid you'll try to get away. Will you promise to stay with me if I loosen up enough for us to move together?"

"Yes."

"Is that better?"

"That's as good as we can do. Now don't move anymore or you'll get sand between us. Let me move alone."

She rubbed against me very delicately, carefully, and after a while raised herself on her hands again to allow herself as much freedom as she needed.

"You're not watching my face."

"Please don't talk anymore."

"If you go on like that I don't know that I can hold back."

"Do what you have to do," Magda said, her eyes still closed. "We'll blame it on the demon of noon."

I was inside her now, and when I knew I had to come out or lose control and tried to press against her with my hands so that she would release me, she shook her head and wouldn't let me go. When I shuddered and called out, she still wouldn't let me go. I stayed there and let her have her pleasure as long as she wanted, almost longer than I could bear it, and when the little sounds she made finally stopped and she backed off me to slide down my legs and float in the water at my feet, I lay still with my arms spread out on the sand and closed out the light again.

We got back to the village in late afternoon. The Russian woman was still having her siesta, but she'd left out a meal of beans in tomato sauce and fried chicken livers, along with a decanter of local wine that she must have chilled in the spring outside. Magda filled my plate and set it in front of me, then poured me some wine, then brushed her hand across my forehead to comb the damp hair out of my face.

"You don't really have to serve me," I said. "I can serve myself."

"I want to do it," Magda said. "In this country that's what you're supposed to do for the man in your life."

"Is that what you want me to be?" I said.

"It's what you are," Magda said. "Young as you may be, and whether I wanted it or not."

"What does that mean?"

She smiled. "It means the demons or gods or fate or whatever you want to call it have made you that, and that's where we are now."

"You can still tell me to go home."

Magda served herself. "I thought I could this morning," she said without looking at me. "But after this noon, things have changed. As you would say, I know that I can't help it now."

She sat down and started eating faster than I'd seen her do.

"Well, I don't know about demons and things like that. But if you yourself don't really want me to stay, I'm not staying."

She looked up at me, then sighed.

"Why do you make me say it bluntly? That's so very Anglo-Saxon. The whole point is that I want you to stay."

Magda went over to the cupboard and came back with a dish of chopped parsley and some other herb in a jar. She took a pinch of parsley for her chicken livers and passed the dish across to me but kept the jar beside her plate after she'd sprinkled it over her beans.

"Don't I get any of that too?" I said.

Magda shook her head. "That's for me. Natasha's prescription for helping fate decide in a woman's favor. After what we did this noon."

"I tried to do what you told me I should do."

"I know. It was my decision. Sometimes at moments like that you have to let things take their course and not worry about the consequences."

"Are you worried now?"

"No, not really. I can pretend it's all a matter of demons and fate and that sort of thing, but I made a choice and I'm ready to live with it."

"You make it sound as though I'm not involved in all this."

Magda reached across for my hand. "You really are so very young. Don't you see that the choice includes you?"

That evening, it was a Sunday evening, Magda decided that she wanted to visit the church that I'd found locked when I first arrived in the village. She said that it might not be the right church for either of us, but it was the one that she credited with helping her recover her peace of mind when she'd hid out with Natasha the first time, and right or wrong for us, it was the one closest at hand. She said that she wanted to go there and light a candle the way she had during her last stay in the village, and she wanted me to light one with her, if my Anglo-Saxon conscience would allow me to do that. I told her my Anglo-Saxon conscience wasn't bothered by that or anything else, except maybe for an occasional touch of guilt about giving my parents something to worry about, but I figured I might light an extra candle for their benefit, though I doubted that lighting candles in a Greek Orthodox church would do much good for any one of us in view of the different religions each of us was supposed to believe in, not counting Natasha, who was at least Russian Orthodox.

"What do you mean when you say supposed to believe in?" Magda said. "Don't you believe in your religion?"

"I don't know," I said. "I don't know what I believe in, but I feel I should believe in something."

"Well, I don't really believe in mine either. Not in my father's religion. Not when it allows him to try to arrange a marriage for money with somebody I've never seen that would have the Rabbi's blessing if my mother happened to have been born Jewish instead of Greek."

"What about your mother's religion? Or your aunt's?"

"That's not much better when it comes to arranged marriages and the dowries that go with them. But I like the Greek churches when they're empty. And I like the icons and frescoes and even the smell of incense when it isn't too strong."

"But what about the God the Greeks believe in? Do you believe in him?"

"I don't know," Magda said. "In a way. In any case, if there is a God, I would say that he must be the same for all religions. And it would be nice to think that he or the Virgin Mary or some other saint might want to bless you and me for what we can't help being. Which is why I thought we ought to light a candle in whatever church we have here and hope for the best."

So we waited until Natasha was fairly certain that it was late enough for the Church of the Sleeping Virgin to be more or less empty, and then the three of us went for a walk that took us through the village square and up to the bell-tower gate, which turned out to be still open. The men sitting around in the two cafes had a good look at us as we crossed through the square, and so did some of the women sitting out in the doorways of their houses on the winding street that took us higher up, though there wasn't a one of them who didn't say a sweet "good evening" as we passed by. When we got inside the church, Natasha dropped a coin in the box near the candles and picked up one of the smallest to plant and light in the candelabrum, then went up front to cross herself and kiss the icons there. Magda dropped enough money in the box for three of the largest candles.

"I have to pay for my own," I said. "It won't count otherwise."

"Oh, all right," Magda said. "But beginning tomorrow we put our money together."

She gave me two of the candles and I dropped some coins in the box without counting them. Magda lit her candle from another in the candelabrum, then lit mine from hers.

"If it's going to mean anything, I want yours beside mine," she said. "I don't care where you put your other one."

"What's it supposed to mean exactly?"

"That we belong to each other now first of all and want the Virgin's blessing. I mean, if you really feel that way."

"I feel that way. Honestly."

"Then I do too," Magda said.

She fixed her candle in the candelabrum and I put one of mine beside hers. The other one I put on the far side. I stepped back beside Magda and watched the candles burn. She took my hand and held it tightly. When Natasha crossed herself in front of the iconostasis and headed back toward us, Magda let go of me and turned toward the doorway, then took my hand again as we stepped outside the church together.

When we got home, Natasha brought out a worn pack of cards and tried to teach us a Russian game that would have been difficult enough with ordinary cards but was totally confusing to me when the face cards had Greek characters. Magda of course got the thing down right away, but she pretended to be bored with the game and very sleepy, so Natasha promised to teach us a simpler game the next day and went off to bed, kissing us in turn on both cheeks.

Magda carried a kerosene lamp into our room and set it down on the commode. She said that under the circumstances she thought it might make more sense for us to put our beds together side by side without the clothes cupboard between us, so we did that, with a chair at the foot of each to put our clothes on, and then we got undressed. When I went over to the commode to blow out the lamp, Magda caught my arm and stopped me.

"Not tonight," she said. "Tonight I want to see every bit of what I belong to first of all. Unless you're too tired."

"I'm not too tired."

"Then lie down and let me look at you."

"You've seen me," I said.

"I mean really look at you."

I lay down on my bed. Magda stayed on her bed, kneeling over me. While she gazed down at me she ran her fingers slowly over my forehead and down my nose and across my cheeks and turned my head toward her so that she could run her fingers into the crevices of one ear and around behind it and down my neck to my throat, then kept going across the top my shoulders and down my armpits to my chest, now using the fingers of both hands and sometimes the flat of her palms, as though there was an unspoken agreement that any part of me she didn't manage to cover that night not only with her eyes but her hands wouldn't belong to her from that day forward. When she got to my feet and even my toes, she said "Now turn over."

"No," I said into my pillow. "I want to look at you the same way."

"You'll get your chance."

I turned over and kept my head buried in my pillow so that I couldn't see where she was but let myself follow the path of her hands entirely by the feel of them, and that path led her to open me to her look and her touch where nobody but I had been since my infancy. She was still kneeling on her bed when she reached my shoulder blades and the back of my neck, but suddenly I felt her straddle my back.

"Now turn over again," she said.

"No," I said. "That isn't fair. You said I would get my chance too."

"Does it have to be tonight? Can't we do that tomorrow?"

"No, I want to see you too. The same way."

Magda climbed off me and lay back on her bed. Her chest was rising and falling and I could hear her breath coming short. She wouldn't look at me as I ran my fingers over her face and her neck, and when I reached her breasts she began to moan softly.

"Am I hurting you?"

"No, but I knew it would be better if we waited for this."

"Do you want me to stop."

"You don't have to yet."

I went on running my fingers over her, trying to be as gentle as I could be, and when I reached her belly and then let my fingers play lightly with her pubic hair, she rose up against my hand and opened to me so suddenly that I couldn't go on and had to stay where she wanted me to. I finally came over on top of her and let her guide me inside her, and when she curled her legs around me, I knew that was where my night's exploration was going to end.

WE SPENT MOST OF THE NEXT DAY INDOORS. OUR VISIT TO THE church and what followed it brought a new calmness into our room, so that both of us slept easily, and by the time Natasha woke us to bring in breakfast, the sun had come up long since. We didn't talk about what we had said to each other in the church, and for the moment, anyway, it seemed that there was no longer any need for either of us to question the rightness of where we were and where we might be going. We were together now, that was what counted, and the only thing we owed was what we owed each other. The rest of the world was somewhere else.

The breakfast that Natasha brought us came on a tray that we put on a chair at the foot of Magda's bed. I felt a little shy about eating breakfast naked, so I put on my underpants, which seemed to amuse Magda. While I was working on my second slice of dark bread and some kind of wild preserve that Magda told me coyly was Natasha's formula for what new lovers needed most, Magda got up and went over to the commode to brush her hair. She stood there with her back turned to me brushing away, and I could see where the sun had shaped a large half-moon of tan below her shoulders and where the absence of sun set her buttocks off from her brown legs and the slightly shaded small of her back to make the cheeks seem a pure white. I went over to stand behind her and run my hand over the curve of one white cheek and then the other. But when I moved to the crevice in between, Magda shook her head without turning.

"No. Not yet," she said. "Not until I've washed and you've undressed yourself again."

I went back to the foot of my bed and took my underpants off and sat there waiting. I could hear Magda washing herself by the commode, but I didn't turn to look. Twice she opened the shutters to empty the basin out the back window, letting in a flood of light, and though she shut them tight again, there were enough loose slats in those shutters and the ones on the other side of the room to let you know how high the sun had moved by then. When she was done, Magda filled the basin with clean water and brought it over to set it down in front of me.

"It's all right to be shy and it's all right to respect another person's privacy," she said. "But when lovers are lovers and they're alone, it isn't right for one of them to be dressed while the other one is naked, is it?"

"I'm not dressed any longer," I said.

"I can see that," Magda said. "So now that we're equal again, would you like me to wash you the way women wash their men in the villages or would you rather be shy and do it yourself?"

"I'd like you to wash me," I said.

"Then we'll start with the feet."

She knelt behind the basin and soaped the washcloth, then worked it carefully over each of my feet and legs in turn and went back over them to rinse off the soap. Then she emptied the basin and brought over clean water.

"Now stand up," she said. "Unless you'd rather go on by your-self."

"I'd rather you go on," I said.

She washed my testicles so gently, using both hands, that it seemed she thought they might break like fresh eggs if she put any pressure on them at all, and it was the same with my penis, though she let that rest for a moment on the washcloth, as though on a plate, so that she could study it a minute. She said something about it in Greek that I didn't understand.

"I mean the skin is cut away clean up here, as though you were Jewish," she said. "I've never seen one like that when it's more or less soft. Except my father's by accident."

"Well, I'm sorry if it isn't Greek enough for you. It's the way they mostly are in America these days. Almost all my friends back there are that way."

"Don't be difficult. I didn't say I wanted it to be Greek or any-thing else. I think it's sweet the way it is."

She bent forward and kissed the tip of it, then went on washing. When she got to my belly, I sat down on the bed again.

"You don't have to do it all," I said. "I can do the rest."

"I like doing it," Magda said. "It's a way of getting to know you that's a bit calmer than last night."

She spread my legs and pushed the basin between them, then moved in to do my chest and neck. When she started rinsing me off again, I grabbed both her hands and brought her in against me.

"That's enough," I said. "I'm as clean as I need to be."

"Not in the places you can't reach. And your ears need washing."

"All right, you can do my ears."

She rinsed out the washcloth and came back to go over one of my ears as though she were cleaning the insides of a watch. When she moved on to the other ear, I took advantage of her being up against me to run my hands down her back and go into the territory that she had stopped me from getting to know before, and then I came back up so that my fingers could play with the hair under her arms.

"Please," she said. "I can't work when you do that."

I took the washcloth away from her and made it into a ball that I arched in the general direction of the breakfast tray, then wrapped my arms around her so that she had to fall back with me on the bed. Her feet tipped the basin over.

"Now see what you've made me do."

"It's only water."

"Water is our lifeblood in this country."

"I thought olive oil was. That's what Natasha said."

"It depends on what you have in mind."

"I have you in mind."

"Then I guess it has to be olive oil. That's supposed to be lifeblood for the newly married. So they say in the villages."

She had eased her way up on me and her tongue was now doing the rinsing on the ear she hadn't quite finished with the washcloth, and though she came away to make a face at the taste of soap there, she went right back to that ear until she thought it time to move on to parts of my face that the washcloth hadn't touched at all. I tried to wiggle out from under her, but that just worked to get both of us well up on the bed so that she could settle on me comfortably and hold my head in her hands to do with it as she pleased.

"You taste of salt," she said, letting go of my head and leaning back. "Is that from the sea or last night's heat?"

"I don't know," I said, reaching up to pull her head close. "Let's see how you taste."

"Where?"

"Here on your neck, for example. Quite salty."

"That's not true. I washed it well."

"And here. And here too."

"You're making it up."

"I swear. And here under your arms."

"Oh God," Magda said. "Are you going to taste me everywhere?"

"If you'd like me to," I said.

She sat up straight. "You know, you really shouldn't ask about things like that. You should just do what you want to do. The way you let me do last night. That's the best way to find out what I like."

"Well then let go of me and lie back so that I have a chance."

"Is that better?"

"Yes."

"And is this better still?"

"Yes. But tell me if I'm being gentle enough. Or maybe too gentle."

"I think you know more about what you're doing than you admit, little brother. Or else you're learning terribly fast."

"All I know is what you've taught me. But I want to learn more."

"Well one thing you could learn is that there are times when you should just go on doing what you're doing and anything else you want to do but not make me talk when I can't keep my mind on what I'm saying."

The light had not only softened but had turned a dying rose color by the time we went out to take a walk that evening, and the church was clanging its bell for vespers. We were headed for the store to pick up some supplies for Natasha because we felt we owed her that and she had to go off in a different direction to make a house call regarding a young woman whose mother had come to her because her daughter was under the spell of the evil eye and refused to eat. The mother reported that her daughter had been given the good fortune of being engaged to a young man from another village who already owned more olive trees down by the port than anybody in Panagia could boast, even if he had only one arm and one eye as the result of a bizarre fishing accident involving dynamite. The mother was afraid the daughter would starve herself to death before the wedding. Natasha felt that her mission was to convince the mother that the evil eye lived inside the groom, as was witnessed by his crippling accident, and that the only way for the mother to get out of her predicament and save her daughter's life was for the daughter's family to cancel the engagement, costly as it might be for the daughter's future marital prospects.

"You see the difficulty I have to live with?" Magda said as we approached the square. "There's no way you can be a woman and still control your future in this country. If you accept what your parents arrange for you, you may have to live with some form of horror until death releases you, and if you don't accept, you're marked for life and probably unmarriageable."

"I can see that's true in a village like this, but is it true in the cities too?"

"It's true in Salonika. At least for those of us who live with people who look at things they way my parents and most others do. That's why I've been thinking of Athens as a possibility for us."

"Athens?"

"Things there have to be more advanced than they are in Salonika. And it may be the only safe place for us when our money runs out."

"Well, that's a thing I've been meaning to discuss with you," I said. "My money has pretty well run out already."

Magda took my hand. "We don't have to worry about that for a while. I brought along all my savings. And since a lot of it came from your parents for those terrible German lessons I tried to give you, the money really belongs to you as much as to me."

"I didn't think those lessons were so terrible."

Magda smiled. "Of course you didn't. But that's just because you were falling in love with me."

"Anyway, I can't say that I'm thrilled about the idea of going to Athens. Not with your old boyfriend there."

"Oh God," Magda said. "Don't tell me that you're going to become the jealous lover already, when we're just beginning to learn who we are. That man means nothing to me."

"Still. He's there."

She let go of my hand. "Still nothing. I refuse to allow you to think that way. We have to be free of worrying about past mistakes and begin to trust each other or we'll turn out to be just like everybody else and end up nowhere."

"All right, I'm ready to go to Athens if you think that's best."

"Can't it be if we think best?"

"That's what I meant."

She took my hand again. "I don't really mind your being a little jealous if it's only part of a game we play. But not if you really mean it. Do you understand the difference?"

"I think so," I said. "And I'm sure you'll let me know if I don't get it right."

That made her stop and kiss me lightly on the mouth, right there in the middle of the cobblestone street. I don't know whether any-body saw us, but it was clear she didn't give a damn, and I can't say that I did either. When we got to the square we went right across to the grocery store, still holding hands. Magda stopped a moment outside the store to slip me the little purse that she carried her money in.

"You can add yours to that when you get around to it," she said. "But as the man in the family, I think you should handle cash pay-ments from now on. At least in the provinces."

We came back home to mix up a stew out of the okra and egg-plant we'd bought, piled around a freshly beheaded chicken that it turned out to be my job to clean. That made me end up concentrat-ing on the fruit course, which was an orange melon shaped like a football that you sliced and ate in bite-sized squares of solid green honey. I passed up the Turkish coffee I was offered. Magda and Natasha sat there sipping theirs slowly without a word, the kitchen windows wide open so that we could take in the cool night air and hear the cry of owls and other nighttime birds in the forest below us. When Magda finished her coffee, Natasha turned the cup upside down to let it drain on the saucer and twisted it three times, then let it sit for ten minutes so the design that settled on the inside would tell her Magda's fortune. She studied it very carefully. The first thing she was sure of, she said, was an open road, always a good sign, especially when it came between green fields, though how she knew the fields were green, she didn't say. Then she saw a large door, which could mean several things, including time in jail, but the best thing it could mean was a gateway to riches. Then she saw some-thing that could be taken for a cross.

"You're making that up," Magda said.

"No I'm not," Natasha said. "Here, I'll show you."

"I suppose you could call it a cross. But what does it mean?"

"That you're going to be a priest or a nun. If it really is a cross."

"In what religion?"

"That it doesn't tell you," Natasha said.

"Well, I don't like that idea very much. What else is there?"

"There's a circle here which could be a crown."

"And what does that mean?"

"Either a marriage or a position of authority."

"Well either one of those could be good or bad, depending."

Natasha was still turning the cup slowly in her fingers. Suddenly she put it down and went over to the sink.

"Enough fortune-telling for one night," she said.

"What else did you see?" Magda said. "You're hiding something."

"The rest is not clear," she said. "Just a dark mess."

"I don't believe you," Magda said. "Let me see the cup."

She got up and went over to the sink, but Natasha had already dropped the cup in the dishwater. She kissed Magda on the cheek.

"You have nothing to worry about," Natasha said. "You've got an open road ahead and you're going to be rich and married. What else do you want?"

"But rich for how long and married to whom and what about Hal here? How does he come into the picture?"

Natasha shrugged. "You can't expect too much from one coffee cup. Tomorrow we'll try another."

But we didn't, and the thing was left hanging. Not knowing about the future in that way wasn't a thing that I took seriously, and I'm sure Magda wasn't so superstitious that she did either, but it must have got her thinking again about what lay ahead of us, because she lost her playful mood. Later, in bed, when I tried to nuzzle her into a different mood, she put me off gently but firmly. And I had the sense that trying to talk to her about what was on her mind would just set us back after what had been the easiest of our days so far. I turned away from her and went to sleep.

The next day we decided we would explore the only other nearby village we could get to without climbing some of the mountains behind ours, and from there we planned to go on to a high lookout point and have the lunch that Natasha put up for us in one of the baskets that the villagers used for beehives. The new village turned out to be even smaller than ours, and it was in the foothills of a mountain that sloped broadly into a spread of low orchard land finally bordered by the sea. When we went through that village at mid-morning, it seemed there was nobody alive in it, I suppose because it was a summer weekday and the villagers were all at work in their orchards and vegetable gardens, but it gave you the feeling of a place that had lost its inhabitants to some catastrophe. The streets were so narrow in places and the stone houses so tight against each other that the air seemed heavy and motionless, so that passing through it made you want to hurry into open country. We decided not to hang around there for a coffee but to head on up through the forest to the lookout on the mountain ridge that Natasha had told us about, a place where she said you could see the southeastern coast of the island and sometimes on a clear day as far as Samothraki, halfway to the Turkish coast.

It was a long climb getting to the place we thought she had in mind, mostly through thick forest. When we finally reached what seemed the highest lookout point, we found the sea again at some distance below us. It was now as calm as it could be, dark polished glass, and from where we settled, on a dome of bare rock surrounded by short fir trees, you could look a long way in any direction and not see a living thing.

I remember that early afternoon as our most peaceful time on the island. We spread ourselves on that smooth rock, with our basket between us, and just lay back for a long time gazing up at the sky, which had gathered some clouds since noon, especially over the range at our backs, and as the clouds swelled out, the sun would pass behind them every now and then to let the air cool down a bit. We didn't even talk as we lay there, and when I glanced over at Magda, she had her head tilted back and her eyes wide open, and her face was so calm and contented that it had the look of an icon. Though she didn't turn her head she must have known that I was studying her, because her hand came across behind the basket to touch my arm and just rest there as though that was a way of passing her mood on to me. I turned my head toward the sky again. Magda finally sat up and wrapped her arms around her legs to look out across the plain below. When she spoke, she didn't turn toward me, and her voice came out as though she were speaking to herself.

"Do you believe in what the Christians call original sin?" she said.

"Original sin? I've never thought about it."

"I don't believe in it, not for a minute, but I still can't understand why so many of us become what we do become when we've been given a garden as beautiful as this to live in."

"Well, I don't know about original sin, but I believe there is evil out there. I mean there was evil in our school, for example. In the way Herr Trauger treated my friend Stephan."

"But why is it out there?" Magda said. "I can't believe there is any evil in what we see around us here, so it must live in people. And I don't understand how it gets into them or why it should."

"Well, it doesn't live in all people. It doesn't live in you, for example."

Magda looked at me. "I know you don't think so, and I can't help liking it when you're so innocent about me, but I know you're wrong. There are people I hate, people I would like to kill sometimes, and that must be evil because it makes me feel ashamed."

"Well, maybe some people deserve to be hated."

"Maybe. But if that's so, how do you decide when it's right to hate and when it's wrong? And how do you decide about other things that might be right or wrong when you're on your own the way we are now?"

"I don't know," I said. "All I know is that I can never think of myself hating you."

She reached over to touch me again. "I can't think of myself hating you either, and I hope it will always be that way. But what about the others?"

"Well, for me there are no others who really count."

Magda lay back again. "I just wish it were that simple. If only it could be."

She closed her eyes as though she didn't want to think about it anymore, and though her expression didn't have the same peacefulness any longer, her face was still calm, and in a moment her hand came back to rest on my arm again. We stayed that way without saying anything for the longest time, and it didn't bother me, because while her hand was there, I had the feeling that whatever she might be thinking to herself wasn't anything that excluded me or could put me at a distance, and with that worry gone, I found that I could be content to let her have her thoughts to herself.

She was the one who finally broke the silence by saying that she was hungry. There wasn't much left in the water bottle we'd brought with us, but we hadn't touched the wine that Natasha had packed with our lunch, so we put that out between us at the top of our rock and surrounded it by everything else in the basket: the fruit and cheese and tomatoes and hardboiled eggs. Then Magda did a strange thing. She took the knife Natasha had put in there for slicing the half-loaf of bread, but instead of going for that, Magda cut the dessert melon in half and used the knife to hollow out one half of it, passing me my share of squares on the tip of the knife until just the rind and a layer of hard green was left. She reached for the bottle of wine and poured some of it into the hollowed half of the melon.

"Our cup," she said.

She passed it over to me, but when I went to drink out of it, she reached over to stop me.

"Wait a minute," she said. "That's very Anglo-Saxon of you. You can't just drink wine without drinking to something."

"All right," I said. "I'll drink to you and me. And I promise never to do anything to make you hate me and feel ashamed about it."

I took a swallow and passed the melon back to her.

"That's nice," she said. "Then I'll drink to the same thing and promise never to do anything that will make you hate me if I can possibly help it."

"Well, that's nice of you too, but I wouldn't say it's exactly the same thing. I mean, what would make you not be able to help it?"

"I don't know. Something I can't control. Maybe something you might do. Or something that comes from whatever evil is out there."

"Well it won't come from anything I do. And I don't see why it has to come at all. It spoils everything to have to think that way."

"I'm not saying it has to come. What I was trying to say is that I would never knowingly harm you or betray you myself. I can't honestly promise anything beyond that and you shouldn't either."

I didn't know how to answer her, but I found I couldn't look at her squarely.

"May I drink my wine now?" Magda asked. "And please don't look so sad. After all, I'm letting you drink out of the same cup I'm drinking out of, which in this country means that you will know all my secrets. What more do you want?"

"Nothing," I said. "Just you."

Magda took a swallow. "Well, you have me. As much as anybody ever has. I can't give you more than that."

Magda put the melon down and picked up the knife to cut two thick slices of bread, then passed me a tomato and a hardboiled egg, using the bread as a plate. We ate without talking, just about everything that Natasha had laid up in the basket, and we got through most of the bottle of wine, each of us drinking at our own pace but not letting the other get very far ahead. When it came to the fruit course, Magda picked up an apple and cut it into quarters. She cleaned each quarter neatly, then dipped one of the quarters into our wine cup and let it soak a second before passing it over to me between two fingers.

"The ancient Greeks say you should dip fruit in wine to keep the fruit from making you too passionate. Everything in good measure is what they say."

"You think I'm too passionate, for God's sake?"

"No, not in the sense you mean," Magda said. "But I think you get too upset sometimes. For example, when I'm just trying to be honest with you."

"Well, I'm not upset any longer," I said. "I'm fine. I never felt better."

Magda took a bite of apple. "Is it the wine in you or have you really forgiven me?"

"The wine is beautiful and you're beautiful and the whole world is a beautiful green mess."

I reached for the bottle and emptied it into our cup, then took a long drink.

"Holy Virgin," Magda said. "What am I going to do? Little brother is drunk."

"Little brother is drunk with love for big sister. What are we going to do about that?"

"We're going to take the wine cup away from him and we're going to make him take a nap, that's what we're going to do."

"I like that idea. Let's take a nap."

"Not that kind of nap. One that will make you sober."

"There is only one thing that will make me sober and I must have that too. The fruit has made me passionate."

I put the wine cup down and reached for Magda's head, but she managed to dodge me, and when I crawled over to grab her, she rolled free and got up to back off the rock.

"My God," she said. "What has gotten into you?"

"I don't know," I said. "Maybe one of your demons or whatever you call them. But you're not going to get away."

When I got to her she turned her back to me, so I put my arms around her and held her close and kissed her neck.

"Are you going to force me? Is that it? While the goat over there watches how like animals human beings can become sometimes?"

I let go of her and stepped back.

"What goat?"

"The wine has made you too dizzy to see. Over there on the rock opposite."

She was right. There was a black-and-white billy goat standing there looking out toward the sea with its tufted chin raised as though smelling the light breeze that had suddenly come up from the plain below.

"I don't mind a goat watching," I said.

"I do," Magda said. "Because where there's one goat there are others nearby, especially when it's a male goat. And behind them there's a goatherd. In fact, if you listen a minute you can hear them around the mountainside higher up."

She was right about that too, the sound a faint mixture of tinkling chimes that would have been very quaint and idyllic if it hadn't come in with that breeze at just the wrong moment. I turned and started gathering up the remnants of our lunch. Magda came back to help me. She put the melon away in the basket, ate what was left of the apple, and when everything else was packed away, she passed me the wine cup.

"Finish it," she said. "I don't want you to get too sober. That could be even worse on a day like this."

I took a swallow and passed it back to her, and she emptied it, looking me straight in the eye so that I finally had to look away. She put the cup down and leaned over to kiss me on the mouth with a little flick of her tongue, then stood up and handed me the luncheon basket.

The goat was still standing there on his rock paying no attention to us when we headed downhill, but the sound of the bells stayed with us for a while, and so did the feel of the wine, which wasn't enough to make me unsteady but made me more careful than usual in the rocky places, and there were times when Magda and I had to help each other climb around some jutting rock or cross through tight underbrush where the path disappeared for a stretch. Partway down we lost the sun behind the mountain at our backs, and once we were in the thick of the forest and the path would split here and there for no clear reason, we made a point of coming out to the edge of the trees whenever they thinned out to make sure we were still heading down in the right direction. When we came out to a clearing some ways above the first houses on the upper edge of the deserted village we'd gone through that morning, the plain below still showed no signs of life, and there was only one caique some distance offshore working its way down the coast. Magda took my hand.

"Are you all right now?" she said. "I mean in the head?"

"I'm fine," I said.

"Then we'll stop here for a nap."

She led me back into the trees, a good distance uphill from the path, and when we came to a place that was just about broad enough to set our basket down on the level, she told me to help her clear the place a little against the slant of the hillside and gather dead pine needles to make a kind of bed. We worked on that until we had a fairly decent spread of pine needles about wide enough to handle one and a half people thin as we were.

"We have to be careful not to stir things up or there won't be much of a bed left," Magda said.

She undid the button at the side of her skirt and stepped out of it, then knelt to brush the pine needles smooth and laid the skirt across them. When she turned toward me, still kneeling, and undid my belt, I took off my pants and laid them out on the pine needles below her skirt.

"And your shirt," Magda said. "Where our heads will go."

I took off my T-shirt and spread it above her skirt as far as it would reach. She unbuttoned her blouse and took it off to fold it and lay it down next to my T-shirt, then tucked in the edges to make the two seem a kind of pillow.

"Now the rest," she said. "But we'd better keep all that within reach beside the basket in case one of us hears goatbells again."

When she was undressed, she lay down carefully on the skirt and trousers and spread her arms open.

"Come," she said. "But remember, we have to move very gently in the beginning or we'll make a complete mess of our bed before we've gotten very far."

The sun had long since gone down by the time we reached our village and the men had come out to sit in the cafes, so we decided it would be better to skirt the square and cross over to Natasha's place by way of the lower path that had taken us to the sea on Sunday. We found the house dark except for a flicker of light in the kitchen, and Natasha had already gone to bed or chose to make us think she had. We found a salad and some sliced lamb set out for us on the kitchen table, but neither of us was hungry at that point. I decided to fill our water bottle with fresh cold water from the spring, and I took the wine bottle along to wash that out as well. When I came back, I found that Magda had taken the lamp into our room and was lying on her bed next to mine still dressed but already asleep. I took off my clothes as quietly as I could and blew out the lamp, then lay there under my sheet listening to her steady breathing. A thought came to me that was an honest thought even if it might have embarrassed me to hear it from anybody else, and this was that if some harm were to come to her and she were to die, I would have to die with her, because I couldn't imagine myself living without that sweet sound from her and the other sweet sounds she made. For a moment the thought elated me, then saddened me, then eased me to sleep. I ended up so dead out that I came to only for a second when Magda moved in next to me at some point during the night, and when I woke in the morning, she was already gone, though the light was just beginning to come in through the cracks in our shutters.

I found her sitting out back below the house on the edge of the path that led down to the sea. She had changed her clothes and was wearing a dress that I hadn't seen, what I would have called a party dress in the city, mostly white but with tiny flowers to give it color and the lower part pleated all around. She didn't seem to notice me coming up behind her.

"Are you going somewhere special dressed up like that?" I said.

She patted the ground next to her. "Maybe," she said. "Sit down. We have to talk."

I sat down. Then I leaned over and kissed her cheek.

"Did you sleep all right?" I said. "You were lying there knocked out when I came back from the spring."

"I slept well most of the night. Until I came in beside you and began thinking and couldn't sleep any longer."

"Thinking about what?" I said without looking at her.

"About a lot of things, but mostly about you and me and where we are and where we're going."

"Why do we have to go anywhere right now? Just when we've found a place as good for us as this."

"Because things can't stay still when they're so unsettled. They never can. And I don't think it's fair to you for me to drag you along with my problems when I don't even know how I'm going to solve them for myself."

"Well, I would have thought by now that your problems are my problems and that what you by yourself might think is or isn't fair to me just doesn't come into it any longer."

"I understand how you feel, and you make it very easy for me to want to feel the same way. But the point is, does it really make sense?"

"I don't know whether it makes sense. All I know is that I don't care any longer what makes sense when it comes to you. And I thought maybe by now you might feel that way about me."

Magda took my hand and kissed it, then held it against her face.

"Dear Hal," she said. "You always make things sound so simple. And God knows, I don't want to give you up. But how am I going to get over thinking that I must?"

"Just don't think it any longer. That's all there is to it."

She was still holding my hand next to her cheek, and when she turned to look at me, the tears started streaming down her face, just like that. I put my arm around her.

"You mustn't do that," I said. "Please."

"I can't help it. I know what we're doing isn't right for you, but I can't seem to bring myself to let you go, and I just don't know what to do any longer."

"You have to stop thinking that way. That's what isn't right."

She wiped at the tears with her sleeve. "But what are we going to do? Where are we going to go? We can't stay here forever."

"I don't know," I said. "We'll just have to figure something out."

"It isn't fair to Natasha to use her place as a hotel. She's a nurse and ought to be helping others."

"Well then I guess we'd better think of moving on somewhere else."

"I keep trying to tell myself that we should go to Athens, that maybe I could get work there giving private language lessons. But you can't just leave your family and go to Athens."

"I could if I have to," I said. "At least for a while."

Magda sighed. Then she stood up without letting go of my hand.

"I suppose if we've come this far when it was really impossible, it means there must be something working in our favor. So maybe the only thing to do is keep going day by day and hope the gods will help us choose the right road in the end."

She didn't sound completely convinced by what she'd said, but the tears had stopped, and her grip on my hand was firm as we walked back inside. At breakfast Natasha told us that she had a little problem, but she didn't want us to worry about it because she could figure out a way of coping with it. The problem was a note she'd received the previous afternoon from a nunnery on the island that was among her contact centers. A girl who was thought to be carrying the evil eye because of a broken engagement had been brought to the nunnery by her parents and left there, but the nuns had found that they couldn't cope with the girl because she kept running away from them and one time was discovered outside the nunnery grounds dancing naked on a rock. Natasha had agreed to take the girl in for a while and see if she could cure her of her madness. That meant that I would have to move into the living room so that Magda and the mad girl could share the spare room which Natasha regarded as her clinic and reserved for the sick first of all, but she promised that this arrangement would be only temporary since Magda's well-being really had priority with her and since she was fairly sure that she could cure the mad girl quickly if she could manage to keep both the girl's parents and the nuns away from her for a certain period of time.

This helped to settle our plans. Magda told me privately that my sleeping in the living room by myself while she slept in the same room with a mad girl who was given to dancing naked just wouldn't do, however much she might sympathize with the girl's condition and its likely causes and however confident she was about Natasha's power to bring the girl back to her senses. What she told Natasha was that we had decided during our excursion the previous day to move on the next afternoon in any case now that Magda's own problem was under control and now that we both felt I owed my parents a visit and an explanation of how things stood. Natasha didn't argue. She came over and kissed each of us on the forehead in turn, then asked that God be with us if that was what we had really decided to do, then crossed herself three times.

Magda and I spent the morning working on a plan and getting ourselves ready for the road. She insisted that at the very least I had to let my parents know where I was going and with whom. This created a serious obstacle since she was afraid to spend any time in Salonika and I couldn't see myself going home for a family conference to outline what I had in mind doing and then just taking off again as though I was a free spirit who had a vote in family affairs relating to my welfare. Since we had to go to Salonika in order to get to Athens, the compromise we reached was a stop in the city just long enough for me to mail a letter that would tell my parents what I was up to more or less, to be followed by a second letter once we'd reached Athens safely. Natasha had a map of Greece that was more detailed than the one I'd ripped out of the *Encyclopaedia Britannica*, and after mulling over that for some time, Magda and I figured out that the least exposed way of getting through the city would be to take a boat from Kavalla to Salonika harbor, mail my letter there, and leave the city by the usual Vardar Square route. That would allow us to keep clear of the busy center of town, and if we could hitch a ride at least as far as the village of Veria, we could avoid using public transportation until we were safely in the provinces and heading south either by bus or train.

It seemed a great plan to me, and it put Magda in a cheerful mood again. She packed up her party dress in the suitcase she'd brought with her and put on a skirt more suitable for travel, then she made me give her what dirty laundry I had so that she could wash it out along with hers and dry it in the sun in time for us to set out after lunch. What we had in mind was walking down to the port village of Thassos and spending the afternoon there getting what information we could about sailings to Salonika and just doing some sightseeing so that we stayed relaxed and didn't lose the feel of still being on vacation.

Natasha decided to wait and have lunch with us before heading off for the nunnery to pick up her new patient, and she made us drink a glass of wine so that she could toast our future in Russian. But when it came to the Turkish coffee, she said that she was in too much of a hurry to take the time needed to read either Magda's cup or mine. Magda pushed hers aside after one sip, and then the two of them left me sitting there at the kitchen table to go into the living room for a parting consultation and a chance for Magda to make a contribution on behalf of both of us to the work of the clinic. When Magda came back, she was tearful again, but she told me that had to do with leaving Natasha rather than what she called things in general.

Getting ourselves to the harbor village proved to be a long haul even if it was downhill all the way. Because Magda insisted on helping me carry her suitcase a good part of the time, we had to learn to keep more or less in stride. But one benefit that came from it was Magda's decision to trade the suitcase for something more sensible that would go along with my knapsack, and this she did by picking up two large shoulder bags from a fisherman's wife in the harbor who thought Magda's suitcase a prize. The shoulder bags not only eased our traveling but gave us a pillow each when there was no other way of providing ourselves with one, and a thing I remember clearly from our time on the road was the smell of wool against my face from the shoulder bag I sometimes took over for sleeping, and the fainter but sweeter smell of Magda's clothes inside it.

The other thing we did in the harbor village was find ourselves a caique captain who would take us over to Kavalla, because we'd missed the only sailing by the regular line. The caique captain was a hard bargainer. He said it was a long trip over there, more than four hours, and he had no particular desire to set out that evening and come back empty, not to mention losing a chance to put out his nets, unless we were willing to make it worth his while, and that turned out to mean paying for his trip both over and back and probably for some of the fish he might have caught if the moon weren't close to full. Magda talked him down to something more reasonable, but only after agreeing to buy a couple of yards of woven material from his wife to make a dress out of someday when she might get around to making dresses. The captain said we would sail after his supper but early enough to get us into Kavalla around midnight, and that left us over an hour to do some sightseeing.

There were a lot of ruins one could see in that harbor village, including some under the water, but I hadn't yet developed a taste for ancient ruins and would have been content to find a high point for a last view of the mountains behind us and the sea ahead if Magda hadn't felt that an archeological tour was important for my education. Anyway, we didn't have time to cover everything there was, just a large spread of stones and broken columns that was once a marketplace and some more dedicated to Apollo and a sanctuary belonging to Artemis and another to Pan, all in terrible condition, and then an ancient theater that was at least recognizable for what it was supposed to be. Even Magda seemed to be getting bored with sightseeing by the time we came down from the theater to a square pile of stones dedicated to the god Dionysus, I think because a statue standing there got on her nerves.

"You see what I mean about the ancient Greeks?" she said at that point. "The statues of the men make them all look beautiful and noble if maybe too feminine sometimes. But when it comes to the women, they give them coy smiles, or have them riding on the backs of fish as though they didn't have a care in the world or a brain in their heads, or just leave them standing there straight up like a tree without any heads at all. It's really very tiring."

"I don't think you can blame the ancient Greeks for not giving that statue a head. It just fell off at some point."

"Or somebody cut it off. Anyway, look at what that miserable thing represents."

"What does it represent?"

"Comedy, of course. That's what it says. What else would they choose to represent comedy but a woman? Tragedy, I suppose, would have to be represented by a man. Especially since tragedy is usually made out to be some woman's fault. Like Helen, or Clytemnestra, or Medea."

She was over my head at that point, so I just nodded understandingly. Maybe she was right about the ancient Greeks and maybe she wasn't, but I decided to get things moving on another tack by showing her the relief of Silenus with the huge erection that I'd come across on my trip out to find her the previous week. That took us back beyond the far side of the village, and though we were running short of time by then, once we got there, she insisted on going down into that sanctuary to have a close look at what I'd uncovered for her.

"That is something," she said. "Very impressive. At least it must have been when it was all there. And you say the villagers think it has magical powers?"

"That's what I was told. If you scratch what's left of that thing of his there and swallow the powder you come up with."

"And what's that supposed to do for you?"

"What do you think?"

"But for women too?"

"How do I know?" I said. "I suppose so."

"Well then give me something to scratch it with."

"You're really going to scratch that thing?"

"Why not? What have we got to lose? And think what we might have to gain."

"But it's just stone, for God's sake."

"Don't argue with me, please. Give me your penknife."

So I gave her my penknife and she scratched away at what was left of the erect phallus until she came up with something, or at least thought she did. Then she wet her forefinger and touched it to the knife and licked the end of her finger, then went back to scratching so that she could pass the knife over to me for my taste of that stone.

The sun was at the horizon as we headed out to sea. We went up into the bow to sit with our legs over the gunwale to watch it slowly sink out of sight and to eat the cheese pies and baklava we'd picked up for our supper. The caique was one of the largest I'd seen close up, probably used for transport as well as fishing, and empty as it was, it rode high on the water. The captain had brought his ten-year-old son along for crew, and he let the boy take the tiller until it got dark and we were far enough offshore to pick up a swell that stayed with us most of the way, the caique rolling just enough to let you know you were on the open sea. When the captain took over the tiller, the boy lay back against a coil of rope in the stern and went to sleep.

It was a clear night, with a view across to the far coast that showed the dark shapes which I took to be the mountains above the Drama plain, and after a while, the town of Kavalla outlined by its lights against the hillside behind it. Though the sky wasn't as bright with stars as it would have been on a moonless night, the lighter background made the constellations and planets stand out from the rest until the moon actually came up and confused things with its greater brightness. Well before that, Magda and I brought our feet in and stretched out side by side in the bow facing the stern, with the shoulder bags for pillows. She pointed out some of the constellations she recognized from an astrological chart she and Natasha had studied during her first visit to our island and she was able to pick out the water carrier that was my birth sign and the lion that was hers, or at least convinced me that she had.

"How do the water carrier and the lion go together?" I asked her. "Did Natasha tell you?"

"I didn't ask her because I didn't know you then," Magda said. "We just worked out my astrology."

"And what did that show you?"

"Good things and not so good things. But with Natasha, the good things always win out."

"Do you really believe in astrology?" I said.

"Not really," Magda said. "Because if you do, it means that you give complete control of your life to something outside you. Which is a good way to talk yourself out of being responsible for what you do."

"On the other hand, if you look very long at what's really up there, the whole spread of it above us, it makes you feel so small that you begin to think you have no control over anything anyway."

"It is a little frightening. And I can't say that I understand how it all got there in the beginning when there was nothing at all anywhere. But I don't think that means you have to let everything be decided by chance or something else completely outside yourself."

"Sometimes I wish I could figure out how it got there in the beginning if somebody or something didn't start it all."

Magda sighed. "God knows, sometimes I worry about that too. But there are other times when I think it's foolish to try to understand what I doubt any human being ever will. And there's some comfort in that."

"Except where does that really leave you?"

"I suppose with what you have. And for the moment that means you and me."

"You don't make that sound like very much."

Magda turned to me and smiled. "Don't I? I'm sorry. I meant that to mean this life and the best one has in it, but it didn't come out right. I guess that's what happens to your mind when you spend too much time looking at the stars, so I'm going to stop now."

She leaned toward me and brushed my hair back.

"So what are we going to do now?" I said.

She ran a finger over my lips. "I don't know," she said. "What would you like to do?"

"You know what I'd like to do, but we can't do that here."

"Maybe we can. If we're very clever."

She sat up and looked through the shoulder bags until she found the dress material that she'd picked up from the captain's wife.

"We'll use this for a sheet," she said. "Which means that you'll have to lie very close, as though we were one person, and pretend to go to sleep."

She handed me the material, then lay down and turned her back to me. I lay down behind her and stretched the material over us from head to foot. It didn't tuck in, but it covered us where it counted and then some. I felt Magda raising her skirt against me very slowly, just using the ends of her fingers.

"You'll have to help me a little before you help yourself," Magda said under her breath. "So don't be in a hurry, whatever that magic powder may be doing to you right now."

I put my free hand under the cover and with my fingertips helped her raise the skirt slowly so that I could then help her ease her panties down enough in the other direction.

"Now," she whispered. "If you want to be really clever, you'll use the motion of the caique to help you hide what we have to do as secretly as possible when we're both ready."

It was after midnight by the time we pulled into Kavalla harbor, and the moon was well up by then. The sound of the motor slowing had woken me from the long sleep I'd fallen into, but Magda didn't stir until she felt me take my arm from around her waist and ease away from her. And even then she didn't turn to pack up our sheet until the captain and his midget crew started to busy themselves with the ropes for docking, which gave her a chance to bring my hand back under the sheet and hold it in against her for a long minute. The sea was completely placid now, a dark mirror for the harbor lights along the pier and the old houses beyond, laid out on the curve against the hillside like the stands in an open-air theater. Except for a few fishermen sleeping in their boats along the pier, there didn't seem to be a living soul in that high town. I stood up to help the boy put out some tire fenders as we pulled in to dock, then threw him a line when he jumped out onto the pier so the captain wouldn't have to come forward. Magda slipped me her purse.

"If you don't mind, you pay the captain," she said. "And give the boy something for sleeping the whole way."

I went back to the stern and stood there while the captain secured the stern line.

"It took a little longer getting here than I thought because of the swell," he said when I paid him. "But that didn't seem to bother you and your sister."

"We were fine," I said. "It was a good trip, especially when the moon came up."

"You take care of her," he said. "She's a smart girl. Well bred. And not thorn-cunted like some of these modern girls. So don't you let her marry a poor man like me or a fool."

"Don't worry," I said. "No chance of that."

"Well, you never know," the captain said. "The world is full of fools and sometimes you don't know who is and who isn't until it's too late. So keep it in mind."

I promised to keep it in mind, though the thought of my arranging her marriage to anybody but myself didn't seem likely to stay with me longer than a breath of bad air. I called the boy over to help Magda up onto the pier, then followed her with our belongings. When I tried to tip the boy, he wouldn't take anything from me.

"I'm a sailor," he said shyly. "Your sister needs to build herself a dowry, I don't."

We stood there until they headed out to sea again. The captain waved once, then handed the tiller over to his son.

"Now where do we go, beloved sister?" I said.

"I suppose we'll have to find some place outside this town to spend the rest of the night, because it looks as though they've locked us out until dawn."

It took us a good hour and a half to find our way through those winding streets and out to a stretch of shore that was clear enough for sleeping. The moon was high and white by then, lighting up the shoreline for miles, and it brought a glaze onto the water wherever the wind died out along the path it made. Magda gazed at the moon's path for a while, then lay back and dozed off almost at once, but I found that I couldn't sleep. I lay there worrying about the letter I'd promised Magda I would write my parents. I hated the idea, wished I had reason to be as free of that kind of thing as she now was, but I knew all the while that she was right to insist on it for me, and that's why I couldn't sleep.

I wrote several letters in my head. In one I told my parents that I had decided to take a short trip into the provinces to get to know my adopted country so that I could adjust to my environment with better results when school started up in the fall. The blatant lie in that didn't bother me as much as the thought of having to face another year at the German School. This led to a second letter that told my parents I had decided to go to Athens and find a summer job that would help them pay for sending me somewhere other than the German School, which I explained was a disgusting place, full of cruel and immoral teachers who picked on anybody who wasn't a pure-blooded German, and this included Jews, Americans, and most of my friends who went there. The problem with that one was that I couldn't think up any job a seventeen-year-old foreigner might get in a city he didn't yet know using a language he could barely read— at least any job convincing enough to keep my parents from believing I must have gone completely out of my mind. Another letter had me working as a sailor on a caique that rarely came into port but would eventually deposit me in Salonika just long enough to mail my letter and sometime after that to allow a longer visit, providing I got a promise that I would be permitted to live my own life from now on and not have to return to the German School or suffer any tyranny like that which the previous school year had imposed on me and my friends. But my sudden capacity for roaming unfamiliar seas professionally when, as far as my parents knew, I hadn't yet been on anything bigger than a finger lake in upstate New York didn't begin to convince even me. Worse, I couldn't find any honest words that would explain exactly what I had in mind when it came to living my own life and who I hoped to live it with. Thinking about that killed the letter-writing but it didn't help me get to sleep.

"What's the trouble, little brother? You've been lying there I don't know how long with your eyes wide open."

"Do you have to call me that? It isn't really funny any longer."

"Po, po. We've gotten very touchy all of a sudden. You called me beloved sister just a little while ago."

"That wasn't funny either. So I won't do it again."

"I don't mind. What I mind is your not telling me what's really bothering you."

"This letter you insist I send my parents. I can't make it come out the way it should."

"You've decided to write them a letter in the middle of the night?"

"I'm just trying to figure out what I can tell them that they'll understand."

"Well, I don't see that you have any choice but to tell them the truth."

"And what's that? That I love my German tutor like nobody else in the world and I'm traveling around Greece with her for a while but they're not to worry because she will get married to somebody else someday soon even if she doesn't believe in arranged marriages or in building herself a dowry."

"You are in a state," Magda said. "May I ask just what has brought this on now? When you were so sweet and tender with me just a few hours ago."

"That's part of the trouble. I can't bear to think of you being that way with somebody else, but everybody seems to think you ought to get married as soon as possible."

"Well, I don't have any intention of being that way with some-body else or of getting married, so you can be at ease about that."

"But you will someday. And someday soon. You'll have to."

"I can't speak for someday, because nobody can. But I'm not going to get married someday soon, I can promise you that. And I doubt that I will ever."

"So where does that leave me?"

"Where you are. Where we are. I thought we settled that back in the village."

"But for how long?"

She was studying me now. "How can I possibly answer that?"

"You can't. That's the real trouble."

She turned and held my head between her hands. "Dear boy. You can't answer it either. You haven't finished school yet. And I have to go to the university. Even if I have to leave this country and go somewhere else."

"Well what happens when you're finished with the university?"

She put her arm around me. "I wish I could promise that we'd still be together. But you must see that I can't. It wouldn't be fair for me to pretend that I know what's going to happen to either of us three or four years from now."

I knew that what she was saying made some sense, but it didn't work to settle me down. I lay there next to her trying to push certain images out of my mind, not of her making love to somebody else because that was too painful, but one of a priest crowning her and some dark, mustached type next to her, crowning the two of them with thin white wreaths that were tied together by a string and then the happy bride and groom circling round and round an altar table, all smiles as the attendant children threw rice at them, like the couple I'd seen married at the school where my father worked. But it came to me that I might have the wrong ceremony. What if Magda were forced to convert to her father's religion in order to bring peace into the family. That brought on an image of a Jewish wedding that was much stranger than the other one because I had to make it up en-tirely. I had a long-bearded rabbi in a dark place like a cave lighted by two candles only, holding a silver plate with a book on it and chanting something incomprehensible over Magda, who was all in white and kneeling with her head veiled, and beside her, standing stiffly, a stern man in a black suit and a skullcap who was meant to be her father. But there was no bridegroom in the picture, and trying to create one only wiped the image away. While these things were going through my head, Magda went on holding me close to her, caressing my hair every now and then with her free hand. I don't know how long it was before I finally drifted off to sleep, but I kept my head tucked in low against her because I didn't want her to see what I was certain must have begun to show in my face.

The sun was up when I woke, and I was by myself. I sat up to look down the shore and spotted Magda leaning against a low rock some distance away with her bare feet in the shallows. She was dressed, but I could tell that she had already taken a dip because her underclothes were spread out to dry on the rocks behind her. I decided to take a dip too before joining her, so I stripped where I was and made my way over the gravel to flop into the sea. Magda waved to me at the sound of the splash, but she stayed where she was. She was still sitting there when I came out, so I got dressed and went down to squat on the wet pebbles beside her.

"I've been writing your letter for you in my head," she said. "But I'm not quite finished yet."

"That's nice of you," I said. "Let's hear where you've arrived so far."

"Of course you should use your own words, but I'll tell you what I think you ought to say in general. I think you should say it's all my fault."

"How's that?"

"I think you should tell your parents the truth about our being together the way we are, but I think you should say that I was the one who began it, and I was the one who made you take it where it's gone, and I was the one who got you to follow me to Athens."

"I can't tell them all that. First of all, because it isn't true, and second of all, because it makes you out to be terrible."

Magda shrugged. "I don't care. It doesn't really make any difference what they think of me. You're the one who has to be protected."

"And after you made me do all that in the beginning, just how did you force me to follow you to Athens?"

"That's where I'm having a little difficulty. One idea I had was for you to tell them that I found I was pregnant by you and that I made you feel responsible for taking care of the problem."

"That's a terrible idea. When did I have a chance to make you pregnant? I mean, it would have to have been weeks ago."

Magda shrugged. "How do they know what might have been going on all those weeks I was giving you help with your German? You'll just have to make me out to have been a dangerous seductress."

"I can't do that. For God's sake."

"Well, you're going to have to do something."

"And just how am I supposed to be solving your problem after we get to Athens?"

Magda smiled. "Ah, Athens. They must know that anything is possible in Athens. I've been told that there are doctors there who make their living solving such problems. And I suppose there are in Salonika too."

"I suppose," I said, nodding wisely.

Magda drew her feet in and brushed them off. "The point is, whatever they may end up thinking of me, it might make them feel a little better to know that you're not entirely on your own. So I don't care what you say exactly, that's up to you, but you have to blame your sudden absence on me and they have to know that we're still together. It's the only way out."

"I don't know," I said. "I'll have to think about it some more."

"Well, I'm going to sit you down in a cafe, and after we've had our breakfast, I'm not going to let you leave until you've written your letter any way you want to write it. And in the meanwhile, I'll see about getting us to Salonika harbor."

And that's what she did, as though she was still my teacher, now brought in by unidentified authorities to make me behave decently toward my parents. I didn't argue with her at that point, but I told myself that whatever letter I wrote would not be the kind she had in mind but my own creation, at least when it came to what I would say about the two of us being together, so that she ended up as protected as she thought I ought to be.

The cafe she found for me was on the upper edge of the town, not far from the local Roman aqueduct but off on a side street and inhabited that early in the morning by only a few ancient men. As a precaution for herself while she roamed the streets below near the harbor, she'd bought a cheap pair of dark glasses that made her look like a blind woman, especially after she wound a kerchief around her head to make herself more provincial. When she left me sitting there among those old men with the pad of broadly-lined paper and the pencil we'd picked up from a kiosk, sitting there as though I'd been assigned to write an essay on what I remembered best from my summer vacation, I felt completely ridiculous. I don't know how many false starts it took to get my letter going, but I'd been there over an hour by the time I got where I had to go. This is more or less what I ended up with after I'd made a clean copy. "Dear folks"— the way I normally referred to my parents in writing, because any-thing else seemed too personal and forced—"It is not easy for me to write this letter because I know that you must be worried about me, and anything I may say by way of an excuse for leaving home suddenly as I did is probably going to sound foolish. The truth is that I left in order to help my German tutor, Magda Sevillas, who was in serious trouble because her parents were forcing her to marry somebody she'd never even seen, and I felt that she needed the moral support of somebody who really cared about her future more than her parents did. So I tracked her down on the island she'd gone off to in order to recover her peace of mind in a private clinic, and now we're on our way to Athens where she hopes to get employ-ment and save some money to go to the university, whatever her parents may want for her to the contrary. We are both well and in good spirits. I promise to write again as soon as I have Magda settled in somewhere decent, and I plan to be back home in time for school in the fall, though what school I go to is a subject I'd like to discuss seriously as soon as I have the chance. One thing I know is that I am

not going back to the German School, about which I will have more
to say when we next meet. I hope you are all well and that Sam is
becoming the best soccer goalie in Northern Greece. Good luck with
everything. Love. Hal."

I addressed the envelope we'd bought, and put the stamp on it
that would get it delivered in Salonika. I was about to seal it when
the thought came to me that since Magda was mentioned in it, she
had a right to have a look at it before I sent it off. Then I ordered
a coffee with extra sugar to have an excuse for sitting in the cafe
awhile longer. When Magda got back there, she was clearly in a
good mood.

"I have a treat for you," she said. "I not only found the ship that
will take us to Salonika but I arranged for us to have a cabin. It's
below decks, but at least it's private."

"That's great," I said. "And I finished my letter to my parents. I'd
like you to read it."

"No need," she said. "I trust you to have said the right thing."

"Go ahead," I said, offering her the letter. "I really think you
should have a look at it since you're mentioned in it."

Magda took the letter from me, held it a second as though weigh-
ing it, then licked the back of the envelope and pressed it shut on the
table. She handed it back to me.

"That settles that," she said. "Now we have an hour to amuse
ourselves before our ship of hope sails away."

I put the letter and pad of paper in my knapsack. On our way
down to the harbor, I insisted on going back to the store that sold
glasses so that I could buy a pair to match Magda's, though she said
that simply made us look like the blind leading the blind. We found
another shop that sold me a black fisherman's cap, and in the same
place Magda picked out a shirt with sleeves that I could wear over
my T-shirt or without my T-shirt, depending on our future laundry
situation. We both got ourselves blue cotton jackets in case we hit
cooler weather at night in the mountains south of Salonika, and we
both bought a novel to read—one in Greek and one in English—in
case we got bored at some point with just looking at scenery.

There wasn't much time left after our shopping, but we decided to walk up to the high point above the town, what they called the Holy Virgin's Neighborhood but with the word for neighborhood still in Turkish. We could get a good view from there, as far as our island and beyond, and that was enough to keep me happy, but Magda spent most of her time up there reading a weekly newspaper of some kind that she'd bought in the harbor area, telling me bits and pieces of recent news out of it, most of it very depressing. While we'd been gone it seems the Japanese had invaded China, and the Sudeten Germans were now calling for the dismemberment of Czechoslovakia by demanding independence for all minorities, and Germany was drafting laborers to complete its western frontier fortifications.

"Do you think this means there's going to be a general war over here?" I asked Magda.

"I think maybe there's going to be a war in Europe someday soon, but if there is one, I don't think it will come as far south as here. Who really cares about Greece one way or another?"

"Well that's something," I said.

"But it's still awful. The whole thing, I mean. It makes you feel like going back to our island and just hiding away while the world falls apart everywhere else."

"You shouldn't buy newspapers," I said. "Not when you have other things on your mind to worry about."

"The trouble is, even if you might want to you can't just close your eyes to the world. Especially when they make you feel somehow that your own people are involved. I mean, listen to this item. This really makes you sick. It says here that they've just had something called an Evian Conference on Refugees, and the representatives of German Jews at this conference proposed that other countries open up their lands to Jews seeking a new home. And guess what the results were? England said it hasn't got any territory suitable for the resettlement of large groups from any country. Australia said that since it didn't have a real racial problem, it didn't want to import one. Imagine. And New Zealand said the same. And France and Argentina said they'd reached the saturation point when it came to refugees."

"What about my country? Since we're made up mostly of refugees, there shouldn't be any problem. My grandfather was a refugee on my mother's side. And maybe on my father's side too."

Magda glanced at me. "I'm coming to your country. Your country said it could accept only those permitted under its normal quota, whatever that means. And some other countries said they could accept only farmers. And four other countries said they couldn't accept any Jewish traders or intellectuals. So the only countries that agreed to accept Jews without any qualification were Denmark and Holland. What do you think of that? It makes you feel that being Jewish means you're carrying an incurable disease. Anyway the half of you that's Jewish. I mean the half of me."

"I'm sorry it makes you feel that way. Please stop reading that thing."

"You're right. No more news of the world. Let's go off and hide away in our cabin and pretend that we're normal human beings like almost anybody else. Even better, let's pretend we're Danish or Dutch."

She rolled up the newspaper and thrust it deep into one of her shoulder bags. I took her hand as we started downhill, and for the first time I found it damp with sweat. She tried to take her hand away because I think she was embarrassed that it was damp, but I wouldn't let her, and when she finally allowed it to relax, I brought it up and wiped it dry against my face.

The ship waiting for us in the harbor was really an old tub, with rust that had been settling on it for some time. And though it was much bigger than the caiques in the harbor and looked as if it was once meant for passengers only, they had the open decks loaded up with crates and baskets of produce of one kind or another that they were transporting, including some goats caged in boxes and a bull tied up with ropes who bellowed out his unhappiness toward the sun like a mournful foghorn. The smell as we got aboard was a mixture of overripe vegetables, stale vomit, and manure, so we didn't spend much time breathing the harbor air but headed down to our cabin to wait until the ship hit the open sea. Our idea was to spend some time reading, because Magda said it was going to be a fourteen-hour voyage and that gave us hours to kill.

The cabin was two decks down from the gangplank level, and it was just big enough to hold two bunks and a small sink, but at least it smelled relatively clean, and the top sheet on the bed was folded as though that was clean too. There was an overhead light, but the bulb was dead. We left the door open and put our baggage down on the floor under the sink. Magda sat on the lower bunk with her hands crossed around her breasts as though she was cold. The truth was that it seemed a degree hotter down there than it was outside, not insufferable, but not exactly restful either.

"We can't read down here even with the door open," Magda said. "So I guess we might as well close it."

"The place may get pretty hot that way," I said.

"It may," Magda said. "Close it and we'll see if we can bear it."

I closed the door and stood there in the darkness.

"You'd better lock it," Magda said.

I locked the door. It was pitch black in there, and I couldn't see a thing for a minute, then only the outline of the bunk and of Magda sitting on it. When I crossed over to feel my way along the upper bunk, Magda stopped me by putting her arms around my waist. She didn't say anything. She just lay her head against my stomach, then reached up to run her hand along my face as though she was trying to recognize me that way, then let the fingers of both hands move down my chest.

"It will certainly get too hot in here if we keep our clothes on," she said.

I took off my pants and threw them onto the upper bunk, and while she was lowering my shorts, I took off my T-shirt and threw that up there as well. Magda was still running her fingers over me as though she didn't know who I was in the darkness.

"You take your things off too," I said.

Magda undressed and handed me her things so that I could throw them onto the upper bunk. I felt a touch cooler standing there na-

ked, but it was still hot enough for me to feel wet in the hollow of
my neck and under my arms. When I sat down next to Magda, I felt
her shiver against me.

"You can't be cold," I said, my fingers testing her arm.

"I'm not cold," she said quietly.

I could make her out more clearly now that my eyes had begun to
adjust to the darkness, but she was still touching me as though she
was learning who I was, keeping her eyes closed while she did that.
And then I felt her lick the dampness in the hollow of my neck and
run her tongue along my collarbone and shoulder, so I did the same
to her, with my eyes closed too. We went on rediscovering each
other that way with hands and tongue as though we weren't just
playing some lovers' game but were really blind and trapped in there
for the purpose of knowing each other the only way we could,
because the illusion that what you were feeling was new remained
sharply intense as long as you didn't open your eyes to see where
you really were and as long as you let what your tongue tasted seem
entirely natural to what you were discovering. And after a while the
illusion weakened and disappeared as we honestly began to know
each other in more intimate ways than we had come to know yet.

The ship was well out to sea by the time we left the cabin to come
up for some salt air. The upper decks were crowded with people
sitting side by side on benches or on the deck itself, especially where
there was a canopy for some protection from the sun or a passage
wide enough for stretching out and going to sleep with a kerchief
over your eyes. The only place we found that had some privacy was
under the bow of one of the lifeboats strung along an upper deck
that you got to by climbing over a gate that was supposed to be for
officers only—and, Magda said, foreigners like us who couldn't read
Greek. Magda sat with her back against the curved arm from which
the lifeboat hung and had me lay my head in her lap so that she
could stroke my hair and hum something to herself that I didn't
recognize. After a while she got up and spread her news of the world
under what shade that lifeboat gave us and brought out a half-loaf of
bread and some delicacy consisting of meat cured in garlic that was
as strong as you might care to manage on a hot day even in a

country where garlic was considered good for lovers and anybody else with a serious malady.

"It may be a while before we get to sleep together again like we did today," Magda said, slicing me some of the cured meat. "So the garlic that will come out of your pores after you've eaten this won't matter that much to either of us as far as the odor is concerned."

"Why will it be a while?" I said.

"I don't know," Magda said. "I just don't think it's going to be easy to be alone once we reach the city. And who knows what to expect after that."

"Then let's not spend any time in the city," I said. "Let's just mail my letter and keep going."

Magda smiled. "Is it so urgent? Sleeping with me again? Aren't you filled to the brim with it by now and a little bored?"

"Are you serious?"

"Do I look serious?"

"Anyway, I wasn't thinking only of that. I was thinking of being free to do what we want to do."

"Well we'll have another look at the map Natasha gave you to make sure we get through the city quickly so that we can be free spirits once more. But first we have to eat to keep up our strength."

"I'm not hungry."

"I'm not either. But we should eat something."

"Let's go below again and maybe we'll be hungry afterward."

Magda took off her dark glasses and looked out across the empty sea. Then she put them on again and packed up our lunch. "As long as we come back up in time to see the Holy Mountain of Athos," she said. "Since women aren't allowed anywhere near the place except by sea, it's probably the only chance I'll ever have to get that close to holiness."

As it turned out, the ship was rounding the western finger of the Chalkidiki peninsula by the time we came back up on deck, and the Holy Mountain was long since behind us. I told Magda I was sorry about that, but she said it wasn't my fault any more than it was hers, since it was clear that both of us were now condemned to be children of godless pleasures. She said this in a way that showed what a good mood she was in, so that it didn't bother her to find that an older couple had taken over our morning lifeboat with no intention of sharing it. We settled against a nearby stretch of wall more or less protected from the sun, which was dropping low in the west by then anyway, and this gave us a full view of the coast that we were now cruising so close to you could have reached the rocky shore by Kassandra lighthouse with a single dive and twenty strokes if you had any wish to arrive at a place as desolate as that one. I spotted only one collection of houses that could have been a village along that stretch of coast. The rest was open country, mostly level but rarely cultivated, as though the best part of that peninsula had been set aside by whatever gods had once been there to remain free of civilization through the ages or as long as gods were still around to keep it primitive and pure.

We sat out there on the deck munching on bread and reading until it turned too dark, and then we sat and just watched the lights come on along the coast as our ship rounded the point that shaped the outer rim of Salonika Bay. The city was still a long way in from there, and it was almost unrecognizable from that distance because it seemed so small, hardly more than another village set into the hillside next to Mount Hortiati, with what might pass for city lights properly lined up only along the quay and a few major streets before the lighting turned dim and sporadic and then disappeared entirely where the walls held in the old city. The smallness of it from that distance made it seem mysterious to me however well I'd come to know some of its more secret places, and that added to the sudden dread I'd felt the minute we'd turned the point and spotted the first of its lights. I had a sense that the city carried some kind of evil threat at its heart that hadn't been there before. I don't know whether Magda felt the same thing, but there was something about our coming into it from that angle that must have got to her as well.

"Your overgrown village," she said. "I can't call it mine any longer. And I used to think it so beautiful."

"It isn't mine either," I said. "Not anymore."

"I don't want to spoil it for you," Magda said, gathering up her newspaper and book. "There are things in it one can love, and you should have a chance to learn what they are in your own good time and not be influenced by what has happened to me."

"There's nothing more I want to learn about it," I said. "Not on my own."

Magda took up her shoulder bag and crossed over to the deck on the other side to look out toward the Axios River and its marshy plain, stretching to the mountains south of the Yugoslav border. The moon had just begun to come up behind us to the east.

She leaned her arms on the railing. "Wouldn't it be nice if we could take our ship up that river and join the Vardar and the other rivers up north that would take us all the way to the Danube and let us keep going on and on wherever fate might take us?"

"That would be nice," I said.

Magda sighed. "Maybe in some other life. In this one ships don't go up rivers like that. And it probably isn't good for us to pretend they might."

Nevertheless she stayed there leaning on the railing gazing out toward the north until we reached the lights on the pier marking the gateway to the inner harbor and I had to leave her there to go below and gather up the things we'd left below in the cabin. She was waiting for me by the gangplank when I came up. I took her hand to help her down the ladder, and when we reached the bottom we kept going in the direction of Vardar Square to mail my letter because that was the quickest way out of town on the road to Veria and regions south. We found a mailbox just outside the harbor area, and though it was the only letter I had to mail and already had a stamp on it, I took it out of my knapsack and checked it over carefully the way I always did with my letters before sending them off into the great unknown. The moon had come up bright by then, as full as it had been the night before, and that was enough to make up for the bad lighting once you got off the main streets. Though the upper parts of the town had settled in for the night, people were still out eating in the tavernas and there was still enough activity around the harbor area and beyond to make us cautious about traveling along the central avenues. When we were partway up the first deserted side street we came to, Magda took my hand again.

"Are you tired?" she said.

"Not especially. We've had plenty of rest."

"Then would you mind if we just keep going for a while until we find a place along the way where we can safely spend the night?"

"I don't mind," I said. "I'm ready for anything."

She stopped to give me a quick kiss on the forehead.

"Then let's keep walking until we're at least far enough out to feel ourselves free again."

And that's what we did.

WE SPENT THE FIRST NIGHT ON THE ROAD TO ATHENS IN THE BARN
of a buffalo herdsman in a village called Vegetable Garden. When the herdsman came along-
side with his wagon, we were still within the
city limits walking hand in hand on the road
that eventually became the narrow motor highway to the town of Veria and the Vermion
mountains above it and on to the south. We'd
been walking over an hour by then, out as far
as the tin-roofed shops with dirt floors and
dusty glazed windows that sold skins for rugs
or winter coats through the heat of summer.
There was nobody on the road at that hour.
Once in a while a loaded truck would go by,
sometimes slowing down to have a look at
us, but we paid no attention to that and just
kept on walking with our joined arms swinging between us as though we could go on
that way all night. And the more open the flat
landscape showed beyond the single row of
shops to our left and right, the easier it

became to think that we were finally clear of the city behind us and on our way to new country with no threat in it.

Something else happened on the road out of town. Magda and I didn't have much to say to each other most of the way, I guess because that feeling of being free and on our own was so strong and so alike for the two of us that we didn't need to talk about it or maybe sensed that talk might spoil it. But after an hour like that, with the houses thinning out on both sides of the road, a new feeling came into me. I wasn't really worried about the two of us being out there alone, but I felt that Magda was now under my care as much as I was under hers, and I had to think about that a bit. I was the one who broke our mood. Instead of asking Magda what she had in mind about where we might camp out for the night, I just told her that I thought we ought to begin looking for an abandoned shed or at least a stretch of wall before we ran out of the built-up area around us into completely open country.

"Is that what you're going to offer me on our first night away from home?" Magda said, looking off toward the mountains. "A piece of empty wall to sleep against?"

"Well I don't see that we have much choice out here," I said. "Maybe you had something more exciting in mind."

"No," Magda said. "I have nothing in mind. Whatever you say. You're the man in the family."

"I'm just trying to be practical," I said. "You don't have to make a joke out of it."

"I'm not making a joke," Magda said, squeezing my arm. "I love not having to be the man in the family any longer or feeling responsible for you. From now on I can be just me."

She let go of my arm and moved off to do a twirl in the middle of the road, then backed off a step and turned back when she saw the herdsman's wagon easing toward us almost silently. The herdsman brought his wagon to a stop beside us and leaned out to ask what in the name of God two young people dressed for the city expected to find for themselves except trouble that far out of the city center in the direction we were headed and at that time of night.

Magda looked at me.

"Tell him, little sister," I said to her. "The whole family story."

What Magda told him was that we were actually dressed for the road since we were on our way to the town of Veria to visit the shrine of the Sleeping Virgin in one of the churches there, because lighting candles to that Virgin had cured the two of us of a terrible family disease that would have left us crippled for life, and we had vowed to offer our gratitude to the Virgin's shrine in the village our mother came from.

"I can understand that's a necessary thing to do," the herdsman said. "But does it have to be at this time of night? What I mean to say is that you won't reach Veria on foot either tomorrow or the day after."

"However long it takes, we have to do it," Magda said.

"Well then you'd better let me take you as far as I'm going. Which isn't very far, maybe eight kilometers up the road. But at least it's better than walking until morning. Even with the moon out to help you see where you're going, you could fall into a ditch from exhaustion and be eaten by wolves."

Magda looked at me, I looked at her, we decided what the hell without having to say it. I thanked the man and climbed up beside him, then helped Magda come up to sit beside me on the far side from the driver. The man had two mules working for him up front, wearing blue beads and tassels at the ears, and in back he was protected by a kerosene lamp swinging under the wagon's rear to ward off any faster means of transportation that might come up on him in the dark. I could tell that the wagon was still carrying some hay from the sweet smell of it, though what else might have been in there behind us was protected by a tarpaulin held in place by baskets full of packaged goods that the man had picked up in the city. When we were settled in, he lit a cigarette and offered me one. I was tempted to take it in recognition of his thinking me man enough to smoke, but not sure I could handle it, I declined on the grounds of having too recently recovered from the inherited infirmity my sister spoke of.

Though the man tried to keep as much space as he could between him and us on that plank of a seat, it was clear right away that he was pleased to have the company even of young people who had been carrying an unnamed disease, because he didn't stop talking from the time we climbed up there beside him until he pulled off the main road to his farm outside the village called Vegetable Garden. We learned a great deal about the problems of buffalo herding in that region, what with the new program for draining the marshes in the Axios-Vardar valley that was meant to kill mosquitoes and the malaria they brought with them but was also killing much of the marshland buffalo used for grazing, so that people who used to prize buffalo milk over cow milk or even goat milk as food for the young were now apparently learning to do without it, and veal had sometime since come to be regarded as more high class than buffalo meat at the tables of the rich. The man himself was quite discouraged, ready, he said, to give it all up and sell his herd while it might still bring a reasonable price so that he could turn to farming on what new land he could find, but it wasn't a choice he liked to make at his age, especially with one unmarried daughter left to torment him with the problem of her future—no disrespect for my sister intended—and a son who had no more interest in farming than he had in raising buffaloes, though the man thought he might do well at breeding mosquitoes, because his son's brain had been turned to yoghurt by the village priest who had in mind sending him to Athos to become a monk, a thought so depressing to our driver that he shut up just long enough to light another cigarette.

I tried to break in at that point with a few wise comments about the problems of keeping young people interested in farming in depressed areas, but when I started to talk about the specific case of Allegheny County, New York, Magda came in to cut me dead by explaining to our driver that we didn't really know what the exact circumstances were in America since our family was in the tobacco business in Kavalla and only knew about American agriculture from the Virginia tobacco people who occasionally visited our home to look over our crop. I quieted down after that, though I wouldn't have found much ground for conversation on the buffalo problem in Greek Macedonia even without Magda's help, because I didn't get to see the kind of animal he was talking about until a group of them crossed our path in the moonlight during the last kilometer of this leg of our trip, and I have to admit I might have taken them for an unknown breed of large-boned, long-horned cows if I hadn't been close enough to cows all my life to see the basic difference whatever the light.

Before dawn I got to know some of the special sounds and smells of a buffalo intimately, and so did Magda. This came about because our driver insisted that we spend the night at his place, even if all he could offer us was the barn he used for housing his herd when it got too cold in winter, not really proper for cultivated people like the two of us, he said, but preferable to the dangers that the highway might have in store for us, from domestic animals on the loose with rabies to the wolves and bears in the nearby hills and the brigands a bit farther out who were not much different from wild animals because they would rob you clean and then leave you in some wounded state for the vultures to feed on when the sun came up. We didn't argue. It was halfway through the night by then, and Magda and I had both come out to a darker view of our future on that road under the herdsman's pitiless monologue and the rocking motion of his wagon as it worked its way between one pothole and another toward the wilderness in front of us.

The barn was not like those I'd been used to. It was made up of a series of sheds with partitions that had been constructed, it seemed, to keep up with the growth of our driver's herd, buffalo by buffalo, partition by partition, with the style of one section unrelated to the next except as boards might be put together to prevent something short of a man's height from getting in or getting out of a space that was about wide enough for the spread of your arms if you kept your elbows slightly bent. The herdsman explained that he was putting us in a section of the barn that he was hoping to renovate and make suitable for housing relatives as soon as he sold his herd, and if it weren't the middle of the night, he'd wake his wife and bring out a straw mattress from the house to add to the straw that was in there already, but under the circumstances, embarrassed as he was, we'd have to settle for a tarpaulin spread double on the ground between one partition and another. He went off mumbling to himself about the failures of man and nature that had come into his life so that it was now impossible for him to treat even strangers like normal human beings.

Magda and I had only a moment of tenderness before the long night's journey put us to sleep fully dressed. But we didn't sleep for long. I woke up as the dawn light was just beginning to thin out the darkness in there, and what woke me was a sound that was both familiar and not of this earth, a moaning that never rose to anything like a bellow but that still seemed to have the pain of the ages in it. The sound was coming from the section of barn one down from ours, and as I lay there trying not to listen, trying not to let that, or the dank smell of rotting straw under my head, or the rich garlic smell of my own sweat distract me from the sleep I needed, there seemed to be no end to that sound. Magda was awake now too.

"Holy Virgin," she said. "What is it?"

"I don't know," I said. "I would say it's a cow, but the sound isn't quite right for the cows I've known."

"Well, whatever it is, it sounds in pain."

"It's a little like a cow giving birth," I said. "Only it's worse."

Magda sat up. "Shouldn't we do something? I can't stand to hear that."

"Well, if it's a cow or a buffalo or something giving birth, there isn't much we can do about it except hope that the thing comes out right. Though sometimes you can help it along if you know what you're doing."

"I'm going to see," Magda said.

She got up and put on her cotton jacket and her shoes. The sun still wasn't up when we stepped out of our shed but there was light enough to let us make our way through the manure along the edge of the yard and down to the open door where the sound was coming from. The herdsman was already in there.

"Shut the door behind you," he said. "This is not something your sister should see. It could make her womb shrink like a dried fig."

I tried to close the door, but Magda put her foot out to keep a crack open. The buffalo was laid out flat on her side in one of the stalls in there, and though the moaning had stopped, her head was bent back and her eyes were bulging, and the bloodied head and forelegs of her calf were sticking out of her haunches. The man was kneeling behind her, pulling on the calf as hard as he could to get it out. I squatted down beside him and grabbed one of the calf's forelegs so that he could take the other and the two of us could work together to get the animal out, as I'd seen my father do with a cow more than once.

"She came in early," he said under his breath. "She wasn't due yet or I would have warned you."

"It doesn't matter," I said. "You can't be sure of things like that."

"At least she waited until I got back from the city. With my luck you'd expect her to calve while I was gone, or anyway try to, so that I could get home just in time to bury her and the calf too along with the rest I've had to bury."

We were making a little headway but not enough, and both of us were pulling with all our might. The man paused a moment.

"It's a devil, but at least it's beginning to come out," he said. "I've had to hook up ropes sometimes and haul the thing out with the help of mules."

That made me work even harder. I don't know how long it took us, but we finally got the rest of the calf out and laid it in the straw so that its mother could help us clean it up. When I came outside for some air, my hands and shirt were covered with blood and muck. Magda was standing there with a hand over her mouth. The man came out behind me, nodded to Magda, and went over to his wagon to bring in some fresh hay. I helped him with that too, then took some hay to clean off my hands and arms.

"You'd better go over to the well and draw up some water to wash," he said.

Magda followed me over to the well. She insisted on rinsing out my shirt in the first bucketful I brought up, and then using the shirt as a washcloth to clean me up as though she was my nurse.

"I don't understand it," she said after I'd begun to smell more or less normal again. "Whatever they say, it's a cruel trick."

"What trick is that?"

"To make it such pleasure in the beginning and then to make you have to suffer so much afterward. Especially when it's a necessary thing."

"Well, it isn't really anybody's fault, is it?"

"The point is, it happens. And it isn't fair. Anyway to females. And it doesn't help when they try to tell you that it's punishment for original sin or eating an apple or some other such nonsense."

"I don't much like the suffering either, but I don't know what you can do about it. I'd say it's the way nature works."

"Well then, nature is cruel and unfair, and you can at least speak the truth about it."

"All right, it's cruel and unfair. Can I have my shirt?"

Magda smiled. "I don't mean you have to speak the truth. I mean mankind. Especially the priests and rabbis."

I took the shirt and put it on wet, then hauled up another bucket of water and dumped it over my head. Magda took off her cotton jacket and used it to wipe my face.

"Don't be angry with me," she said. "You were very good in there, helping like that. I just can't stand to see that kind of mean-ingless suffering. In an animal or anything else."

"Forget it," I said. "I understand."

"No you don't exactly. But I like your being more down to earth about such questions than I am. It's one thing that makes you a man, I guess."

I didn't know how to answer that, so I didn't. I filled the bucket again and poured it slowly so that she could wash her hands and face, then filled the bucket again and left it there so that she could wash anything else she wanted to. The sun was up by then and neither of us had much heart for sleeping any longer. I gathered up our things and went back along the barn to thank the herdsman again for his hospitality, but he'd slipped off and left the calf stand-ing beside its mother to get used to its new world as best it could on its own.

We decided not to go into the village but headed back to the main road, and when we got there we took out Natasha's map to see just where we'd ended up in the middle of the night. As far as I could tell from the scale on the map, we'd done about ten kilometers of the seventy-five that were needed to get us to Veria, and there was some question as to whether we wanted to get to Veria at all since the railroad branched off south about halfway there.

"I'm not sure we want to get on the Salonika-Athens line just yet in any case," Magda said. "That's the one sure way they have of tracing us. I mean by now there could be some kind of notice to look out for either you or me in every train station along the main route."

"Well there could be a notice in every bus station too."

"Maybe in the towns," Magda said. "But not out here in this wilderness. Maybe we should use local buses at least until we get farther south."

"So that means we keep going to Veria?"

"I'd like to do that anyway," Magda said. "I'm still a bit superstitious after what I told that herdsman. And my aunt told me that Veria is full of churches, so there's bound to be a fresco of the Virgin somewhere that we can light a candle in front of."

"Well, I'm all for keeping the Virgin on our side if we can," I said.

"And in Veria we can stay in a hotel," Magda said. "I'm ready for a hotel, aren't you?"

"I don't know," I said. "I've never stayed in a real hotel."

"How nice," Magda said. "That means there's still something really new for both of us to look forward to."

The thought put us in a good mood again. We headed down the road holding hands until that became too sweaty, and when we got to the bridge across the Gallikos River where there was only one-way traffic, we decided to sit by the riverbank beyond the bridge until a local bus came along to take us as far in the right direction as it might be going. There wasn't much to look at out there, a mixture of farmland and swampland stretching flat for miles ahead of us and sometimes a line of poplars to mark the road's path after the broken surface of it was no longer in sight. But the air was clear enough in that early sunlight to let you see the outer edge of Salonika Bay to the south and the mountains above Veria to the west merging into others that must have been as far north as the Yugoslav border.

Neither of us bothered to turn around to see the lay of the land behind us. We sat there thinking our own thoughts, then read for a while, then Magda had me stretch out with my head in her lap so that she could pick my face clean of some blackheads that she'd spotted when she'd last had a chance to look at me close up.

It was a sound as sick as I'd ever heard from a working engine that made me vault out of Magda's lap and get to the road in time to hail what looked like it had once been a bus as it came clattering across the bridge. The driver had to get down to open the door on the passenger side, which was held shut in two places by thick wire that he had to unwind to let us in and then wind up tight again to keep the door from falling off.

"I'm only going as far as Plati," he said, working to get the wire unwound. "You'll have to go on from there by the train or some other bus, depending on where you're going."

"Veria," I said.

"Well, I'm not going as far as Veria," the driver said.

"Don't worry about it," Magda said. "We'll take care of ourselves after Plati."

"I'm just warning you," the driver said. "This bus doesn't go as far as Veria and never has."

"Don't worry about it," I said.

I paid the man what he asked for, and we climbed up to find that there was no room for sitting in the bus and the only place for standing was on the step that we'd taken to get partway inside, which meant that the two of us had to stay on that step side by side and hope the door didn't give way behind us on a sharp curve and release us into that wilderness before we were due. Once we were on the open road, at high speed, the vibration in the bus tingled your flesh through to the bone, and when the thing would slow down to avoid a cart or wandering beast and then gear up again, the rasping shift from one gear to another brought a tremor through the aged metal of that step that made you want to dance free of it as though it was suddenly covered with hot coals. Nobody in the packed bus was talking. You couldn't hear your own voice no matter what pace that motor chose for itself, and most heads were bowed either with sleep or motion sickness or fright.

The bus stopped twice before we reached Plati, both times to let people out who had come up to the aisle to tell the driver that they were sick, and both times we had no choice but to free our step and climb out with them as quickly as we could after the door was unwound and stand by the roadside until they'd finished vomiting. Our only choice was to give the bus up during one of those stops and walk to the next village, but when we asked the driver at the second stop how far it was to the next village up the road, he told us there was no such thing as a next village up the road because the villages out where we had arrived were all on the railroad line some kilometers off the main road and we should just relax because we wouldn't find a better bus than his to get us to Plati since his was the only bus there was.

It was while we were sitting in the one cafe we found open in the village of Plati having a late breakfast of coffee and honeyed yoghurt that we decided it was time to let ourselves get more reckless, since playing it safe was what had condemned us to that stinking bus ride. We had our map out in front of us again and could see not only the main railroad line to Athens that turned south from where we were, but also another line heading west to Veria and then north all the way into Yugoslavia. The reckless idea we discussed was taking the train as far as Veria and going on to Athens from there by bus, because the train ride would be outside the main line and therefore ought to be reasonably safe and the bus we could then pick up in Veria would supposedly be the kind that connected major towns and therefore ought to have a decent motor and four round wheels and doors that could be shut by hand.

I volunteered to scout the railroad station just beyond the village while Magda picked up some provisions from the local general store. The attendant at the station was asleep inside his booth, so I decided I wouldn't disturb him. I covered the outside and then the inside of that station looking for something that might pass for a schedule of the trains to Yugoslavia, but all I could find posted on the walls was a photograph of King George of the Hellenes and another of General Metaxas. As I was about to drift out of the station, the attendant woke up.

"There is no train to Yugoslavia today," the man said. "Why do you think I'm taking time out to rest my eyes?"

"The truth is, we don't want to go to all the way to Yugoslavia," I said. "We just want to get ourselves to Veria."

"That's another matter," the man said. "Who is we?"

"We is I and my sister," I said.

"Well, you and your sister won't find a train to Veria today," the man said. "But there's one to Edessa that stops in Veria."

"That's fine," I said. "When does it leave here for Veria?"

"That depends on when it gets here," the man said. "And about that I make no promises. Though things have gotten much better under General Metaxas, I can assure you of that."

"Well, can you give me a general idea of when it might get here?"

The man was studying me again. "A general idea?" he said. "Are you a foreigner or something?"

"I suppose you could say that," I said. "My father is Dutch."

"Dutch?" the man said. "I don't know any Dutch people to speak of. Though some pass through here once in a while I'm sure."

"So do we just come out here and sit down and wait for the train to come along sometime before it gets dark, is that it?"

"You can do that if you want to," the man said. "But I wouldn't bother beginning to do that for an hour or two. Because that train never gets here before midday. Even when there isn't much to slow it down but a buffalo or a goat between the Salonika station and this godless place."

We were the only ones waiting for the train to Edessa that came along just after midday, and when Magda and I arrived in our dark glasses and head-cover to sit on the bench outside and read our novels, the attendant didn't bother to give us more than a glance, in fact, didn't come out from behind his desk until the train was easing into the station. It was a regular European-style train, with a separate door for every compartment, and the second-class coach we ended up in still had upholstery on the seats, though the dust had gathered there over the years in a way that didn't make it inviting as a head-rest unless you kept your hat on. We walked the length of the coach until we found a compartment with only one other person in it, a gray-haired man dressed in a white linen suit and a fedora hat who looked so respectable that Magda figured he wouldn't be the kind to ask questions or look for opinions during such a short trip.

But the train turned out to be a toy train when it came to speed, moseying along as though it had been sent out on a special mission to carry schoolchildren and their parents on a sightseeing tour through the northern wilderness and into the mountainous regions for a holiday. That seemed to be the mood down the line, with people of all ages but mostly the very young and the middle-aged hanging out of the compartment windows to the right and the left, taking in the slight breeze our motion made and gazing out endlessly across the fields and the swampland as though they expected strange plants and animals to show up on the horizon. And since that was my mood too, nothing out there would have surprised me. What startled me while I was hanging out of the compartment window was hearing the man in the white suit suddenly say something to Magda behind me.

"Your schoolmate looks very pleased to be on holiday," the man said in a soft voice. "Will you be spending all of it in Edessa?"

"We won't be going as far as Edessa," Magda said. "And he isn't my schoolmate, actually. He's my brother."

"I'm very sorry," the man said. "May he live long for you."

"That's all right," Magda said. "We're also schoolmates in a way. That is, we go to the same school. Though in different grades."

I don't know exactly why, but the two of them talking like that behind my back about what I was and wasn't suddenly got on my nerves.

"The truth is, we're not really brother and sister," I said. "We're something more personal."

The man didn't say anything. He just bowed his head slightly.

"My little brother is very good at making jokes," Magda said. "And he has a great imagination. But sometimes he can be infuriating."

The man looked up again. "Well, I wish you both a good holiday. And if you get as far as Edessa, you must stop by my summer home."

"We'll certainly do that," Magda said.

"I don't have any children of my own, but I am very fond of young people. Even after teaching in the gymnasium for thirty years."

"You teach in a gymnasium?" Magda said.

"In Salonika," the man said. "I've just finished grading my share of the entrance examinations for the university. And I suppose that yearly torture being over explains why there are so many young people on this train."

"So the entrance examinations are over," Magda said, really to herself.

"What a business," the man said. "It's really disgusting. They give you so many examinations to grade and you have to be so careful because so much depends on it."

"Well, that's that," Magda said.

"I beg your pardon?" the man said.

"Magda is planning to go to the university," I said. "I guess not this year, but maybe next year. And maybe I'll end up doing the same."

"Is that right?" the man said. He took off his glasses and cleaned them slowly. Then he looked at Magda again as though seeing her for the first time.

"And what will you study at the university?" the man finally asked her.

"Psychology," Magda said. "Child psychology. So that I can become a teacher and maybe teach young people when to speak and when not to speak."

"Isn't that interesting," the man said. "I didn't know they taught psychology at the university. Of course my field is religion and ancient Greek."

"This will be in Athens," Magda said. "At the American college there. Where I think they are a little better about admitting women to study difficult subjects."

"I see," the man said. "Of course. Athens is a completely different world, isn't it?"

"I hope so," Magda said. "We're counting on that."

"I'm sure that the two of you will do well in Athens," the man said. "Where there's a will there's a way, as the Anglo-Saxons are fond of saying."

He said that gently, as if assigned to tell us that even though we'd failed this year's examination, there would always be another chance next year. Then he picked up his newspaper and read it for a while without reading it at all. Magda joined me at the compartment window. She didn't say anything, but her fingers came against the outside of my thigh and pinched me so hard that I cried out as though stung by a wasp or other vicious insect, and that's what I had to pretend had happened while Magda just stood there ignoring what she'd done. The man glanced over at us above his glasses, then flipped his newspaper over to scan the headlines on the back page.

The Veria station was east of the town and well below it because the train suddenly veered north at that point to follow the outer edge of the plain that ended where we got off. As we left the compartment, our fellow passenger rose up suddenly to shake hands and wish us a good journey, and I looked back to see him standing in the doorway watching us with a smile that seemed to hover somewhere between amusement and disapproval, but how you saw it of course depended on your frame of mind. It seemed mine was still fairly mellow. I decided to make my peace with Magda as we climbed the steep road toward the white town on the mountainside ahead.

"I'm sorry," I said. "I don't know what got into me back there on the train. I guess I just get tired of having to pretend all the time."

"Well, I get tired of it too," Magda said. "But what choice have we got?"

"I don't know," I said. "Suppose we just choose not to pretend any longer."

"How can we do that?"

"Suppose from now on we tell people that we're married."

Magda took my hand. "But isn't that pretending too?"

"Well it isn't as bad as pretending we're brother and sister. Which is not only a lie but makes it sinful just to hold hands. Besides, I thought we were married in our own way."

"We are in our own way. And isn't that what matters? What you feel inside rather than what you show people on the outside?"

"But does what we show people on the outside matter so much that we have to pretend to be something we really aren't all the time?"

Magda sighed. "All right. If it will make you feel better, when we go to the hotel we'll pretend that we're married."

"Well, what about how it will make you feel?"

"I don't know. At this point it all seems a little hopeless. I'm not afraid to take risks for what I believe in my heart, but I don't seem to have many choices left. I can't really have you and I can't go to the university this year or probably next year and I don't know what there is ahead for either of us."

"You can have me. You do have me. Why do you keep saying that?"

"Talking to that man just made me begin to feel lost again."

"Well stop feeling that way. I mean it."

Magda sighed again. "All right, from now on we'll pretend that we can have everything. At least for a while. And I suppose we might as well begin by pretending we're on holiday like other normal human beings at this time of year."

The hotel we chose to go to may not have been the biggest of the three in Veria but it was the closest to the town square, which was the only open space we came across among the steep curling streets of the town, except for the space around the occasional gushing fountain or springhead. The square was as grand a place as you were likely to find in a town that small, with large plane trees and planted flowers and its segment of ancient wall leading to a castle. We decided to have a drink of fresh lemonade in the square before heading over to the hotel we'd chosen. The only other people in the cafe were a middle-aged couple and their two children, city people by the look of it, and as new to the region as we were because I heard them ask the waiter what, if anything, there was of interest to see in the town of Veria. Magda didn't seem to notice them. I got the impression that she was a little nervous about how we'd decided to present ourselves at the hotel, because once we were seated she certainly took her time with that lemonade. Not that I wasn't nervous too, but in the other direction, more like what an impatient bridegroom is supposed to feel. By the time we finally got to the hotel, Magda seemed to have settled down, because she didn't hesitate to walk up to the front desk with me, though she let me do the talking. I asked the man at the desk for a double room with a double bed.

"For how many of you?" the man said.

"What do you mean, how many?" I said. "For me and my wife here."

"Your wife?" the man said

"That's what I said."

"You're sure you don't have a brother and a sister to go along with your wife? I've had bad experience with some of you young people from the city who like to pretend that a double bed is made for a whole family just because the bed is bigger than any you've been in."

Magda took off her dark glasses. "You don't have to worry about us," she said sweetly. "We don't have a family with us and we've seen plenty of double beds before."

The man studied her. "Don't misunderstand me, I'm just doing my job," he said to the register book. "Will you please sign here and leave me your identity cards."

I looked at Magda. She was still smiling sweetly at the man.

"Identity cards?" I said. "We don't have identity cards. Nobody does in our country."

The man looked up. "What country is that?"

"Denmark," I said.

"You learned to speak Greek like that in Denmark?"

"We learned in this country," I said. "We're students at the university."

"In any case," the man said. "Then let me have your passports."

I looked at Magda again.

"Why would we have passports with us?" Magda said. "We don't plan to cross any borders."

"Well, I need some sort of identity verification," the man said. "I don't know what happens in Denmark, but in this country the police require it."

I took my knapsack off and went into it to find the address book I was carrying with me in case I wanted to send a postcard to somebody back in the States, and inside the flap of that I had certain documents that I didn't feel would be safe in my wallet while I was on the road—my YMCA membership card, a worn ten-dollar bill, and a certificate from Camp Cory, New York, stating that I was a qualified lifesaver. I decided to give the man the lifesaving certificate, because the lettering on it was tiny and it had a blue-and-red Camp Cory seal for a background.

The man glanced at the certificate. "What's this?" he said.

"My state scholarship certificate," I said. "It's all I have that's official."

Magda went over to sit on the chintz settee they had in the entrance lobby. I didn't dare look at her.

"Well, you'll have to write out the details I need because I don't read or write Danish," the man said. "Name, address, date of birth, nationality, how long you plan to stay, where you plan to go from here."

What I wrote out on the form he handed me were the only Danish names I felt I could be sure of, Horatio Hamlet, and I put the address as Elsinore, Denmark. When he turned the register toward me, I scribbled "Mr. and Mrs. Hamlet" as illegibly as I could. I told the man he could put down that we would be staying just one night and then moving on to join friends in Edessa. When I reached over the counter for the lifesaving certificate, the man palmed it.

"No," he said. "This stays with me. Until you've paid your bill."

"But it's the only identification I have."

"That may be," the man said. "But as long as you're in this hotel, only you and I and the police need to know who you are. And once you've paid your bill, neither I nor the police will care any longer."

The man swung around and studied the wall behind him. He

picked up a key from one of the pigeonholes there and put the certificate where the key had come from. Then he made a little bow toward Magda and signaled her to follow us up the stairs. Our room turned out to have both a double bed and a single bed off to one side, and it looked out on the square. It wasn't luxurious, but there was plenty of space in there, and it had its own bathroom with an old-fashioned tub that had some rust stains at one end where the water dripped down steadily but was as large a tub as any I'd seen. The man opened the brown drapes, then the gray lace curtains, then the green shutters. He handed me the key.

"I've given you the suite we normally give priests and political dignitaries," he said. "It may not be the equal of what you're used to in Denmark, but I can promise you it's the best we have to offer in this small Macedonian town of ours."

He gave Magda another little bow and closed the door softly behind him. Magda flopped down on the double bed and lay there with her arms behind her head, smiling at me as though she had a taste of honey in her mouth. I went over to look out across the square a minute. The light had turned soft, and people had begun to come out and gather in pairs and larger groups for the late afternoon ice cream or cake before their evening stroll around the square. There was a bougainvillaea vine climbing the wall under our window, and somewhere nearby there was jasmine or honeysuckle to sweeten the air every time the breeze that had come up brushed by our window. Across the square, where the old walls of the town cut straight through the winding streets, you could see the rounded roof of a leftover mosque with its minaret still beside it. I was about to call Magda over to look at that curiosity and breathe in the general feeling of contentment the town gave you at that hour when I felt her arms circle my waist from behind.

"You're a great liar," she said. "Where did you learn to lie like that about who you are?"

"I guess I must have learned from being with you," I said. "I never used to lie like that before."

"Is that right? And just how is anybody supposed to put their faith in you if you've learned to deceive people like that?"

"I don't know. How is anybody supposed to put their faith in you when you're the one who taught me how?"

"I didn't teach you anything," Magda said. "You remember how all this started? With the scheme you made up to get me to the beach?"

"Well, that was your fault too. For making me feel about you the way I did."

"I made you feel that way?"

"Yes. Just like you're doing now."

Magda flicked her tongue into my ear. "Then I think there's only one solution. I think both our souls need a thorough cleansing."

"I don't know how to do that," I said. "You'll have to teach me that too."

"Let me think," Magda said. "In most religions you have to cleanse the flesh before you try to get through to the soul. So maybe the first thing we do is wash ourselves thoroughly."

She let go of my waist and stepped back. Then she undid her blouse and took it off to lay it on the bed.

"Come," she said. "Take off your clothes so that we can help each other wash off our old sins before we add any more new ones."

I took off my clothes. When Magda finished undressing, she went in and ran the water in the bathtub. The water came out rusty at first, but it came out full throttle, so that it cleaned itself in a hurry, and there was enough heat left in the pipes to make it lukewarm. Magda sat on the rim of the tub while it was filling up and turned every now and then to let one hand play with the water as it rose, but her eyes were mostly on me standing in the doorway—that is, until she seemed to become shy and took her eyes off me because she saw something in the way I was gazing at her. I don't know what it was she saw, but I know what went through my mind as she sat there with the afternoon sun from the high window slanting across the top half of her body, and this was that I couldn't ever expect to see anything more beautiful in a woman than the line of Magda's neck and shoulders when she turned against the light, and the long line her legs made when she stretched them to lean back and touch the water.

Magda turned the tap off suddenly while the tub was still only half full and sat there on the rim with her knees tight together and her legs tucked in against the tub's underbelly. I went over and knelt in front of her and kissed first one knee and then the other. She took my head in her hands and gazed at me. Then she bent to kiss my eyes. She let go of my head then and swung her legs over to sit on the rim facing the other way, with her feet slicing the water, then slipped in all the way and settled back against the slanting end of the tub.

"Come in," she said. "We can both fit easily."

I climbed in facing her, but she took hold of my legs and turned me around.

"This way, silly man. Otherwise you'll have your back against the faucets instead of against me."

I eased in that way and settled back against her. She wound her arms around me and put her chin on my shoulder to lean forward and pick up the soap from the tray in front of me. Then she leaned back again and used the soap on my shoulders and as much of my back as she could get to easily, and when she had rinsed me off, she brought the soap around front and went over my chest and belly and as far as she could reach underwater. I turned my head to brush my lips against her cheek just to show her that I liked what she was doing, but that made her draw back up.

"Not yet," she said. "We still have me to do."

She put the soap back in the soap dish, then put her hands on my shoulders to raise herself and ease over me leap-frog fashion so that she could lower herself into the water again and settle back against me with her head bent forward, waiting for me to work on her back.

"You have to pick up the soap yourself," she said. "I told you that it's bad luck for me to hand it to you."

So I leaned forward to pick up the soap from the dish, then settled back to soap her shoulders and her back, and when I'd rinsed them off and moved my hand around front to run the soap over her breasts, she held my hand and had me go over them twice, then let go of the hand so that I could soap under her arms and gradually work on down and into the water as far as I needed to in order to soap all of her in front. Her head was bent back against mine when my other hand came around front to rinse her off, and she didn't seem to mind now when I turned my head to put my lips against her neck and then her ear.

"What do we do now?" I said into her ear.

"Now you put the soap back in the dish and then we let the water run out and then we do anything we want to do."

I put the soap back in the dish and she leaned forward and pulled out the plug under the faucets. I held her there, one hand on the ridge of her shoulder and the other on her neck under the hair, where the down was still damp from my washing. As I caressed her neck she turned her head to bite gently into my hand, but she stayed where she was even after the water had run out and after I'd taken my hand off her shoulder and picked up the soap again so that I could go below in back where the water had been and soap that intimate place as well, and when I stopped soaping her there but kept the soap beside me and eased her back against me, she knew just what I wanted and arched her back slightly as though to help, then let out a little sigh of the kind that has only pleasure in it.

By the time we woke from our late afternoon nap, it was dark in our room, and when I went over to the window to have a look outside, the square seemed almost deserted, with very few strollers still working the two sides of the evening promenade to show off who they were or make eye contact with somebody they wanted to get to know better and only a few scattered groups sitting outside the sweet shops and the cafes along the periphery of the square. I was hungry by then, but it took a while to get Magda out of bed so that we could go out and find some place still open that served decent food. She told me that since we'd decided to pretend we were on vacation like everybody else, there was no need to hurry to do anything any longer, even to feed ourselves, and all she really wanted was for me to come back and lie with her awhile in that grand double bed so that we could enjoy the luxury of it as long as possible. So I went back to bed and just lay there holding her close and not talking. Magda finally said that since the only thing I seemed to have on my mind at that point was eating, she thought it might be nice for us to play a new game she'd just invented, which was to pretend that we could go someplace and order anything we wanted of the meals we remembered as the best we'd ever had.

The first thing that little game did for me was to make me excruciatingly hungry, and the second thing it did was make me secretly jealous, because the ideal menu I came up with was a simple boring one based on Christmas meals my German grandmother used to turn out in upstate New York, with various kinds of poultry and potatoes and pies, while Magda came up with a menu so exotic and French that she couldn't settle for just naming the fish and meat and vegetables she had in mind but had to describe everything that went into the sauces those things floated in, and the cheeses that followed, and a couple of desserts too complicated to be real. The more she went on the clearer it became to me that she must have learned about all this luscious food in somebody's company, and this made me wonder what other more personal things she may have learned from whoever that somebody was. I finally had to ask her where the hell she'd gotten to know so much about French cooking in Salonika, Greece, for God's sake, where there wasn't a single restaurant that served food like that as far as I knew, though of course somebody could have cooked it up for her in his own home. Magda must have realized that her little game had worked to put me in the wrong frame of mind, because she suddenly admitted that she hadn't actually eaten everything she'd described but had gotten it out of studying a French cookbook that her aunt had given her to cheer her up after the first time she'd run away.

"That's cheating," I said. "I could have made things up out of a book too. If my mother happened to have one around the house instead of learning all she had to know from her mother."

"You're just jealous," Magda said. "I can tell. Otherwise why would you force me to admit that I'd never been to a restaurant or anywhere else where they serve that sort of food?"

"Because it's one thing to make up an imaginary meal out of things you've actually eaten and another to make it up out of a book."

"What difference does it make if it's imaginary?"

"I don't know," I said. "I'd say the one is honest pretending and the other not so honest pretending once we've set up the rules of the game. But I'm not in a mood to argue."

"That's a foolish distinction. Very Anglo-Saxon. Because it's still only a game meant to entertain one either way, and the better one makes things up, the better it entertains one."

"O.K. It's only a game, and you win because you can make things up better than I can. So how about going out now for something to eat. Please?"

"I think you were just jealous because you thought I'd eaten all those things with somebody else. And maybe I had. Some of the things. Only it wasn't with the man you think it was."

"What man was it with?"

"My father. When I was fourteen years old. He took me on a trip to Belgrade for a birthday present and we had a wonderful meal in a kind of French restaurant there. Only I don't remember exactly what we ate."

"Your father took you on a trip?"

"Yes. That was when he was still an ordinary human being who loved me because I was his pretty little daughter and not this rebellious whore I've grown up to be."

"Is that what he calls you?"

"He called me that once and maybe now he'd call me something worse."

"Well, if that's what he thinks of you, what would he think of me if he knew about us being together like this?"

"I don't know. If he could forgive you for not being Jewish, he'd probably think you a fool for having anything to do with his one-time daughter. And about that he might be right."

I took my arm out from under her and sat up to look at her. "Do you really think that?"

"Sometimes. I guess sometimes when I'm most happy, like right now, I can't help wondering what I've done to deserve it. And that makes me wonder if it's real, and what will happen if it turns out not to be."

"Of course it's real," I said. "And why shouldn't you and I deserve to be happy?"

"Because the truth is that I've lost one year of school because I was reckless, and now I've lost another not only because I wouldn't do what my family wanted me to do but because I fell in love with my own student the first chance I had to become a teacher. So maybe I'm incorrigible."

"You're no such thing. In fact, what you are is the only person I've ever known who is really free."

Magda sat up beside me. "Am I? Well, it's nice to know that you think I am, because you're the person who matters now. But the one thing I learned from the last time I was in love is that you're only free when you're enough in command of yourself to choose what you can do and not do. And even then you have to hope that fate or luck or whatever you want to call it is on your side."

"Well, we're both free to choose what we want to do," I said. "And we're both lucky besides. Otherwise we wouldn't have made it this far."

"Maybe you're right. Anyway, we must pretend it's so as long as we're on holiday, mustn't we?"

She kissed me on my forehead and then on the tip of my nose and then on my lips, there as though she meant it, and then she stood up and got dressed. What she put on was the party dress she'd worn when I found her sitting by the road below Natasha's place brooding about where we were and where we might be going, but this time she said she was putting that dress on because it was Saturday night and the first night of our real vacation together. So I put on a clean pair of pants and my shirt that had sleeves. We still didn't go right out because Magda wanted to wash a few things of mine and hers and leave them to dry on the rim of the bathtub, and then she wanted to put on some jewelry that she'd packed up in a hurry when she left Salonika. What she wore turned out to be a necklace and earrings from Turkey with amber stones in them that her aunt had given her and my filigree bracelet from our afternoon above the ravine. Seeing that on her lightened my mood again, not just because she chose to wear it at that moment but because it told me that she'd chosen to take it with her when she'd left the city for Thassos, sometime before I found her there. While I was standing in the doorway watching her put those things on in front of the bathroom mirror, tilting her head to get the earrings through her ears and adjusting the necklace so that the jangles on it fell comfortably in the hollow between her breasts, she must have caught something in my look again because she turned and tried to dab some perfume on me from a tiny bottle that she carried in her purse, and when I got it away from her and tried to dab her here and there, it caused a bit of wrestling that ended up almost sending us temporarily back to bed.

The place we found for our Saturday night dinner was not as foreign to my life at that point as a French restaurant would have been—it was just an ordinary outdoor taverna with a barbecue pit— but once we'd settled in there, we ordered three dishes that seemed to me as rare as anything Magda had created out of the mix of her memory and imagination: a portion of the charcoal grilled entrails of an unnamed animal filled with its own spiced spleen, then the intestine-bound liver, lungs, sweetbreads, and other unidentified inner parts of what must have been one of the smaller varieties of grazing livestock that roamed those hills, and finally a plate covered with thick fried slices of breaded pork gonad. Magda assured me that however you might choose to name the parts of those grilled concoctions, each and every one of them had been safely tested over the years by popular consumption, and some of them had been proven to carry either medicinal or aphrodisiac powers.

When we got to the fruit course—cherries and early grapes and two kinds of peach—we decided to ask the waiter's help with our holiday plans for the next day and maybe a few days thereafter. Magda's idea was to spend the next morning looking at what there was to see in Veria and then maybe heading for the mountains above the town.

"We still have plenty of money," she said. "And if we're going to be normal like other city people in this country, we should have some time in the mountains to breathe the pure air now that we've had a number of healthy cleansing baths in the sea and in other places."

"I'm game for anything," I said. "It's still only July. And I told my people back home not to expect me much before the opening of school in the fall."

"You told them that?"

"I told them I felt a responsibility to get you settled in Athens."

She took my hand and held the back of it against her lips.

"It's so nice to have somebody feel that sort of thing for you," she said. "What can I do to show your parents that I feel a responsibility toward you that's just as strong? I mean without having to send you home."

"You don't have to worry about my parents," I said. "They're my problem. And I'm not going to worry about that for at least a month or two."

With what seemed like so much time on our side, we couldn't see any reason not to stop for a while in the mountains to take in the high air and green forests after the flat swampland we'd been through. We decided we had to try for a place that was civilized enough to be safe and preferably near the main road south in case we got bored with too much mountain purity and wanted to move on toward the sea halfway to Athens. That was when we brought our waiter, the only waiter in the place, into our discussion. He was a tall man with a thin black mustache and dark hair split in the middle and brushed down on either side, and he was a professional juggler when it came to carrying food, balancing plate after plate along one arm from the tip of his fingers to the pit of his arm and using his other hand to carry a spread of dishes flared out fan-like and wafting the air to keep his balance as he moved with quick grace from the barbecue cage to one table and then another.

The first thing we asked the waiter was what there was for us to see in Veria, and he told us that there was nothing for us to see in Veria besides the old walls and the old houses, especially those in the Jewish quarter, and the old churches, of which there were too many to name but five of which had frescoes that we shouldn't miss, and those he was willing to name, which he did. And when we asked him if he knew of any place in the mountains nearby where we might spend some time comfortably taking in the clean air, he said there was no place in the mountains that was comfortable except one place that he could speak for, which was the home where he had grown up in the village of Kastania on the road to Kozani at a high point of the mountain behind where we were sitting. I got out our map so that he could pinpoint the village for us, and it turned out to be about fifteen kilometers from Veria, just off the main road to Athens.

"Of course it's only a village," the waiter said. "With nothing but village life in it. But it's safe from brigands and wild animals, I can assure you of that."

"What sort of wild animals do you find near here?" Magda said.

"No wild animals in this region," the waiter said. "Except for the occasional wolf or bear."

"And are there really brigands in these mountains?" I asked.

"Not in the village of Kastania, I promise you. But sometimes they come across from the mountains nearer the border. Slavs more than Greeks, on the whole, but godless thieves whatever the nationality."

"And is there any place to stay in your village?" Magda said.

"If you mean a hotel, there is no place to stay in the village," the waiter said. "If you mean a house, then the only house I would stay in is my own."

"Well, where might the rest of the world stay?" Magda said.

The waiter shrugged. "Who can speak for the rest of the world? If you want to stay in my home, my mother and father would welcome you, I'm sure. But it wouldn't be in my heart to recommend that civilized people stay anywhere else in that village."

Magda and I looked at each other.

"We'd be happy to stay with your mother and father," I said. "As long as they will let us pay something."

"That's up to my mother and father," the waiter said. "Since my profession is being a waiter, I never allow myself to act as an agent for anybody, my family included."

When I paid the bill, I added a tip that made the man look away from the money and put it quickly in his pocket as though there was enough there to constitute a bribe; then he wrote out a note to his mother and father on the back of a blank bill, the handwriting huge because he said they were both weak at letters and anyway half blind but still the cleverest old couple in the village of Kastania. Magda asked what the best way was to get to his village, and the waiter said that the only way for foreigners to get there if you didn't use a taxi was to go by bus, by which he meant the bus to the town of Kozani, since that one was new enough to have all its seats solidly in place and a motor that wouldn't boil over more than once or twice on its way up the mountain.

We missed the bus to Kozani the next day. That was because our evening meal stayed with us in a way that made us sleep in late and take as much advantage as we could of our giant bed before going out to face what was bound to be a simpler life ahead. And after adding up our cash on hand, we decided we had enough to splurge and take a taxi to the village of Kastania. This left us as much time as we needed to see the abandoned mosque with its minaret, and some stones surrounded by a fence marking the place where the Apostle Paul preached against pagan sin to the people of the town long before the Turks came in to try and impose their way of life, and the old houses of the Jewish quarter perched on the edge of a ravine like birdhouses and separated off to confine still another way of life. There were more Byzantine churches of different sizes and different ages than somebody unfamiliar with churches of that kind could take in during a single morning, one of them with a fresco of the Sleeping Virgin attended by holy men as she lay on a bed covered by beautifully embroidered cloth and set on a slant so that the whole of her could be seen lying there peacefully in blue with eyes shut as she waited to be carried up to heaven and wakened again for the only life that was meant to last forever.

The fresco had a candelabra close enough to it to allow us to use it for a private shrine, though neither of us called it that. We lit a candle each and stood back a minute to watch them burn, then Magda lit a third that she said was just for good luck down the road. We were silent on our way back to the hotel, as though saying anything more about it would spoil the intimacy of what each of us took it to mean. Magda waited outside while I collected our things and paid the hotel bill. When I headed out the door, the man behind the desk called me back and handed me my fake identity card with a look that told me I shouldn't go away thinking I'd put anything over on him.

The taxi we found had new tires and new orange paint on its chassis, but it looked to me a lot like the Model A Ford my grandfather had parked on a hillside behind one of his barns next to the Model T Ford he'd discarded there to rust some years earlier. It was the general shape of the taxi that made me feel that way, because whatever identification there had once been on the front and the wheels had long since vanished, and some parts of its outer shell now appeared to belong to another race of car or had been made up in a local blacksmith's shop to fill needed space. But the taxi driver, who had deep lines across his forehead that looked to have been carved there by years of bitter experience, turned out to be a born optimist.

"You're sure we won't have trouble making it that high up the mountain?" I said to him when we'd settled on a reasonable fare.

"Why should we have trouble?" the man said. "A team of mules might have trouble, but not a machine as powerful as this one."

He patted the hood with his hand as though it was a favored horse's neck.

"It's just that I heard the bus to Kozani sometimes boils over going up there even though it's a new bus."

"The bus to Kozani," the man said. "The bus to Kozani begins in Salonika, so what do you expect it to know? It hasn't been up and down this mountain the way my limousine has."

I looked at Magda. She looked away and stood there surveying the road out of town as though to say the whole thing was entirely up to me. So I put our baggage on the front seat beside the driver, then helped Magda into the back. The road that climbed out of the village was as steep as any main road I'd been on, and it didn't let up until we came to a plateau several kilometers out of town that gave the driver his first chance to shift down to second gear. But almost as soon as he did so he came to stop by the side of the road.

I leaned forward. "What's the matter?"

"Nothing's the matter," the driver said. "I thought you and the lady might like to get out and have a look at the view since it's the only one on this side of the mountain and we won't be stopping again."

Through the back window it looked as though you could see the whole of the town below and the plain beyond as far as the first river we'd crossed on the road out of Salonika. While Magda and I moved to the edge of the road to take it all in, the driver opened the hood and poured water from a demijohn into his radiator.

"Did you smell the engine while we were climbing?" Magda asked me under her breath.

"I smelled something. But I'm not sure it was the engine. It could have been the gears."

"Do you think we should say something to him? Once we get up in the mountains, there may be no turning back."

"Well, we can always spend the night in the backseat and coast down in the morning."

Magda smiled. "And fight the wolves all night?"

"I think we ought to give the man a chance," I said. "We still aren't even a third of the way to the village according to how I read the map."

The taxi broke down the first time just as we were about to crawl over a ridge that would have given the driver another opportunity to shift down one gear and maybe provide the boiling engine enough relief to get us around a few more bends in the road and possibly over the next ridge, though exactly where that would have put us on our map, I could no longer tell after the way the winding climb had muddled my sense of distance. The driver stood there gazing under the raised hood with his hands on his hips because the one time he'd reached for the radiator cap, it turned out to be a hot coal. I got out to have a word with him.

"I really don't understand it," he said. "There is only one explanation. The garage that was supposed to flush out the radiator and purify the cooling system must have cheated me. And that garage is owned by my brother-in-law."

"So, how long do you think we'll be stuck here?"

The driver looked at me. "We're not stuck," he said. "How can you say we're stuck when I stopped voluntarily to let the engine rest a little?"

"Well how long do you think it will it have to rest?"

"Only as long as it takes to cool down," the driver said. "Which is a thing I'm sure you realize is not in my hands but in the hands of God."

I went back to sit beside Magda. She smiled sweetly at me.

"Are we here for the night?"

"No. Just until the engine cools down. Which he says is a thing in the hands of God."

"Well, I'm glad he's a Christian. And since you're a Christian also, maybe you could help him by offering a little prayer."

"That isn't funny. Whatever you want to call me, I'm no different from you."

"I'm not really trying to be funny. Just practical. In a country that has as many gods as this one has, the man should get what help he can from those who know his god the best. But if you want, I'll try to help as well."

When the driver was finally able to unscrew the radiator cap, he started the motor up again and poured water into the radiator until his demijohn was empty. That got us another four kilometers up the mountain before we boiled over again, and by that time we were climbing up a pass, with steep slopes on both sides of the road and no sign of a village anywhere. When the driver pulled over, the steam was coming out of both sides of the hood, so he decided not to bother opening it up for the moment.

"We're very lucky," he said, getting out the empty demijohn. "No more than a kilometer up the road there's a spring. I'll be back with water before this beautiful thing has even had a chance to cool down again."

Magda and I got out to sit on the hillside facing the gorge that the road had been following. She put her head on my shoulder.

"You see what comes of your not praying?" she said.

"Who says I didn't pray?"

"I don't believe you did. I'm afraid that being with me has turned you into a heathen."

"That's not true. Being with you has turned me into a believer."

"In what?"

"In you. And in what you and I are together."

"That's what I mean. I don't think that's really at all Christian."

"I don't care. It's what I really am."

Magda didn't say anything. She turned her head to kiss my cheek, then swung around and laid her head in my lap. She closed her eyes and kept them closed as I stroked the fringes of her hair. I don't know what she was thinking, but she bit her lower lip for a second at one point, so whatever was on her mind couldn't have been as peaceful as her face made her look.

When the taxi broke down the third time, the engine cut out with a sound that seemed to me as close as an old car could get to a death rattle. We were still climbing when it boiled over and sputtered to a stop, but at that point we'd come out of the narrow part of the pass and were on the far side of the mountain, with a view of the Kozani plain below that stretched all the way to the high mountains on the Yugoslav-Albanian border. The driver stood there beside his taxi gazing out at the view as though it was infinitely fascinating, then turned back abruptly and opened the near side of the hood.

"We're lucky again," he finally said. "The engine block hasn't cracked open as far as I can tell, so the problem must still be confined to the cooling system."

"Is that an easy problem to solve on top of this mountain?" I asked, keeping my voice cool.

The driver looked at me. "Everything is easy in this country if you know what you're doing and if you have a little patience," the driver said.

"Well how long do you think it will take for you to fix the cooling system?"

"Let's get one thing straight," the driver said. "I'm a taxi driver, not an automobile mechanic."

"O.K.," I said. "You are what you are. But where are we likely to find an automobile mechanic where we happen to have ended up? We haven't even come across another automobile on this side of the mountain."

The driver lowered the hood flap. "As your good fate and my good fate would have it, we happen to have ended up not far from a village where there's a man who is a master like no other when it comes to fixing motors of all kinds."

"What village is that?"

"The village of Kastania. Where you said you wanted to go."

The man took my hand and led me a few feet up the road, then pointed up the mountainside.

"That sheepfold up there belongs to the village of Kastania. So where we happen to have ended up is very close to where we wanted to be. Not more than an hour away by foot."

The village turned out to be an hour and a half away, but it was a fairly pleasant climb getting there, at least when we decided to leave the road and take a shortcut through the forest of pine and spruce and chestnut trees, the taxi driver choosing a path for us up ahead and using a stick he'd found to flail the underbrush every now and then like a safari guide. The air was certainly clear on that mountain, and there was a breeze that brought down the smell of thyme from the clearing where the forest gave way to cultivated plots on the lower edge of the village. It was a village that had been cut into the mountain at a steep angle, one house on top of the other so that every one of them had its own clear view of the landscape below, each built out of stone gathered from the surrounding slopes and each with a terrace at the side or the back covered by thick vine leaves for shade, already heavy with grape clusters ripening for a later season.

Our driver took it as another sign of the gods' favor that the old man named in the note our waiter had given us the night before proved to be the mechanical genius the driver had in mind soliciting for help. We found the old man at work in the courtyard of his home at the top edge of the village. He was a thin man with white hair that was turning yellow and with a strong jaw that needed a shave, and he had a thin gray mustache that was shaped like his son's. He was wearing thick rimless glasses that made his eyes seem twice the normal size, and he was sitting on a straw chair that had its legs cut short to keep him close to the ground. The courtyard around him had an earthen floor, and it was walled in by things meant to provide the essentials of life so that there would be no need to go outside to survive in case of attack by man or nature: an oven for bread, a cistern for water, a pit for treading grapes beside two large barrels for holding the year's wine, a goat in the shed for milk, a barrel of olive oil, a walled plot for growing vegetables, a fig tree and a lemon tree and an almond tree. One side of the courtyard had a workbench along it and a collection of tools and parts from old machines that would have made my father's mouth water.

When we looked in through the doorway, the man was bent over a container he was making out of meshed wire to trap bees by enticing them to drink from a dish of syrup at the bottom of the container they got to by crawling through a tiny tubed hole in the mesh they were meant never to find again when they tried to get out. He had a container of that kind protecting each cluster of grapes that hung from the roof of his arbor, and all but the newest had become a mass grave for marauding bees born with the bad luck to cross the old man's threshold in search of ripening vines.

"I told you the man is a genius," the taxi driver said while the man was slowly making his way through the note from his son. "Just make sure you stay on the right side of him, because he has been known to turn mean, as you can see from the way he treats the same bees that bring him honey on the far side of his wall."

The man stood up suddenly and bellowed for his wife to come out of the back room, then disappeared inside with the note. He came back out with a table and set it in the center of the courtyard, then his wife appeared with a plate of cheese and another of quartered tomatoes in olive oil, and then the man came out again with a liter bottle of wine and a tray of small glasses. The wife had grown to look like her husband over the years, much heavier but with the same yellow-white hair, her own kind of strong chin, and glasses that made her eyes larger than life. She spread herself on her straw-seated chair near the doorway with her hands folded in her lap and gazed at us endlessly as though our light skin and hair made us creatures carved out of gold. After I'd paid our driver what we owed him and he'd gone off with the old man to see what might be done to revive the dead taxi we'd abandoned on the main road below, the woman brought out another chair and made Magda come over and sit next to her so that she could touch her hair and her skin and talk to her about the wonder of it. Magda was wearing my T-shirt, and when she put her head back at one point and raised her arm to rub the day's tiredness out of the back of her neck, the old woman reached over suddenly to touch the hair under Magda's arm as though testing silk.

"This is good," she whispered. "They tell me the modern girls in other countries cut this off. But once you're married you'll learn that it helps to remind your husband of what there is lower down."

Magda let her arm drop. "I'm already married," she said.

The woman looked surprised. "Where did you leave your husband?"

"There," Magda said. "That's my husband."

The woman stared at me. "This young man?"

"He's not so young," Magda said. "He just looks that young because he's Danish."

"Well, may he live long for you," the woman said. "And may his hair always be as gold as wheat so long as yours stays copper."

The sun was down by the time the old man came back. He said that he hadn't quite fixed the taxi but he'd made the motor work so that the driver could turn around and coast down to Veria with the help of at least one gear to keep his breaks from burning out on him, assuming God was with him all the way. The man sat down at the table in the courtyard and had himself a glass of resinated wine from what was left of the bottle he'd brought out earlier, then filled it up from the barrel in his storage shed and poured out a glass for each of us and another for himself. He signaled his wife with a nod of his head and she went inside to get dinner ready.

"So," he said, clicking Magda's glass and then mine. "Welcome. And to the good health of all of us. God knows we'll need it the way they're getting things organized in Athens."

Magda took a long swallow of wine. I could tell she was in a good mood now.

"Tell us about Athens," she said. "How are they organizing things in Athens?"

The old man studied her. "I may have been born in this village and I may die here without going anywhere else, but sometimes I see things others don't. And what I see right now is that they're organizing things for war."

"You really think there will be a war?" Magda said. "Who needs to attack a country as small as ours?"

The old man looked across at her above his glasses. "Why else do you see troops moving up and down the road out there all the time? Truckload after truckload going up full and coming back empty? And mostly at night or early in the morning?"

"Where are they moving to?" I asked.

"Who knows?" the old man said. "But they're not moving soldiers up and down this road just to chase brigands, I can tell you that. Those that are moving up are heading for the border."

"Which border is that?" Magda said.

"Who knows?" the old man said. "Albania, Yugoslavia, Bulgaria. We have plenty of borders in our neighborhood."

"But they don't all belong to enemies," Magda said.

"Of course they do," the old man said. "Choose any one of them. One's worse than the next."

"Well, I hope you're wrong about going to war," Magda said. "But you may be right. Things are never good when the army takes over your country and a general ends up running it."

The old man dipped his head. "You're wrong there, my sweet thing. It doesn't make any difference who's running the country. Metaxas, Venizelos, Pangalos, whoever it may be. They'll all go to war if you give them the chance, and the rest of us will have nothing to say about it. But I'll tell you one thing. They'll never get to me or anybody else in this village because the Turks didn't and the Allies during the Great War didn't and our own people didn't when they went off to Asia Minor. We're a fortress up here."

His wife came out with a huge platter of mixed vegetables cooked in olive oil.

"Take that dish for example," the old man said. "You could live on a dish like that for a year. And if you got to the end of the year still in good health, you could throw in the goat as an offering to the God who got you there."

The woman set a clean plate in front of each of us. "Don't listen to him," she said. "After a while the wine turns his brain into feta cheese."

The old man looked at her. "Just because I offered you a blank piece of paper that gives you the freedom to leave this house anytime you want to doesn't mean you're free to insult me in front of foreigners."

The woman brought her chair to the table. "What kind of freedom is it when the truth is an insult?" she asked Magda and me.

"Freedom is anything you make of it," the old man mumbled. "At this particular moment, you're free to button up your mouth."

"And you're free to keep yours open and talk nonsense about slaughtering our goat."

The old man looked at her, then must have decided that their private war had been going on too long to matter to them or anybody else, so he filled a glass for his wife and clicked it with his own.

"To the modern woman," he said. "May her mouth always be open to speak whatever the devil puts in it and may the goat always remain safe enough to die in his pen."

By the fruit course the old man was beginning to nod to himself, no longer at all argumentative, more and more slow-voiced and philosophical to the point where I couldn't understand a thing he said. When Magda finally tried to hide a yawn with her hand, the woman took her by the arm and led her into the cottage, then came out to say that it was time for all of us to go to bed.

It turned out that there was only one bedroom, in fact, only one room in the cottage besides the kitchen, and that room had a raised platform at the back where the old couple slept, and on the level below, split by the fireplace, two stone benches built against the wall. The stone benches were covered by rugs and small pillows, and Magda was already asleep on one of them, under a white hand-woven cover. That left the other bench for me. I was so groggy by then from the wine and the talk and the day's traveling, that I just lay down dressed as I was and turned to the wall so that I was actually half asleep when the old woman arrived with my own woven cover and a pitcher of water I was meant to use for washing up in the kitchen sink. She decided to leave the pitcher on the ground at my feet, then took off my shoes and spread the cover over the lower half of me, tucked in one side of it, and patted my cheek.

By late afternoon of the following day, Magda had become restless. I could tell something was wrong even earlier, when we went out for a morning walk, because she seemed to have lost the excitement about our village that she'd shown when we were coming into it. The truth was that we couldn't find much that was new to see there once we'd climbed up and down the few main streets and some of the passageways between the houses, because the houses were walled in, protected from the street and as much as possible from neighbors. And it wasn't the time of day when people sat out to greet those going by, which might have given us a chance to ask for a look into their courtyards so that we could admire all they'd built there to keep themselves isolated from the winter and those fellow villagers they didn't care to see. But what was really bothering Magda was our own isolated cottage on the upper edge of the village. She said she'd woken up in the middle of the night and had hardly slept after that.

"I don't think I can stand another night in there," she said. "I ended up feeling claustrophobic. Imprisoned. And the old man snoring half the night."

"Well, I can't say that I'd choose to sleep on stone if I could avoid it."

"It just isn't fair for a newly married couple like us to have to sleep that way. I couldn't even touch you with my feet. And you'd be surprised how much like hands one's feet can become when they have to."

"I guess I wouldn't be surprised," I said. "Not anymore."

"I mean, he talks about how secure he is and how he lives his own life, and maybe in a way he's right, but how free is that old woman to choose how she lives? Or even the old man himself?"

"They both seem to me to be living pretty much the way they want to."

"Maybe. But do they really have the freedom to choose some other way? And what about the freedom to think about things beyond their village and all the enemies they believe are out there?"

When we got back to our cottage at mid-morning, we tried to organize a picnic lunch that would take us not only outside our cottage but someplace clear of the village. The old woman refused to hear of it. We were her guests for all meals, she said, and anyway it wouldn't be safe to go wandering very far from the village except maybe on the road that joined the main Kozani road lower down, because there were still brigands crossing the high ridge behind the village and sometimes Gypsies and other migrant groups looking for anything they could steal. I didn't know anything about brigands, but I'd had enough experience with Gypsies to believe that they could mean trouble when they hadn't settled in to help work the land somewhere, so I convinced Magda we had to stay home at least that first day.

During the afternoon, once siesta time was over, I sat in the courtyard helping the old man make more bee-trap containers to protect his grapes, neither of us saying much to each other because it turned out that talk for him came only with wine late in the day. Magda chose to lie on her stone bench and read while the light still held inside. And when she came out, she sat at the far end of the courtyard with her knees propped up to go on reading. That clearly bewildered the old woman, who tried to get her to sew something out of the material she herself was working on, then retreated to her chair outside the doorway with one eye on what she was creating in her lap and the other on Magda, as though expecting her to jump up any minute and start climbing the grape arbor to prove that she was a young bride who had truly gone out of her mind. While I was sitting on the ground concentrating on the bee-trap between my crossed legs, I felt Magda's hands kneading my shoulders. Then they slipped down to caress my chest for a second.

"Can we go for another walk?" she said in German.

"Where to?"

"Where we can be alone."

"That is not easy," I said

"Come. We will find a place."

The old man looked up from his work. "What language is that?"

"My husband's native language," Magda said. "We practice so that I'll be able to please his family when we next visit them."

"That's a good thing," the man said. "The only foreign language I know is some Turkish, and what good is that to anyone?"

"It's not always a bad thing to know your enemy's language," I said to him. "The point is—"

Magda pinched my shoulder hard. I gathered that she wasn't in the mood for another political discussion or even for polite conversation.

"I don't know what the point is," I said.

I handed the man my half-finished bee-trap and thanked him for teaching me how to make the thing. He took off his glasses to look at me as I stood up, then put them back on again. Magda went inside to pick up the shoulder bag that had our money in it. When she came out, she was also carrying the blue jackets we'd bought in Kavalla. She said we might need them after the sun went down and handed them to me, then she told the woman that we were going down to the village store to buy some soap.

"But we have soap," the woman said.

"Special soap," Magda said. "To keep my hair copper."

The woman studied her. Then she made a face that had a coy smile in it which said she understood, more or less, that this must be a woman thing that foreigners did.

When we were on the path outside, Magda sighed and took my arm.

"I couldn't wait to get out of there," she said. "I wasn't even reading the last hour or so. I was sitting there plotting."

"Plotting what?"

"Our escape from prison. I can't bear to stay there any longer."

"Well, we don't have much choice at this point, do we?"

"Of course we have a choice," Magda said. "We always have a choice. You must have learned that by now."

"I mean I don't see how we can just run out on them the first day we're there as their guests."

"But we don't belong to them. Or to their village or to anybody else. That's how we've chosen to live now, isn't it? And this is my plot to set us free again."

Her plot came down to a simple thing. We would make sure that we didn't drink as much wine with dinner as we had the previous night but that our hosts drank even more, and at some point before dawn, when we were sure they were both sound asleep, we would leave enough money on the kitchen table to buy them a vacation in Veria and then slip out and walk down to the main road to wait for the early bus to Kozani that we'd missed the day before. I still couldn't help feeling guilty about running out on the old couple like that, but not guilty enough so to make an issue out of it, and my going along with the idea clearly made Magda lighthearted. She took my hand and made me skip down those narrow stone streets to her step as though teaching me some new dance that had come into her head, and every time we came across somebody with an open court-yard door, she would wave as we went by and sing out a "good evening" in the hope that she could draw whoever was in there outside to see what crazy dress and manners the young foreigners who'd come to town were showing off now. And whenever it worked and somebody came to the doorway to look out, Magda would throw a kiss back over her shoulder, and wave again, but still not lose a beat of her skipping dance until we both ended up out of breath and had to stop and cling to each other to keep from falling flat.

At the general store we bought three bars of soap as a present for our hosts and some rusks and cheese to store in Magda's shoulder bag for the breakfast we planned to have once we were again on the road to Athens. The sun was low by then but not nearly gone, so we decided to walk to the lower end of the village and keep going on

the road out of town to see if we could find a place that was shel-
tered from the village but would give us a view of the Kozani plain
and the mountain ranges beyond it in case there were clouds enough
on the horizon to make it worthwhile watching the sun go down all
the way. When we cleared the lower houses, the afternoon breeze
turned cool and strong across the plotted fields there, and Magda
asked for her jacket. I put mine on too so that we matched each
other, and when we came to the beginning of the forest that the
road cut through, I drew her over to the edge of the road and kissed
her the way we did when we had more than just play in mind.

"Be patient," she said, breaking away. "We'll find the right place.
Where nobody can see or hear us."

What we found was a good ways below the village and on the far
side of the main road, a jutting rock ledge on the ridge of the
mountain overlooking the whole of the plain, the ledge close to the
road but with a stretch of tableland next to it that was covered with
grass and brush and had the remains of a circular sheepfold at its
outer edge. There was an abandoned hut that had once been part of
the sheepfold, its piled rock base broken through on the side opposite its doorway and a section of the reed roof missing. We crossed
the road to the rock ledge and moved along it to its high point, then
put our things down to sit there awhile and watch the sun go down.
There weren't enough clouds to make that very exciting, but you
could see every square in the checkerboard of small-crop fields that
made up the plain below and the spread of yellow wheat mile after
mile beyond that to the distant grazing land on the mountain slopes
to the northwest, where the rose light was now turning them purple
before it faded off into another country. Right below us there was
nothing but wild brushland down the length of the mountainside to
the plain, and though we could see a few of the village houses well
behind us, there was nothing to see above them but barren rock face
following the ridge of the mountain until it disappeared into the
blue-gray dusk. The wildness of that high country would have been
frightening if the village had been any farther away and the changing
light less pleasing to watch.

Magda stood up suddenly from her perch beside me and moved

back down the ledge to a point where it made a slight bend that gave you a clearer view of the valley to the south and the mountains we would have to cross on our way to Athens. She stood there so still as she surveyed that bit of territory ahead of us that I figured she wasn't just studying the view but had other things on her mind, so I let her stand there alone awhile, and when I finally got up to move down the ledge to join her, she didn't turn as I came up, but just kept on standing there, and then suddenly reached back and took my hand.

"Come," she said. "There isn't all that much time, because we shouldn't wait until it's dark before we start back home."

She led me back off the ledge and across to where there was a break in the crumbling sheepfold and through that into what was left of the abandoned hut. There was still the smell of goat or sheep dung in air, but not inside the hut, where the floor looked clean, as though it had been meant for the use of men rather than animals. Magda spread her jacket on the ground and then asked me for mine and spread that below hers. She knelt on her jacket to take off her blouse and her brassiere and laid them down on the ground behind her. I knelt down in front of her, and as I did so, she straightened her back.

"Your eyes look so hungry," she said under her breath. "Take it. This is your body as much as it is mine, so have your fill of it."

I did, as she did in turn, as though we were making up not only for the time we'd lost but some time we might lose in the future. I don't know how long we were in that hut, but it was long enough so that when we lay back to rest beside each other, I could see that the light beyond the open doorway was moving from dusk to night. When I turned to take a last slow taste of Magda's neck and shoulder, she suddenly sat up and held my head tight against her breast so that I couldn't move it.

"Oh my God," she said.

"What is it?"

"My shoulder bag. I left it up there where we were sitting to look out over the valley."

"Don't worry about it. I'll go find it."

But I could see that she was worried.

"It has everything in it. Our money and my jewelry."

"Don't worry about it."

I got my shirt and pants on and put my shoes on without any socks. When I got outside there was still just enough light to let me see where I was going, and as I made my way over to the rock ledge and along it toward the place we'd first settled, I couldn't see anything like a shoulder bag on the ground in that neighborhood. And getting up close didn't help. The thing was gone. I circled around the back of the ledge and followed it down to the point where Magda had stood to look south, though I knew that wasn't going to make any difference. The only thing in sight was a flock of sheep on a level below ours farther down the road that had brought us up from Veria. When I went back inside the hut, Magda was sitting there already dressed with her hands over her face. She took her hands away to see what my face told her.

"It's gone," she said.

"I don't understand it," I said, sitting down to finish dressing. "How could somebody come along and just take it? It couldn't have been a shepherd because we would have heard the sheep coming ahead of him."

"It was out in the open and close enough to the road so that anybody could have taken it who happened to go by and see it there."

"Well maybe it was somebody from the village. Maybe we can track it down when we get back."

"It could just as easily have been bandits or Gypsies or who knows what kind of people move through these mountains. It could have been somebody watching us out there the whole time."

"Well if it was people like that, maybe we're lucky they settled for the shoulder bag and left us alone," I said, trying to lighten her mood.

"We're not lucky," Magda said. "Everything valuable we have was in there. I don't have anything left but some clothes and a book in the other shoulder bag and we can't live on that."

"Maybe we can borrow some money. At least enough to get us to Athens."

"Who would lend us money in this godless place? They don't have enough money to live on themselves. And I can't go back home now to get more money and you can't either."

Magda sat there staring at the ground. I moved over beside her and put my arm around her. She let her head come against my shoulder.

"It's all my fault," she said. "I left it out there. I was thinking too much about our trip tomorrow and what was ahead of us. And now I don't know what we're going to do."

"We'll think of something," I said, holding her close. "We've got to. We'll go back to the cottage and rest up a little and see if the old couple has any advice to give us."

Magda shook her head. "I knew our luck would turn," she said. "We were just too happy and free. That's the way it always is."

"We'll be all right again," I said. "I know we will."

But I couldn't say what that conviction was based on except my young hope, and that didn't seem to work for Magda. She took her head off my shoulder and just sat there with her hands covering her face again because she'd begun to cry and didn't want me to see. I finally slipped out of my jacket and used the sleeve to wipe the dampness off her face, then made her stand up and follow me outside. The dusk was almost gone, and it was still too early for what was left of the waning moon, so we had to pick our way carefully along the path through the brush as we crossed to the grassy slope on our side of the main road. We'd just reached the edge of that when I heard a dog begin to bark a ways downhill on the level below ours where I'd seen the herd of sheep, and then suddenly the dog was over the ridge and onto our level, coming at us at top speed, a black-and-white dog who looked bigger than he was because he had a heavy coat. I told Magda to get behind me and stand still, not to move a finger. She let go of my hand and stayed where she was, as though fixed there by her fear, and when I yelled for her to get behind me, she still wouldn't move.

I don't know whether it was the mood that had come on her after we found the shoulder bag missing or this being her first time with a sheepdog, but something made her panic, so that when the dog kept coming at the same speed and showed no signs of stopping, barking as viciously as I'd heard any dog bark, Magda whirled suddenly and ran back along the path toward the sheepfold. The dog got to her before she'd taken ten steps, and by the time I got there she was on the ground and he had her leg in his teeth. I straddled the dog and got hold of his head, with one finger in his eye socket, and I managed to pull his jaw loose and stuff my jacket into his mouth. The shepherd was up at our level now whistling for his dog. I yelled for him to call the dog off, and the shepherd came running. I was about to lose my hold on the dog's jaw when he backed off with my jacket in his mouth. Magda was holding her leg, moaning, and the color had gone from her face. I pried her hand away to see the bite, and it was bad, the bite marks jagged and outlined in red and the blood coming freely now but not spurting as it might if an artery had been cut.

"Why didn't you call off your dog?" I yelled at the shepherd.

"I called him off when I could see," he said. "How was I to know he was after a girl instead of a wolf?"

He'd taken my jacket out of the dog's mouth and had sent the dog traveling with a wave of his crook. He came over and bent down to see the bite, then shook his head.

"I've seen worse," he said. "But I've seen better too."

Magda was lying there with her eyes closed and one hand against her mouth to make herself stop moaning. I touched her forehead, and it was wet. Then I took out my handkerchief and wiped the bite clean, and when the blood started coming right back, I padded the handkerchief and held it against the wound to stop the blood even though that made Magda cry out. I told the shepherd to help me off with my T-shirt so that I could keep my handkerchief against the wound, and when he had the shirt off me, I told him to tear it into strips. I touched Magda's forehead again.

"It's going to be all right," I said.

She opened her eyes and then closed them again, but that was enough to show me that she was still very scared, so I went on gently wiping her forehead. The shepherd handed me strips from my T-shirt, and I used those to bind the handkerchief against the wound, then put what strips were left over in my pocket to use when the wound had stopped bleeding completely. I got the shepherd to cross his hands with mine to make a chair for carrying Magda, and when he had that learned, I brought Magda up to a sitting position and put her arm around my neck so that we could ease our crossed hands under her and carry her out that way to the main road. She tried not to let her head fall back as we moved off, but she must have passed out at some point, because I could feel it bobbing against my neck, and when we reached the road and laid her down on the slanting shoulder, her eyes were still closed. I propped her head up with my jacket and wiped her forehead again with a strip of my T-shirt. Her breathing was too fast, but at least it was steady. She still had her eyes closed, and when I touched her forehead with my hand, it felt cold. I told the shepherd he would have to go for help, because I couldn't leave her there like that, and when he went off across the road heading up toward the village, I just sat there stroking Magda's forehead and praying that she would open her eyes and show me that she was going to be all right.

IT SEEMED THAT LUCK *WAS* TURNING BACK IN OUR *FAVOR AS* SOON as the shepherd left me to go for help, because he had barely disappeared into the forest heading for Kastania when an army transport truck came barreling out of the bend in the main road a short distance up the mountain. I got up from where I'd been kneeling beside Magda and vaulted into the center of the road, waving my arms like mad. The soldier behind the wheel just kept on coming as fast as that truck would let him, as if he thought me a maniac who'd come out of the forest naked to my waist to confront him with the fearlessness of the insane, but at the last minute he or the soldier in the cab beside him must have spotted Magda lying by the side of the road. He slammed on the brakes and veered to the far side to avoid running over either her or me. The truck skidded to a stop a full length past us, and the soldier sitting beside the driver stuck his head out of the window to look back. He had his rifle pointing out of the window at the sky.

"What the devil is the matter with you?" he yelled. "Are you looking to find your head separated from your neck just because you can't find a better place to fuck your girl than the middle of the road?"

"We need help," I yelled. "She's been bitten by a dog."

The soldier opened the door and climbed down. He left his rifle on the front seat.

"What kind of dog?" he said when he came up to me.

"What difference does it make?" I said. "A sheepdog."

The soldier went over to stand above Magda.

"I'll tell you what difference it makes," the soldier said. "It makes a difference if the dog has rabies. And that's a lot of difference, I can tell you that, though you might not think so being a foreigner."

"Well the dog didn't have rabies but it wasn't exactly tame either," I said.

Magda opened her eyes suddenly, then closed them again. The driver had climbed down now too and had come around the back of the truck to see what was happening. The soldier beside me knelt down to study the bandage I'd made, then looked up at the driver.

"We'd better get her to the camp doctor," he said. "You never know with these dogs up here. They're half wolf, and they could be full of poison."

"What will the camp doctor do for her?" the driver said. "I wouldn't let that doctor touch one of our women, let alone a foreigner who hasn't had the benefit of fighting off all the germs our women have known."

"She's not a foreigner," I said. "I'm the foreigner. And it doesn't make any difference what she is, in the name of God."

The soldier stood up. "He's right. Foreigner or not, it's better that she see our doctor at this point in her life than that she die here in the road. So let's get her into the truck."

And that's what we did, the three of us making a kind of stretcher out of our arms and raising her up to slide her into the empty back of the truck. We laid her out on one of the benches along the side that they used for transporting troops. The back of the truck had a canvas roof, but I began to shiver as soon as we were in there, so I put on my cotton jacket, teeth marks and all. I sat on the bench with Magda's head in my lap. The driver got down and brought a knapsack around to hand up to the soldier. The soldier put the knapsack gently under Magda's wounded leg to keep it raised, then took off his army jacket and spread it over both legs.

"I want that back when we get into the camp," he said. "Otherwise they'll have me arrested for being out of uniform."

He climbed down and closed the back of the truck.

The moon was up by the time we reached the camp outside Veria, because the driver took his time winding his way down the road, trying to keep the ride as smooth as he could with some effect but not enough to keep Magda from moaning again and, when we hit a bad bump, crying out in a way that cut right into my gut. Partway down, when there was a break in the steep hairpin turns as we crossed a short plateau, she opened her eyes and spoke to me, asked me where we were, and I lied to her, told her we were on our way to a clinic in Kozani. I couldn't face her knowing that we were heading back in the opposite direction, at least not yet. She did her best to smile, then closed her eyes again, and I bent to kiss her forehead, which was hot now, as though she had a fever. I brushed the damp hair back off her forehead and told her not to try to talk, it was going to be all right, she needn't worry now because once we got to the clinic we would get her leg fixed up in a hurry and be on the road to Athens again. The way I said that didn't sound right to me, but Magda didn't show any signs of hearing the lie in it.

The camp was on the far side of Veria, at the edge of the plain we'd crossed to get up to the town. It looked like a very temporary army camp to me, put up for maneuvers of some kind, because it consisted mostly of tents, with a few huts here and there made out of plywood and metal sheeting. The driver got through the camp gate with barely a pause by telling the guard that he had wounded personnel in back from the training exercise in the mountains, and he drove right up to the door of the hut that I figured served as the field hospital. The other soldier came around back to collect his army jacket, and he told me to stay put where we were because that hut was no place for a woman to enter, given the half-naked and diseased bodies that went in and out of there, which was why he planned to bring the doctor out to have a look at Magda in the back of the truck.

The doctor was a man in his fifties, bald and heavy and slow, and he sweated a lot. The two soldiers helped him climb up into the back of the truck, then handed him the kerosene lantern he was carrying and an army flashlight. The doctor told them to go off and get themselves something to eat. As he knelt to take the bandage off Magda's leg, I smelled garlic coming from the huge wet stains under his arms. He put the flashlight beam on Magda's wound, then shook his head.

"This is not good," he said, looking up at me. "This needs stitches. External and maybe internal. And there are certainly damaged nerves. But the first thing it needs is to be cleaned by a hot iron."

"A hot iron?" I said.

"A poker. Anything that can stand the heat. That's what we do in the field for bad bites."

"Well, how about just cleaning it up with alcohol so that we can move on someplace where we aren't in the field."

The doctor was studying the wound. "And she'll need rabies shots," he said.

"But the dog wasn't rabid," I said. "It was just a sheepdog protecting sheep."

"Still," the doctor said. "I don't know what happens in your country but in this country you can't ever be sure enough with rabies."

"I'm certain the dog was all right," I said. "I'm willing to go back and find him. Bring him in on a leash if I have to."

"That won't be necessary," the doctor said. "I don't have the rabies shots out here anyway. And I don't have the equipment to operate on a wound like this one. We're just a first aid station and dispensary, not a hospital."

"Well then, how about just cleaning it up so it doesn't get infected and I'll take care of the rest."

The doctor looked up at me again. "That's what I have in mind doing. Are you some kind of trained nurse? Or maybe you'd like me to be the nurse and you be the doctor?"

"Fine," I said. "Go ahead. Do what you have to do. I'd just like to make sure my wife doesn't have to suffer a lot and stays alive, that's all."

"Your wife, as you call her, is going to be fine if you take care of her and get her to a hospital," the doctor said. "I'll just sterilize this wound with a little peroxide and clean it up with a little gasoline, and then you can take her along to the hospital for everything else that's necessary."

"Gasoline?" I said.

"It's the best thing for cleaning dead skin, and I've had plenty of experience with it in the field, so don't you worry your young blond head about it."

Magda suddenly sat up. "Please don't let him do anything to my leg," she said softly. "I just want something for the pain."

"Have you got anything for the pain?" I said to the doctor.

"I have aspirin," the doctor said. "And I have morphine. But the morphine is not for civilians. The morphine is for wounded soldiers."

"Can't you make an exception? Just this once? In the name of God. Don't you see how she's suffering?"

The doctor stood up. "You don't want me use gasoline which is legal, but you want me to use morphine which is illegal. Do you understand what position you're putting me in?"

"All right, we don't have time to argue. You can use the gasoline if you use the morphine as well."

"Don't let him do anything to my leg," Magda said, her eyes closed again. "Please."

I stroked her forehead. "Don't worry. It's going to be all right."

I helped the doctor climb down from the truck and stood there waiting. He came back with his black bag and two bottles, a brown one with peroxide in it and a soda bottle with gasoline in it. When he knelt down to begin cleaning Magda's wound, I put my hand on his shoulder.

"First the morphine," I said.

The doctor looked up at me. "Christ and the Holy Virgin," he said. "What's the matter with you?"

"I just don't believe in causing people pain," I said. "It's a weakness we have in my country."

The doctor sat back and opened his black bag. He took out a syringe and a small bottle with a rubber cap on it.

"You'll have to roll her over and bare her bottom for me," he said.

Magda opened her eyes again.

"This will help the pain," I whispered to her. "Be brave for just a minute."

I sat down on the bench and put her head in my lap again, then eased her over on her side, cushioning her head and chest against me. She moaned as she turned, but she didn't resist. I reached down and pulled her skirt up in back and held it out of the way. The doctor lowered the band on her panties to bare one buttock and jabbed the needle in. Magda gave a little cry and shivered.

"You'll have to change her underclothes when you can," he said. "She's made something of a mess."

I pushed her skirt down again and let her lie where she was. When the doctor got his roll of cotton out and went for the peroxide bottle, I reached out and touched his hand.

"Not yet," I said. "If you don't mind, we'll wait for the morphine to take hold. That's how we do it back home."

The doctor gazed at me, then sat down on the bench opposite to dab his forehead with a tuft of cotton.

The morphine took hold quickly but not all the way, so that Magda still had to show how brave she was while the doctor worked on her, pressing her head hard against my belly as I held her and clutching my arm when a wave of pain came through the morphine, but hardly letting out a sound. When the doctor had her bandaged up, I could feel her relax, and at some point while I was holding her there and the doctor was packing up his things, she went out completely. I thanked the doctor for his help and asked him what we owed him, though I had no idea how I would pay him if he wanted it that moment in cash. He looked up at me and told me to forget the payment, as a foreigner I could consider it all courtesy of General Metaxas. So I asked him if General Metaxas would mind if we borrowed a blanket from the army to wrap Magda in and assigned the truck driver or his companion to watch over her while I went off to find some way of transporting her into the city. He said he thought that might be arranged. Then he gave my cheek a pat, picked up his bag and sat down heavily on the back of the truck to edge himself off onto the ground with his two bottles in one hand and his bag in the other.

I didn't feel right about going off without telling Magda what I was up to, but I couldn't bring myself to wake her, and in view of her condition and our having no money, I couldn't see how I had any choice at that point but to get her to a hospital in Salonika and worry later about what that might do to our long-range plans. So I hitched a ride into Veria with a group of soldiers going in for a night on the town, and I headed for the main square to look for the taxi that had taken us to Kastania, because I figured that was one driver I might count on to wait for his payment until I got hold of some cash. The taxi was nowhere to be seen, but the driver was sitting in a cafe on the side of the square where his taxi used to be parked. When I told him the story of what we'd run into on the mountainside below Kastania and how important it was that I find some way of getting my wife to the hospital in Salonika as soon as possible, he said that was no problem, it only involved something like a two-hour ride at that time of night, in fact the only problem was working out some way of arriving there, which was unfortunately no longer a matter under his control because his taxi was now back in the hands of his unprincipled brother-in-law for the purpose of seeing if that godless man might finally fix the cooling system that he had already failed to fix twice that year.

"Well, do you know of anybody else who might get me to the city at this time of night?"

"I know of only one other person in this town besides myself who would be able to do a thing like that at this hour without making you buy his automobile first, and that is a person who has a limousine that's big enough to be an ambulance but who happens to be somebody we can't ask for help."

"Why can't we ask him?"

"Because he's my brother-in-law. And at the moment he and I are not speaking."

"Well you don't have to speak to him," I said. "I'll do all the talking."

"Fine. And who will do the driving?"

"Can't your brother-in-law drive?"

"Of course he can drive. It's just that he's not a driver, he's the owner of a garage. What used to be the best garage in town."

"Well, in the name of God, can't he make an exception? This is an emergency case."

"Of course he can make an exception," the driver said. "The question is, will a man of his nature make an exception, and that is a question I obviously cannot answer. You'll have to get the answer yourself."

He took out his box of cigarettes and removed the white paper lining, then wrote out a phone number on the paper and handed it over without looking at me.

The brother-in-law turned out to be a reasonable man, older than the taxi driver, but with the same drawn look to his face, as though he was constantly sucking in his cheeks on a cigarette even when not smoking. He also had a tic that made him squint his eyes as though in pain whenever money was mentioned, as I found out when he picked me up as agreed near the kiosk on the far side of the square from where the taxi driver hung out. His limousine was a long black De Soto with a bright grill up front that looked like a giant shark's teeth, and when I climbed in back and asked him how much he wanted for the truly invaluable service he was providing so late at night, he squinted at me and said money was simply not a question to be raised in an emergency, though as a friend of his brother-in-law, I might understandably think otherwise. Since I didn't have any money on me and wasn't sure how I was going to come by any in the immediate future, I decided to let the subject die. When we came up to the camp gate, I told him to tell the guard that he was serving as an ambulance to remove the wounded personnel that had arrived earlier in the evening. The driver told that to the guard, and when the guard started cranking up the field phone to get to higher authority, the driver said that the son of an important foreigner was involved and there was no time to make an issue of the situation, because that might get both the guard and the driver in serious trouble with authorities even higher than those in the camp. That made the guard come over and look in back. He studied me, then waved the De Soto on through.

I found Magda still asleep. With the help of the truck driver and his buddy, we were able to lay her out in the back of the De Soto without her coming to enough to feel what was happening, and she slept right through the ride into the city. So did I, eyes open or not, my head bouncing against the back of the seat and the side window as the driver used his new status to honk his way around every stationary or moving object we came across at a speed that gave no quarter to the constantly changing surface of the road. When we got to the outskirts of Salonika, he began to use the horn as though it was a siren, a steady drone whether there was anybody in front of us or not, and he kept to the center of the road all the way into Vardar Square and out the other side. I didn't know anything about hospitals in that city, so I told him to head for the biggest and best he knew.

"That would be the Municipal Hospital above the cemetery," he said. "They gave my mother a new hip there that would be good enough to get her up Mount Olympus if she had any need to climb mountains at the age of eighty-five."

As we drove up to the hospital, I turned to find Magda lying there in back wide awake.

"Have we reached Kozani?" she said.

"We've reached the hospital," I said

"What hospital?"

"The Municipal Hospital," I said. "It's supposed to be the biggest and the best."

"Oh my God," Magda said. "You've brought me back to Salonika?"

"I had to. There was no other choice. You need an operation."

"Oh my God," Magda said.

"Please don't say it that way," I said. "It's going to work out fine."

"No it isn't," Magda said. "How can it?"

I didn't have an answer to that, so I reached back and took her hand and just held it. Magda began to cry.

"I couldn't help it," I said. "There just wasn't anything else I could do."

She shook her head. "It's over then. Our vacation and our trip to Athens and everything else."

"No it isn't," I said. "You mustn't think that."

"But how can we go to Athens now?" Magda said.

"We just can't worry about that right this minute," I said. "First we have to get you well, and then we'll figure something out."

"My God," Magda said.

The driver had pulled up to the emergency entrance and was sitting there tapping the steering wheel with his palm. I let go of Magda's hand.

"I'll be out in a minute," I said. "Please be good and try to go back to sleep."

"My God, my God, my God," Magda said quietly, her eyes on the roof of the car.

Just inside the emergency entrance there were three orderlies sitting around the front of a desk sharing an ashtray. I told them what had happened to Magda and what the army doctor said might still be needed, but I told them no rabies shots were necessary because the dog was just a sheepdog. Two of them went off with a wheelchair to bring Magda in, and the third moved his chair around to the back of the desk and signaled me to sit down. He was a pudgy young man in his thirties with thin hair plastered across the top of his head, and he had a long fingernail on his little finger, which meant that he had arrived at a station in life that limited his responsibility to paperwork and that precluded menial tasks.

"You're a doctor then," the orderly said with a half-smile as he brought a clipboard out of the front drawer of the desk.

"Of course I'm not a doctor," I said.

"I thought you might be a doctor because you seemed to think you know whether the patient needs rabies shots or not."

"I may not be a doctor, but I know the dog involved," I said.

The orderly adjusted the blank form on his clipboard.

"In any case," he said. "May I have the patient's name?"

"Magda Sevillas," I said.

"Address?"

"25th of March Street, Harilaou."

"The number on that street?"

"I don't remember the number," I said.

The orderly looked up from his clipboard. "May I ask who is responsible for this patient?"

"I am," I said.

"But you don't know where she lives?"

"I know where she lives. I just don't remember the number."

"And what is your relation to the patient?"

"I'm a friend," I said. "A very close friend."

"That is not enough," the orderly said. "This form should be signed by a relative."

"Well, I'm close enough to her to be a relative."

The orderly looked at me. "You either are a relative or you are not a relative. There is no such thing as being close enough to be a relative."

I stood up and leaned forward on the desk. "You mean you can't admit an emergency case in this hospital unless you have the signature of a relative? Even in the case of an accident?"

"Of course we can admit the patient," the orderly said. "We just can't release the patient."

"Well, can't we worry about the release later? At the moment I just want to make sure she gets the best care possible."

"The patient will certainly get the best care possible," the orderly said sweetly. "It is simply a question of who will pay for the best care possible."

"I will see to that," I said. "I swear."

"There is no need to swear. You will simply have to find a relative to sign this form. Though I will accept your signature for the time being."

"Where do I sign?"

"First I will need your identity card."

"I can't believe this," I said. "I don't have an identity card. I'm a foreigner."

"You may not be able to believe this, but may I ask you how I am supposed to believe that you will see to the payment of the hospital bill for this Magda Sevillas when you're a foreigner without an identity card who doesn't know the lady's address?"

"I have a foreign identity card," I said. "I thought you meant a Greek identity card."

I took out my wallet and gave the orderly my lifesaving certificate. While he was studying it, the other orderlies came in with Magda in a wheelchair and headed toward the elevator. They had stretched Magda's leg out in front of her, and I could see that she was in pain again, because she was biting her lower lip. I rushed over and grabbed the arm of the orderly pushing the chair.

"Where are you taking her?"

"To the emergency room. Where do you think?"

"I'm coming too."

The orderly looked toward the desk. His friend there raised his chin and eyebrows in a negative gesture.

"Only relatives go to the emergency room," the orderly behind the desk said. "You're not a relative."

"I'm coming too," I said. "You have no right to stop me."

The other orderly on the far side of the wheelchair came around and held my arm.

"Don't make things more difficult," he said. "You're wasting valuable time."

Magda reached out and touched my free arm.

"I'll be all right," she said. "You wait down here for me. I won't let them keep me any longer than they absolutely have to."

I didn't know what to do. Magda took my hand and held it to her cheek, then let it go. The orderly behind the chair pushed her into the elevator and waited with his back turned for his friend to come in behind him. As the door closed, Magda turned her head to see me standing there.

I went over to the desk and sat down again. The man handed me the form to sign, and when I'd signed it, I asked for my lifesaving certificate.

"If you don't mind, I will keep that for the time being," the orderly said. "You may have it back when you produce a relative to sign the form under your signature."

"In the name of God, what do you do in cases where there are no relatives?" I said.

"In the name of God, I don't understand what you're saying," the orderly said. "Whatever may happen in your country, in this country there are always relatives."

I signed the form without looking it over because I couldn't have read what it said anyway. I felt drained now, somehow defeated even though I'd gotten Magda where she had to be, and it depressed me even more to sit at that desk facing the orderly sitting behind it. When he leaned back in his chair and lit a cigarette, I told him I was going off to find a relative of Miss Sevillas, so I'd appreciate it if he told her not to worry, I'd be back as soon as possible.

The orderly smiled. "I will certainly tell her when I have the chance, but there's no need for you to hurry back. If this emergency is what you say it is, Miss Sevillas won't be coming down here tonight or tomorrow night either."

That depressed me even more, as I figured it was meant to. When I got outside, I found the driver resting his head against the back of the seat with one arm crooked out of the window and a cigarette in his fingers that had an ash on it longer than the smoldering butt that was left. I climbed in the front beside him.

"They've taken her to the emergency room," I said. "I don't know when she'll be out."

The driver looked at his watch. "It's after midnight," he said. "I'm willing to wait an hour or two, but I don't think I can wait through the night. I didn't even tell my wife where I was going."

"The problem is, I also have to find a relative," I said. "If you can stay with me until we find my wife's aunt and bring her back here, then we can settle on what I owe you and you can go home."

The driver squinted. "Please. The question of what you owe me has been settled. You owe me nothing, except maybe the cost of the gasoline. Please understand that I do not make my living as an ambulance driver, or as a driver of any kind, and my character is not to be confused with that of my cheap-minded brother-in-law."

Magda's aunt was not at her home on the road heading up to the village of Kapudjida. I came back to the De Soto and climbed in front to sit there staring out of the windshield while the driver smoked another cigarette. There was no way I could escape the feeling that our luck, Magda's and mine, had now soured, though I still didn't want to believe it. And I couldn't see any way out now except to go up to her own house and tell her parents what had happened to her, unless I went to mine, and that wouldn't solve the problem of getting her released from the hospital, quite aside from the damage it would do to my morale. The only outside chance I saw at that time of night was checking to see if the aunt might be visiting her sister, and if she was, somehow getting her to talk to me alone.

I got the driver to turn back to the 25th of March Street and to park down the road a ways from Magda's house, then got out and crossed over to the narrow street beside her house where there was a stretch of rose garden leading up to the porch that ran the length of the house on that side. The garden had a low stone wall around it, topped by a grating half my height. The side street was deserted, so I cut across it to the garden wall, stepped up on it and swung over the fence on my arms to land on my ass between two rosebushes. I crawled over to the porch and waited up against that. When it looked as though nobody had heard me, I eased up to one of the windows along the porch and looked in. There were at least five people in there, and I recognized two of them as Magda's mother and her aunt. It looked cozy inside the house. They had food spread out on a table in the middle, and people were still eating off plates on side-tables spread around the room, talking to each other in low voices, nobody laughing as they might at a party, but talking amiably, full of understanding gestures. I hadn't eaten anything since noon, but seeing that quiet homey atmosphere didn't stir my appetite. In fact, it made me feel completely outside of things. I crawled back off the porch and went into a crouch to make my way back between the rosebushes to the fence, then vaulted over it into the side street, this time landing on hard ground but at least on my feet.

The driver was taking a snooze when I got back to the car. I decided not to wake him. I also decided that there was no way I could bring myself to walk up to Magda's front door and just announce who I was and then launch into the story of where I'd been all this time with the daughter of the house. That meant that I had no choice but to wait for Magda's aunt to come out and head home, if that was what she had in mind doing sometime before dawn. So I sat on the sidewalk catercornered to Magda's house and waited. It must have been close to an hour before she came out, and when she did, she was with another woman. The two of them turned up the street heading for Harilaou. I went back to the car and shook the driver awake.

"I've found the aunt," I said. "Only she's with somebody else and I'd just as soon wait until she's alone to give her the bad news."

I told him to follow the two ladies up ahead but to keep his distance, and if they split up at some point, to follow the one whose hair was gray and in a bun. The driver turned on the ignition without saying anything, I think because he was still half asleep. We cruised along behind the two ladies to the top of the 25th of March Street, at which point they paused and then separated, Magda's aunt turning right to head toward the road that took her home. I told the driver to follow her to the right and then park for a moment while I got out. I caught up to the aunt as she was crossing the street to turn uphill but I decided I'd better circle around her and come at her from the front so as not to scare her, and though I did that, it didn't keep her from stopping dead in her tracks.

"Holy Virgin, what are you doing here?" she said.

"Magda's had an accident," I said. "We need your help."

"What kind of accident?"

"If you can come with me, I'll tell you all about it on the way," I said. "My car is down the street."

"Where is Magda? You must tell me."

"She's in the hospital, but she's all right now. You don't have to worry."

The aunt looked grim, not at all happy to see me, but she came with me without saying another word. As we crossed to the De Soto, she asked me where I'd gotten myself a dangerous car like that one. I told her that I'd hired it in Veria.

"In Veria? What in the name of God were you doing in Veria?"

"Well, that's part of what I have to tell you. But I'd better begin at the beginning."

I didn't do that, partly to protect my own privacy but mostly to protect Magda's. On the way to the hospital, I told the aunt about our visit to Veria and Kastania and our stay with the old couple in the village and about being robbed of a shoulder bag and attacked by a sheepdog during our outing below the village, but I didn't say anything about my finding Magda on Thassos or our days on the road or anything else about our personal life. And the aunt didn't ask for more details than I gave her, I suppose because she was the kind of woman who felt it wasn't her business to hear more, at least not from me. When we got out of the car at the emergency entrance, I explained about the form she would have to sign inside, and I asked her if I could borrow some money on behalf of Magda and me to pay for the hired car.

"How much do you need?" she said.

"I don't know," I said. "He insists that I pay him only for the gasoline he used."

She opened her pocketbook and picked through it. "This ought to be enough," she said.

I went over and handed the money to the driver.

"This is too much," he said, squinting. "Half of this is too much. I absolutely refuse to be considered a professional driver on a scale with my you-know-who."

He kept several bills and handed the rest back to me. I thanked him and gave his arm a squeeze.

"May things go well for your wife," he said out the window. "And may God be with the two of you."

As he drove off and we headed toward the entrance, I handed Magda's aunt the leftover cash.

"What is this wife business?" she said.

"It's just that Magda and I consider ourselves husband and wife," I said. "But I'd better let her explain that to you."

"Husband and wife?" the aunt said. "That is nonsense."

"Well, it may seem so to you but it doesn't seem so to us."

"Maybe in your country you could consider yourselves husband and wife but not in this country," the aunt said.

"In any case," I said. "I'm not in a mood to argue about it right now."

The aunt stopped me to study my face. "You look very tired," she said. "You should go home and get some sleep."

"I'm not going home just yet," I said. "Not until I'm sure Magda's all right."

"I'll make sure of that now," the aunt said.

"Well one thing you can do for her is see to it that they don't give her rabies shots because that's a terrible thing for her to have to go through. I mean, forty days of shots in her stomach when she doesn't need it?"

The aunt stopped me again. "And just how am I to prevent it if the doctors insist? They never take chances with rabies in this country unless you can prove the animal is all right."

"I can prove it," I said. "If I had the animal I could prove it."

"But you don't have the animal," the aunt said. "And you can't get the animal. And even if you could, it would take days to prove that the animal was all right."

I don't know what came over me, but I felt completely defeated again, and I couldn't bring myself to go inside the hospital and face that smirking orderly, so I just sat down suddenly on the pavement outside the entrance and covered my face with my hands. Magda's aunt came over and touched my head.

"I'll do everything I can for Magda," she said. "You don't have to worry any longer. So go home and get some sleep."

And then she was gone. I sat there trying to keep the tears back, and then I got up to walk it off. I could see the city walls from where I was standing, a short ways off to my right, so I decided to head in that direction, and when I came up beside them I kept on going uphill until I reached the old path I used to take with my foreign friends from the German School to our winter hideout. Hardly four months had gone by since we were last up there, but it already seemed to belong to some other life of mine, and I didn't feel any great pull drawing me back to that roofless ruin with the goatdunged hut next door to it. On the other hand, hanging out there awhile was a more appealing idea than heading home, so that's where I ended up spending the night, and not only the night but part of the next morning, because once I got settled in on what was left of the straw floor in that hut, nothing was able to wake me up until the mid-morning heat turned my cotton jacket into a wet mess. I bolted upright and looked out to see the sun higher in the sky than I wanted to believe. My jacket had straw clinging to it, and it had picked up the smell of goat dung along with my sweat. The thought came to me that I had no choice but to go home eventually to change my clothes and see if I could pick up some cash, but I wasn't ready to face that until I'd checked in at the hospital to make sure they were really taking care of Magda the way they should.

There were three new orderlies sharing the ashtray at the desk when I got there, and one of them had a long fingernail on his little finger, so he was the one I went up to.

"I'd like to find out what room Miss Magda Sevillas has been assigned," I said to him.

He went around behind the desk.

"That's the girl who was bitten by a mad dog?"

"It was not a mad dog," I said. "It was a sheepdog."

"In any case," the orderly said, checking down his list. "I see here that she is not accepting visitors."

"What do you mean, she's not accepting visitors?"

"Only relatives," the orderly said. "By decision of the family. Some of whom are with her now."

"Well, doesn't she herself have the right to decide who she wants to see?"

The orderly looked up at me as though to make sure I was asking the question seriously.

"She is hardly in any condition to decide things for herself," the orderly said. "She is still recovering from an operation, after all."

"Well, can you at least tell me what they did to her?"

"What who did to her?"

"The doctor, or surgeon, or whoever?"

"Obviously that is not information I could give out even if I were privileged to have all of it," the orderly said.

"Well, how do I find somebody who's privileged to have all of it?"

The orderly shrugged. "You're free to get in touch with the girl's family and see what they might be willing to tell you. But not in the patient's room while she's recovering from an operation and under care for rabies."

I stood there looking at him. He put the list aside and reached for his cigarette.

"May I at least have my identity card back?" I said. "The one that was taken from me and put away inside the middle drawer?"

The orderly opened the middle drawer and began shuffling through what was there.

"That's it," I said. "The one written in English."

The orderly picked up my lifesaving certificate and studied it.

"What's the name on this?" he said.

"Gogarty," I said. "Henry Gogarty."

"Since I can't read English well, Mr. Gogartis, I'll have to trust you," the orderly said. "But the rule in the hospital is that identity cards should be in Greek."

"Thank you," I said. "I'll keep that in mind if I'm ever bitten by a mad dog and need your help."

He went on studying the certificate awhile longer, then handed it to me authoritatively as though a customs officer returning my passport.

I left the hospital heading for Harilaou in the hope of finding Magda's aunt there, the only way I could see of breaking through the family circle that had closed Magda in, especially now that they appeared to have her sealed off by the need to take a daily rabies shot at least until she could get up and walk away from that horror on her own two feet. I figured that if the aunt had found a chance to talk to Magda about who I really was in her eyes at least, maybe she would be ready now to think of me as something other than an aggressive enemy of the Sevillas household and worthy of some news about the one person in the world I cared for more than I cared for myself. But halfway out to Harilaou, walking fast in the city heat, I started getting a regular whiff of the way I smelled, and that made me realize that it wouldn't do my case any good to show up at the aunt's house in the condition I was in. I decided to take the back road home with the intention of returning as soon as I'd washed up and changed into the best clothes I had left.

After what Magda and I had been through together during the past weeks, it didn't occur to me that anybody in my family would still think of themselves as being in charge of my life the way her family seemed to think they had the right to be in her case. It took a family conference that my mother called during the first hour I was home to set me straight on that score. There didn't seem to be anybody in the house when I got there, so I went right up to my room and undressed and got into the shower. I wasn't halfway through soaping myself when my mother came into the bathroom in her gardening clothes without even knocking first.

"So the prodigal son is home at last," she said without the trace of a friendly smile.

"Hi," I said. "I'll be right out. Just give me a minute to finish soaping myself here."

"Well, I'm glad you've decided to stay long enough to have a shower and get dressed again," my mother said. "Can we count on that?"

"Sure thing. I'll be right out."

My mother just stood there in the doorway looking at me, and when she finally turned to go, she didn't shut the door behind her. I went on soaping myself, several times over, and I took my time washing and rinsing myself off. When I stepped out of the shower, I went over and shut the door, and when I was through drying off, I kept the towel wrapped tightly around me while I brushed my teeth with an old toothbrush I'd left behind. I hadn't shaved since I was in the Veria hotel, and even though my beard was light-colored, I needed a shave badly now. That meant I had to go out with the towel around me and borrow my mother's razor from her bathroom, but I didn't run into her because she had gone off somewhere, which I figured meant that she'd gone down to the machine shop to find my father. I had one long-sleeved shirt folded up in my dresser drawer, and I decided to wear that, along with a pair of dark corduroy pants and a pair of black shoes that I kept for the few times I was required to go to church and for proms, weddings, and funerals. I put a lot of Vitalis on my hair, which was in bad need of a haircut, at least so they would have told me at the German School, and for that reason I decided I liked my hair just the way it was.

On my way to the stairs, I saw Sam's door was open, so I went over to say hello to him, but he wasn't in his room. When I got downstairs, I found my mother and father waiting for me in the study, she still in her gardening clothes and he in a pair of overalls covered with oil stains that were linked here and there by smears of rust. The two of them were sitting side by side on his leather couch, my mother with her back straight but my father slouched over his knees and gazing at the floor in a way that made him look as uncomfortable as I'd ever seen him. My mother signaled me to take a chair across from them, but I decided to stay standing because the way they had the chair set up in the middle of the room reminded me too much of a witness's chair in a courtroom. While my mother sat there staring at me, I noticed for the first time that there were streaks of gray in her hair, and that made me suddenly very sad because she didn't seem the same young mother I remembered.

"You look dressed up fit to kill," she said to me. "Are you planning on going to a party or something?"

"Not really," I said. "Just an important visit."

"Well, I hope it won't be asking too much of you to put it off for a while, because your father and I have a few things we'd like to talk over with you."

"Sure," I said. "I'm in no great hurry. As a matter of fact, there are a few things I'd like to talk over too."

"So I gather," my mother said. "We got your letter. And I'm sure it will come as no surprise to you that it hurt us deeply. Your father as much as me."

She nudged my father, and he looked up, but he didn't say anything.

"I'm sorry it hurt you," I said. "That was the last thing I had in mind."

"Well, I'd like to know what the first thing was that you had in mind, going off like that suddenly with just a scribbled message that didn't tell us the truth. What were your father and I supposed to think?"

I decided to sit down after all.

"I guess I didn't think much about that at the time," I said. "I guess I was too worried about what had happened to Magda when I couldn't find her that day."

"Well, I'm glad you were worried about somebody other than yourself. But I hope you realize that your father and I cannot be much impressed by this relationship with your German tutor. In fact, we find it quite embarrassing."

"I'm sorry you do," I said. "Because Magda means the world to me and at the moment she's having a hard time of it. But I guess there's no point in talking about all that if you find it so embarrassing."

I started to get up, but my mother told me to sit down again, she and my father hadn't finished. Then she turned to my father.

"Aren't you going to say something, Ralph?"

I suddenly felt sorry for my father. He'd been sitting there nodding with his eyes lowered as though agreeing with some deep thought inside his head. Now he bit his lower lip.

"I guess I have to say that I'm a little disappointed in you, Hal," my father said. "But I also have to say that I'm disappointed in myself. Because I've never been able to express myself to you boys."

"It's all right," I said. "You don't have to express yourself. I understand why you're disappointed."

He was looking down at the floor again. "The point is, I should have been able to talk to you two, but I never could, so I didn't. And now it's too late."

"I understand," I said.

"No, I don't think you do exactly. What I'm trying to say is that I thought you and Sam would like coming to a new country and learning new things that few other people your age would have a chance to learn, but the truth is, I never asked you."

"It's all right," I said. "Sam and I love being in this country. Maybe it took a while, but we've ended up being as much Greek as we are anything else. It was just the German School that got on our nerves."

My mother sat forward in the couch.

"What your father means is that we may have made a mistake in bringing you over here. In fact, we clearly made a mistake. It hasn't been good for you and it hasn't been good for us. And the way you've ended up shows it."

"Well, I wouldn't go so far as to say it hasn't been good for us," I said. "Some of it has been unbelievably good and some maybe not so good."

My mother stood up and straightened her dress.

"Whatever you may think it's been, we've decided that the time has come for you and Sam to go back to the United States and get some proper schooling before you become strangers to your own country. Especially when there's all this talk of war."

That made me stand up.

"How can you just decide a thing like that?" I said. "I refuse to go along with it."

"You see what I mean?" my mother said to my father.

"And you see what I mean when I say it's too late?" my father said.

"Let's not talk anymore right now," I said. "We're all a little upset. I'll be happy to talk about it later when I've solved a few personal problems I have to deal with."

"I suppose you think your personal problems are no longer of any interest to your parents," my mother said. "Is that it?"

"No. Not exactly. I just don't feel in a mood to talk about them right this minute."

"Well, your father may not want to tell you what you'd better keep in mind; but I'll tell you. If you go off again without letting us know the truth about where you're going and why, you're on your own, and that's it."

"I understand that," I said. "It's no longer an issue."

"Well, you may find it is an issue," my mother said. "You may find that you can't earn your living in this country as an underage foreigner, and you may find that you have no way of continuing your education in any country without our help. So you'd better think about it."

"I will think about it," I said. "I can promise you that."

I felt sorry for both of them now, and for myself too, but that didn't keep me from having to get out of there as quickly as I could to get myself into the open air. And that's what I did. On my way out, I spotted Sam leaning against the banister at the top of the stairs. He'd obviously been sitting up there listening to everything we'd been saying, and it irritated me that he hadn't been allowed downstairs to hear firsthand what my parents had decided about his future. But I wasn't ready to talk to him about it right at that moment, so I just waved to him and called out that I'd be back to have a word with him later on.

I cut out across the farm fields at the back of the school and headed uphill toward the village of Kapudjida. It was noon by then, and I was famished, but without a drachma in my pocket, the only thing for me to eat on that road was a bunch of still unripe grapes from a vineyard halfway to the village. I ate the whole bunch, though it made my stomach feel as sour as the taste of the grapes, and to counter that, I decided to go into the village and take a long drink from the village spring before heading downhill again to face Magda's aunt. On the road down, I stopped at a place where Magda and I had paused to get a clear view of the city that late spring day when we'd gone up to the hillside above the ravine, but the midsummer heat now covered the outskirts of the city with haze, so that you could no longer make out the road heading across the plain to Veria, and the mountains beyond the bay were just shadowy forms in some other country.

Magda's aunt was home, working in her kitchen, and that was where she sat me down so that she could go on cleaning the string beans she dumped into the apron across her lap. She told me that Magda was all right, she'd spent the whole night with her so that she was there when they'd taken her in to sew up her leg and she was there when they'd brought her out still under the anesthetic several hours later with a cast covering her leg from the ankle to the knee. Then she'd felt it her obligation to tell Magda's parents what had happened, so she'd left Magda sleeping there in the early morning and had come home to find her sister and her brother-in-law, who went back to the hospital immediately and were there now to take their turn with others in the family. The surgeon said that Magda would have to stay there from five days to a week, assuming no post-operation problems with infection and the like.

"So that means I won't see her for at least a week?" I said. "And maybe not even after that?"

The aunt went on stripping the bean in her hand.

"Did Magda at least say that she wanted to see me?"

"Of course she wants to see you," the aunt said, looking up. "And if you're patient, maybe it can be arranged. But at the moment there's no point in your seeing her because she isn't herself yet."

"Well, how can it be arranged when the family has her in prison like that? And when they obviously hate me."

"They don't hate you," the aunt said. "They don't know about you. And I told Magda if she has any sense, she won't tell them about you. For her own good and yours as well."

I got up and started walking around the kitchen.

"What did she tell you about me?" I said.

"Enough," the aunt said. "Too much. Now will you please sit down and calm yourself?"

"And you let them start giving her rabies shots. That much I learned on my own."

"I didn't let them do anything," the aunt said quietly. "They didn't wait for my advice."

"So now I suppose they're going to go on giving her shots for forty days."

The aunt shrugged. "That's up to Magda," she said. "After all, once she's fully awake and herself again I suppose she can refuse to have the shots."

"And what about me? Will seeing me be up to Magda too when she's herself again? Or is the family going to keep her locked up from now on?"

The aunt stood up and emptied her apron onto the kitchen table. "You're a very stubborn young man. Very impatient."

"I'm not stubborn," I said. "You just don't understand. Magda means everything to me."

"I do understand," the aunt said. "I just don't like what I understand. And you're not going to make me change my mind about that."

I sat down again. "So I guess I have no hope," I said. "You're just like the rest of her family. And mine too."

"I'm not like anybody but myself," the aunt said. "What you don't understand is that I want the best for Magda, and to me that means that she does not complicate her life with love affairs or get married to anybody yet but goes to the university."

"Well, I want her to go to the university too. But I don't want to be cut out of her life as though I don't count for anything. And I don't think she wants that either."

The aunt came over and stood above me. Then she reached down and brushed her hand across my forehead to straighten my hair.

"She's made you grow up too much already," she said. "Taught you to think the way she thinks. Made you believe that you can always choose to do just what your heart wants you to do. And that is not a good thing in someone so young."

I sat there feeling trapped again, sure that anything I said would just make things worse.

"I will arrange for you to see her," the aunt said finally. "When the time is right, you can come to the hospital with me."

I looked up. "And when will the time be right?"

"That is a thing you will have to let me decide. And since I'm really not a cruel woman, you won't have to wait very long."

As I was leaving, she said I should come back to see her at noon two days down the road. She also said that one thing I might do in the meanwhile was find some way of recovering the clothes and other things that Magda had left in Kastania, and if I succeeded, I should deliver those to her directly so that no questions would be raised. I told her sure, I'd do my best.

It wasn't until I was well along the road home that I became relaxed enough to take in some of what the aunt had said. When she told me that she'd advised Magda not to tell her parents about me, I'd seen that as an outright rejection on her part, but even if there was some truth in that, it came to me now that the aunt was also saying she herself had decided not to tell Magda's parents about what there was between Magda and me. This meant that unless Magda chose not to follow her aunt's advice about keeping me out of the picture, I wouldn't be an issue in the Sevillas family so long as the aunt herself didn't make me one. And what the aunt had said about my bringing Magda's leftover things to her directly made me think she wasn't planning to make me an issue, for Magda's sake if not for mine. What this told me in turn was that I might have some freedom left to get together with Magda after all, at least once she got out of the hospital and was on her feet. The tiredness suddenly fell away from me. The only worry I still had—and it didn't last— was that Magda might not be as shrewd as her aunt and might decide for one reason or another that she had to tell her mother and father the truth about us the way I had done with mine.

I spent the next two days working hard in the dairy barn to earn the equivalent of what I had borrowed from my mother's purse when I went off to find Magda. I was feeling so much on top of things during those two days, especially after making up in full for the several meals I'd recently lost, that I must have put in more time hauling heavy new machinery around than any day laborer would have given that school. And I milked enough cows morning and evening to give the regular staff extra time out during their cigarette breaks for some serious political conversation about what Metaxas and Mussolini and Hitler were all up to, which everybody seemed to agree was getting more and more dangerous in the case of Mussolini and Hitler but still wasn't all that clear in the case of Metaxas, who had his good points and his bad points, depending on your point of view. During those two days my mother and father left me much to myself, sharing some meals with me but neither of them saying anything aimed specifically in my direction, as though the wrong word might set me to barking violently and ruin everybody's peace of mind.

I did get to talk to Sam privately at one point. He told me that my going away had created a lot of heated conversation and some bad blood in my parents' bedroom and had resulted in their paying more attention to him than he had any need or desire to take in, but he didn't seem as upset as I was about the idea of heading back to the States to go to boarding school. In fact, he said that anything was better than the school we'd been sent to in Salonika, and now that he'd mastered the game of soccer, he could see himself making first string on any American prep school team he might end up trying out for, since the competition in that sport wasn't the greatest in the States. As far as he was concerned, the only condition he was ready to make a fuss about if they decided to uproot him again was that my parents choose a school for him that had a decent soccer team. Sam and I were clearly not seeing things in the same light any longer, and I didn't feel that I could come clean with him about why I was ready to fight the idea of going off to boarding school against my will, because even though he knew my feelings about the German School well enough, I wasn't sure what he knew about my feelings beyond that. I settled for telling him that I'd be grateful if he didn't commit himself one way or the other until both of us had more time to mull over this sudden change in plans our parents had decided was best for us, and though he nodded, I could see from his look that he had begun to think a screw had come loose somewhere in the relatively solid head I used to have.

Late in the afternoon of my first day back, before I went down for the milking, I looked through my wallet for the cigarette box lining with the phone number of my ambulance driver in Veria, then went over to the school office and put a call through to him. The man didn't seem at all surprised to hear my voice, and we chatted away about Magda and me as though we were family friends. I finally got around to asking him if he could get his brother-in-law the taxi driver to recover what Magda and I had left behind in the village of Kastania since he knew exactly where we'd stayed, and the man told me he certainly could not do that under any circumstances, but his wife might agree to do it, and if she succeeded in getting our things back to him in Veria by way of her unspeakable brother, he himself would take responsibility for getting them to me personally since he had to make a trip to Salonika in any case to pick up some vital car parts for his donkey-brained brother-in-law's broken-down excuse for a taxi.

The De Soto arrived at my father's school late in the morning of my third day back, as I was about to go into town again to meet Magda's aunt. My mother was at one of her weekly gatherings with wives of the school staff, so she didn't see it arrive, but the deaf-mute did, and just as he had when Magda arrived at the school in a taxi so many weeks ago, he immediately pulled his donkey cart well out of the way as though this great black car in the middle of the road carried invisible death inside it. Sam was also much impressed by the De Soto. He followed me out of the house when I went out to meet my friend the non-driver.

"Wow," he said. "Who ordered that thing?"

"I did," I said. "He's a friend of mine from Veria."

"Wow. Is it a hearse?"

"No, for God's sake. It's a private limousine."

Sam ran his hand gently over the rear fender. "Well, it looks like a hearse to me. Personally, I wouldn't even be caught dead inside it."

I shook hands with the driver and introduced Sam, then climbed in back and told the driver that I'd ride in with him as far as Harilaou if he didn't mind. He had Magda's second shoulder bag and my knapsack on the backseat, along with a huge yellow basket full of peaches and apples. That turned out to be a gift for Magda and me with a personal blessing from the old couple in Kastania after they'd learned from the taxi driver that Magda and I were all right, just mistakenly attacked by a sheepdog and not kidnapped by brigands, which was the rumor that had circulated in the village after the shepherd had returned with several villagers to find that we'd vanished in a matter of minutes from the place he'd left us sitting by the side of the road.

"And the sheepdog must be healthy," I said. "Or they would have said something about that to your brother-in-law, isn't that right?"

The driver looked in his rear-view mirror. "Of course the sheepdog is healthy. Dogs don't get sick from biting human beings. It's the other way around."

When we got to Harilaou, I tried to get the driver's address so that I could send him a present in return for all his help as soon as I found a way to earn some cash, but he was too clever for me. He said that I had his phone number, that was good enough, and when I next passed through Veria, I could treat him to an ouzo someplace other than the town square, unless in the meanwhile I had any acquaintances in need of a first-class garage with a large selection of foreign parts for whatever car was built in this century and not the last, in which case he would appreciate my passing his phone number on to them. He offered me a parting cigarette and I took it without thinking, then held it between two fingers to give him a farewell salute and stuck it behind my ear so that I could use both hands to pick up the things he'd brought me from Kastania.

When Magda's aunt opened the door for me, I could see that she was dressed up and had her hair neatly combed, which I took to mean that she was ready for our visit to the hospital. When I approached her with the idea of kissing her formally on both cheeks, she stiffened in a way that told me it was not a good idea. As I stood there she took the things I'd brought out of my hands, then gave me back my knapsack after she'd figured out what it was.

"I'll take Magda some fruit if you wish," she said. "But only a plateful at a time so that it doesn't raise any questions."

"That's fine by me," I said. "Can I help you get it ready?"

"No, I'll do it," she said. "What you can do is remove that cigarette from behind your ear because it looks ridiculous."

We took a taxi to the hospital. Magda's aunt didn't have much to say to me during the ride down there, and I found I didn't have much to say to her. In fact, I was quite nervous the whole way, I suppose because I had a strong feeling that she wasn't on my side any longer, however much she might be on Magda's, and that left me confused about what I could and couldn't say in front of her. Back in her house I'd asked her how Magda was when she'd last seen her, which had been the evening before, and she'd told me that Magda was doing well, her original cast had been changed for a lighter half-cast that the doctors could change as the swelling went down and no infection had appeared so far, but she tired easily and I was not to stay with her at the hospital any longer than I had to. Since I wanted to stay with her that day and the next and the next after that, lie beside her on the hospital bed and take care of her any way I could as long as they would let me and then stay some more, there was no way I could speak my mind. And as I sat in the back of the taxi holding a bowl of fruit in my lap, the one thing I really wanted to say was that I felt Magda belonged to me as much as she did to her aunt or to anybody else in the world, and I couldn't stand being treated like an unwanted outsider who had to be kept at a safe distance from her because of some danger I supposedly carried. Since I couldn't say that, I commented on the size of the fruit that our friends in Kastania had gathered for us, then learned how poorly the aunt's own garden was doing in Harilaou, then both of us clammed up.

Magda was no longer in the emergency section of the hospital, so we went in by the front entrance and were cleared through as relatives at the main desk, the aunt as what she was and I as her nephew. Magda was on the second floor, with a small room to herself and a window that looked out on Mount Hortiati. She was lying on her back with a sheet covering her except for the wounded leg, which was in a sling that raised it slightly above the level of the bed. She had her eyes shut when we came up to stand in the doorway, and she looked pale but quite peaceful. The aunt put a finger to her lips and slipped in to remove one of the two chairs at the foot of the bed. She brought it out and set it down in the corridor, then told me she would sit outside awhile since Magda was asleep and I could do as I chose. I chose to go in and sit at the foot of the bed, with the bowl of fruit in my lap. I hadn't been there two minutes before Magda opened her eyes.

"Hal," she said. "My God, where have you been?"

I put the bowl of fruit down and went over to her. She put out her hand to grab mine.

"They wouldn't let me in to see you," I said. "They only allowed relatives."

"They didn't tell me that," Magda said. "Nobody told me that. I thought you'd just decided to abandon me because I only have one good leg."

I bent down and kissed her gently. "You're crazy," I said.

"And you smell good. Some girl has put her perfume all over you."

"It's just Aqua Velva," I said. "An after-shave lotion."

She reached up with her hand and felt my cheek. Then she passed her fingers over my lips. That made me close my eyes.

"I've missed you so much just lying here," Magda said. "I didn't know I could miss anybody that much."

I held her fingers against my lips. "Your aunt's outside," I said. "She's the one who got me in here. Only she said I couldn't stay very long. And I don't think she approves of me any longer."

"Don't pay attention to her," Magda said. "I made the mistake of telling her too much."

"I know," I said. "I just hope you didn't tell your parents anything."

"I wouldn't do that," Magda said. "They can barely bring themselves to talk to me as it is. I'm such an embarrassment to them. Especially after I refused to have rabies shots."

"You refused? That's great."

"The second time. The first time I was still groggy and didn't realize what they were doing. The second time I told the doctor I'd break the needle off while it was in me. And when he said what will we do with you young lady if you go mad, I told him I'd search him out and make sure he was the first one I bit."

"You're really crazy. I wish I could have been here to see his face."

"You should have seen my mother's face. And even my aunt's."

I decided to sit down on the edge of the bed. "The trouble is, we need your aunt now. It's the only way I have of seeing you."

"I'll talk to her again," Magda said. "I'll make her approve of you."

She glanced toward the corridor, then took my hand and put it under the sheet, then brought it up under the nightie she was wearing and held it against her bare breast.

"I can't tell you how awful it's been," she said. "Not just the pain, because you get used to that after a while, but being alone. Or being with all of them and not being able to talk about you and everything that really matters."

"I had my problems too," I said. "I had to have it out with my parents. And now they want to send me away to school in America."

Magda brought my hand out and put it to her face.

"Oh no," she said. "They're sending you back to America?"

"They're trying to. But I'm not going. Don't worry."

"They know all about us then," Magda said.

"Not all," I said. "They just know how I feel. I couldn't hide it."

Magda wasn't looking at me any longer, but she didn't let go of my hand.

"So what are we going to do now?" she said.

"I don't know. My mother says I can't get a job in this country. And she says they won't help me any longer if I go off on my own."

Magda shook her head. "I knew it would be impossible if we had to come back to this city."

"We'll work something out," I said. "We have to."

Magda looked at the corridor again. Then she told me to come up beside her on the bed and hold her close.

"Your aunt must be getting nervous," I said. "She's bound to come in any minute."

"Let her come in," Magda said. "I have nothing more to hide from her."

I eased up beside Magda and put my arm carefully around her. She kissed my face and neck and then put her head on my shoulder.

"Can't we go back to Thassos?" she said. "Or even that hotel in Veria?"

"Sure we can," I said. "As soon as your leg is all right again."

"I wish we could. How I wish we could."

"Don't say it that way. You've got to believe we can."

"I do believe it," Magda said. "I know we will someday."

I looked at her to see if she really did believe it, and that made the tears start rolling down her face.

During the taxi ride back to Harilaou, unlike the ride coming in, Magda's aunt turned out to have a great deal to say. She told me right off that she wasn't going to help me visit Magda in the hospital again because that morning's visit had obviously upset her niece terribly, even though she'd denied it and had pleaded to be allowed to see me again the following day. Then the aunt said that she felt the time had come for her to be perfectly honest with me and make it clear that it was only her affection for Magda, who was really more a daughter to her than a niece, that permitted her to go on acting as the go-between in a relationship that she was certain would do neither Magda nor me any good. But she also said that much as she didn't like the idea, she had promised Magda to get in touch with me as soon as she was out of the hospital the following week and well enough to move around on crutches, and since she was a woman who always kept her promises to those she loved, she would arrange for the two of us to meet in her own home at a convenient time, since meeting in Magda's home was certainly out of the question. And that meeting would be it, as far as she was concerned. She said unlike Magda's parents, and especially her father, she wasn't about to decide what Magda should do with her life or try to prevent Magda from doing what she felt she had to do, however foolish some of what she did might appear to herself and others. But at the same time, she didn't feel she had an obligation to help Magda travel down a road that was sure to lead in the end to her unhappiness, especially when a girl with her talents had a better road clearly marked out for her. What she meant by that, she said, was Magda's going to the university and eventually getting herself a position that would bring her all the long-range benefits of a civil service career as a teacher and eventually a husband old enough and settled enough to be worthy of her accomplishments.

I don't know whether she expected me to make a speech like that in my defense, but all I found I could say was that I was sorry she felt the way she did about my love for Magda, and whatever she might think of me, there was nothing in the world I wanted more than Magda's happiness.

"And what that means to you is that she give up everything so that she can go off and live with a seventeen-year-old foreigner, is that it?"

"I don't want her to give up everything," I said. "I just want her to be free to do what she wants."

"And just how is she going to be free to do what she wants while she's taking care of you?" the aunt asked.

I didn't know how to answer that, so I clammed up again. And I guess the aunt felt that she'd said her piece and didn't really need to say any more, so we rode on in silence, and when we got to her house, she told me to wait at the door while she got my knapsack, and then she came back and reached out to hand the knapsack to me as though it were my severed head.

"I'll find you when Magda is ready to see you," she said. "There's no need for you to come looking for me."

When I got home I went up to my room and shut myself in. I didn't want to eat and I didn't want to talk to anybody. I lay on my bed and stared at the ceiling, but what I felt I was staring at was a deep black hole with no bottom to it. I knew that there had been times, especially in the beginning, when Magda had felt guilty about where she and I were heading because she thought it was bad for me, and even on the road there had been times when she'd worried about where we'd ended up and said so. Yet somehow she'd worked her way out of that, or at least had learned to live with it, and that had helped to build my own faith that it was right for us to do what we both felt we had to do to be free. But alone now, I found that what her aunt had said had gotten to me in a way that made me feel guilty about where Magda and I were hoping to go, and about what our going there might do to her life, whatever it might do to mine. I could now see the two of us arriving in Athens and my sitting around some apartment in a strange neighborhood without anything to do while Magda went off to work so that she could support me and the place we were living in, and no university for her, no school for me, nothing for either of us but the burden of my being too young and foreign to find work that would help set both of us free. I got up and started pacing around my room, turning over the idea of our living together in Salonika or Athens or someplace else in Greece, and I always came back to that same feeling that wherever we ended up, she would be the one taking care of me rather than the other way around, and that was a feeling I found I couldn't live with easily.

I stayed in my room through supper time because it was the only place I really felt at home, and my mother finally had to knock on the door to see if I was still alive. She had a tray with her that had a plate of Greek meatballs on it and a dish of potato salad of a kind she knew how to make like nobody else I'd run across, and next to all of that was a stack of books. When she handed me the tray, she said there was homemade ice cream downstairs if I felt the need at any time to return to civilized life, but in view of my new independence, she didn't want me to feel that I was being pressured to do anything I didn't want to do, even to eat and talk and dress like other normal human beings. I thanked her for making the potato salad and said that I still had a few personal problems I needed to sort out and would be coming down regularly as soon as I'd straightened them out in my head.

I set the tray down on my bedside table and ate most of what was there, saving a couple of meatballs in case my appetite came back in the middle of the night. The books she had stacked there were stamped as belonging to my father's library, which meant that they were new arrivals from the States, not for the school's use but for our family's.

They were thin books on the whole, and every one of them turned out to be a catalogue describing why this or that prep school was generally thought to the best in its particular state if not always the oldest, with the broadest all-around curriculum and the largest number of graduates accepted into major universities. I decided I owed it to Sam if not to myself or my parents to have a serious look at some of them at least, and that is what I spent the evening doing whenever my mind could turn away for a moment from gazing into its dark hole.

It was a full week later before I saw Magda again. I spent that week working at the school, no longer because I owed it to anybody but because it kept me from just sitting in my room and brooding on and on about Magda and me and our problems. And working hard that way from morning until night clearly raised my stock with the family, so much so that toward the end of the week my father decided that he could begin supplementing my laborer's hourly wage out of his own salary, which was his way of giving me a small allowance without calling it that. I still had some trouble communicating with my mother, but when my father called me in to his study to make his offer of reimbursing me a bit more for the hours I was giving the school's farm machinery operation and the dairy barn, I took that chance to have a serious conversation with him on a subject that I'd been turning over since the evening I came back from visiting Magda in the hospital.

"As I understand the way things work in the States," I said, "you have to go to most of those prep schools over there for a minimum of two years to be accepted, right?"

"That would normally be the case," my father said. "What school have you got in mind?"

"I don't have any school in mind," I said. "I'm just thinking in general terms. And I was hoping there might be some school that would take you in for just a year."

"Well, that might be a little difficult this late in the game," my father said. "Those schools start up in a little over a month and you're out here where you can't be interviewed and they don't really know who you are."

"I was hoping they might make an exception in my specific case because you're in the business, so to speak. And maybe Sam and I could get back early enough for an interview."

"Anything is possible," my father said. "But if you're speaking about your specific case and not in general terms, your specific case is that since you haven't made up any time over here, you would have two years to go before you could graduate anyway."

I decided to sit down and relax a bit. "What I was sort of mulling over in my case as distinct from Sam's was taking a year in the States and then maybe finishing up here for my final year."

"But I thought the whole point was that you didn't like the German School," my father said.

"I wasn't thinking of the German School," I said. "I was thinking of Anatolia College, for example. Since Jackson Ripaldo ended up going there."

"Well, I don't know," my father said. "I imagine you'd have to learn to read and write Greek for one thing. Their classes are mostly in Greek."

"I could do that on my own in the meanwhile. I'd like to do that anyway."

"I don't know," my father said. "We'll have to think about it. Your mother and I."

"If it's all right with you," I said, "I'd just as soon we kept it between you and me for the time being."

My father studied me in a way that showed me he thought I was somehow testing him.

"Sure," he said. "Right. We'll keep it between you and me for the time being."

He lowered his eyes then, and I figured that was because he felt he was somehow betraying my mother by what he'd just said, but his having said it made me feel closer to him than I'd been able to feel at any point since he'd taken us away from my grandfather's farm.

Magda's aunt got in touch with me by coming to our school and tracking me down one morning in the farm machinery area where I was cleaning up what was once a stable to make it ready for some new equipment that my father had ordered from the States. She had a young boy by the hand, a nephew from her brother's branch of the family, and she was supposedly out there to show him all the farm animals and the rest of the school in the hope that he might want to apply to go there someday, an idea that I was fairly certain had sprung out of Magda's imagination. I was embarrassed by the way I looked in the misfitting dungarees I'd borrowed for my work down there, and I said so, but Magda's aunt told me very soberly that there was no need for me to worry about the way I looked, I had plenty of time to wash and change into something better before I was due in town for my German lesson, which could be a long lesson because the aunt would be taking her nephew to lunch by the sea and wouldn't be returning home until late afternoon. While she stood there still holding the boy's hand, I wanted to say something that would show her I was honestly grateful for what she'd arranged to give Magda and me, but she turned away before I could come up with anything that sounded right, so I ended up saying thanks to her back.

When I reached the aunt's house in Harilaou, I found the front door slightly ajar, and as I pushed it open I saw that Magda was stretched out on the settee in the living room. She had her bandaged leg flat out in front of her, and her other leg crooked so that she could curl her arms around it. There was a pair of crutches leaning against the settee beside her head. Somebody had washed and trimmed her hair for her, and she was wearing a neatly ironed white blouse and a green skirt that I remembered from our travels. I shut the front door and bolted it. Then I went over and kneeled by the settee to put my arms around her and just hold her for a minute with my head pressed against her so hard that I could smell how clean the skin was where her blouse opened.

Magda ran her hand over my hair. "We've been betrayed," she said.

"How's that?"

"My aunt has told my mother and father about you and me."

That made me look up. "You're joking," I said. "Why would she do a thing like that?"

"She thought it was for my good," Magda said. "Because she used that information to bargain with them."

"Bargain for what?"

"My freedom. She said she'd tell them where I'd been and with whom I'd been if they'd promise to leave me alone from now on and let me go to the university."

"And they agreed to that?"

"Yes. Except that my father cheated and used what she'd told him to try and bribe me."

I laid my head against her blouse again. "I don't think I want to know about this."

"He came into my bedroom yesterday morning without even knocking first and told me that I could go to the university and he would support me while I was there so long as I agreed never to see you again."

"Oh God. So now it's me or the university."

Magda took my head in her hands and gazed at me for a second. "I hope you don't think I would agree to anything like that."

"I don't know," I said. "Sometimes I get confused about us and don't know what to think."

"Well, I'm not confused," Magda said. "I told him what you and I did was none of his business and I didn't need his support any longer anyway. And when I said that, he threatened to throw me out of the house."

"Now? While you're still recovering? He can't throw you out."

Magda let go of my head. "I didn't wait for him to throw me out. I picked up the shoulder bag you got back from Kastania and stuffed as much as I could in it and some more in a pillowcase and came over here."

"I don't understand," I said. "Why do people make our lives so difficult when it's our lives and we don't mean anybody else any harm? Especially people who are supposed to care about us most."

"Because it's usually their own lives they care about most."

"Can't we talk to your father at least? Try to explain?"

"It wouldn't do any good and might make things worse. Besides, I couldn't stay in that house a minute longer and now I'm not going back. Which makes my life simpler."

I stood up. "So where does that leave us? Your aunt won't let me see you here after today. She told me this one time was it. And we can't go very far to be alone while you're on crutches."

"I'll make her change her mind," Magda said. "It may take time, but I think I can do it."

I went over and sat on a chair. "That's not going to be easy," I said. "She thinks I'm bad for you. And I'm beginning to think she may be right."

Magda was looking at me steadily. "Is that what you mean when you say you're confused? Is it because my aunt thinks you're bad for me?"

"Maybe that's part of it," I said. "She told me I would just keep you from going to the university and having a career and marrying somebody older who was worthy of you."

"And what's the other part of it?" Magda said.

"I don't know," I said. "I just can't think of any way to go to school in this country and still earn enough to support you so that you're free to do what you want to do and don't have to spend all your time supporting me."

"So now even you think I have nothing to say about any of this? It's all settled that you and I are no good for each other, is that it?"

"I didn't say that. I just said I was confused. And I don't want to become a burden for you."

Magda was still staring at me in a way that made me feel two inches high.

"Hal, why are you sitting over there?"

"I just thought it might help me think straight."

"Please come back and hold me. I promise not to let that confuse you."

I went back over and knelt by the settee. Magda edged over to give me room to lie beside her.

"That's better," she said. "Now will you be honest with me and tell me what's really on your mind?"

"I just thought it might make more sense if I went to school in America for a year and then came back here for another year and then maybe just stayed on over here to go to the university myself. That way we could be together and support each other and neither of us would lose out on an education."

Magda had her arm around my neck and was stroking my shoulder.

"And you think your parents will agree to that?"

"I don't know," I said. "I think my father might."

"Have you talked to him about it?"

"Sort of. Not about the university but about coming back here after a year. Or two years at the most. After I've graduated from the gymnasium in America."

"And you would want me to wait for you?" Magda said. "Is that it?"

I tried to sit up but she wouldn't let me.

"You would wait for me, wouldn't you?" I said.

"I don't think I have to answer that," Magda said. "I'm not the one who's confused."

"But you would wait, wouldn't you?"

"Yes," Magda said. "If you would promise to come back."

"I would promise," I said.

"And if I was certain you were choosing to come back freely."

"You could be certain," I said.

"So that is that," Magda said.

She took her arm from around my neck and sat up, turning carefully to keep her wounded leg from rubbing against me.

"Now that we've agreed to be faithful to each other and not to betray each other with confused thinking about what we can and can't freely choose to do, we shouldn't waste what little time they've given us to be alone."

She unbuttoned my shirt and helped me get it off, then worked with me to get my undershirt off. I stood up and tried to back off a little at that point to make it easier for both of us.

"No," Magda said. "I want to help you do it all right here, and then you're to help me, as slowly as is necessary, the way we used to in the beginning. And then I want to do all the things we learned to do together, so that when you go away, you won't be able to forget me even if you choose to."

SAM AND I LEFT BY TRAIN TWO WEEKS LATER FOR THE PORT OF
Piraeus, where we boarded an American Export Lines ship bound for New York. I saw
Magda a final time just before leaving Salonika.
I met her at a cafe in Harilaou near her aunt's
house to say good-bye and to give her a new
filigree bracelet to replace the one that she'd
been robbed of in Kastania. She was using a
cane rather than crutches at that point, walking with only a slight stiffness, and in the
sunlight outside that cafe, her trimmed copper hair had a glint more golden than any I'd
seen in it.

When I'd stopped by her aunt's place earlier in the week, I was let in to talk to Magda
without any fuss because I explained to the
aunt that I would be leaving for America shortly.
That quick encounter with Magda had given
me a chance to tell her that my parents, after
much debate between the two of them that
apparently roused the willful side of my

father in my defense, had finally gone along with my plan to return to Greece for my last year of high school providing I learned enough Greek in the meanwhile, and if I did well in prep school during the year ahead, they agreed to support my application to the university of my choice. I told Magda I was sure that at least in my mother's mind, this didn't include any university Magda and I might hope to attend together, but that was a detail I didn't plan to bring into the family debate until it was too late to be debated.

While we were in the cafe for our farewell meeting, Magda and I figured out that when she and I did end up at the university two years down the road, we might even be able to sit in on some classes together, since she had to wait another year before she could take her entrance examinations and that meant there would be only one year separating us at that level. She said she was no longer in any hurry to get started because she needed time to earn enough money to be completely independent of her family, even if her aunt had promised to give her an allowance to help her out once she was living on her own. Our plan for getting together again seemed to be a good one now, the best possible solution the more we got used to the idea, and both of us tried very hard to be cheerful about it while we sipped an ouzo and discreetly held hands under the table. But of course we weren't really cheerful at all. When I gave Magda her filigree bracelet, she put it on right away and then took my hand in hers and slipped a ring on my little finger. It was a fairly heavy ring made out of a Turkish gold coin that her aunt had given her for her last birthday, and it had a design cut into it that I figured out were an interlocking H and M.

"So that you remember," she said. "And if you don't, you can always melt it down to make your wedding band."

"Of course I'll remember," I said. "Don't make stupid jokes like that."

"Would you rather have me cry? Then I'll cry."

And she did, without a sound, still holding my hand in the open, and when I had to turn away because I couldn't look at her any longer, we got up and walked arm in arm to her aunt's place. I didn't go in. I held on to her arm halfway down the garden walk, then took her cane so that she wouldn't have to hold it and could hold me instead while I put my arms around her and kissed her face where it was wet, then handed her cane back to her and waited for her to turn and go on down the walk so that I had no choice any longer but to go away.

Sam and I reached the States that August in time to visit three prep schools in the East, and we settled on one in New Jersey that was supposed to have a first-rate soccer team and that was the closest of the three to our relatives in upstate New York near the Finger Lakes, where Sam planned to spend the following summer. I had other plans for that summer, discussed and settled well in advance through correspondence with Magda. I planned to work from the minute school let out in June until I'd earned enough for my passage to Greece, then arrive there in time to enroll in one or another of the Greek cram schools that might give a foreigner the best chance of perfecting his Greek in a hurry, especially with the added help of a trained language tutor at his side.

The correspondence with Magda was my lifeline during the first dreadful term in that sweaty monastery that passed for a civilized place to incarcerate virile young men, even though she had to write me in German when her English failed her and I had to write her in simple English while I was still mastering a way of spelling Greek that was one stage better than the phonetic rendering of an illiterate housemaid. I got some help with the Greek from a local restaurant owner who had left school in Greece too early to be a master speller himself but who was impressed enough by my command of village vulgarity to hire me as a part-time busboy when I had recreation time to spare. The trouble was that he couldn't be of any use to me when it came to the personal things I wanted to say for Magda's eyes alone, and these must have come out on the page in a shape that chilled whatever substitute for the missing intimacy between us I might have hoped to promote through my increasingly horny imagination.

A short vacation visit that Sam and I paid to our aunt in upstate New York helped for a while to cure the loneliness of those first months because we both ran into old friends. And the second term

started out better, in Sam's case because he made the school basketball team and in my case not so much because I was getting used to
my monastic life but because I felt the days were moving me faster
and faster toward the time when I would have Magda in the flesh
again and could do my best to keep her amused without having to
use any form of written language, foreign or domestic. Magda didn't
write as often as I did, I suppose because she was busy day in, day
out earning money with her tutoring. But she saved her weekends to
write me long letters, full of talk about Greece and what was going
on there, full of things she was learning from her reading and wanted
me to learn too, and always ending with a sexy tenderness about
what she would like to be doing to me where, which made me
tremble with desire sometimes and other times just brought on tears.

I think it was mostly the influence of her always asking whether I
was doing well at school that helped cure my constant daydreaming,
so that by spring I was actually becoming a good student again. I
read everything I could get my hands on, mostly fiction and history,
because I seemed to have hours to myself that nobody else had. And
what I read became something I could talk about in my letters just as
Magda always did, so that she didn't think my brain was still turning
to mush from lack of sex the way it surely must have struck her in
the beginning. Then one day in late April my mother suddenly came
home.

It was the war scare that brought her back to the States. She came
to see Sam and me in early May, as I was working hard to get ready
for my final examinations that term, and she stayed in a hotel in
town for two weeks because she still wasn't sure where she was
going to settle, though it seemed likely she would start out living in
our aunt's house in upstate New York. She said that after Germany
had marched into Czechoslovakia in mid-March, she had become
convinced that war was imminent and had tried to get our father to
commit himself to returning home as soon as his school year was
over, but she said she'd had no more luck talking to him about that
than she'd had talking to him about anything lately. When Italy
invaded Albania on Good Friday in early April, it apparently brought
war close enough to Greece to get even my father worried, but he

still couldn't make the decision to turn his division of the school over to others who had to stay behind while he pulled out for home. By June my mother had decided that enough was enough and had booked her passage on the next ship out of Piraeus. It was at that point, after her irrevocable decision to leave, that my father agreed to pack up what there was worth saving in our house and to join my mother as soon as he could decently pull himself away from the school and transfer his responsibilities to some member of the Greek staff.

I tried not to let this news interfere with either my studies or my plans, but it made me begin to feel trapped again. Without my saying a word, my mother told me that I ought to clear my head of any thoughts I might have about going back to Greece that summer because of course that was now clearly out of the question. I just looked at her with a little smile that I hoped gave no clue at all to what thoughts I might have in my head and then went off to write Magda about what had happened and how much it worried me. Magda wrote back that things did not look good in Europe but she was still convinced that Greece was safe from any war, because Germany was surely after bigger things and nobody in Greece took Mussolini or the Italian army very seriously, however close they might choose to come to Greece's border. She was in a good mood in that letter, playful and flirtatious and very personal, because she said that she felt she'd done as well as was necessary on her entrance examinations for the university and would soon be on her own in all ways, ready to help me with my Greek and anything else I might want from her the minute I got back.

Her letter brought me out of my depression at least enough to get me through my own exams respectably and to give me what strength I needed to resist my mother's efforts to make me live with her and Sam at my aunt's place. Instead I went to work in a small bookstore a good thirty miles away in the college town of Alfred that I'd scouted when Sam and I had passed through there during our mid-year break. Quite aside from needing to earn as much cash as I could, I wasn't about to let myself be boxed in somewhere that would interfere with my corresponding freely with Magda, and fair or not, I was sure that my mother wasn't above intercepting my mail if she thought it was the best thing for me and her view of my future. So I spent the best part of the summer in Alfred by myself despite the bad family blood this stirred up once again and despite my having to pay for my own room and board out of what I was now earning.

My father still hadn't come home by early August, though he had written to tell my mother that he was virtually on his way. By that time I had saved up enough from my work as a busboy and book-store clerk to pay for my passage to Piraeus, so on the 15th of August, what I took to be a lucky day because they would be cel-ebrating the Feast of the Holy Virgin back in Greece, I got on a train for New York City to visit the passport office there and make sure my passport was still valid for the traveling I had in mind, this on the advice of the travel agency in Albany that I'd phoned for infor-mation. And after I'd done that, I planned to see what the American Export Lines office had to offer by way of a passenger ship or a freighter heading for the Mediterranean, since the travel agency couldn't find any other line out of New York that would get you to Greece now that anything once sailing there via Italy was no longer accept-ing passengers.

"You must be out of your mind," the passport clerk said. "Haven't you been reading about what's happening in Poland? Not to men-tion Albania? We're advising people to return home from Greece and you're planning to travel there?"

"That's my plan all right," I said. "I have vital personal business."

"Well it had better be so vital that you can get special dispensation from the Secretary of State, because if this war situation gets any worse, we'll be bringing our diplomats home, not to mention every-body else, and you'll have nobody to see to it that you don't get your head blown off the minute you get over there."

"I can take care of myself," I said. "I'm not new to the country."

"Well, you may be able to take care of yourself, but what interests us is that we may not be able to offer you our good offices, which happens to be the business we're in."

I stared at the man. "Are you trying to tell me that my American passport isn't valid for Greece any longer?"

"That's not a decision that's up to me," the clerk said.

"Well, who is it up to?"

"I told you. The Secretary of State."

"And how do I get to the Secretary of State?"

"You don't get to the Secretary of State," the clerk said. "I get to the Secretary of State. By way of the State Department in Washington. So if you'll just leave your passport with me, I'll do my best to look into the matter."

I had no choice but to leave the man my passport, though I felt I was leaving him the key to my life, and when I went over to the American Export Lines office to see what might be heading out to Greece in the near future, they told me a ship was scheduled to go there in late September, but they couldn't write me out a ticket until I presented a valid passport, and even that wouldn't do me much good if things heated up over there so that we got ourselves into a war.

I went back to Alfred to wait for my passport, trying to stifle the feeling that fate had begun to challenge me at every turn. The next morning at the bookstore they told me that my summer work couldn't last much beyond August because there would be students coming in to the university there who expected to get their old jobs back as soon as classes started up again. On the first of September I got the official word that I wouldn't be needed any longer. Heading back to my room that afternoon, hardly feeling on top of the world, I decided to stop in at an ice-cream parlor run by a local Greek to see if a bit of village talk might raise my spirits. The family and a couple of customers were gathered around the counter listening to a news report on the radio they'd brought out from their living room in back. Germany had invaded Poland, and the correspondent from London said that war with England and France now seemed inevitable.

That was a Friday afternoon, and news like that was all I needed to blacken what looked like a bleak weekend ahead under any circumstances. And black it turned out to be, except for the part of it that I spent writing Magda. I hadn't told her about my visit to the passport office in any detail yet because I didn't want to show her what it had done to my mood, but now I thought I'd better. I tried to make it sound as though the passport business was just a minor problem, a temporary delay, there were still a good three weeks before the ship I planned to board would be sailing for the Mediterranean, plenty of time for the passport to arrive and for me to get my things together, so she wasn't to worry. But there was no way I could keep myself from worrying once I'd written that letter and had time to brood about my situation, especially after a telegram from my mother arrived on Saturday requesting that I come home immediately, as though the German troops were banging on the door of my aunt's place in upstate New York with bayonets at the ready. I decided to pretend the telegram hadn't arrived. I also tried not to pay attention to all the war talk that was circulating in the neighborhood, though it was difficult to keep aloof from the excitement it stirred up, and the tension it left in me, after England and France kept announcing what they planned to do to show Germany that they weren't going to let Hitler get away with it this time. By Sunday morning I found myself drifting over to the Greek's place more or less on the hour to hear the news reports in case something came up to help me believe it was all going to blow over soon.

On the following Tuesday, not long after I heard a report that the United States had declared its neutrality in this latest European conflict, my father appeared at my door. As we shook hands awkwardly, he apologized for arriving unannounced like that. He said he hadn't been able to figure out a way of getting through to me ahead of time since my mother had told him when he'd arrived at my aunt's place on Monday that it seemed neither the post office nor the telegraph office was delivering messages to the place I was supposed to be living, and though he didn't want me to feel that either he or my mother was invading my privacy, she was clearly worried about the lack of information coming out of Alfred, New York.

"Have a seat," I said. "I'm fine. You can tell her I'm fine. I'm just depressed by all this war news."

My father sat down on the chair at my writing desk, which was the only chair I had.

"Well, the news isn't good, that's for sure," my father said. "But with Britain and France heavily in it now, it shouldn't take long for the thing to be cleaned up."

"I wish I could believe that," I said. "But from what I know of the Germans, they're ready to take on the whole world."

"Yes, maybe, but they don't have the British stiff upper lip. The Germans are just a well-oiled machine that's bound to dry up. I give the whole thing six months at the most."

"That would be great if it's true," I said. "Because between you and me, I'm still planning to go over there as soon as my passport arrives."

"Over where?"

"Greece. Salonika. The way we agreed last August."

"Well, I wouldn't think of going to Greece right now," my father said. "Your friend Jackson has headed home from Salonika, and they're not letting the Consul and the rest of the family go back to Greece from home leave."

I decided to sit down on the edge of the bed. "I've got to go over there," I said. "I have very important personal reasons."

"I'm sure you do," my father said. "But can't you postpone things a bit? At least see how the war goes?"

"But what if it gets worse rather than better?"

"Well, personally, I wouldn't want to get caught over there if it gets worse. And if it does, at some point they'll just send Americans back home anyway."

I got up and started pacing the room. When I finally glanced over at my father, there must have been something in the way I looked at him that showed how desperate I felt, because I saw his lined face suddenly scrunch up as though he was suffering, the way it did when he had to work on a sick animal.

"Of course there's no way of really knowing how the war's going to go," my father said. "But even if things get better, it wouldn't do you any harm to go over there after you've had another year of school behind you and have a better idea of where you are."

I sat down on the bed again. "I'll just have to think about it," I said.

"Well, you do that. And take your time. Don't you let anybody rush you. And when you're ready to come back home to your aunt's place, you can be sure that your father and mother will be there waiting."

I wanted to go over and embrace that man, tell him that I knew he was on my side and that I appreciated what he was trying to say, but I couldn't bring myself to do it. I just went over and sort of touched him on the shoulder and said thanks, and what that did was make him lower his head and hold it there for a minute as though with some deep inner thought that wouldn't come out.

On Friday my passport arrived by registered mail. It was stamped as invalid for travel in Germany, Italy, Czechoslovakia, Poland, and Albania, and there was a mimeographed note enclosed with it that said United States citizens traveling in some other countries of Europe and the Near East could no longer be guaranteed, in all cases, the full services provided by U.S. Consular or Embassy facilities and should apply to the Department of State or the closest passport office for the latest travel advisories regarding areas of potential conflict.

I decided that the only person I wanted to apply to for a travel advisory was the one person I trusted more than I trusted myself. I sat down that Friday and wrote Magda about my father's unannounced visit after his coming home from Salonika and what he had said about the war being over soon in his opinion, even though Jackson Ripaldo had gone home from Salonika and the American Consul had not been allowed to return to his post with the rest of his family. I also told her about my father's advice that I postpone my trip for a while until we saw how things developed over there because they would just try and send me back anyway if the war got worse. Then I told her that, thank God, my passport had arrived safely, though it was now invalid for some countries and there was a note enclosed from the Department of State about American citizens no longer being able to travel with guaranteed protection in some other regions. I asked her, finally, to think about all this and to write me her view of the situation and what she felt was best. I said that she was the only person I trusted to give me honest advice about what I should do, and if she thought I ought to come to Greece whatever the war circumstances, I would come, and if she thought it would be better for me to postpone my trip until the following summer when things might have settled down a bit, I would do that too, much as it would break my heart to have to wait that long to see her again. I asked her to write me immediately so that her answer would get to me before the next American Export Lines sailing if possible, though I was sure there would be other sailings after that, and to send the letter to my old school address, where I planned to go, after a short visit home, and just stay put until I heard from her there.

I didn't hear from Magda again. I went to my aunt's place and lounged around for a few days, which was as long as I could stand it, then went back to school and took up my old job as a busboy at the Greek's. When nothing arrived from Magda by the middle of the month, I sent her a telegram asking her to please send me a yes or no telegram in return, and when nothing came of that, I decided not to let the school know quite yet that I was planning to withdraw any day. I didn't withdraw, but I didn't go back to school either, not in a way that counted. I rode out the first month in a nervous daze, listening to the war news and waiting, unable to read or even think about anything but my situation, and that only confused me and finally unnerved me to the point where I began to be afraid to check on whether any mail addressed to me had arrived. And then it gradually began to come home to me that I wasn't going to hear from Magda then or maybe ever again.

I tried to think through the possible reasons for that in the days that followed. Maybe Magda had been brought under pressure by her father and had gone off to hide away as she had before. But if that was so, she could have found a way to write me about it after more than a month on her own, especially since she'd been the one to insist that I write my parents while we were on the road together. Or maybe she'd gotten sick and was hospitalized, so that she wasn't able to send out letters, or those she'd sent out were intercepted on her family's orders. But wouldn't her aunt have broken down and written me about that if Magda had been seriously ill all that time?

And wouldn't that also be true if the unthinkable had happened and she had suddenly died? I found myself returning to the one thought I'd wanted to avoid most initially but that kept coming back with more conviction as the school year moved through the fall, and that was that Magda had deliberately decided not to answer my letter or my telegram and that was the end of it.

What I still couldn't figure out was why she would suddenly decide to do a thing like that after all we'd been through together and the faith we'd put in each other. And the more frustrated I became trying to work it out, the more angry I got, first at myself for being too stupid to be able to find a reason that didn't damage the image I had of her, and then angry at Magda in the simplest way. When that happened, I not only decided I wouldn't write her again as I'd been planning to for weeks but also convinced myself that I really didn't give a damn, which pushed me back to work at school with a vengeance. Of course I really did give a damn, and when the anger cooled as the year went on, it was replaced by a growing sense that I had been the one who had done something wrong, though I couldn't any longer decipher the past clearly enough to see just what it might have been or remember just what it was that I'd written in my last letter that could have caused her to choose not to answer it. If it ever occurred to my conscious mind that my having chosen to write a letter like that was cause enough, I apparently had ways of burying that kind of knowledge when it became too painful, so that what I ended up with was a deep sadness and a sense of wasted possibilities that I never quite understood or got over completely.

In June I graduated high enough in my class to get myself admitted to Cornell University, where I had in mind working my way toward a career in agricultural education, but after America entered the war, I enlisted in the V-12 unit there and eventually graduated as an ensign in the Navy. My two and a half years of service toward the end of the war and a little beyond were mostly on an aircraft carrier in the Pacific, in the Fire Control Division, which bored me to death most of the time but gave me plenty of chance for recreational reading, so that when I got out of the Navy I decided I was more suited for a career in journalism than in anything having to do with

either agriculture or education. That decision took me to the Columbia University Graduate School of Journalism for as long as I could
stand it, which turned out to be some time before I came within
sight of a degree, let alone a professional commitment.

Greece was much with me during the war years and even after.
While I was in college I kept a scrapbook that I filled with news
clippings whenever something appeared in the papers about what
was happening over there—the Albanian Campaign, the fall of Crete,
the German Occupation and the starvation it brought. And since the
papers didn't offer nearly enough to satisfy my longing for news
from that country or any way of easing my worry about what it was
going through, I would go out of my way to find a Greek restaurant
or ice-cream parlor whenever I hit a town of some reasonable size
just to have a chance to talk the language again and to pick up any
recent word that might have come that way from someone in touch
with relatives back in the home country. But while I was in the
Pacific, I had a lot of other things on my mind as well, and all
personal contact with things Greek disappeared, so that by the time I
was discharged from the Navy and was into graduate school, I found
that I'd even forgotten how to speak Greek, except for some useless
phrases of rich village obscenity.

What stayed with me even as my longing faded was a nostalgia for
certain images of the Greek landscape and some of the people that I
remembered best from my trip with Magda, but for a long time that
did not include Salonika at all. I suppose since I really didn't want to
blame either myself or Magda for what had happened between us in
the end, I took it out on the city, which I saw as a walled-in fortress
of middle-class intolerance that had made life miserable for the person I'd loved most in my life and that had given me too many bad
days both in school and out at a time when the young are supposed
to be at their most carefree. And just when the two of us had found
ourselves liberated from that city and on the road to some other life,
we'd ended up having to go back there to be swallowed up again by
the same intolerance that had driven us away in the first place. Of
course it wasn't the city's fault, but that's where I let the blame rest
for a long time, and that was why I swore I would never go back

there—that is, until this resolution was confronted by the news that began to come out, well after the war was over, about what had happened to the Jewish community in Salonika.

Most people wanted to pretend that the news couldn't be as bad as it gradually came to seem because the reports, never really detailed, hadn't come from the Salonika Jewish community itself. That was because there no longer was a Salonika Jewish community. I got the full truth from my friend Jackson Ripaldo, who had managed to get back to Greece as soon as he had his Navy discharge papers in hand and was now in Salonika making his living by teaching English in a Greek cram school while getting in some practice as a free-lance journalist on the side. When he'd learned that I was at Columbia, he'd written me to ask whether graduate school there was a thing worth pursuing if you were serious about journalism, and if it was, whether I'd send him a catalogue. I'd written him back to say he'd be crazy to give up a chance to do the kind of work in the field that the Greek Civil War might provide for him in order to do what I was doing in New York City.

Whether or not that was sound advice, it came entirely out of envy on my part, which led to further correspondence with Jackson that had the secret motive of my using him to try and get some news about Magda. I was afraid to ask him directly about her, afraid of what I might learn, but what I did find out was that people in Salonika were saying that only some two thousand members of the Jewish community had survived out of the fifty-five thousand who had been deported to the camps, and those two thousand were scattered now, their original homes looted and long since occupied by others, their synagogues mostly gone, their cemetery now a quarry for stones to help extend the local university across their once sacred portion of that city.

I left Columbia without finishing the term I was in and sailed for Piraeus nine years to the month after I'd sailed back to the States with Sam. I didn't have a clear plan in mind. I figured I could do the same kind of thing that Jackson was doing, teach English for a living and do what journalism I could fit in on the side until I had enough experience to try and become a stringer for somebody somewhere in the Middle East. On the way over, I sat out on deck a lot and worked on recovering my Greek, a thing I'd been doing for several months already with more passion for language study than I thought I still had in me, because I wanted to make sure I would be able to talk to Magda as freely as I used to when I succeeded in getting together with her. And that was a thing I came to believe would happen.

I spent a lot of time during that voyage convincing myself that Magda was still alive somewhere and that I would eventually find her if I could just bring back enough of that young faith in possibilities that had led me to track her down against all odds on the island of Thassos in 1938. Even if she had been deported by the Germans, I was ready to think that she had disappeared somewhere between Greece and Poland in the spring of 1943 as some others who made it back to Greece apparently had, and her having vanished into no-man's-land to settle in another country became a convenient way for me to rationalize her not having been in touch with me even after the war was over. And then it became even more convenient to think that she had just gone into hiding before the German army got to her and had then melted into one Greek community or another, with no more will to return to her city after the Occupation than I myself had and no desire to reveal her ties to that segment of her past. But by the end of the voyage, my conviction had worn a bit thin. I was left with a mix of hope and regret, with the mystery of not really knowing any more than I'd known during that eight-year silence, and with all the sharp, sharp memories that had now begun to come back.

I caught the first flight north out of Athens, because I didn't see any point in wasting time there, much as the thought of returning to Salonika brought on a conflict between elation and dread. The first thing I did was pay a visit to the school near the airport where my father had worked before the war, and though the staff had changed and the families of those who had retired were now living in the city, I came across a few people of my generation working for the school who remembered me. There was only a shadow of physical recognition in the case of most, since all of us had grown much older too quickly, but the names, the nicknames and diminutives, were enough to call up our green past for a moment, and even though the names didn't really fit any more, we would embrace and say them to each other as though we were still as young as ever and there had been no war to turn us older than we wanted to be.

There was no one left at the school I might have asked about Magda, because she hadn't ever become part of that small rural community, and when I went into the city to scout out the fellow foreigners I'd come to know well at the German School, some of whom must have known Magda too, I found that they had all disappeared along with the Germans who had run the school, which was now closed, the gate to the schoolyard locked. So there was no one obvious to ask even in the city. At least not outside the Jewish community, and I found precious little of that left, just as Jackson had reported.

I did what I could to trace Magda through those few survivors I managed to find who were willing to talk to me in Greek, but what I got from each of them was another version of the same ghastly story without any specific news of Magda. I always went away feeling that I had intruded on someone's bottomless grief for my own selfish purposes. One survivor, who had come back to claim his family home near the Arch of Gallarius and who twice showed me the tattooed number on his wrist to underline his credentials, said he seemed to remember that several people with Magda's last name had been among those rounded up with the rest in the Ayia Paraskevi district of Salonika the day the German occupation army surrounded that area and marched those living there to the Hirsch quarter to ready them for the trains. But when I told him that Magda hadn't lived in that district but near Harilaou, he said he couldn't be sure that his memory had it right, and I got the impression that he didn't much care any longer one way or another. I also took a walk to where the Jewish cemetery used to be, but the wilderness I found there, not a single headstone left in place, just made me depressed and angry without helping me get any farther with what was beginning to seem a hopeless search.

I think the hopelessness came with my sudden recognition of how devastatingly cruel and complete the slaughter of that old community had been. And that made me feel like an awkward outsider, a kind of nosy tourist, who hadn't shared any part of that terrible past in a city I had once lived with intimately and had then escaped from in time to be spared even any knowledge of what had gone on there under the German Occupation. I also couldn't fit my image of Magda into that history, because thinking about her as having been part of what had happened in Salonika now brought her back in ways that distanced her from me. It made her appear to have returned to her own people, her father and her mother and what they may have been through during those days, which I was able to understand on the level of sympathy but was unable at that moment to face on a more private level, where it only made Magda and me each seem to be foreign to what the other had become.

That first afternoon I took a walk up the 25th of March Street to Harilaou and a ways beyond. Magda's house was still there, but it was all boarded up. It looked as though it hadn't been lived in for years. And her aunt's house on the road going out of Harilaou had been razed. The whole neighborhood had begun to change, with new buildings going up here and there to replace older ones, and the new ones taking up space that used to be given over to gardens and open lots. I turned back before I'd made it very far up the road that led to the village of Kapudjida because that walk depressed me beyond what I'd known since the first weeks after Magda had gone out of my life. Not finding any trace of her in that neighborhood made her disappearance seem final, and if I wasn't ready yet to believe it at the center of my dying hope, I had no heart for hanging around where the evidence appeared inescapable.

When I got back to Jackson's place on the waterfront, he saw that I was low but he didn't ask any questions. He said whether or not I felt like it, he was going to take me out on the town to lift my spirits, though given the town and the political climate we were in, he'd have to do some planning about where we might go for some honest relaxation with the right kind of company. At the time, the civil war situation around Salonika was still considered dangerous enough by the government to keep the city under curfew after dark. Reports had the region surrounded by Communist guerrillas who were not only trigger-happy but had artillery large enough to reach from the hills into the center of town. Jackson himself was no longer much impressed by the guerrilla threat up there, not since Truman had come out with his Doctrine and American Helldiver aircraft were arriving in Greece.

"All you've got to do to get through the curfew these days is speak American," he told me when he got around to explaining his plan for the evening. What he had in mind was a trip out of town to the far end of the shore that shaped Salonika Bay, a little beyond the beach where Magda and I had learned to rub each other down with sun-tan oil during our first really private meeting. Jackson said he never went out after dark alone, at least not beyond the checkpoints at the outer limits of the city, and we would therefore be going in the company of two Greek nurses, who were actually sisters, trained by the British when the British were still the foreign power in charge of Greece for the Allies.

My sense of cultural disorientation after such a long absence from Greece began the moment we picked up the nurses outside their hospital in town. There was a question about the seating arrangements in the jeep that Jackson had borrowed from some buddy of his in the American mission. I don't know what he'd told those nurses about whose jeep it was or where we were going in it, but they weren't in uniform when we got there and they weren't dressed for the beach either. They had on skirts and blouses and high-heeled shoes, and both were wearing earrings. The sister who was supposedly my date was the younger of the two, a dark-haired beauty, though a touch overweight. When I tried to climb in beside her where I thought I belonged after I'd helped her step into the back-seat, Jackson caught me by the arm.

"We have to pretend they're nurses on duty," he said to me in English. "We can't go out there as couples. So they have to sit together."

"Pretend to whom when they're dressed like that? In the middle of a civil war?"

"Don't worry about trivial details. I'll take care of all that."

At the checkpoint beyond the Depot where the streetcars used to turn around, two soldiers with rifles came up on either side of the jeep and peered in. The rifles were M-1s, unmistakably, so I assumed they had come over under the Truman Doctrine.

"American Mission," Jackson said in English to the soldier on his side and flashed his wallet. I don't know what he had in there, his press card, or his social security card, or maybe his livesaving certificate, but he didn't show it long.

"American?" the soldier said.

"Right. Now you have yourself a good evening, hear?"

The other soldier came around. "What's he saying?" he asked his buddy in Greek.

"He says he's American," the soldier said.

"And the women in back?"

"So we'll see you around, O.K.?" Jackson said, gunning the idle. "You take it easy, hear? That goes for you and your pal both."

The soldier in charge pointed into the backseat and made a question sign by twisting his wrist.

"American Mission," Jackson said. "Nurses." He smiled at the soldier, then reached out to give him a quick mock injection on his arm. The soldier pulled his arm away. Then he looked at his buddy. Then he smiled.

"What the devil, go ahead, half the shame is yours and half mine," the soldier said and waved us on.

It was close to nine, but there was still enough light to see the whole stretch of the bay in front of us, the land at the far end rimmed by layers of rose and gray and then a line of black like heavy smoke that finally died out to make a clean break between the fading dusk and the clearer night sky. There wasn't much more out there beyond the checkpoint than there had been before the war, just marshland between the road and the sea for several miles and then a broad clearing where Jackson said they were planning to put a new airport someday. We hardly spoke on the way out. The seating arrangement didn't make it easy for small talk, and I got the impression that our nurses were a bit uncomfortable about being that far out of town, anyway until Jackson turned off the main road into what seemed a wagon track and explained in Greek that he knew exactly where we could get some wine and sit outside to have a bite to eat next to the sea. He said he was acquainted with a family at the end of that dirt road that owed him a carafe of wine or two whatever the hour, because he had sent a lot of people out there during daylight hours to help them put their single-room taverna on the local map.

And he was right. The owner was all over Jackson when we arrived, full of loud good wishes and gratitude, with a handshake and an embrace that could cause damage if you didn't prepare yourself for it. He set out a wooden table on the beach some fifty yards beyond his house, with four straw-seated chairs and a clean checkered tablecloth to cover the filthy one that seemed to have glued itself to the tabletop by way of a complicated pattern of murky stains. We barely got seated before his ten-year-old son began to bring out the appetizers of marinated octopus, fried squid, and finger-sized fish to go with a round of throat-rasping raki from the owner's village near the military airport. And before we were halfway through that, a carafe of resinated wine from the family barrel appeared, along with fried zucchini and eggplant and sliced sausage, and some cheese floating in olive oil surrounded by sliced tomatoes, so that Jackson had to catch the boy by the back of his shirt and tell him to tell the owner that it was all wonderful, he really meant it, but it was too much, and maybe the time had come for us to slow down a bit.

It had turned dark by then, and from where we were sitting you couldn't make out the road that had brought us out there or a clear curve of shore until it began to be shaped by the city lights some miles away. And even then the outline didn't become distinct until you came to the streetlights along the quay where the Americans had their offices and where the apartment buildings were mostly new and brightly lit. There was no enforced blackout, but you couldn't make out enough lighted houses for a city of that size once you left the quay and followed the ancient walls uphill to the prison towers at the top of the old quarter. The feeling wasn't exactly of a city under siege, but it wasn't a natural feeling either, and the long dark stretch of flat country between where we were and the first cluster of lights on the outskirts of town gave you the sense that you were not only cut off from whatever normal nightlife might still be going on near the waterfront but that you were easy prey to those open spaces outside the city limits where there was nothing but darkness.

It seemed I was the only one at the table who felt that way, or cared to think about it. Jackson was having the time of his life telling his lady friend some very tall war stories from his career as captain of the seamen's head on a cruiser that had taken him to the Pacific just as the Second World War was winding down, and since his Greek was quicker than mine, I had trouble getting my date to pay much attention to what I was saying while he had the floor, which was most of the time. But when he and the older sister decided to take a walk up the beach while we were waiting for the plates to be cleared away and the fruit to arrive, I had as much conversation as I could manage.

Katerina—that was her name—talked too fast for me, but even though I had to slow her down occasionally, I learned a great deal about the stint she'd put in working in a hospital toward the end of the German Occupation, which is when she began to pick up English, because not long after she became a nurse there she fell in love with a British officer who had worked for the resistance and had got himself machine-gunned during some factional dispute among the guerrillas that almost cost him both his legs. That was why he ended up in the hospital long enough not only for her to get to know him and his language quite intimately but to create the major problem that he handed her and that was still too much on her mind.

"I was foolish," she said. "Too young. I believed what he told me."

"Well, things sometimes get confused during wartime," I said more or less just to say something.

"No, he simply didn't tell me the truth. He told me that he loved me and that we would be together after the war was over when the truth was that he had a wife from long before the war even started."

"Well, I don't mean to sound unfeeling, but odd things happen to people when war comes along. I mean, things do happen to people that might not happen to them during normal times."

"It won't happen to me. Not again."

"Well, let's hope there isn't another war to complicate things," I said. "The point is, he may have felt that he was speaking truthfully under the circumstances. About his feelings, at least."

"What you mean is that he told me his kind of truth, not mine," Katerina said.

She was half-smiling as she said that, and it was the wrong kind of half-smile, too much irony in it. I found myself looking away, partly because I was embarrassed by her being so personal so soon, but more than that, because the way she said it was too much like the way Magda would have.

"At least that won't happen to me again with a foreigner," Katerina said. "Where I'm not sure on what ground I stand."

I looked back at her. "How did you find out he was married?"

She shrugged. "When the war was over he invited me to come to England. That had been the plan. And when I got to England, you know, I was only seventeen at the time, he met me in an old car that he must have had from before the war because it barely worked and he drove me to his village in Kent and the cottage he lived in with his wife and eight-year-old daughter. The woman was standing there in the doorway smiling. Can you believe it? And I just walked right in."

"You stayed with him and his wife?"

"She said she was happy if he was happy. The only person who wasn't happy was me. And maybe the eight-year-old daughter. It just took me a while to see how impossible it all was. So never again."

The half-smile appeared, as though in warning.

"That's a sad story," I said. "I guess we've all had sad stories of one kind or another in the beginning."

"You were lied to like that?"

"No," I said. "Just cheated. Not by anyone in particular. Just the war. And fate."

"Fate? What a silly thing to say. You believe in fate? You who are an Anglo-Saxon?"

That made me smile. "Why shouldn't an Anglo-Saxon? You think fate is only for Greeks?"

"Fate is only for fools," Katerina said. "An excuse to let things outside yourself govern your life and the choices you haven't got the courage to make."

She was the one who looked away at that point, off toward the open sea. I couldn't find an angle that would let me keep the conversation going even if I'd wanted to, and once I'd recognized the ghost in her tone of voice, it unnerved me to hear any more. I really wanted to get out of there, but I suggested that maybe we ought to take a short walk ourselves since the others hadn't come back yet. Katerina shrugged. "What's the point?" Then she reached over and filled my wine glass. "Why don't you tell me all about how fate cheated you during the war? I promise I'll do my very best to be sympathetic."

However little that evening at the beach raised my spirits the way Jackson had hoped it would, one thing it did do was fill me with restless images out of the past that kept me from sleeping most of that night and had me out of the apartment for a long walk early the next morning. I found myself going by Magda's boarded-up house again and the lot where her aunt's house had been and on up the road toward the village of Kapudjida. It was hot by then, and I decided to hail a taxi and go on up to get a high view of the city from the village farther up that used to be called by the Turkish name of Arsakli but was now called Panorama to go along with the few high-class villas up that way that had survived the war and the new ones they hoped would begin to sprout along that road. From up there the city looked much as I remembered it, especially the old quarter, but there were a lot of new concrete hotels and apartment buildings along the quay near the White Tower, unvaried in the rigid square monotony of their shape and their lined facades, as though a mad architect with a love for piling up balconies had been told that he could play as he pleased along that stretch of land as long as he restricted his stylistic impulses to the design of the railings he installed. And the city was already growing out along the road that led to open country and the beaches of Chalkidiki, mostly one-story houses but beginning to fill the cleared spaces that used to be fields for wheat or grazing right up to the outskirts of the city.

I decided to walk downhill a ways before catching a taxi back to Jackson's apartment on the waterfront. That brought me by Anatolia College and the outdoor basketball court where Jackson and I used to play one-on-one and where I first realized Magda could hurt me in a way that meant she was already deep into my blood. But the image that came back to me in a rush as I passed the school gate was that of the hillside above the ravine that cut through the open fields at the back of the school grounds. There was no easy way for me to bring my downhill route near an opening that would show through to that hillside, because the school had a wall all around it and the main road below the wall was now mostly lined by private lots. But I decided I had to try. I kept on going down the broken asphalt substitute for the gravel road that Magda and I had climbed in the spring of 1938, and not very far down I found a dirt road that carried me over to the ridge we had followed that afternoon of our long-gone awakening. The ravine was still there, though much smaller, and there were houses going up along the far ridge beyond it, where the outskirts of the city were now extending south. The near hillside, where we'd found tall grass and poppies to hide us from the road, had been partly leveled to make way for a football field, and beyond that, you could see a new school of some kind surrounded by a yard that was vibrant with the voices of young children.

There was no longer much room for nostalgia in that sight, but I sat down anyway to take it in, and while I was sitting there listening to those voices the thought suddenly came to me that I was a fool, something that had been on my mind ever since Katerina had chided me for blaming fate rather than my own choices for where I'd ended up. Of course a war had complicated my life just when I had been ready to make what had seemed in retrospect a courageous move for an eighteen-year-old, but what courage there may have been in it vanished when I didn't board that ship for Greece, and if I chose to blame that on fate, this didn't change the fact that I'd been the one who had decided not to move until I'd heard from Magda about whether she thought I should or not. That complication had ended my part in our joint venture. But what about Magda? It struck me now that my not showing up back then didn't necessarily mean that she had given up on the plan we'd worked out together. And if she hadn't, it meant that I'd completely missed the most obvious way of tracking her down, which was not by way of her house or her aunt's house or even what might linger in the memory of survivors in her father's community, but the one place where she was certain to have left some trace because that was where she was heading to turn herself into a schoolteacher when she disappeared from my life. I stood up and made my way back to the main road on the run and kept on going downhill at a steady pace until I was out of breath and then kept on anyway, walking as fast as I could, right through the village of Kapudjida and on down to Harilaou, where I caught a taxi for the university.

The main office of the Philosophical Faculty was open, and the assistant in there was very helpful, patiently going back over the records of students who had studied foreign languages under that faculty from 1939 onward for as long as was possible under the Occupation. There was no Magda Sevillas on record. The assistant suggested I try the Law Faculty, but I had no more luck there. I went out and had a coffee across from the main university building, a bad choice because my table was perched on the edge of a section of the old Jewish cemetery that still showed where it had been dug up for masonry to serve as lintels and stoops in the houses that were crowding the hillside behind me on both sides of the city walls. I sat there trying to figure out what could possibly have happened to Magda in the fall of 1939 that would have kept her from signing up to go to the university after she'd been so sure that she'd passed the entrance exams and by that time had been set to go there for over two years, anyway long before she met me. And if she hadn't made it that year, what about the one following? How could she just change her life so completely?

And of course that question gradually became its own answer. She hadn't changed her life completely, she had changed it exactly the way she and I had planned for it to change all along. What came to me with the force of a conviction now was that she must have decided at some point during that fall eight years ago not to wait for me any longer but to go ahead and finish the trip the two of us had started out on, and had ended up in Athens, probably at the university there, probably teaching on the side to support herself, probably there through the Occupation and, God willing, still there now. I paid for my coffee and took off for the airline office to see if I could get a flight out that day, and when I found that I could, I took it for a sign that my luck had finally begun to change for good in the right direction.

I didn't wait for Jackson to come home from his classes at the English cram school but packed up and left him a note saying that I had to go back to Athens on urgent business and would be in touch with him again as soon as I'd settled in somewhere. Then I went down and walked along the waterfront from the White Tower at one end to the harbor at the other, back and forth I don't know how many times until the airport bus was ready to head out of town for my flight. And I could have gone on walking that city until dawn the next day and then some, inside and outside the walls and up Mount Hortiati as far as the local guerrillas would let me and back down again, given where my mind was now and where it planned to stay.

I was right about Magda and the University of Athens. She had enrolled there in the fall of 1939 to study French and English after doing so well in her university entrance examinations that she was given her choice of which university to attend. And the records showed that she had completed two years initially and had returned after the liberation of Athens to finish her course work and take her final examinations, receiving her degree in 1946. The University had no record of where she had gone after that, and they had no advice to give me on how I might find out except by way of the last address they had in the file. That address was on Patission Street, and the number was theoretically still there, but Magda wasn't. The house she'd lived in, apparently a two-story remnant from the turn of the century judging by those next door, had been torn down the previous winter to make room for the skeleton of a faceless concrete apartment building that was still far from completion and belonged in large measure to the ancient civil engineer who had designed it and who had no idea who might end up living there. The only consolation that emerged from my first week's effort at tracking Magda down was the sure fact that she had survived the German Occupation and had been alive at least as late as the previous year.

It took another two weeks for me to come any closer to her in my search, and that happened only by hard work on the pavements and some restless thinking after I'd taken out a lease on a so-called Kolonaki area apartment that was actually never meant to be an apartment but was the partially converted and unheated ground floor of an old house at the foot of Lycabettus. A large and noisy family lived above me, including two highly-strung cats that adopted me immediately because I fed them more regularly than I fed myself.

When I wasn't out hustling for part-time work as an English tutor and walking the streets to get myself familiar with the city, I sat in that apartment with a cat on my lap trying to work my way through Magda's recent history to uncover a clue as to how I might find her despite her having no relatives I could approach for help, no friends I could identify, and no place of employment that was obvious. The first thing I'd done after my visit to the University was check out every one of the various foreign language institutes that had begun to spring up in Athens as part of a major postwar industry for the largely unofficial employment of transient foreigners like myself and the education of whatever local citizens aspired to find a reasonable job outside the civil service. From that canvassing I learned that if Magda was teaching foreign languages in Athens, she was doing so out of her own quarters, wherever they might be. And I could think of no way, short of going from door to door in the neighborhood where she used to live, that I might discover where those quarters were, a strategy that seemed hopeless when all I had to work with was a name that went with a face which still had a power over me far beyond any other I might draw up out of my past but surely was not the same face now, at least not one likely to stir the recollection of some stranger I might try to describe it to as I'd known it nine years earlier.

What finally provided me with a kind of clue was one part of the very little I'd been left to work with: Magda's last name. I'd seen Sevillas as a strange name from the start, exotic for a Greek even before it took on the shape and colors of the face that went with it. And as I sat in my apartment with a cat in my lap saying that name to myself once again for the pleasure of its sound, I began to wonder if that too might have changed now along with the face, changed into somebody else's polysyllabic monstrosity of a male Greek name that I would make a point of mispronouncing if I ever had the chance. I let that thought go as soon as it came to me, and what struck me then was that the strangeness in the name might be the thing that could make it useful to me now, because Sevillas was surely Sephardic, and that would not only make it rare in Athens but could link it to others equally rare and therefore maybe open a way for it to be traced.

It was a long shot that depended on where Magda had ended up during the years I'd been gone. I had no way of predicting what had happened after that break with her family and the decision to go on to Athens and the period during the Occupation when she'd disappeared, but one thing that seemed possible was that she'd had to go into hiding when the Germans began rounding up the Jewish communities all over Greece. However independent and self-sufficient her thinking might have been at that time, she may well have found herself tied once again to the people she'd cut herself off from in greener years, whether it was fate that had decided that kind of move or her own choice. I had to hope that she'd established some link to the Athens Jewish community at one point or another, because that possibility now seemed the last open road I had left.

I got what information I could about the Athens Jewish community through the good offices of Jackson Ripaldo's father, who had been reassigned to Greece after the liberation as Counselor at the American Embassy in Athens. I learned from the Embassy that the synagogue serving what remained of the Jewish community was in a two-story building on Melidoni Street, just beyond the sunken Byzantine church of the Saints Incorporeal, and that the top floor was used for religious services as in the old days, while the ground floor was now a temporary administrative center for the Council that had been established recently to represent the community in civil affairs, especially the restoration of confiscated property.

It turned out that Melidoni Street was hardly more than a block long, on the border of the ancient Keramikos cemetery, and you got there by going to the far edge of the Monastiraki shopping area. That was the one part of central Athens I came across that made me feel in familiar territory, because it had the look of the prewar road out of Vardar Square that Magda and I had taken that night in 1938 when we thought we were leaving Salonika behind us for as long as we might care to. The shops in the Monastiraki area had the same open one-story facades all in a row, and as you moved along them you could find just about everything there was that could be made out of wood or wire or wickerwork or leather, all the specialty craft shops in competition with each other lined up side by side, so that you could head straight for the group offering what you were looking for, whether a chair or a fence or a basket or a handmade stove or a pair of shoes, the price whatever you could bargain for as you went down the line, take it or leave it, and if you didn't take, you could just come back some other day and work the competition again. Drifting down the lower end of Ermou Street let you forget, for the ten minutes or so it took, that a war had come and gone and had changed almost everything.

The rabbi I found on duty at the Melidoni Street synagogue was a man in his thirties with a short beard and heavy sweat on his forehead because he was helping a workman clear out the frame of a building across the way from the old synagogue. When I told him I'd been sent down there by the American Embassy in the hope that I might be able to find the answer to a question I had about a missing person, he went on working as he talked, as though against the clock. He apologized for doing so but said that the groundwork had to be prepared for new cement that was to be laid that afternoon as a major step forward in building the new synagogue that had been started before the war but had only progressed far enough to serve the Germans for a convenient place to gather as many Jews as they could round up after the Italians, God be with them, withdrew from the war and their occupation zone in Greece, which they had administered with almost total disregard for the German policy concerning the harassment of the local Jewish communities under Italian jurisdiction. That tolerance had saved many, he said, but of course not enough. My question?

"I wonder if your records list one Magda Sevillas as a member of the local community here."

"During what period?"

"The Occupation or after," I said. "She came to Athens from Salonika in 1939, and she was a student at the university here as late as last year."

"Then she's lucky," the rabbi said. "Luckier than most. As I myself am, coming from Zakynthos, where the Archbishop and the Mayor managed to save every one of us. A miracle."

"But you don't happen to recognize the name?"

"Sevillas? I may have heard it, but not so that I can put a face to it. And there is a Sevillias who is a survivor from Auschwitz, but that is not the same name. On the other hand, I'm new to the community here, so I don't yet know everybody either by name or by face. You should check the lists across the street at the administrative office."

There were three unlabeled offices on the ground floor across the street. I chose the one nearest the door. The clerk in there was a middle-aged man with only a tuft of hair left in the center of his forehead and thick glasses that were apparently not thick enough to save him from a deep squint. I asked him if he would be good enough to look through the records since 1946 to see if one Magda Sevillas was listed among the members of the local community.

He studied me above his glasses. "Why do you want to know?"

"Personal reasons," I said. "I'm a friend from before the war."

"Well you won't find a Magda Sevillas listed now," the clerk said. "What you will find is a Magda Nahmer."

"Magda is married?" I said.

"If it's the same Magda you have in mind. And I would guess that it is from the look on your face."

"When did she get married?" I said, my voice showing more irritation than I would have wanted. "I mean how long ago?"

"That of course is none of my business whether or not it may be yours. In any case, she has a child of three or maybe four."

"Three or four?"

"Please. It is not my position to provide personal information. Unless of course you are Jewish and need this information in connection with some claim you wish to make."

"I don't wish to make any claim. I'd just like to find her. An address. A phone number. Anything."

The man was still gazing at me above his glasses. Then his eyes shifted to his right and came back.

"I will take the responsibility of helping you to find Mrs. Nahmer. If you are patient, you will find her in the office next door. Maybe in an hour or so. She is among those who work for us whenever she can free herself from her family obligations."

The man shifted his eyes again and made a slight gesture with his head toward the chair opposite his desk. I decided to sit down. I sat there staring at the floor. When I looked up, the man behind the desk was bent over some document, reading it with barely a hand's width separating him from what he was reading. I stood up and excused myself, said I had some errands to do and would be back before the lunch hour, thanked the man for all his help—even if my restlessness must have told him that the information he'd given me wasn't exactly the kind I'd most wanted to hear.

I went back to the Monastiraki area on Ermou Street to wander among the shops there without bothering to pretend that I was interested in buying anything. I was angry, and not being certain why I had reason to be so angry didn't help. How could Magda have gotten herself married long enough ago to have a three- or four-year-old child? Say the child was three, that still meant she'd married somebody before the war was over in Europe, or anyway just as it ended. Admittedly that would have been more than five years after I'd left Greece, but it was well before I might have had a chance to get back in touch with her. Why had I been foolish enough to think, to hope, that she might have waited for me to come back even if it had taken me nine years to keep my adolescent promise and even if there were times when I barely thought of her during those nine years? And given how long it had been, why did I care so much now?

I couldn't rationalize my anger, especially when I found it stimulated by an image of Magda in what I saw as some kind of domestic bliss, a whitewashed cottage somewhere with a garden up front of rosebushes and fruit trees and maybe a palm tree, all of it modeled on her aunt's place, and a corner of it set aside for her copper-headed kid to swing his or her days easily into some brilliant future. And on the front porch, vaguely watching over the swing, the young couple in intimate conversation, the dark, mustached father leaning forward slightly on his straw chair to brush a mosquito off his wife's warm cheek. I tried to take it lightly, tried to make fun of my own too literary image, but it didn't quite work. The thing still hurt.

When I made it back to the administrative offices opposite the synagogue on Melidoni Street, I found the door to the second office slightly ajar, as though to let in air, so I eased it open farther. A woman was sitting in there behind a desk piled with stacks of folders that had been spaced so that there was an opening just large enough to allow her room to fill in the document she was working on with an old-fashioned pen that she would dip into a small inkwell, and after filling in a line or two, would put down so that she could go over what she had written with a blotting rocker. She seemed completely preoccupied with her work, punctilious in the way she handled the pen, almost somber in her concentration. Her hair was shoulder length, a rather dull copper color, and she was wearing black-rimmed glasses.

"Yes?" she said, glancing up at me when I knocked.

"I'm trying to trace a missing person," I said. "A member of the Jewish community named Magda Sevillas or possibly Magda Nahmer, though I don't know how the latter is spelled exactly."

"I'm Magda Nahmer," the woman said. "And as you see, I'm not missing."

She took off her glasses and studied me. It was Magda all right, the same wide eyes, the same speckled green pupils, the same elegant nose, but with a darkness under the eyes that hadn't been there once and that seemed too deep for her age, and there was more flesh in her cheeks and her neck now so that some of the grace was gone there but none of her mouth's sensuality.

"You don't recognize me, do you?" I said.

"No, I don't think I do."

"I'm Hal," I said. "Hal Gogarty."

She put her glasses on again, then took them off. Then pushed them aside.

"Hal," she said. "My God. You're my Hal?"

"That's right," I said

"It can't be you," she said. "What are you doing here?"

"I came back," I said.

"You came back?"

"I thought that was the plan," I said.

She stood up and came around the desk. Then she reached out and took my hands. She was still studying me.

"You've grown a mustache. How am I supposed to know who you are when you've grown a mustache?"

"I forgot to shave it off," I said. "No, that isn't quite right. I'd planned to shave it off if I found you, but the last place I expected to find you was here. Now. Today."

Magda was still studying me. "I sort of like the mustache. You shouldn't shave it off just for me. That would be a shame."

"Since it doesn't make much difference what I look like any longer, is that it? And since your husband probably has a mustache that you're used to by now, right?"

"So you've found out I'm married. And that bothers you, does it?"

"Just a bit," I said. "Yes, it bothers me. What did you expect?"

"What did I expect?" Magda said, and there was a touch of sharpness in her voice. "What, after all, did you expect?"

I didn't know how to answer that, and I found myself looking down to avoid the way she was looking at me. Magda had let go of my hands, but now she took hold of one of them again.

"Come," she said. "We have a lot to talk about and we can't really talk here. I'll take you to lunch."

She told the clerk next door that she was going to lunch, then she came back to lead me out into Melidoni Street. When we got outside, she stopped me and stood there looking at me again.

"I can't believe it," she said. "Even without the mustache I don't think I would have believed it. You've grown up so much. And your hair is longer."

"So is yours," I said.

I reached out and touched it, then took my hand away. Magda didn't move.

"I don't have time these days to take care of it," she said, running her hands through it. "I work down here much of the time and then I have other obligations."

"Like having a four-year-old daughter," I said.

"A three-year-old daughter," Magda said. "Though my mother-in-law takes care of her whenever I need it."

"So you've been married for four years," I said.

"Yes. Almost four years now."

"How could you be married that long?" I said.

Magda must have heard everything I didn't manage to hide in the way I said that, because she took my arm without answering me and turned me so that we were heading back toward Ermou Street.

"I know a small place overlooking the ancient marketplace where we can have an ouzo and what passes for mezedes in Athens these days," she said. "Would you like that?"

"That would be nice," I said.

"And on our way there I'll tell you everything I think you should know about me, all right?"

"That would be nice too," I said.

She tried to speak carefully, patiently, but what she told me did not always come easily for her in the telling, and though I was too churned up now to keep my mind focused on all the details, I ended up hearing more than I could easily accommodate. She said that after she passed her entrance examinations and chose Athens University, she had managed to get through the first two years without any difficulty and with some pleasure, though they were lonely years on the whole because she didn't have many friends in Athens, just a few fellow students, and frankly she couldn't get entirely used to being without me, whether in person or through the letters we used to write each other. But there were also some thrilling moments during the Albanian campaign in the fall and winter of her second year when Greece pushed the Italian army back almost to Tirana. Then it all came to an end in April 1941, when the Germans invaded Greece and after three weeks raised the German flag over the Acropolis. At that point, she said, everyone in Athens knew that the war had come home to them in a way that would stay for a while, though nobody was prepared for the mass starvation that devastated the city the following winter, so that one couldn't walk the streets without brushing against those ready to fall from weakness and sometimes one just had to step around those already dead on the sidewalks.

When that began to happen, Magda had left the city with two schoolmates and had gone to live in a village tower that belonged to the family of one of them in the Mani region of the southern Peloponnese, high above the sea, where even the Turks hadn't managed to travel during their four hundred years of occupation and where no enemy arrived while she was there. That place gave her and her companions more than enough to eat, but they were short on books to read and people to talk to in the village, and she eventually became restless, especially after not having heard a word from her aunt in months, which meant that she also hadn't had any news of her parents with whom she communicated indirectly through her aunt. And what this also meant was that she had no money coming in any longer and was forced to live largely off the charity of her schoolmates and others in the village. So she'd decided to go back to Athens during the spring of 1943 to get in touch with her aunt.

In Athens she found that her aunt was gone. She learned through a cousin who had come south that winter that the aunt had become sick with cancer the previous spring and had eventually moved back to her village because that was where she wanted to be buried, and she had just made it back there in time. The news of Magda's parents arrived in May by way of the daughter of one of her father's business associates who was rounded up with her family by German soldiers when the Salonika Jews were lined up in the streets on March 15 and told to ready themselves for a trip north and resettlement in Cracow, Poland. Some fifty-five thousand of their community took that trip in a series of freight car convoys over the next two months. But the daughter was lucky. A Greek friend in her neighborhood spotted her waiting in line with her parents and followed her during the march to the Hirsch Ghetto in town, then came up beside her and told her to remove the yellow Star of David attached to her coat, and when she'd done that and the guard in front of them was looking elsewhere, he told the girl to take his arm. She looked at her parents, her mother nodded, and with that gesture the girl's life was saved. In the confusion of that first day, a few others managed to leave the march and save themselves by going into hiding, but this woman never saw any member of her family again, and when she moved on to Athens with others who had escaped the roundup, she brought news that she had seen Magda's parents lined up among those who had been forced to walk that day to the Hirsch Ghetto to prepare themselves for the Polish resettlement program. Magda never heard another word from anybody about either her aunt or her mother or her father.

We were sitting at an outdoor table with a small carafe of ouzo and some olives and bread squares in front of us when she finished that part of her story, and I hadn't been able to take my eyes off her to notice the grand view of the ancient ruins that opened out below us, and she hadn't looked that way either.

"Do you know what it does to you when you suddenly realize that you have no one left?" Magda said into her glass. "No lover, no close friend, no relative of any kind, and when your mother and father have just disappeared that way, however distant you may have become from them over the years?"

"I can certainly imagine what it must be like," I said. "It must—"

"No, you can't imagine it," Magda said. "How could you? And it's not really your fault that you can't."

"I'm trying," I said.

She was still looking at her glass.

"And I don't think you can imagine what it feels like to lose all touch with what you were brought up to believe in when nothing else has come along to take its place except a belief in yourself and the one or two people you have honestly loved who are no longer there for you."

"I think I know something about that," I said. "I'm not seventeen any longer."

Magda looked up at me and tried to smile.

"I don't mean to be critical," she said. "I'm just trying to help you understand why it was important for me to get married when I did, and have a child, and choose one of my own."

"One of your own?"

"Of course that too is difficult for you to understand. How could I expect it to be otherwise? Our life was so different when we were together. Before this cruel war changed everything."

"What you mean is that you married into the Jewish community, is that it?"

"I married a Jew like myself," Magda said. "A survivor without a family who had to go into hiding when the Germans under General Stroop issued an order on the eve of Yom Kippur in October 1943 that all Jews in Athens were to return to their place of residence and to register within five days at the community offices. Those of us from Salonika knew by then what this would mean sooner or later."

"So you went into hiding with your husband?"

"No. I went into hiding with an Athenian family that was willing to take me in along with two others, one of whom became my husband. Would you like to know more about him?"

I looked away from her. "No, you don't have to tell me more," I said. "I don't want you to think I'm prying into your private life."

Magda reached over and took my hand.

"You sound so bitter," she said. "I suppose that's understandable. I was bitter for a while too. Not so much against you as against what the war did to us. But I had to get over it."

"So you're over it now and happily married and that's that."

"Happily enough," Magda said. "And I have a lovely child."

"So I guess what's left for me is to swallow my disappointment and stop asking questions, right?"

"Maybe if I tell you one thing that even my husband doesn't know, it will help you understand better. I didn't have to register under the order from General Stroop because that order didn't consider a person Jewish if that person had only two Jewish grandparents rather than three or four."

"And you knew that all along?"

"I knew it because it was part of the posted order. It just didn't make any difference to me at the time."

"I guess you're right," I said. "I don't really understand your doing a thing like that. I mean, choosing to go into hiding when it would have been safer not to."

Magda was running her fingers over my hand. "Don't you see that I had to go along with the others who were threatened? I felt guilty enough as it was about my parents and the other people I'd grown up with who had disappeared, and if I hadn't gone along with the others in Athens who went into hiding, there would have been no way to justify my survival. I mean, it was a thing I felt I had to do. The right thing."

"I do see now," I said. "So one thing led to another, like working for the community after the war instead of teaching school the way you and I had thought you would when we made all those wonderful plans together."

"I will teach eventually," Magda said. "There's just too much to take care of right now. Too many claims that people need help with."

"And marrying one of your own without telling him that you were only half Jewish is part of the same thing, I suppose."

Magda let go of my hand.

"It wasn't only that. My husband's a good man. Hard working. Honest. A good father and a good provider."

"And I guess that's enough for you now, right?"

"Whether it's enough or not, it has to be," Magda said.

I poured myself another ouzo and studied her.

"And since it has to be, I just have to get used to the idea whether I like it or not, is that it?"

Magda tried to smile again. "Aren't you used to some such idea by now? It's been eight years since you decided not to come back to me. I would have thought you'd gotten used to the idea long ago."

"How can you say a thing like that? I didn't decide not to come back to you."

Magda took my hand again.

"Poor Hal. Of course you did. But I guess you didn't realize what you were doing at the time."

"Well, I'd appreciate it if you'd enlighten me. I mean, as far as I'm concerned, when you didn't answer my letter or my telegram, you just left me hanging out there not knowing what to do."

She had the Turkish gold ring she'd given me between her thumb and forefinger and was turning it slowly on my finger one way and then the other.

"Then I'll explain. Whether you realized it or not, you gave me an impossible choice when you wrote me asking my opinion about whether you should come back to Greece after the war broke out in September. And when you sent that telegram asking for a yes or no reply, there was no reply I could send you."

"I don't understand that either. All you had to say was yes. I would have come. I thought I'd made that clear."

Magda stopped turning the ring.

"How could I possibly say yes? Bring you back to Greece when you and your parents seemed so worried about the war? There were others who came back or just never left, and of course some of them eventually got trapped in Greece and had to go through the Occupation just as the rest of us did. But how could I be the one to force you to come back and share whatever danger I might end up being in when you had the choice not to?"

"But I was ready to share it. I just wanted you to tell me what you thought I should do."

"Dear Hal, that's the whole point. You wanted me to make the choice for you, and I couldn't do that. Don't you see that it had to be your choice?"

I couldn't look at her. I knew she was right, but I couldn't give up either. I stood up and went over to stand in front of the full spread of those ruins below us without seeing a thing.

"You could have written," I said. "You could have told me just what you told me now."

"I couldn't have done that either," Magda said behind my back. "Don't you understand? You'd already made your choice by writing me as you did. I guess you didn't see that then, but once you'd written, I knew it wouldn't work for you to come over here, and I didn't want to confuse you more than you were already."

"I was only eighteen," I said. "For God's sake."

Magda came up and took my arm to stand beside me.

"Please don't think I'm blaming you now," she said. "You were doing what you could do at that time, and maybe it just had to be that way. We were both so young. And there was this terrible war. Let's just blame it on the war and leave it at that."

"All I can tell you is that not hearing from you broke my heart."

"Just as hearing from you broke mine," Magda said.

I turned to look at her.

"So what do we do now?" I said. "Now that we're not so young any longer and understand things better?"

"I don't know," Magda said. "I guess we have to settle for what the past may have taught us and now try to learn to live with what we have left."

"Well that may be good enough for you, but it isn't for me," I said.

"Not even if what we have left includes what you and I had together before the war? That is a thing that belongs to the two of us alone, and I don't plan to let that part of my past disappear whatever you may do."

Magda turned her look away from me to gaze out over those ruins the way she'd gazed across the Kozani plain and farther south along the road to Athens the evening we'd lost her shoulder bag at the Kastania pass. It seemed to me that what she was seeing was mostly inside her now, and just as I had let her stand alone then, I let her look across the valley of ruins below us without saying any more and finally turned aside so that she released my arm.

As I left Magda I promised to get in touch with her again as soon as I was settled into a steady job and had a decent place to live in so that I could invite her and her husband over for a drink or something. She said no, she was the one who would invite me to come to her home because she very much wanted me to meet her daughter as well. She knew I would love the daughter, who was actually learning some English and even some German under her tutelage, and who was a very bright little thing. So I was to call her at the office when I felt the right time had come because she didn't have a phone at home.

The right time never came. In the days that followed I began to understand what Magda had meant by saying that what the two of us now had left was the past we'd had together. At first I'd tried to make that support my still incomplete yearning, the lingering romantic hope that had brought me back to Greece. But as I thought about it, the sense of it became clear: that past was what the gods had given us, time as precious as it comes yet also as final, as contained, which is what our parting so many years ago had necessarily made it be. It allowed no room for a future now. Hers was obviously elsewhere and had to stay there, and I think she was trying to tell me in her special way that it was time for me to take that past for what it was, be grateful for it, and move on as she had. Anyway, that is what I did. I sent a note to the place where she worked telling her that I wouldn't be seeing her again because I was leaving Greece and didn't expect to be coming back soon. I also told her that whether or not I ever found someone else in my life I might love as I had her, I would remember her as the one who had taught me all that was possible and impossible about it in the beginning, and I still couldn't help believing that our beginning was the best there was likely to be.

ABOUT THE AUTHOR

Edmund Keeley is the author of six novels, fourteen volumes of poetry in translation, and five works of nonfiction. His first novel, The Libation, was awarded the Rome Prize of the American Academy of Arts and Letters. In 1982 he received the Howard T. Behrman Award for Distinguished Achievement in the Humanities, and in 1992 was elected Fellow of the American Academy of Arts and Sciences. The recipient of numerous grants and fellowships, he was a Guggenheim fellow in fiction at the American Academy in Rome, where he wrote his second novel, The Gold-Hatted Lover. His poetry translations have earned the Columbia Translation Center/PEN Award, the Harold Morton Landon Award of the Academy of American Poets, and the First European Prize for the Translation of Poetry awarded by the European Economic Community. Excerpts from his fifth novel, A Wilderness Called Peace, were selected for the Pushcart Prize anthology and the NEA/PEN Fiction Syndicate Award anthology.

A graduate of Princeton and Oxford, Keeley has taught English, creative writing, and modern Greek literature at Princeton since 1954. He is currently Charles Barnwell Straut Professor of English and Director of the Program in Hellenic Studies. During 1991–1993 he served as President of PEN American Center, the association of writers, and on four occasions as delegate of the Center to international PEN congresses.